To Ron,

PUPPET

ON A

STRING

Victoria Rose

A catalogue record of this book is available from the British Library

First Edition: March 2004

ISBN: 1-84375-094-5

To order additional copies of this book please visit:
http://www.upso.co.uk/victorrust

Published by: UPSO Ltd
5 Stirling Road, Castleham Business Park,
St Leonards-on-Sea, East Sussex TN38 9NW United Kingdom
Tel: 01424 853349 Fax: 01424 854084
Email: info@upso.co.uk Web: http://www.upso.co.uk

PUPPET
ON A
STRING

BY

VICTOR RUST

UPSO

For Jane
For whom the words 'long' and 'suffering' were
intended to be hyphenated

PUPPET ON A STRING

INTRODUCTION

T he following manuscript was found in the cell of David Richard Loughton in the early spring of 1993 and used as evidence in the re-opened and posthumous trial of the aforementioned.

I have taken three liberties, which I hope is agreeable:

first, I have changed some of the names to protect the innocent, who verified most of what follows;

second, I have chosen an odd name for the "author", so that people will not buy it for the sensationalism attached to David Loughton's name at present;

third, I have called it Puppet on a String, because the phrase or allusions to it appear so many times in Mr. Loughton's writings

The short note below prefaced this epistle to malpractised justice and to an old man's sadness and it is this that sparked my interest in verifying and publishing the manuscript.

M. S. (Lawyer)
May, 2003

To anyone who is interested:

I am a musician. Amazing, really! I just looked at that bald statement and realized how strange it must seem twenty years after...it happened. All the Fleet Street hoo-hah, my name and face flashed across television screens and radio sets around the world and nothing but hate and spite to be remembered by.

The truth of the matter is: I <u>was</u> a <u>singer</u>. Until, as I say, twenty years ago.

The headline from that seedy paper, The Investigator, is the one, which nags at my brain, which pushes poisoned pins in to my heart and which squeezes my stomach with anguish. It was the edition on Monday, 15th April, 1968:

SINGER MURDERED IN BED

With a small, sub-headline:

Contemporary to be charged

Just that! In eight words, I had been divorced from my position of lover to common murderer.

Now, as I sit here in this all-too-familiar, grey cell, with the watery moonlight straddling these tawdry pages of scrap paper as I write, I want to set the record straight – if not in your mind, then at least in mine. Maybe it's my brain vomiting the ageing guilt and despair on to these bits of paper or maybe... well, when I am finished, I will do what I must do. You may believe what you read; you may not. I don't care; to be honest. I am young-ish (fifty-one last birthday) but I look and feel much older. And I'm scared, not of dying, but I'm scared.

This story will be told and then posterity can examine me under whichever light it chooses.

David Loughton
12th April 1993

PUPPET ON A STRING

CHAPTER 1

It was only the male members of the *Coro di Londinium* who were in Paris and, although there is very little for the chorus to sing in *Tosca*, there are a few other (prestigious?) rôles, which were more character-acting than anything else. I had the dubious fortune to land such a part. Marie was playing the eponymous rôle and sang it, although I could be accused of bias, very well. You may not remember the voice of Marie Duvois – it was like listening to a nightingale call; it was aural silver. She did not possess one of those awful, oscillating voices too omnipresent today. When she hit a note, it was as clean and as straight as a die, if that is the right comparative.

I had made it a practice to ask the conductor and principal soloists in every performance that I was involved with to sign their autographs (on the programme, if I could get hold of one). In retrospect, it was unclear to me whether I was doing it for the ego trip or whether it would provide me with conclusive and unnecessary proof that I had been present at that performance. Either way, I had decided that, above all, Marie Duvois's autograph was an essential addition to the collection.

* * *

After the performance, still in my sweat-scarred make-up, but changed into a casual pair of trousers and a long-sleeved tee-shirt with the *Coro di Londinium* logo on it, I made my way to Mademoiselle Duvois's dressing-room, heart pounding like a pneumatic hammer at its rib-cage walls. All I wanted was her autograph and yet I was behaving like a schoolboy asking a girl out for the first time.

I stood at her door, looking at it as if it had just spoken to me, furrowed in brow. Why was I being so hesitant? I considered walking away and trying again the following night but that would have been defeatist. The small – very small – brave part of my brain crunched suddenly into gear, over-riding any other feelings and misgivings, and I knocked.

"Entrez, s'il vous plaît!" said that voice, with which I would soon fall in love.

I waited a moment, then grabbed the handle and pushed the door open, trying to decide what to say to her. What I saw, I was not expecting. Marie was sitting in her gown at her dressing-table, frowning into the mirror, while dabbing at her face with some sticky, pink gunge on a cotton-wool pad and pulling her face about to whisk out the make-up from its hiding-places.

"Oh, sorry," I said, jumping a little at catching her in such a state of down-to-earth disarray, "I'll come back later."

"No, no, please," she said quickly as I turned to go and put her cotton-wool down on the table. "I'm only taking off my make-up. I don't know what you think but I find it gets so ingrained." She leaned towards the mirror, stretched the skin of her cheek down, leaned back, frowned and then shrugged. "Then, of course, you break out in spots. So you cover it up with even more make-up and then your face ends up looking like a mountain-scape in the Andes."

I looked at her, mouth agape and momentarily forgot the purpose of my visit. Realistically, it was unclear what I had expected of Marie – perhaps to find her sipping champagne, draped voluptuously across a *chaise longue*, with press men urgently battering her with questions or, perhaps, shouting instruction and direction to or executing chastisement of a personal assistant – but here was the world-famous Marie Duvois, the international singing star Marie Duvois, telling me about problems she encountered with make-up in her pores.

She seemed to give up resignedly with the mirror, the frown disappeared as she turned to me, obviously noticing the catatonic look of bemusement on my face as her eyes widened a little. "Oh, I'm sorry," she said, smiling embarrassedly, "I'm so rude. What can I do for you?"

I forced my mind back to some semblance of reality and what I was there for. "Er…my name is David Loughton. I'm a tenor in the *Coro di Londinium* –."

"Oh, your chorus," she interrupted, "it's so good. Rarely have I seen or heard such an articulate and well-rehearsed chorus."

My turn to be embarrassed. "Thank you," I said modestly, "even though *Tosca* doesn't provide us with anything that's too taxing."

"Some choruses would become bored with that amount of singing and it would come across to the audience. The *Coro di Londinium* does not."

"Well, thank you again." Redness was seeping unchecked across my face. "Anyway, I was wondering if I could possibly have your autograph. You know, something to show the grandchildren in later life."

"Of course, of course! Give me a pen and something to write on and I'll give you a very *special* message." Her emphasis on the word *special*, wrapped warmly in her Gallic accent, caused a tingle to run sprightly up the spine and to unhinge my eyebrows upwards.

Marie was definitely oozing sex appeal and I think it was that moment that I started falling in love with her. She had very dark brown – almost black – shoulder-length hair and strikingly hazel eyes, which seemed clear yet undefined, warm but unknown, very deep, intelligent and understanding. Her figure was unsurprisingly like any other soprano I had seen. You know the usual type – six feet of rippling fat and diaphragm muscle; the typical Wagnerian Brunnhilde – but Marie was a sylph. Not skinny but slender. Well, Brunnhilde might be just right for you but Marie Duvois was absolutely perfect for me. Here and there, dotted on her face were small freckles. She was almost twenty-nine but they lent her such youthfulness that you would swear that she was at least ten years younger. Finally, she had a permanently happy disposition, a wicked twinkle in her eye and so (I suppose you could say) it was then that she became my *femme fatale*.

I felt acutely embarrassed and not only because I was aware of staring at her. "Now you come to mention it, I...er...I haven't got anything to write with or on. I don't think I thought about it – if you see what I mean."

"Oh, what a shame!" She scanned around the room quickly. "Neither have I."

A thought struck me and I reached into my pocket. "I tell you what. Use my handkerchief and your lipstick. Who said autographs needed pen and paper?"

Surprise crossed her face and she laughed lightly. "You English are so eccentric. I love it."

"We do our best to please."

"Give me your handkerchief, then."

I passed it to her and she picked up the lipstick, telescoped half-an-inch out of the tube, stared thoughtfully through the wall and wrote clumsily across the material:

To David
Thank you for a wonderful evening
Love, Marie Duvois X

"There," she said, punctuating her handiwork with a flourish of lipstick to underline the message, and sat back, "that'll get your friends thinking." Dimples appeared on her cheeks, a twinkle appeared in her eyes and we both laughed.

"Thank you. I don't suppose you get many lipstick-autograph-hunters, do you?"

"Not in my whole experience of music."

"Well, thank you very much for this." I waggled the handkerchief carefully and paused. I realized that I would never have another opportunity to talk to her and she had instinctively made me feel at ease. "Would it be a rude question to ask how many years that might be? The music?"

"Yes," she replied, smiling, "let's just say too many but not yet enough."

"Very cryptic! Can I ask you something else?"

"As long as it's not too personal!" Marie gave a slight wink and then leaned over to clear papers off another chair. "Sorry, I am so rude. Please sit down."

I pulled the chair up and sat down, glancing at my watch. Originally, I was supposed to have gone to some seedy *brasserie* in Montmartre with Pete and Gary (short for Garfield, would you believe?) after getting the autograph, but all thoughts of boozing the night away in some French sin-bin melted as I chatted with Marie Duvois. I had even brought my jacket with me to avoid the necessity of returning to the dressing-room.

"Why did you decide to become a singer? I mean, what was the main attraction?"

"Well, that's a loaded question. Would you believe me if I told you that I had never meant to be a singer?"

"Really?"

"Oh, no. I wanted to be an artist. I had this romantic notion of sitting on the banks of the Seine in a hazy summer, drawing some everyday Parisian scene in some style or other – *pointillist* is my favourite. Or to sit in the market-square by the *Sacré Coeur*, painting while tourists came and went and looked over my shoulder. You know, while away the day a bit like Toulouse-Lautrec and his *protégés* did."

"I'm sure that would have been very idyllic. So how come you're singing on the world's finest stages and not squatting in front of an easel now?"

"It's a long story. Basically, I tried to enrol in a local art college here in Paris at the age of seventeen but without success. There were no places available at that time."

"Maybe everyone else wanted to sun themselves silly on the river-banks."

Marie laughed. "Yes, maybe. Anyway, rather than do an honest day's work at some boutique and sink obsequiously into obscurity, I decided to bide my time by studying music at the Paris Institute."

"In a way, I suppose, you were still training to be an artist. What you might call an aural artist."

"What a lovely way of putting it. Very poetic. Well, to cut a long story short, I fell in love with music and put my name down for singing courses. My tutor was the late, great Pierre Croumeux."

I whistled appreciatively. "That explains why you're so good then!"

"Flattery will get you everywhere with me, David," she responded, smiling.

"I try hard," I replied, my cheeks reddening once more. "So, the great Monsieur Croumeux? I'd love to have had some lessons with him. There are lots of big names from the Croumeux stable, aren't there?"

"Oh, yes. Quite a few were studying at the same time as me. There was Guido Estente, for one – a very fine singer. Beth Jackson studied under him for a while and, of course, there's Roberto Metrino."

"Yes, yes. I remember singing with Metrino. I did *Così fan Tutte* with him. Well…I was in the chorus. Obviously."

"The problem was that there was a…a…what's the word?…a glut; a bottleneck. Too many soloists and not enough work. So I was left with the option of either being a boutique sales-girl or joining the local opera company. Monsieur Croumeux insisted that I waited. Of course, I didn't need that much persuasion. Through his contacts, he found me a position in the soprano section of the *Choeur d'Opéra* in Paris. That was when I was twenty-three." She paused and then added mock-wistfully, "all those years ago!" She tutted.

"You're looking good on it. At least, you seem to be wearing well."

"I'm beginning to really like you," she grinned, "keep it up. You are making me feel younger by the minute."

"I'll try. Flattery is my middle name – I was ridiculed at school for it!"

Marie giggled prettily.

"So how did you manage to break free of the shackles of the Chorus?" I continued.

"Oh, I stayed there for quite a while. Four years, I think. I mean, I was enjoying every moment of it but I could not help but feel that solo work was becoming more and more unlikely. Then, out of the blue, I was 'discovered' by Sir Charles Minton. From that point, my career went up and up" – she demonstrated by circling a pointed finger towards the ceiling –"I have a lot to be grateful for."

"Well, I'm glad you made the Big Time. I think you've got a great voice."

"Thanks," she said and winked slightly again. "Well, the practical upshot of it all is that now I am back at the *Opéra*, singing solo. It feels like my second home. In fact, I remember once, when I had to get back to my hotel from a late night reception here. It was about eleven o'clock or half past..." She trailed off, looking at her watch on top of the dressing-table.

I jumped up. "I'm so sorry, I've kept you away from another appointment." Surprisingly, a jolt of disappointment churned my stomach.

"No, no," she replied quickly, as she strapped on her watch, "I am just hungry and it's almost a quarter to eleven. Talking about the time and receptions woke my hunger up."

"Well, in that case, I had better go and find my hotel," I said, feeling no urge to leave. "Pete and Gary will have already fallen over drunk somewhere."

"Oh, please. I insist," she said.

"What?"

"Dinner."

"No. I couldn't let you. After all, I –."

"Alright. I insist you buy me dinner. Just let me get ready. I know a very good restaurant at the back of Boulevard de la Madeleine. It's about ten or fifteen minutes' walk away. Pierre knows me."

"Why are all *maîtres d'hôtel* called Pierre?" I asked.

Marie laughed. "I love your sense of humour. Now, go. Go. I must get ready."

"Certainly," I smiled, reaching the door. I turned: "Do you mind if I borrow your pink stuff? It'll save me going back to the dressing-room."

"Of course," she said, handing me cotton-wool and the tub of cleanser. "Now" – she waved her hands – "shoo!"

* * *

On the other side of the door, I grinned to myself and folded the handkerchief carefully to avoid smudging the autograph. This was indeed going to be a night to remember, I thought, dabbing the cool cream on to my face.

PUPPET ON A STRING

CHAPTER 2

Considering it was mid-April, the evening was very mild; mild but still cool enough to raise a few goose-bumps when the wind became more than a breeze. Marie had changed into a sky-blue dress, which left her arms and calves bare. Draped over one arm, she carried a white woollen jumper.

As we left the Opéra, via the administration block, a barrage of newsmen met us. Protectively, Marie rested her hand in the crook of my arm as I tried to put my best confident face in place. I had never been subject to this attention before and it was a little unnerving. Marie answered all their questions pleasantly, although my grasp of French left me a little in the dark. Finally, the flash-bulbs started popping – I am sure that my face must have had that startled, rabbit-caught-in-the-headlights look.

"Mademoiselle, regardez-moi!"

"Monsieur, Mademoiselle, par ici!"

"S'il vous plaît, tous les deux devez dire le mot "Cheese"!"

I relaxed at that. "That's incredible," I said, when we managed to get away from the throng, walking towards Boulevard Haussmann. "I didn't realize that the French said "Cheese" as well, when their photographs were taken."

"There's not much else we could say. 'Suisse', 'dix' or 'Nice', I suppose."

I smiled. "It's an odd feeling hearing it. And I suppose that *fromage* isn't a very smiley sort of word."

She laughed. "You're weird. Do you know that?"

We arrived at the Hôtel de la Cavalière at about quarter past eleven. Marie led the way and was immediately confronted by a dapper penguin-suit and bustling formality in the shape of the person, who was obviously Pierre.

"Ah, bonsoir, Mademoiselle Duvois. Monsieur."

"Bonsoir, Pierre. A table for Mr. Loughton and myself, s'il vous plaît."

"But of course," fawned Pierre, stepping aside, showing the way with a sweep of his hand, bowing and catching the attention of the cloak attendant simultaneously, with a brisk click of the fingers. This hired hand, in a white tuxedo, took my jacket and Marie's jumper as we were shown to our table.

The restaurant was a large room, filled with white damask cloth-covered tables, most of which were occupied by puffing, overweight, overdressed Parisians, dribbling gravy and *Steak Diane* sauce down their ample chins and shirtfronts. Around the ceiling ran a cornice with crenellations and indentations; here and there, almost randomly, were plaster creations of bunches of grapes, grotesque masks and Rubenesque cupids. The entire cornice was painted white and the remainder of the ceiling and walls was coloured a gentle olive, giving the impression of sitting in a vast, inverted Wedgewood ornament. Ostentation appeared to be the watchword here. In a few alcoves, the wall was adorned with signed photographs of the restaurant's more rich and famous clientèle. The light was subdued without being gloomy, giving the effect of a small, cosy, candle-lit room rather than the ballroom grandeur it was. In the corner, a string quartet played softly, something soothing by Handel or Albinoni. This was in the days before piped music became the norm.

As if reading my thoughts, Marie laced her fingers and rested her chin on them, leaned towards me a little and smiled. "It *is* a nice place, isn't it?"

"Very nice," I replied, subconsciously playing with my fingers under the table. On the walk to the restaurant, Marie had told me that the gist of the press questions was to find out about me, whether we were a courting couple and what they could print. She had not divulged her answers to me. Since that episode with the press and now sitting in the restaurant, reality had seeped into what had been hitherto another world and I was suddenly and completely overwhelmed and unsure of myself.

"We used to come here a lot after a performance in the Opéra," said Marie.

"Yes." My lap had become an extremely interesting point of focus.

Marie sat back. "Why suddenly so ill at ease?" she asked, concerned, two or three crinkles furrowing her forehead.

"Oh, I'm sorry," I stuttered, feeling my cheeks burn a little, "I'm not used to having dinner with such a...a world-class singer." I had wanted

to use the word 'beautiful' but Marie might have requested a bucket in
which to throw up.

"No?" Her face contorted further into its mesh of concern and then
relaxed into an engaging smile. "Please don't worry. Enjoy yourself. The
problem is – with most people anyway – that they fail to think of a so-
called star as a human being. They think I come out of a little box to
sing some opera or other. Then, when the applause has died down and
the bouquets of flowers have been collected, they put me back in my box
until the next public appearance." Her smile had disappeared. "But I'm
not that wooden. Look, give me your hand."

Dumbly, I held out it out to her. She took it gently by the wrist and
rubbed it over her hand and forearm. A thrill squeezed from my
stomach, banged recklessly past the heart and embedded itself
irrevocably in my head. If she had meant anything sexual in the gesture,
it was not overtly apparent, but when I left my hand on her silky arm
longer than perhaps I should have done, she did not protest.

"I'm only human!" she continued, turning my hand over. "See? Flesh
and blood. No splinters. It's one of the reasons why I took hold of you
in front of the press." She gave my wrist a light, affectionate squeeze,
released it and laughed. "I'm sorry but the stardom tag wears a bit thin
and sometimes I feel incredibly lonely, because no-one wants to talk
with you. They think you're in a totally different world. Unreachable."
She paused and smiled. "And I'm sorry I keep saying, "I'm sorry"!" I
returned her smile and she laughed again. "Now, some wine?"

"Excellent idea," I replied and relaxed a little.

She snapped her fingers towards a deferential Pierre. "A bottle of the
Salon le Mesnil, please."

Pierre fingered the air, giving a slight bow, and scuttled off to the
cellars like a trained, moustachioed, greasy-haired rat, working his ticket
as hard as he could for a tip. When he returned with the bottle, he
uncorked it with a Gallic flourish and proffered me the cork.

"No thanks," I said meekly, waving him away, embarrassed at this
surprising gift.

"Go on," urged Marie.

"Thanks," I acknowledged and promptly pocketed the cork, fearing
that the other diners may be watching this strange enactment of an even
stranger French custom.

Pierre let his composure slip a little, being slightly taken aback, while
Marie covered her mouth, shaking with silent laughter. The problem, of
course, was that I was not well-versed in the etiquette and art of

viticultural consumption; how was I supposed to know that I should sniff at the proffered cork to register its suitability for drinking and to get a foretaste of the wine's bouquet?

Pressing on, unruffled and composure sealed back on his demeanour, Pierre tipped a little of the liquid into my glass, hunched over and awaited a response. Determined to show Marie that I knew exactly what I was doing – which I most certainly did not – I sniffed noisily over the rim of the glass, raised it into the light for closer scrutiny, sipped a little and sloshed the faintly acidic liquid around my mouth, like a mouthwash. All the while, Pierre's moustache twitched and widened over an obsequious grin, as he nodded at each thing I did. Marie still had her arms arched on the table, her knitted hands covering her quiet and irrepressible laughter. Her eyes belied the fact that that she was genuinely amused with my shenanigans – she had guessed that I had no clue about what and what not to look for in a good wine.

"Very good," she said, covering her smile with the length of a finger.

"Very good," I said, pushing my glass forward for more wine.

"Very good," said, Pierre, tipping the bottle over Marie's glass.

Marie collapsed in a fluttering series of giggles. It was an infectious laugh as lethal as nitrous oxide, which soon had me laughing at the absurdity of it all. Pierre, on the other hand, could not understand the humour of the situation, finished pouring the wine, excused himself and retreated to a safe place, looking over his shoulder as if we had unexpectedly grown teeth in our ears.

"I'm sorry," said Marie finally, drying her eyes gently with the corner of her serviette. "It was just so funny watching you pretending to know what you were doing and then we all said the same thing."

"That's alright," I replied, breathing hard with the effort of getting under control again. "I like a woman who enjoys herself."

The menus came and went. Over the starter of escargots in garlic butter, we returned to our previously interrupted conversation.

"So what did you mean when you said Sir Charles Minton" – I raised two fingers and crooked them twice to indicate the inverted commas – "'discovered' you?"

"Well, we were at the last but two rehearsals for *Il Trovatore*. That's my favourite opera after *Carmen*. Everything was going well. No problems."

"You were in the chorus?"

"Yes, I was. Fame lurked nowhere near me at that point. Anyway,

Jemima Shaw, who was playing Leonora, suddenly became ill with laryngitis."

"Poor woman. One of the worst things to happen to a singer."

"Precisely, but she was susceptible to it, apparently. And this wasn't the first time that she had been forced to cancel an appearance."

"Oh, yes! I remember that time at Covent Garden. The music press had a great time pulling her apart. But I guess that susceptibility is quite career-limiting."

"Quite so. Hardly fair, really. She can't help her illness."

"I think the press sticks its unwanted nose into other people's affairs far too often. So were you asked to stand in?"

"Not immediately. I can tell you that Sir Charles was frantic. Pacing up and down and literally pulling at his hair."

"I'm not surprised."

"You know that all leads have an understudy, specifically for such an occasion?"

"Yes."

"Jemima Shaw's understudy was Katrina Belsavo. Unfortunately, during the last few dress rehearsals, Katrina got to the part where she's running from her suitors, when she tripped on the dress hem and badly twisted her ankle."

"Yow! And I bet that she couldn't walk on it and had to pull out herself?"

"Absolutely right. So Sir Charles aged about one hundred years and sent the Opéra minions to the telephones to find a replacement."

"Oh, God! Don't tell me – no-one was available."

She smiled, raised her eyebrows and nodded slightly. "Absolutely right again. The plot thickens. So, as a final measure, he appealed to the chorus for a stand-in."

"And that's where you came in?"

"Not precisely. My friends in the chorus reckoned that I had a pretty good voice. *Il Trovatore* being one of my favourite operas, I knew the part of Leonora almost backwards. They knew that I was…*au fait*? That I was *au fait* with it and said that I should volunteer to do it. Of course, four years in a chorus with no solo work had eroded my confidence."

"But you did it anyway?" I was on tenterhooks.

She laughed, dabbing her mouth with a serviette. "Not quite there yet. After I had refused a few times, I received a note from Pierre Croumeux, which said 'If not now – *never*', with the word *never* in capitals and underlined several times. That swayed me!"

"Well, Sir Charles could only say 'no'."

"Which is what I thought. After a lot of agonizing. But you must know what it's like."

"Only too well," I nodded sagely.

The plates were removed and the next course arrived. Being as consummate a gastronome as I was a wine connoisseur, I thanked Marie for awaiting the end of the meal before telling me it was frogs' legs. I am not squeamish as such but I figured that I would have refused them if it were known what they were nonetheless. And the taste was not too bad; a case of mind over matter.

"So," she continued, sipping her wine, "eventually I decided that I had nothing to lose, except a bit of pride, and I auditioned."

"Were you first choice?" I asked eagerly.

"It's terribly immodest to say so but, yes, I was. In fact, as soon as Sir Charles heard my voice, he refused even to listen to the other girls' audition pieces."

"No, that's not immodest."

"Thank you."

"A starlet overnight, were you?"

"More or less. The critics raved about my performance. At least, they seemed to like me – they were very positive. Then, Sir Charles insisted on using me at every available opportunity."

"I'll bet that you had to work hard for that."

"Yes. Good heavens! There were so many new and different pieces to add to my repertoire. I had six or seven months in which to learn them. It was exhausting. Fortunately, Sir Charles helped me at every stage – he has become a sort of uncle to me."

"And now you are Marie Duvois, international singing star, up there with Maria Callas."

Marie frowned admonishingly and shook her head. "I wouldn't quite put myself in the same bracket as her. I have a long way to go before I reach her status. Having said that, I could retire now and live off my earnings. Particularly now that making records is increasing in popularity."

"Yes, the *Coro di Londinium* is always being signed by the large record companies these days. Mostly on the Music Masters label."

Marie wiped her mouth and put her hand up towards me. "How very rude of me. Here am I, talking about nothing but myself and I have not asked anything about you. You English have a quaint expression for people like me – I can talk the back legs off a donkey. And I can usually persuade it to go for a quick canter afterwards too!"

I laughed. "There's very little to tell about me, really."

"Oh, surely not. If there were nothing to tell, you would not be a member of that fine chorus."

"You have a point there."

"So. What made *you* take up music?"

"My mother, I think. She recognized that I had a good treble voice and, at the age of five, I joined the local church choir."

"Ah. An angelic little choirboy, were you?"

"I may be some things but I don't think I could, by any stretch of the imagination, be called 'angelic'. Even at the age of five. I was terribly mischievous."

"Figures," she said cryptically, a dimple flirting on one cheek. I raised my eyebrows but continued.

"I didn't sing again after my voice broke until my early twenties. Except for bath-night concerts, of course. I was actually training to be a lawyer, which takes about three hundred years and is as boring as a very tedious thing. Anyway, I read an advert in one of the papers for a relatively new amateur chorus, affiliated with the London Philharmonic Orchestra."

"Good orchestra."

"Yes. So I was in the London Phil. Choir from about 1955 to 1959. Then I moved on to the Philharmonia Chorus because there was more opportunity for foreign tours, even though I had recently gained my articles as a lawyer. Through a mutual friend, I met up with Pete Phillips, who is the *Coro di Londinium*'s bass section manager. That is, he manages the section and acts as the voice for them at what passes for committee meetings. Where was I?"

"The Philharmonia," she smiled.

"You'll get used to constant digressions and back-tracking. It's part of my training as a lawyer to get the facts absolutely straight but, in so doing, it sometimes is difficult to see how you got to the conversational *cul de sac* you end up in. Erm…"

She giggled. "The Philharmonia?"

I clicked my fingers melodramatically. "The Philharmonia! Anyway, Pete was taking singing lessons and eventually suggested that I do so as well. I was uncertain. A young lawyer doesn't get paid very much. But I went to one lesson and was hooked – I enjoyed it so much I signed up for a course of ten."

"You had been bitten by the music bug."

"Exactly. So, after a while, Pete went to the Royal Opera House chorus, auditioned and was accepted. About five years ago, I think, Pete contacted me, suggesting that I should audition. Pete's a bit like a fairy godmother…no, god*father*, although he'll hate me for saying that for a number of reasons – and not the least calling him a fairy."

Her grin broadened to show a perfect set of white teeth. "He was your guiding light?"

"I suppose so. Well, I don't think I would be sitting here now if it had not been for him."

"I must thank him," she said and smiled warmly.

"Then I auditioned and, much to my surprise, was given a three-year contract. It's a bit more involved than that but you have the essentials."

"And what about your present Chorus?"

"Once again, Pete had a hand in that. A wealthy businessman – an opera-loving, philanthropic millionaire – approached him and Gary, our secretary, who was also at the Royal Opera. I don't know why he talked to those two specifically but it worked. What he wanted was to create a freelance opera chorus, which would perform for approximately cost price. He also gave enough cash to pay for the *Coro*'s headquarters, their own wardrobe for each opera and he would also pay the personnel's salaries. But he didn't want any publicity."

"I wonder why that was?"

"Just eccentric, I think."

"Aren't all Englishmen?"

She smiled and I mouthed "Thank you" as the waiter cleared the plates in preparation for the fish course.

"What was I saying? Oh, yes. Then Pete asked me to join the CdL. I refused, because I still had two years to run on my Royal Opera contract and I wanted to gain a bit of experience before resigning. Plus I didn't know if this *Coro di Londinium* thing would actually have the legs it needed to work."

"Wise move."

"However, it was thriving by the time my contract expired. I was offered an extension of a further five years but I chose to join the CdL."

"Why is it called the *Coro di Londinium*?"

"That's lost in the mists of time but it is an unforgettable name. I think Gary came up with it, reasoning that anything in Latin would sound more prestigious and important. To my mind, sometimes it's pompous and pretentious – a bit like Gary really so no surprises there!"

"And do you do anything on this committee? I mean, all your friends seem to be on it."

"No, no. It's not that I don't want to; it's just that I'm not really a political animal and I would want to make things happen. I would get very frustrated very quickly because I couldn't do what I wanted at the pace that I would like. You know what they say about committees? 'A camel is a horse designed by a committee'." I paused. "And it would give me the hump."

A quizzical look passed over Marie's face, before she made the connection for the poor pun and grimaced. "Do you think you'll move on from the *Coro di Londinium*?"

"Not for a while. It's too new and exciting so I'd like to wallow in it for a while longer. Not being tied to an opera house or orchestra does mean that we have the freedom to do what we like. We can pick and choose. We're also very busy so there aren't any slack periods. There's a lot of job satisfaction, if you like."

"Have you ever thought about going solo yourself?" Marie asked after a pause. Neither of us had eaten much of the fish.

"Hmmm, I'd love to! But you need to be discovered or have the right succession of breaks or be born into it. Plus, I'm not absolutely happy with my voice."

"Neither am I. With mine, I mean. I tell you what. Let *me* listen to your voice some time."

My heart stopped for what seemed to be an eternity and then I smiled. "Maybe."

We finished our meal and the best part of another bottle of *Salon le Mesnil*, talking about the various aspects of the work we enjoyed, the conductors and artists with whom we had worked. It was an unbelievably delightful feeling to be talking to someone who was internationally famous in the same field of work as myself.

In fact, I was in such high spirits that I did not mind paying the horrendously over-priced bill. Feeling heady and an inner warmth, a concoction possibly attributable to the fine meal, the conversation, the wine or Marie (or any combination of those), we left the Hôtel de la Cavalière. Pierre exuded subservience as he fawned and bowed around us, holding out my jacket. As I put it on, I passed the sweating Frenchman a few francs and his face lit up, spurring the subservience to new depths. I am sure he was expecting more but I figured that his wages did not need further underpinning.

We stepped into the freshening night air. A few insipid fingers of light pierced the navy cloak of the sky and danced among the branches of the budding trees. The moon, with its lopsided grin, watched us blindly as we walked along Boulevard de la Madeleine towards Marie's hotel in a comfortable silence.

When we reached the hotel, Marie turned to me and smiled. Suddenly, the fidgety feeling overwhelmed me again. Her eyes twinkled. "I've already written about this evening."

"I'm sorry?"

"The handkerchief," she almost breathed. She smiled again and made her way up the few entrance steps, before turning at the top, where she waved, mouthed "Thank you", smiled and…was that a pout?! Yes it was!

And then she was gone, the night's silence interrupted only by the chuffing of the hotel's revolving door slowing to a stop. I stared at her after-image, thinking.

Happiness grew inside from the catalyst of that pout, burgeoning from my stomach outwards, mixed with a twinge of worry about the next day. If this had been a cheesy Hollywood musical, I would have skipped away, while the string section scraped their way up several *crescendi* to a fortissimo rendition of "I Could Have Danced All Night". But this was reality and I silenced the urge, the parishioners of that *arrondissement* of Paris would have been glad to know.

The concerns I had were pushing at my nerves – at once worried but at the same time thrilled. Would she say anything tomorrow? Would I, for that matter? Was I in love? Was she attached to anyone? There was no ring on her finger but that meant nothing, did it? Did that bring hope? Would I see her again? Would it be an evening like tonight?

So many questions, I thought, reaching into my pocket. A slightly smudged

To David
Thank you for a wonderful evening
Love, Marie Duvois X

glowed redly in the moonlight. Turning towards my hotel, hope battled constantly with pessimism in my brain.

I comforted myself with the thought that, if nothing else, I still had the handkerchief.

PUPPET ON A STRING

CHAPTER 3

At that time, the *Coro di Londinium* was gaining popularity at a very fast rate. The people involved in what was supposed to be the governing body, a sort of committee or council, were mostly, as I far as I had witnessed, there for the ego-trip of having a title in a large, glamorous organisation. It seems odd that people work (for years, in some cases) with ogres pushing them towards a position, a position which entitles them to do nothing at all, except become an ogre themselves and tell other people to pull their fingers out and do something (or, in a brilliant and unintentional Lewis Carroll moment by our chairman, "pull your dos out and finger something"; more of him later). Nowhere was this ego-massage more apparent and endemic than in the infancy of the CdL. That is not entirely fair on some members of the Committee but I would have fancied placing a few rich bets that most had gained the titles in the ladder of success to boost themselves towards the top – perhaps, even, to attain a more obvious and prestigious title: OBE, MBE or even a knighthood for 'services to music', when the best service they could supply to music would be to leave it well alone and emigrate!

The Committee was formed from this disparate bunch of characters: Sydney Althorpe, first chairman of the ill-fated *Coro di Londinium*. He was a military man, something to do with the Para's he said, although there were rumours that he had never ventured nearer the front lines than a desk in Whitehall and the highest point from which he had descended was in a lift from the fourth floor. He looked a little like Harold Macmillan (hence his predilection for misquoting "I've never had it so good", which, in retrospect, was probably a Freudian slip), with his Hitleresque, clipped, white moustache but his features were fuller, like an aged hamster gathering food. However, unlike Macmillan (or even Hitler), Althorpe had very few, if any, abiding leadership qualities, preferring to bury himself under the self-importance his title awarded

him and to make pointless observations at the open Annual General
Meeting (what he thought was an inspirational speech was littered with
mixed metaphors and strange, inappropriate imagery – the best
examples were "you've hit the nail on the button", "we must ensure the
left hand knows what the right hand is saying" and "we must drop the
anchor and steer the ship"). It would be fair to say that the great skill he
did bring to the company and to the proceedings was incompetence. It
must have taken years of training and hard graft to attain those dizzy
heights, to which others could only aspire from afar;

Gary Adner, the Secretary, was a man in his early forties and one who
did not seem to mind taking on the 'woman's job' (as he and others of
the men's sections put it). His hair was always brushed back, slightly
Brylcreemed, ending in curls at the collar. From above, you could see
why he tortured his hair in that way; a monk's tonsure hid under the
comb-over. He would become flustered and angry if you suggested that
he was going bald and stated that, even if he were, he would go bald
gracefully rather than cover up. He had a thinly-cut moustache, always
wore a dark suit with thick pin-stripes and darker shirts. The overall
package was reminiscent of a World War Two spiv, even down to the
dreadful, filterless cigarettes, which incessantly dangled from his lower
lip, spewing ash whenever he talked. Gary was always joking and always
drinking. There were rumours abounding, when I joined the Chorus,
that Gary had an alcohol problem, something again that he strenuously
denied when the subject was broached and was believable because of his
apparent lust for life. If the problem existed then, it was not obvious to
me, at least, not at this stage. There was something else curious about
Gary. Although he appeared to get things done, no-one was really sure
whether it was he who had done it or, if he had, how he had done it. In
other words, Gary was a charmer, a con man, who revelled deep in the
glory of others' achievements. But for all that, I considered him a friend
and his charm over-rode any misgivings I had about him;

Jane Hoare, the CdL's one and only soprano section manager.
Although the male voices were in more demand for opera than the
female, all the sopranos and altos received a handsome retainer as well as
a salary for the work they did. The free time allowed them to
supplement this further with extra-curricular work, an arrangement that
embittered some members of the male half of the Chorus, without
mentioning names. Oh, what the hell? Gary. Jane was blonde, a true
blonde with no dark roots. She was stunningly attractive with azure blue
eyes and a slightly upturned nose. With an almost eternal tan and long,

perfect legs, she was the object of desire for a number of the men. She was indeed a pleasure to look at but what God gave her in looks, he took away in spades in intelligence. During conversations, she would nod sagely to whichever point that was made and side with the majority. As the majority changed position and opinions, she must have experienced violent sea-sickness as she swung from side to side. As a section manager, then, she was next to useless since she did not represent her section but agreed with the consensus;

June Whiley, the overbearing alto section manager. She was a dumpy, almost-grey-haired woman with more frown-lines than laugh-lines and a large wattle that moved about improbably as she sang in a reedy, warbling voice. As a member of the committee, she took her job seriously but never quite made the grade. June had a habit of turning up for everything, regardless of whether the altos were required or not and this, more than anything, drew ridicule rather than pity. Whatever her aspirations, with barbed comments from Gary and others, she would never achieve anything, since it had the effect of pushing her further into her lonely hole;

Bob Holden, the ultimate tenor section manager and a father figure to me. He was getting old, of course, if you could call fifty-seven old. He had grey hair on the bits of his head that were not bald (which was very little) and liver-spots surfacing on his face and hands. Unfortunately, Bob rarely did any performances, because he was a regular in the surgical more than the operatic theatres, having suffered two heart attacks before the age of fifty, which curtailed his brief career as a tenor virtuoso. He had taken the decision that, although it would kill him to do solo work, it would kill him to do nothing and had therefore opted to join the *Coro do Londinium*. It had always bugged me why he had taken on the additional stress of a committee post but the only obvious answer was that Bob was a workaholic, wanting to be involved in as many aspects of the performance as possible. He was, though, an extremely effective manager, who never pulled rank but had his section well organized and fully supportive of whatever he was positioning the Chorus to do. As my manager, I found him a good *confidant* and he had become a close friend as a consequence;

Pete Phillips, the bass section manager and my esteemed friend, who had brought me into this strange world. He was my true friend and he was the only one to stand by me during my ordeal, despite the effect it was having on him. Pete was a tall, lanky youngster of twenty-five, but he was already thinning on top. He always looked permanently worried with knitted eyebrows and a furrowed forehead and with it came a permanent thirst at the pub. Unlike Gary, though, he used to take months at a time off drinking and would always know when to stop. Pete was a joker; well, not so much a joker as a witty cynic. In his management style, he made everything look easy, was modest about his achievements, knew how to get the best out of people, giving them space to make mistakes and, crucially, learn from them and he knew how to keep order without resorting to threats;

Finally, a wardrobe manager, which was an awful job, but which probably explained why it was rarely filled (as was the case on the Parisian trip). It meant that the incumbent had to stay behind after each performance and dress rehearsal, tidying the wardrobe, inventorying the contents and ensuring that everything was ready for the next time it was needed. It cut into the social life, revolving around the Chorus, especially since most of the performers, disappeared to the local watering hole for a celebratory drink or two. It was, therefore, a post that was not filled for long, if at all. For the Paris venture, Gary had volunteered (in his words) a few people to keep the wardrobe in order, amidst scowls and protests, pending the arrival of someone with the good grace to fill the vacancy.

So that was the committee. The members of the *Coro di Londinium* had to supply their own music, this being written into the contracts. This was partly a measure to cut down on required storage space but also to cut down on the costs of hiring scores and employing someone to co-ordinate the lending and return of the music.

Pete and, I suppose, Gary were the mainstays of the chorus. It was they who had managed to settle tours, mainly through sheer audacity. Pete had persuaded our charitable entrepreneur to expand in Paris and use us as a sort of springboard. Several associated Parisian companies had donated money to the evening. There were problems as the date drew closer as one chief company had withdrawn its support because of its own financial troubles. Instead of cutting performances, Pete had organized for the Chorus to stay at cheaper hotels in the Cité des Bergers just of the rue Montmartre.

* * *

While I had wandered off to get Marie's autograph, Pete and Gary had cleared up some last-minute administration. After that, they had hung around, kicking at specks of dirt and sighing with boredom outside the

Choral dressing-room, before deciding that I had probably met and gone off with some voluptuous French tart. They had given up waiting for me and had disappeared to *La Parisienne* in the famous rue Montmartre without me.

Now, the morning after, they were mooning mournfully over their coffee – their *black* coffee – at breakfast, hunched over their cups like death and his brother, bemoaning their state and vowing never to introduce their brains to alcohol again (at least, not this side of lunch).

Pete groaned again. "My liver doesn't understand me," he said morosely, in between sips from his second cup.

Gary winced in agreement, sitting straight and rubbing his chest with a balled fist, and taking another gulp of what passed in the hotel for coffee. "I think it understands you very well," he rejoined. "If you will pour that muck down your throat in the name of a good time, what do you expect? Either way, mine has gone out in sympathy with yours."

They groaned again in unison, burped insignificantly and put the cups to their lips again. Pete frowned in disgust. He said: "What on earth does this hotel think it's serving us? This stuff only tastes like coffee in the sense that coffee normally tastes like sump oil, is gritty, and almost completely unlike coffee."

Gary laughed and stopped quickly, frowning. "Because it was ground this morning. Sorry, that's the wrong joke."

Pete examined the contents of his cup closely. "Well, it's not quite coffee and it certainly isn't tea. But then, neither is the tea. I think we should congratulate this wonderful hotel on its cups of brown."

"You get what you pay for," said Gary. "Mind you, I don't think this was in the contract."

They were laughing carefully so as not to interrupt the pounding in their heads, as I entered the dining-room. There were two other people in the room. It was a late breakfast, even by our standards, but it was nice not to have to deal with the bustle of too many breakfasters.

Gary perked up a little as I sat down next to him. "Anyway, Dave, where the hell did *you* get to last night, you old devil?" He moved to elbow me in the ribs, grimaced and caught his head before his brain could escape through his ears.

"Nothing much."

"'Nothing much'? I don't call arriving back here at three o'clock in the morning 'nothing much'! I know it was that time because that was when I got up to the toilet to throw up." He paused and contemplated briefly. "You probably didn't need that information. Anyway, I saw you coming upstairs, with a faraway look in your eyes and a stupid grin on your face. Who was she?"

I shook my head. "I just went out for a bite to eat, something to drink, a bit of conversation…"

"Yeah," said Gary with forced patience, his eyes darting like a ferret's on the prowl, "but who with?"

"Well," I replied, watching hypnotised as I turned the cup slowly in its saucer, "even if I told you, you wouldn't believe me."

"Oh, I see. Someone special," said Gary, knowingly, giving a half-wink and forgetting that he had just opined that there was not only a mother and father of an ache in his head but they were now the parents of a healthy set of twins with another well on the way.

"Come on, Dave. Try us," said Pete, sitting back carefully and folding his arms. His eyes were bloodshot and the arm-folding was an attempt to stop the inevitable *delirium tremens*. But he looked significantly better than Gary.

"Okay," I said, looking away from the tea-cup hypnosis, "you've asked for it. You ready?"

They both nodded and Pete leant forward again, elbows on the table.

A long pause. "Marie Duvois!"

Stunned silence, just as I had anticipated. Pete turned quickly to Gary, who was slowly frowning, storm-clouds gathering over his brow. Gary said, "Pigs on the runway, fuelled and ready for take-off! Saving its bacon, no doubt! Chops away!" He pointed vaguely in the air and traced it across the room. "Yes, there it is! A flying pink pig!"

"Flying pink elephant, more like," said Pete, under his breath and ignored Gary's glare. He turned back to me. "Was it really Marie Duvois?"

I was about to respond but a hostile Gary interrupted me. "Of course it wasn't," he said, derisively. "Come on, Dave. Who was it really?"

I smiled resignedly and shrugged. "I told you that you wouldn't believe me."

Gary put his elbows on the table, ran his hands through his hair, brought his head up and pulled at his cheeks with the palms of his hands and said: "What the hell would someone like Marie Duvois want with you? She's way out of your league." Temper rising, he frowned a little more. "You're starting to sound like old Whatsisname!"

"John Puttnam?" suggested Pete.

"Yeah. He's always going on about the people he knows, the royalty he's met, people he's sung with, the recordings he's made. Everyone knows that he's talking out of his arse."

"Come one," said Pete, trying to be fair while still intrigued, "no-one's as bad as old Puttnam. Eighteen years old and soloing with megastars in back-street theatres? At least Dave's only saying that he had *dinner* with Marie Duvois. It's hardly the same thing." Pete raised his hands, as if weighing one imaginary substance against the other and then shrugged.

"That's as maybe," said Gary, gruffly. He turned to me. "Okay, have you any proof?" he asked, implying that he could see a confidence trick a mile off. The other two people left the dining-room, scowling at us for the disruption.

"Do I need any?" I asked quietly, aware that this was really antagonizing Gary. I leaned back slightly on my chair, crossed my leg, ankle on knee, and returned to revolving the cup on its saucer. It was wonderful to be in this position and I was relishing having an occasional one up on Gary, competitive as he was. Gary – he of the massive put-down. Gary – the man who hated anyone being more in the limelight than he. And I was in a good position: I knew that the dinner with Marie had occurred (although I had wondered, on waking, whether it were all a wonderful dream), Pete and Gary knew that it was possible but they – and Gary in particular – were jealous enough to tell themselves that I was lying. I decided to wind them up further.

Exasperatedly, Gary said: "You have to substantiate your claim."

"Actually, I don't," I said and paused, smiling inside. Then I sat forward quickly and regarded both of them seriously. "Okay, that's rubbish. Here's the situation. A French harpy, by the name of…Charlotte is waiting round by the stage door –."

"Ah!" exclaimed Gary, rubbing his hands and sitting back, "now we get to it."

"Yes. Beautiful girl: blonde, pretty and looking like she could be really dirty" – Gary was almost apoplectic with glee – "I come out, autograph of Marie Duvois in sweaty paw. She – the harpy – speaks to me in broken English and I agree to go to a restaurant in the centre of town. To cut a long story short, then she invites me back to her place –."

"There you are!" exploded Gary, throwing his hands melodramatically in the air and slapping his thighs loudly as they landed in his lap, as if he had told this story earlier and no-one had believed him.

"Ssssh," Pete hissed angrily and turned back to me. "Go on. What happened?"

"I go back to her place, as I said, for a *digestif*."

"Is that all?" asked Gary, incredulously.

"And another *digestif* or two and to swap some spit."

"Oh, ho, ho!" whooped Gary, like a rather sickly Father Christmas. He leaned back in his chair and smiled, nodding overtly, lips pursed and eyes wide.

"But," I continued, starting to reel them in, "it was when we got undressed that I noticed one strange thing about this girl."

"What?" asked Pete, confusion etching into his face.

"She wasn't one of these…wotchermacallits…these transvestites, was she?" asked Gary, disgust screwing up his features.

"He," corrected Pete, as an aside.

"No," I said, almost breathlessly, "worse than that."

"What?"

"Come on."

"She," I said slowly, "didn't exist." In the palm of my hand, I thought, and swatting them.

"Eh?" said Gary, completely confused, after a pause.

"A total figment of my sub-clinically neurotic and deranged imagination. The true and original Phantom of the Opera. So when I got back here, I was concocting what I hoped to be a believable story, something that I could say to Gary and Pete that they'd believe when they asked me what I did… I think I did quite well. That's why I had that faraway look and was smiling when I came in last night, Gary."

"And?" asked Gary, eyes bulging and temper slipping a further notch.

"Well, I decided to tell you that I had wined and dined Marie Duvois. It was easier than explaining that I had got off with a dream…a ghost."

Gary pushed his chair back noisily and stood up. "I've had enough of this. He's talking in riddles. Pete, when you've got the story straight from him, come and tell me, will you?" He sighed tersely and left the room angrily, shutting the door with a bang.

One of Gary's main failings – one of Gary's many main failings! – was that he always wanted to be in control. Jealousy is a tough, powerful, dangerous and ultimately detrimental mistress to court, particular when it is unclear whether there is anything to be jealous about. Even more so, if there might be more than one thing to be jealous about – a woman, a relationship, a well-known singer, fame. Pete, Gary

and I styled ourselves on being angry young men who had a good laugh.
A bit oxymoronic but we enjoyed ourselves. We were getting on in years
and we were none of us having much luck with the opposite sex.
Therefore, we formed a slightly bitter group and we found amusement
and stimulation in each other's company, purely because we could bitch
about a woman or women in general and their attitudes, in the safe
knowledge that no remedial action would be taken. When this group
was rocked by one of its members having a modicum of female success,
therefore, jealousy always sprang to the fore like an Icelandic geyser on
double-rated overtime.

On top of that, Gary was disconcerted further, in this case, by the
knowledge that the woman in question was famous and, although he
made the quip about me being Puttnam-esque, he was the one of the
three most guilty of name-dropping. He could not stand anyone else
being able to name-drop better than he could. Especially in this
situation, where I had suggested a romantic closeness.

"Touchy," I said as the slamming door echoed around the room.

Pete sat back, lacing his fingers behind his head, and watched me still
playing idly with the cup. Then he sat forward and looked confidentially
over both shoulders. "Are you telling the truth?" he asked,
conspiratorially.

"You know that Grand Canyon?" He nodded. "Well, that's the width
of the great divide between what you're hearing and what you want to
hear. Both of you – well, Gary, mainly – wanted to hear that I had tried
to catch something nasty from some French tart down a back alley
somewhere. So, when you heard about Marie Duvois, you didn't want
to believe it, thinking I was lying. But, here's the question: what
percentage would I get from lying?"

"None, I suppose."

"I mean, you could ask her yourself. Although, if it weren't true,
you'd make a complete ass out of everybody. You, me and her."

"So is it true?"

"Look," I said and reached into my pocket, producing the slightly
smudged, red message in Marie's lipstick. Pete took it and stared at it for
several moments. I was going to tell him to remember this moment in
acting classes because the whole gamut of emotions ran across his face:
jealousy; anger; frustration; resignation and amusement.

"You lucky old bastard," he said, eventually.

I stopped short of telling him that Marie had written the autograph
before our date and then something occurred to me. "Also, if you and

Gary had cared to read any of the French newspapers this morning, you'd see me stepping out with Marie Duvois."

Pete shook his head violently, cheeks slapping against teeth, like a wet dog. "I'll say it again: you lucky old bastard."

"It was a once in a lifetime experience. Nothing will come of it." Involuntarily, I crossed my fingers.

"Yeah," Pete nodded, knowingly. "Sure. And I'm the Queen of Sheba."

I put my hands together, as if praying, closed my eyes to slits, top front teeth over bottom lip and I bowed slightly: "Velly nice taw meet yaw." I laughed and Pete grinned. "Where is Sheba anyway? Is it just south of Lambeth? I must look it up to ensure I get the accent right."

"Yeah. That was an appalling American accent, if I may say so."

"It was supposed to be Australian!" I protested.

We sat in silence for a while, before Pete got up, pushing the chair across the carpet and clapped me on the shoulder. "Well, congratulations, old man. I'm jealous as hell – she's a pretty lady – but I wish you luck." He handed back the kerchief. "Queen of Ayers Rock or not."

He turned to go and then turned, looking thoughtful, a finger across his lips and said: "Did you...?" He made a sweeping gesture with a hand, an enquiring look on his face.

I smiled. "Very euphemistic, but...didn't even get close to it." The image of stroking Marie's arm popped into my head and stemmed the smile, palpitating my heart a little with the thrill of the memory. "Nowhere near it, Pete."

"Just wondered," he said, brightening a little. "See you later."

With that, he smiled, winked and left the dining-room by its central double-doors.

I was alone.

Alone with my handkerchief.

Alone with my marvellous thoughts.

PUPPET ON A STRING

CHAPTER 4

I have always been innately insecure. But, to counter that, I am naturally optimistic and work hard. The upshot of this is that I am never really satisfied with what I achieve, because of the constant battle of optimism chipped and scarred by the drive for perfectionism. Some distant observers have accused me of viewing my life's glass as half-empty accordingly. My usual response is that my glass is not at all half-empty but drained, washed up, dried thoroughly and put away at the back of the cupboard because I know that I have another full one waiting on the bar.

That afternoon, I had gone back to my room and had slept fitfully for a couple of hours, dreaming in hope of all the good things that could come out of a liaison with Marie. I rose at around three, my head a little thick with unsatisfactory sleep, feeling as if feathers had replaced my brain. I decided to have a long bath.

I think the French have no appreciation of what proper baths should be like; my knees were almost up to my ears and the only derived comfort was from the hot water. The bath was more a tall-sided, square box about three feet deep. Eventually, having dressed and groomed myself, I felt presentable and more like a member of the human race than a walking corpse – still, with hope waging war against insecurity in my head and now losing rather badly.

A walk seemed to be a good way to clear my head of everything. Leaving the key at reception, I walked deep in thought, hands in pockets, along the rue de Richelieu to the Tuileries and then along the north bank of the Seine, which glittered nonchalantly in the intermittent sun. It reminded me of our conversation about artists and I tried to imagine what that would have been like. It was almost certain that I would not have met her had she taken that particular course in her life and career, so could that be taken as fate?

A gust of wind caught me and I shivered. Walking was supposed to clear these thoughts from my head! I crossed the Seine by the Pont d'Iéna towards the Eiffel Tower, where I decided to rest a while and, stopping only to buy copies of *Le Monde* and *Figaro*, I made my way to one of the many seats positioned in the shadow of the Tower.

Flicking through the pages of *Le Monde*, I found page thirteen (fortunately, not being triskaidekophobic in any way, the superstition surrounding that number meant nothing to me – touch wood!), which had a large picture of Marie holding on to my arm and a bemused look on my face. I gazed at it dreamily and slowly formulated my resolve.

* * *

I love the excitement generated by an orchestra tuning up over the buzz of the audience chattering. It somehow gets the adrenalin flowing quickly, heightening the anticipation of the forthcoming performance. Then the audience hushes as the leader of the orchestra stands up, raising his bow for silence. A single concert 'A' floats across from the principal oboe, soon to be joined on that note by the rest of the orchestra, before dissolving into an apparently atonal cacophony of sound. The audience conversation starts up again like a reincarnated hive of bees. Finally and slowly, the auditorium lights dim, the place is hushed once more, broken by the explosion of applause like hailstones on a green-house roof, which greets that night's conductor. He shakes hands with the orchestra leader, bows, maybe raises a hand in a modest manner of thanks, turns to the orchestra, picks up his baton from the lectern, waits for absolute silence, shoots his cuffs, raises the baton for attention and then enters the overture in his own inimitable style. The opera has begun.

With this cocktail of anticipation for the night's performance, excitement for its eventual execution and the knowledge of a good resolve founded under the Tower, I walked up the Avenue de l'Opéra and down the side of the Opera House to the Artists' Entrance to ply the make-up and get ready. We were normally made up and dressed by about five o'clock or half past for a half past seven start of the performance – a very laborious and sometimes very tedious process.

"Hello, Dave," said Pete, as I flung the door open and assumed a theatrical pose, arms raised and head turned away as if in pain. He was sitting on one of those imitation patent leather chairs, with his feet up on the dressing-table, sipping unenthusiastically from a paper cup. "How are you?"

"Oh, *allegro ma non troppo*."

"Beg pardon?"

"I mean: life is moving at a fast pace, but not so fast that I can't handle it."

"Very witty. Where have you been?"

"I didn't know you cared so much," I replied, throwing myself at another chair and landing with a satisfying groan of wood on linoleum and farting cushion air. I smiled and chucked the papers casually on to the table. "No. I had a couple of hours' kip and then went for a canter. How's the head?"

"A little better. I went to the bar and had a hairy dog at lunch-time. But I still feel a little rough."

"What? Like a chihuahua?"

Pete shook his head a little.

I explained. "A chihuahua. A little ruff!" I barked the last word.

"God, your sense of humour is going down-hill fast, Dave." He paused and added, questioningly: "In fact, it's going to the dogs?"

I picked up a cushion and chucked it at him. "Christ, that's awful, Pete." He ducked the cushion. "How you can say my sense of humour is bad…"

He chuckled and, noticing the papers, picked one up, which was mysteriously open at the correct page. He whistled quietly, before saying: "My God! It is true! Oooh, dear… Gary's not going to like this!"

As if waiting for the cue, Gary entered. "Hello, boys," he said campily, brushing his hair back delicately with one hand, the other on his hip. "Ooh, I do love to be theatrical."

"Hello, Gary."

"How's your head?" asked Pete sympathetically.

Gary slumped and rubbed his eyes. "Like I've had a brain transplant with a king-size pillow. I've tried to sleep it off but it's still there. The headache; not my brain. Or the pillow. Well, my brain's still there. Obviously. That goes without saying. Oh, shut up, Adner, for God's sake. You're rambling." He gave a sideways nod to me. "Did Dave get his story straight in the end?"

"Well," said Pete, winking at me slightly, "he got the autograph."

"Yes, yes," replied Gary, tetchily, "but did he do anything else?"

I pinched my arm dramatically three or four times. "Oh, good, I am still here!"

Gary tutted and became more flustered. "Well?" he asked impatiently.

"Not even close to it." Pete winked at me again and we began laughing, causing Gary to flinch slightly. Pete brought himself up and said: "Sorry, Gary. Have a look at this."

Gary took the proffered paper and his face seemed to darken. He threw the paper petulantly on to the table. "Oh, I'm going to get my stage clothes," he said, hotly and left the room, just as two petite, attractive-but-not-pretty French girls, aged about eighteen or nineteen, wearing small, green artist's smocks, entered. Gary banged the door shut, which made them jump slightly.

"Now, gentlemen," said one with a seductive accent, "let's see what we can do for you."

Pete looked at me, one eye widened, the other half-closed, rubbed his hands together and licked his lips lasciviously. The poor girls looked confused and smiled nervously as we snorted with laughter, which only served to make us worse.

* * *

Gary was very taciturn towards me for the next hour, on the occasions when he actually deigned to talk to me. Being a very conceited person and consistently petty when not being in control, it rankled with him that I had spent the evening with Marie Duvois. His usual approach to this was to belittle me with a grander anecdote of his own or to make a remark that hit home in the epicentre of my insecurity. But, in this case, it appeared that he was struggling to get the upper hand.

By seven o'clock, however, his mood had completely switched. Laughing and joking with Bob Holden, when I walked up the steps, stage right, he beckoned to me. "Here, Dave," he called, "come here a moment."

I eyed him warily, in case this was the set-up he was looking for to bring me down or to take advantage of my hatred of being patronized.

"Did you hear the one about the two fleas?"

I shook my head and began to smile. His apparent good cheer was infectious and it appeared that my earlier misdemeanour of overstepping my mark with him was forgotten temporarily.

"They were going out for dinner and one turned to the other and said –:" he switched range to falsetto at this point – "'It's such a lovely evening dear. Shall we walk or take a cat?'" Gary was almost bent double, laughing at his punch-line.

It was reasonably funny but we were guffawing, with tears rumbling haphazardly over our make-up. It was one of those situations where the heightened atmosphere is tense with expectancy for the evening's performance, the adrenalin has already started flowing, everyone is on a knife-edge and someone says something that deserves little more than a smile. The width of that smile and the relative measure on the Richter scale of the belly laugh is exactly proportional to the level of adrenal hormone being pumped around the blood. But, for one thing, I was glad that it had seemed to break through Gary's sombre mood.

* * *

That night was the second and last of the performances of the French tour and it started promptly at half past seven. I had wanted to go to Marie's dressing-room beforehand but the bravado I had built up by the Eiffel Tower had burnt away to a thin streak of yellow, which fitted my spine perfectly. Incredible, is it not, that I could happily go on stage and sing to three of four thousand people over and over again but I could not make that short journey to her door just once more? I had wondered more than once over the day, and considered again now, what Marie was thinking and whether she was as troubled as I.

In Tosca, there are three acts. The Paris Opéra is designed in such a way that the sets can be changed as efficiently and quickly as possible. Under the Opéra are several rooms in the cellar, which house all the boxed sets. When one set is finished with, it is literally dropped from the stage and carted away and the next set is wheeled into position and winched up. There are five levels under the stage, a labyrinth of tunnels and rooms – the perfect setting for Leroux's *The Phantom of the Opera*.

The first act had gone down very well with the audience and we had reached the torture scene in Act Two, where Tosca pleads with Scarpia for her lover's (Cavaradossi's) life. Years later, the shame and self-criticism mean that I cannot recall exactly what happened but I can only think that I must have had some sort of mental aberration. Acting and singing take an immense amount of concentration and anticipation. A slight moment of forgetfulness and the whole thing can fall flat on its face. And it happened, almost disastrously, to me that night.

Pete and I were holding Pietro Visconti, the tenor playing Cavaradossi, who was in supplication. We were playing the silent parts of Scarpia's policemen, who are in charge of torture, creative disposal of people and general 'doing very bad things'. We were wearing long Quaker-like coats, white-collared black shirts, pointed shoes with brass buckles and, on top, long-haired, greasy wigs, which came down to our shoulders. We looked very silly.

In the story, Scarpia had just ordered that Cavaradossi's torture be increased (offstage, of course). Marie, as Tosca, was pleading with Scarpia for Cavarodossi's life and a halt to the continuation of torture. And she was wonderful. I think she actually believed she was Tosca when she was on that stage – she sounded and looked in the very depths of despair. Which is when it happened.

Pete and I had dragged Pietro Visconti in and I stood, transfixed, gazing at Marie as she sobbed on her knees. She was wearing a sky-blue, low-cut, ankle-length dress, very similar in style and colour to the one she wore to our dinner the previous night. It was simple but so appealing. A surge of love, compassion and sympathy swept over me and I had an insane urge to step forward to hug and comfort her –.

There was a subtle nudge in my ribs from Pete and the trance was broken. At this point, Cavaradossi was supposed to have been dragged out. Surreptitiously, Pete whispered for me to snap out of it and move, whereupon we began pulling the whimpering Visconti off the stage. Fortunately, for me at any rate, I was no longer required for further appearances during the rest of the opera. This was just as well, since my confidence was in ribbons and shame was battering my beleaguered senses. I could have become famous, being the person to rewrite Tosca by allowing one of Scarpia's heavies to cuddle Tosca, before overseeing the murder of her beloved. Famous, indeed, but I would not work again in the theatre.

Pete and I let Visconti go to moan and groan in the acoustic box behind the stage under the direction of the stage manager. When he was out of earshot, Pete turned to me and said earnestly: "Hey, Dave! Wake up! You're a professional, remember?"

"I…I'm sorry, Pete," I stuttered. "I don't know what went wrong there. I've done this opera, what? A dozen times? And I've never forgotten to move or sing once."

"Well, be careful, eh?" Pete relaxed and smiled. "Look, we're going to La Parisienne again after the show. Will you be coming? Last night and all that?"

"I might do. I've got someone to see first. Say goodbye."

"I've got the picture," he said, winking. "It wouldn't be a certain Mademoiselle Duvois, by any chance?"

I smiled a little. "Yeah, it might just be."

"Well, we might see you down there for a drink. If not; good luck!"

He left me to wander up to the dressing-room, my heart pounding with a mixture of self-loathing and anticipatory nerves.

* * *

After the fifth curtain call, Marie left the stage, her arms laden with flowers, to return to her dressing-room. My heart began tripping over itself with nerves as I followed her at a reasonably discreet distance, determined to see how things were after the previous dinner date and, depending on that, to say a fond farewell. Hey, maybe even swap addresses! Perhaps another meal tonight? Then back to her hotel for a nightcap, put my feet up on the sofa and we could talk about –.

A hand came down unnecessarily heavily on my shoulder like the proverbial long arm of the law. I jumped, startled, partly out of the guilt, partly in surprise, but mainly because I was still feeling the confidence-draining shame of my inadvertent slip. It was Gary.

He watched Marie until she had disappeared around the corner into the labyrinthine path to her dressing-room, before he released my shoulder. Anger stabbed hotly at my temples and throbbed dully. So this was how he was going to maintain one-upmanship over me; stopping me seeing Marie to take whatever relationship we might have further. I had made a resolution, I had weakened before the performance and now Gary was attempting to thwart me from seeing it through to its conclusion. The last person I wanted to be stopped by was Gary, because I knew what was coming next.

"What?" I asked peremptorily and whirled round on him.

"Don't be so tetchy," he said, in a kindly way as if in bewilderment as to why I should be reacting this way. "I just wanted a little word about your attack of amnesia back there on stage."

In the background, I could hear the stagehands and scene-shifters already hacking the sets apart and winching the next evening's performance set into place. The sawing and hammering seemed excruciatingly loud and it exacerbated and stretched my foul temper a few notches further still towards breaking-point. "Yeah," was all I could muster, "I'm sorry. I was thinking about something else." I kept glancing at the corner, the last swish of Marie's taffeta dress having died some moments before.

"You're paid to sing and act, Dave," patronized Gary, with an attempt at sincere concern on his face, "and not to forget your movements by getting an eyeful by looking down the lead singer's cleavage. Just imagine what would happen if every chorister did that. There would be damned near anarchy. You need to be more professional, Dave, and I'm not saying that just as Secretary but as your friend."

Once again, Gary was pushing all the right buttons. Resorting to condescension and preying on the guilt that I felt for almost making an horrendous mistake. Treating me like an aberrant six-year-old was the best way of raising my blood-pressure. I clenched my teeth in an attempt to contain the anger. "I was not looking down Marie's...her dress," I said slowly and carefully, hands clenching and unclenching in fists, fingernails digging painfully into my palms. More calmly, I added: "I'm just a little tired, that's all."

"We're all tired, Dave," Gary continued. "It's not good enough to blame it on other things than yourself. If it was anyone else, I would seriously consider kicking them out on their butt. But just this once, I'll forget it; but don't let it happen again." He was actually waggling a finger at me by this point in the admonition. "You could be out, otherwise, and I've got far too much work to do without having to wet-nurse you."

Another button pressed – the pretence that he was doing me a favour but I had no comeback. I took a deep breath, remembering what I had planned to do. We appeared to be at the other side of the castigation and I wanted the evening to be back on the track I had devised and dreamed of during the afternoon. Summoning up more reserves and pushing the urge to claim unfair treatment away (thus falling into his trap of talking to me as if I were a toddler), I said stiffly: "Right, Gary. I'm sorry." I attempted a humble smile, which felt more accurately like a vicious leer. He stood disapprovingly, hands on hips, shaking his head slightly, before relaxing and smiling again.

"Right. Air clear?"

"I guess so," I responded meekly, even though my innards were still a boiling, frenzied maelstrom of mixed and negative emotions. Nothing, at that precise moment, would have given me greater pleasure than continually hitting Gary's face with a paving slab. Gary 'I'm God Almighty' Adner had managed to get the better of me again. He had stopped me seeing Marie as I had planned, he had my career by the testicles and was unafraid to squeeze them occasionally to ensure I stayed in line, and he had got me into such an emotional state that it would take time to be the same David Loughton I was the previous evening, who had knocked timidly on Marie's door.

This was the first chink in our relationship but Gary paid little regard to that, because he felt – no, knew – he had won. "Are you going to La Parisienne with the rest of us?" he asked now, imperiously.

"Yes…yes, I am. I just need to go back to the hotel for some money – I didn't bring enough out – and then I'll join you." A weak and feeble excuse but I wanted Gary to disappear. I still fully intended to see my resolution through, strengthened by this altercation.

"OK, I'll see you later then," he said, ambling off around the corner that Marie had disappeared not five minutes earlier. It seemed like hours ago. I breathed a sigh of relief tinged with anger and the desire for vengeance and leaned against the wall, eyes stinging with welling tears of frustration and filled my lungs slowly and deeply to get myself under control.

* * *

After ten minutes or so, I had calmed down enough to be pleasant and with renewed trepidation and nerves, made my way down the same path I had trodden the previous night. Excitement had gripped me as I foresaw another wonderful evening ahead. Abruptly, it all dissipated like water down a plug-hole as I turned the corner. I heard Gary laugh, thank someone and then saw that it was Marie's door he was shutting.

He looked up from the piece of paper he was holding. "Dave!" he said, affecting surprise, "I thought you'd gone back to the hotel."

"Yeah," I tried to say lightly, desperately keeping the resurgent emotions in check. "I wanted to see Marie."

"A proper autograph, eh? Well, I've got one now. Look." He proudly showed the studio photograph of Marie that he was holding. It had the message:

To Gary,
Nice to have worked with you
Best regards, Marie Duvois

"No, I just thought I'd say goodbye. You know. Last night to see her before we go back."

Gary took my arm and pushed me back up the corridor. "I don't think you'd better. She's got a visitor." He glanced back. "Come on, I'll buy your drinks at the bar. No need to get your money."

Damn him in perpetuity! He was still winning. Just a few more strings pulled and I would be dancing for him. "Who's the visitor?" I asked, in a dreadful, shaky voice that was meant to sound light and casual and shrugged him off my arm.

"Oh, some chap. An admirer, I expect. And I don't blame him for admiring her." Gary nudged me, leering. I felt nauseated.

"No," I cleared my throat, "neither do I." I tried to laugh but the brain's messages were just not getting through to the facial muscles.

"What I could do to her if I could have one night. I could be so dirty, it would be gruesome." He shook his head. "Not that I'll find out but I'm sure that chap in there will."

The next big chunk of our relationship fell away. Not only was he on top and loving it, but also he would not stop until I was down and out for the count. I remember my feelings precisely; and it made me feel like crying. There was a deep, malignant jealousy revolving in my stomach, gnawing at my brain at the thought that some other fellow was in the same position as I had been the previous night. I had to swallow queasily to stop the growing peristaltic movements ejecting embarrassingly the scant food I had had that day. Just twelve hours before, for once, I had had the upper hand on Gary but he had now skilfully and painfully reversed that situation. While I had relished being in the winning position of one-upmanship, at least I had not been perverse in the enjoyment. It was all so bloody unfair.

Just as this new piece of information was being ingested, the door opened. I heard Marie say something indistinct like, "Vite! Vite! Courons!" and then laughing. Following her was a man about five years her junior. She saw Gary and me standing up the corridor, stopped momentarily and waved, smiled and called, "See you again soon. I'm sorry I can't stop."

I caught Gary looking at me, a half-smile on his lips. If Marie had said anything else or had played charades in the corridor or danced a nude can-can, it would have swept past me in complete ignorance, for I had turned away, feeling sick and anger, frustration and fury at Gary. He reached out to put a hand on my shoulder and maybe attempted to say something soothing. I think he realized that he might have taken things a little too far, as I buried my face in my hands to hide the tears, shying away from him. I had another, more immediate resolution now as we headed disconsolately to La Parisienne. It would solve all my problems.

I was going to get blind, lying-in-the-gutter-singing-at-the-sky drunk.

PUPPET ON A STRING

CHAPTER 5

Of course, I had been wrong. Getting drunk does not solve your problems. It makes them seem unimportant, so you forget about them. Until you sober up. Then the problems appear to increase exponentially in size, as the resultant hangover and sobriety put everything too starkly back into perspective. I can quite see how weaker people become alcoholic.

The next morning, waiting for the ferry at Boulogne port, seated on my suitcase, with head in hands and a migraine-level headache, I thought that I had been an incredible fool and actually Gary had inadvertently done me a favour. What right had I to assume that I had any kind of hold over Marie Duvois? Not only was I not in the same league as she, as Gary had pointed out in such a vitriolic manner, but I had only gone to dinner with her only the once. Granted, it had been a very nice – nay, wonderful – evening; I had even caressed her in a small way and she had written me a very nice message, which I still had (getting more and more smudged – a point not lost on Gary, who had the ballpoint-written version on a picture of her). Furthermore, I had the press reports with the photograph of me with Marie outside the Opéra. That should have been enough to assuage any small fantasies I might still have had, but I still had no rights over Marie Duvois. There was a yearning burning away at me that I had never felt before and could not explain, even ineloquently. I put it down to latent jealousy since that was the closest emotion from past experience on which I could peg it.

I was still angry with Gary. In fact, still livid with him, because of his attempts to control what I wanted to do and moreover the poisonous way he went about it. The anger had subsided to a sort of frustrated fury as the train left the Parisian suburbs – Marie was out of sight and it was becoming easier (not simple) to put her out of my mind.

The night before, Pete had said he understood, as I huddled over my beer, red-eyed and repeatedly slurring the same muttered imprecations.

On the return trip, he was avoiding me; maybe to allow me to get my thoughts more straightened out or maybe because I had insisted to anyone who would listen that Pete, no listen, Pete was my best mate, before promptly and lavishly adorning my surrounding area with half-digested Continental beer.

* * *

Back in the real world, with the Paris tour behind us, the *Coro di Londinium* were planned for a rest from a demanding schedule. Every Tuesday and Thursday, we were required for rehearsal; the morning for acting, the afternoon and evening for music and libretto, singing techniques and general musical activities. If there were a performance or a recording coming up, the number of rehearsals would be increased. The remainder of the time, we were supposed to rehearse privately, although most people took the opportunity to teach singing or musical instruments or to write books and articles. This was not a contractual problem, as long as it did not interfere with the quality of performance.

For the choral and vocal training, the *CdL* hired the services of Sir Norman Pettinger, the world-renowned Mahlerian expert, whose input to the chorus was an enormous and positive impact. He was a tall, thin man with white hair receding at the front and bushy sideburns. He always wore a suit and tie, only removing these when everyone else was almost in a coma from heatstroke and dehydration. Sir Norman gave the impression that he always had fifteen different things running concurrently on his mind and ignored attempts at humour, although he himself was a witty man. For this reason, Pete and Gary were always trying to throw him off-balance with an unexpected remark or joke to make the old man laugh. It had never worked yet. Although he was hired as the vocal coach, he took a great interest in the running of the *CdL* and acted as a Music Director, providing invaluable help and assistance in obtaining performances and recordings where he could. His long history started as a music academic before taking up the conductor's baton, and later taking the job as a classical music producer at EMI. Through this experience, Sir Norman had many contacts in both the music and recording world, which was an asset to the chorus to keep them busy.

* * *

Most of the conversation and occurrences in the next part of my story rely on discussions with Pete (and a couple of others), gleaned over a couple of glasses of fermented hops. They are included here for chronological accuracy and continuity. Some of it (or all of it) could be exaggerated hearsay. But, as I said earlier, I care not. It seems right, it fits the facts as I know them and I will write it down word for word as it was told to me and as I can remember.

On the Camber Road in South Mimms (of all strangely-named places), was the purpose-built hall and studio in which we rehearsed. There were two large rooms on the ground-floor: one with two grand pianos and several of those awful, tubular-metal, material-covered, uncomfortable chairs normally associated with church halls and the bain of orthopaedic hospitals' waiting lists, I should not wonder, which made up the room for music rehearsals; the other was a larger but long room with a mirror down one side and an upright piano, which was used for acting rehearsals. Underneath these rooms, was a vast cellar, divided into a large storage space, where the huge and untidy operatic wardrobe and selection of props were stored and a pristine, rarely used sound-proof room and engineering suite to manage any recordings the Chorus required. Up the stairs from the music rehearsal room was a kitchen annexe with half a dozen Formica-topped tables, the same back-breaking chairs and a small room, which was used as an office – that is to say, it looked small but was actually quite spacious under the piles of papers, posters, contracts, programmes and other paraphernalia associated with running the *Coro di Londinium*.

Just off the Camber Road, two minutes' walk from the halls, was a quaint old-world pub called the Goat and Dramatist, at which we drank prior to and following rehearsals. The deduction of the link between the pub's two symbols never produced anything other than the pornographic or surreal. It was a small, cosy, one-bar pub, with oak beams, wattle and daub walls, booths for privacy up one end, a red, beer-stained carpet and brown nicotine stains on the once-white ceiling. The pub was run by a gruff but amiable chap, called John. He did not enjoy people messing him around (such as changing your mind halfway through an order or not giving the entire order in one go), but enjoyed a chat with customers of longevity on anything from the limited list of the weather or the upcoming football match.

On the Tuesday after we had returned from Paris, just before the evening rehearsal, I wandered into the Goat and Dramatist for a pre-prandial drink. As it was drawing near April's finale, at six o'clock the

sun was sinking but still brightly orange on the horizon. Pushing the
door open, I observed Gary standing at the bar alone. The burning
resentment I had continued to feel towards him on the return journey
from Paris had lessened but was still present. I knew that the right word
(or wrong word more accurately) or action would make me lose my
temper with him. Therefore, having avoided him at the earlier rehearsals
that day, I managed to keep my cool and smiled generously at him as I
approached the bar.

"Oh, blimey," he whined. "They all come crawling out of the
woodwork on my round, don't they? And a pint of best please, John."
John nodded as he placed Gary's drink on the beer-mat and disappeared
to pour mine, at which point Pete came in through the door. Wearily,
Gary said: "Oh, no! Are you trying to ruin me?"

Gary rarely bought a round, preferring to sponge off others who were
either trying to ensure that he returned other unsubstantiated favours in
the future or had the misfortune to be at the bar. This, then, was a rare
privilege, caught as he had been at the bar on his own.

"Sure am," answered Pete, "time to wake up the wallet-moths, Gary.
Pint of cider please!"

Gary turned to the bar and called the order to John, who returned
with my drink. Banging it unnecessarily on the bar, he said: "Right. Is
that everything? I don't want to be running up and down this bar all
night for you." Gary nodded meekly and it occurred to me that John
appeared to be the only person who had any control over Gary.

"How's things, Gary?" asked Pete.

"Rolling along. You know," replied Gary, sucking froth from his
moustache. "I've got over my ship-lag."

"Hangover, you mean."

Gary laughed. "Yes, that's true. No, I've started doing some
preliminary work on this *Carmen* recording. If we get to do it, that is.
Norm's still trying to pull that one for us and I've got to go to all these
business meetings."

"That should be good."

"What the business meetings?"

"No the recording. Anyway: "business meetings"? An excuse for
liquid lunches, more like!"

Gary shifted uncomfortably, the uneasy silence broken by John
returning with Pete's cider. "That's two shillings exactly, please. Unless
you've decided to extend your order again?" Gary shook his head and
groaned as he delved deep into a trouser-pocket, producing a half-

crown. John took it with disgruntled thanks and went to deposit it in the till.

"Yeah, so," Gary continued, "I've got a lot of underground work to do on it at the moment. To be honest, it's a wonder how I can fit it in along with everything else."

Feeling my anger rising again with Gary playing the martyr, I tried to lighten my thoughts by saying: "That sounds a little shady!"

"What does?" Gary looked a little nervous.

"'Underground'. Sounds like the Mafia!"

"The Chorus…Underground. Yes, I like that."

"Well, you've got a nose for that type of thing," added Pete. "Perhaps it could be called the 'Cosy Nostril'."

"At least we wouldn't look suspicious carrying violin cases around," I countered and we laughed.

John returned with Gary's change, re-grunted his thanks and walked to the other end of the bar to remonstrate with a man in a pork-pie hat, who had been banging his glass irritatingly on the bar for service.

The conversation returned to the recording of *Carmen*. Pete whistled a snatch of the *Mélodrame* from the first act and said: "It's simply constructed but it's lovely music. I think it's amongst my favourite operas."

"It also happens," said Gary, knowingly nodding at Pete but giving me a sly sideways glance, which put me on my guard, "to be Marie Duvois's favourite opera. She told me that." His tongue poked into a cheek.

The button pressed, the strings pulled, I tried to keep my calm.

"I'm always mixing with the stars, you know," continued Gary. He crossed the middle finger over the top of his forefinger. "Me and her, we're like that." He reversed the fingers and added: "Or is it like that?"

I knew he was deliberately trying to wind me up and was achieving just that until a thought popped into my head. The emotion dissipated and was replaced with a smile. "I'll bet, though," I said, staring steadily and straight into his eyes, "that you don't know what her second favourite opera is. She told *me* that."

His face faltered momentarily and he struggled to retain his smile. "That's true," he admitted, before draining his glass and waving it at John for a refill.

* * *

At about half past six, we strolled leisurely to the rehearsal rooms. We were due to go over the technique of producing tone and pitch, while singing *pianissimo*. Not too exciting stuff but it was a test of the endurance of the diaphragm muscles, blood pressure and lung capacity. It may sound odd but in order to sustain a note, especially quietly, for any length of time, requires a good level of physical fitness. As the singer holds any particular note for longer than a few seconds, the body is quietly starved of oxygen, filling up with carbon dioxide instead, which results in the desire to breathe heavily. Therefore, the fitter you are, the slower the natural breathing rate and the lesser the need to gulp like a beached fish.

The chairs were set out in a rough semi-circle of five rows radiating outwards from a central podium, upon which a lectern and chair was placed. Behind the podium was one of the grand pianos, which was being played by an accompanist employed by Sir Norman, who I had seen several times but whose name escaped me. Sir Norman was standing by the end of the piano, looking in an opened briefcase, lying on top of it. Several other people were already there and seated, talking to one another, reading the paper or flicking through their scores.

He glanced up as we entered, laughing and joking about the *Mafioso* we would be setting up. "Peter! Gary! Good evening! Please will you join me for a moment?"

I left them and sat in the second row of the tenor section, next to a person whom I had never met before, while Pete and Gary went over to the piano to talk with Sir Norman.

"Hello, darling," said Pete, grinning.

"All right, love?" asked Gary.

Not even a twitch across Sir Norman's wizened features. "Yes. Look. I've obtained agreement for the Chorus to do this *Carmen* recording, finally. Just getting the contracts sorted out *[when I heard this from Pete, I thought back to the pub conversation: so what exactly was it that Gary was supposed to be doing with this recording again?]*. If we are going to do this well, we will need one-hundred-and-fifty percent co-operation from everybody."

"Great!" said Pete, genuinely, "nice going, Norm-mate."

"So, I'll need you to sort out the admin. side, Gary. And Pete, maybe you could talk to the other section managers. I've yet to see them today. We're going to need a lot of people to fulfil this EMI contract. Possibly, we need to think about persuading them not to take holidays just yet. How many basses have we on the books?"

Pete turned his mouth down and shrugged: "Regularly? About thirty, thirty-five."

"Yes. Good. I think nearer forty should do it. And a similar increase in all the other parts."

"Right," said Pete, professionalism kicking in. "Leave that with me and I'll get together with the other section managers. Do you wish to go through auditions for the extras or shall we rely on people we've used before?"

"If we can get away without auditions, that would suit me better."

"Consider it done."

"Right, thank you. Let's get the evening started."

* * *

During Pete's and Gary's tête-à-tête with Sir Norman, I had tried striking up a conversation with the new person sitting beside me. He had squinting, shrew eyes, a long, pointed nose, under which a besom appeared to be growing, a deeply lined forehead and a strong flavour in body odour. "Good evening," I said, holding out a hand, "my name is David Loughton."

"Good evening," he responded, slightly irritated and ignoring my hand. He sucked nervously on the long, straggling hairs of his moustache.

Putting this down to nerves, I withdrew my hand slowly. "You haven't been in the Chorus long, have you?"

"No," he responded peremptorily.

"What? So, is tonight your first night?"

"Yes." He had not even looked at me. He appeared to be staring into the middle distance somewhere over by the piano.

"So you weren't here this morning?"

"No."

This was tough. "And have you met anyone else?"

"Not really."

"Would you like me to introduce you to a few people?"

"Who's the Chairman?"

"Oh, he's an idiot," I replied, conversationally. "It's not worth wasting your time talking to him."

"Well, he's in charge, isn't he?"

"No, not really. Only in name. He's just a figurehead with a title. You might as well have a stuffed cat sitting in his chair for all his effectiveness." I laughed but this odd chap maintained his focus on the middle distance and did not even smile.

"So who runs this organisation, then?" he asked.

"Well, Gary Adner thinks he does, although no-one's too sure. That's him over by the piano."

"He's not the chairman?" For the first time, my new acquaintance looked at me, surprise registered on his face.

"No. He's the Secretary."

"And he's your friend?"

I lifted up this troublesome lid cautiously, weighed up my most recent feelings and covered them over again. "Yes, he is. Would you like to meet him afterwards?"

"Yes," he was now following Gary and Pete to their chairs with his eyes.

"What did you say your name was?"

"I didn't," he replied curtly.

Before I could pursue it any further, Sir Norman stepped up on the podium, raising his hands for silence. I raised my eyebrows and shook my head a little at the peremptory attitude.

"Good evening, ladies and gentlemen," said Sir Norman. His rich voice carried well.

A few disconsolate mumbles returned the greeting.

"Er...Now, I have some good news for you. Or bad news, depending on which way you look at it, because it means more work. EMI have signed a contract with us to record *Carmen*."

Some surprised gasps oscillated around the Chorus and conversations sprang up.

"Sssh, please," said Sir Norman waving his hands for quiet. "I am producing it, which means it is my neck if I don't train you to the highest standard."

A group of sopranos and altos – or Norm's Gorms, as Pete called them - tittered at this. Because of Sir Norman's stature and general power in the music industry, some women found this very attractive and seductive. As a result, they could be relied on to hang on Sir Norman's every word and, irritatingly, laugh at everything, either intentionally or unintentionally funny that he said.

"We have not done *Carmen* for almost two years," he continued, "so I'm afraid we shall be doing a lot of work and stepping up rehearsals. And of course, all the work that I know you'll be putting in during the week."

Groans and titters, like broken glass tipped over an accelerating diesel engine.

"It's what you're paid for. The recording itself is next month, in the last week of May. The final details have yet to be settled or, if they already have, no-one's told me."

More titters.

"I must ask everyone to attend as it is an historic recording. And I'm not taking it lightly, so please rearrange your holidays, if you can, and reserve another time of year for being ill."

On cue, another round of hand-covering-mouth sniggers – it was like stamping on a nest of mice.

"Right," he continued, suddenly getting to his feet. "Enough of that for now. I understand that you had excellent *Tosca*s, gentlemen. Congratulations. Er…tonight, I should like to do some breathing exercises, but first we'll try some individual *pianississimo* scales to see how good your breathing is."

Groans.

"That should sort out the men from the tenors."

Judging from the Norm's Gorms' laughter, there could not have been a dry seat left in the house. I saw Pete pretending to machine-gun them and stifled a laugh.

Sir Norman began by standing everyone up and telling us to take deep breaths and letting them out slowly. Pete had the misfortune to be standing next to Sydney Althorpe, an habitual pipe-smoker in the sense that he seemed to produce as much pollution per day as a standard factory chimney, and who sounded therefore like a steam-train leaving Paddington station during the exercises. Then Sir Norman pointed at each individual person, giving them a starting note and asking them to sing an octave scale as quietly as possible. When it came to my turn, I started on a low note but, singing quietly, just eight notes later, my heart was pounding, my lungs were fit to bursting and my eyes bulged with the effort.

"Good," he said. "Sit, please."

I sat, relieved, having gained redemption to the state of 'good', following my *faux pas* on the Paris stage. Even after a week, I was still feeling very ashamed and paranoid that things would be taken further. Knowing Gary, with the benefit of the bright light under which I now saw him, I would not have put anything past him and would not trust him as far as I could dribble let alone spit.

Sir Norman continued randomly around the Chorus until he

reached my rudely anonymous acquaintance. Sir Norman slapped his forehead with his right hand. Shaking his head, he said: "I'm so forgetful."

Pete's machine-gunning had obviously failed.

"Ladies and gentlemen, would you greet our new tenor..." (he fumbled around for a piece of paper in his briefcase, leaning at a very precarious angle from the podium to the piano) "...Adrian Hilton."

A ripple of applause.

"Adrian Hilton, eh?" I said silently to myself. His initials were not lost on me.

"Now, we shall have the pleasure of Mr. Hilton showing us what he can do."

He was nervous but sounded good for a tenor on his first solo and I felt sorry for him being put through those hoops so early. Little did I realize that I would end up hating him with a vengeance.

PUPPET ON A STRING

CHAPTER 6

Fortunately, the rehearsal ended fairly early and, because it felt as if I had just taken part in a laryngitic assault course, the wonderful oesophageal therapy that is beer beckoned. It must have affected a lot of other people the same way, because more than the usual number came to the Goat and Dramatist after the rehearsal.

As we were leaving the halls with Adrian Hilton in tow, I attempted to introduce him to Gary, Bob and Pete. Before I could get past Gary's name, Adrian had interpolated himself between us, holding out his hand, which Gary shook. "Adrian Hilton," he said, smiling.

"Gary Adner," replied Gary and introduced Pete and Bob.

"Let me buy you all a drink," volunteered Adrian as we neared the pub.

Standing by the bar, I waited expectantly as the drinks arrived and were passed out to everyone except me. Adrian started counting out small change.

"I don't believe this!" I said under my breath.

"What?" said Adrian, unnecessarily terse, before smiling over his shoulder to the others.

I held my hands up in surrender. "Nothing. Just wondering whether you could get me a drink."

Adrian frowned and was about to say something.

"If I pay for it," I added.

He tutted and agreed reluctantly. Then he gave me the money he had counted out and said: "Here, you pay for the others as well."

I ordered my drink, added cash to Adrian's carefully established money and joined the others, who were drinking thirstily. Pete swallowed noisily and sighed ecstatically: "Ah, that hit the duodenum in one bounce."

"Those rehearsals are a hard slog, aren't they?" asked Adrian.

"Oh, you get used to it," responded Gary, touching the back of his head affectedly. "Particularly when you've done as many performances as I have."

Adrian edged oleaginously in front of me, squeezing me out of the small group, as if to indicate that any contribution I might have made to the conversation was now worthless. He asked: "How many performances does the *Coro di Londinium* do a year? Roughly?"

Bob replied: "We do about fifteen to twenty operas with an average of three or four performances for each. And five or six recordings on top of that, although that is increasing."

"Quite...overworked, then," Adrian hazarded a nervous laugh.

"So, Adrian," I started, pushing myself back into the group, "what's your background? How did you get to join this Chorus?"

He turned towards me and, as if he really did not care for this unnecessary interruption, said quickly with a touch of irritation: "I went to the Bristol Opera House Chorus, before reading an article in the Times Sunday Supplement about the *Coro di Londinium*." Then he turned back to the main group and began seeping in front of me again.

"Sorry I asked," I said, quietly. Gary screwed his face up as if in pain and nodded slightly to indicate that I should remain quiet and allow Adrian to talk. I was dumbstruck: I could not believe that Gary and Pete were so taken by this rude little man. Although, of course, it was only I, to whom he was rude; to them, he was sweetness and had started massaging their egos.

"It must be hard work on the committee. Especially as Secretary," he now said to Gary.

"Yes, but I manage somehow," said Gary, theatrically playing the martyr. "Muddle through as I do, because the show must go on." He placed the back of his hand against his forehead, sighing dramatically, and then laughed.

Pete punched him playfully on the shoulder and said: "It's harder being section manager." Bob agreed enthusiastically.

"And how would you know?" protested Gary, "you never do anything!" Gary, Pete and Bob started laughing, and they were soon joined by Adrian.

I withdrew to a bar-stool and watched this strange group and Adrian in particular. There was something about him, apart from the rudeness and the cold shoulder, which I did not like but could not put my finger on it. It was not even that he knew how to stroke Gary in particular. He was dangerous in some way but I put that down to the dislike that I had for him. I continued observing him as they talked about how important they were to the Chorus.

Adrian asked: "Do you get paid more for being on the committee?" He smiled.

(I can't put my finger on it)

Pete answered before Gary could chip in: "No. It's voluntary. But you can work a few perks, if you're shrewd." He winked at Bob and Gary, who laughed.

"So you're doing it for the love of it, as it were?"

(What is it about him?)

"Hardly *love*," replied Gary. "More for the power, I think." Bob and Pete snickered in response.

"And are all the posts elected by the members?"

(What is *it?)*

"All of them bar one," said Pete. "The wardrobe manager is co-opted by consensus from the committee."

"Now that is a dreadful job," Gary chipped in.

"No social life," added Bob.

"No thanks," said Pete.

Gary: "No nothing."

"Which is why we haven't got one," said Pete, "and it's a complete mess in the vaults."

Adrian had been imperceptibly puffing out his chest through this conversation. "How do you go about getting on this committee?"

(SNAP!! That was it! He was after power or control and, until now, that had washed over Bob, Pete and Gary because of the manipulative and flattering interest he had taken in them)

"Oh, no," Gary whined wearily, "you're not another power-hungry devil, are you?"

"No, no," replied Adrian a little too quickly, "I'm just interested in the dynamics of the Chorus and am trying to get a picture of the wonderful work you guys are doing." An oil-slick of a smile secreted itself across Adrian's lips.

"Well," said Gary, "to get on to the committee, you have to be very nice to Pete, Bob and me."

"And buy us drinks," offered Pete, hopefully.

"Oh, yes. Buying drinks goes without saying, of course."

"And be voted for co-option by the committee or by the Chorus itself," added Bob.

"Well, yes. Obviously, there is the democracy angle too."

I sensed that Adrian was going in for the kill as he said: "Are there any vacancies on the committee right now?"

Gary laughed. "Now hang on a minute. You haven't been in the Chorus for three hours and you're already planning a coup."

"No," said Adrian quickly, "I'm just making conversation. Your jobs are very interesting and I'm just trying to understand how they fit into running of the Chorus." That smile again. "But you were saying that the wardrobe manager's post is free?" he nudged calmly and without a hint of shame.

"Yes. But it's a really horrible job. We have difficulty even volunteering people to do it."

"What does it involve?"

"Generally ensuring that the costumes and props are readily available for the next performance," replied Bob.

"And making sure we have no last-minute panics," added Pete.

Adrian countered: "I used to do a similar job at Bristol. I used to find the job a cathartic experience, keeping everything tidy. Admittedly that was just music scores but, having a tidy mind, there is nothing better than to see things neat and tidy."

Gary looked at Pete and Bob, who smiled encouragement. "Well, if you're interested, I could probably swing it for you," he rejoined, turning back to face Adrian.

Adrian smiled triumphantly. "That's very generous, Gary. It's unexpected but I would be interested. Perhaps we can talk about it some time soon?"

The conversation turned to other points of interest but I remained where I was, perched on the bar-stool, shaking my head in disbelief at what had just gone on. Effectively, the three of them had allowed this nasty little man to interpolate himself on to the committee (there was no way that the committee was going to turn down the opportunity of co-opting a willing volunteer rather than finding ten pressed men), with little or no knowledge of his abilities, attributes or ambitions.

Adrian Hilton drained his glass, swapped addresses and numbers with Gary and bade everybody farewell, looking straight through me as he did so. When the door swung shut, I rejoined the group and said: "I can't believe you just gave him a committee post, just like that, Gary." I clicked my fingers.

"Well, he's keen. And you know how difficult it is to get people to do it voluntarily. It's a disgusting and dirty job, scrabbling around in that cellar." Gary's voice was rising in pitch and speed, as he edged desperately on to the defensive. "Anyway, why are you getting so upset? I don't see you doing anything to help this Chorus. Besides, he probably won't last long." Interesting, I thought, that Gary felt cornered because I was questioning his decision.

"I'm not getting upset," I said calmly, as if to prove the point, "but maybe the Chairman should –."

"That twit!" spat Gary. "He's as much use as an inflatable dart-board. Do you know, earlier this evening, I found him doing the caretaker's job and putting out the chairs for the rehearsal. Gives a new meaning to chairman, I suppose. No, if this Chorus is to go places, we need to leave him out of decisions like this."

I tried again: "Well, that's not the correct –."

"Look!" said Gary violently. "I've made a decision on behalf of the committee and it's sticking. Christ, Dave, you've been nothing but sour grapes since you failed to get off with that Marie Duvois woman and forgot to be professional."

Once again, Gary had turned the argument back on my one misdemeanour and the raw feelings I still had for Marie. My blood started to boil and all the animosity and more that I had felt under the Opéra stage in Paris returned with a sickening lurch. As then, my hands were making fists and releasing, the pain of nails digging in my palms remembered again.

"Gary," I said, fighting to keep calm, "that's not fair. You know as well as I do –."

"You see," replied Gary, smiling to Bob and Pete, "he's already started jumping down my throat."

"Forget Marie Duvois," I tried again. "Forget Paris. I'm talking about Adrian Hilton. He'll stab you in the back."

"No, Dave," Gary continued to protest. "He's a nice fellow and, as I say, he's also keen."

"Only because he wants power." Pete and Bob shifted uncomfortably at this.

"Sour grapes, Dave," countered Gary, "sour grapes."

"It's not bloody sour grapes. It's a matter of principle. The constitution says –."

"Oh, the constitution –."

"Yes! The constitution. Remember? The democratic constitution? Pah!" I spat. "Twit or not, the chairman –."

"For God's sake, Dave," shouted Gary, receiving a warning from John, the barman, "let it drop. I have made a decision."

I sighed and tried one more time. "Gary, will you –?"

Pete grabbed my shoulder and took me aside, while Gary shot his cuffs and moved his neck around to uncling it from his shirt collar. "Dave," Pete said, quietly, "I agree with you that Adrian was coming on a bit strong and that the Chairman should have been consulted, but both are harmless and Sydney Althorpe is a pain in the backside. He's next to useless –you've said as much yourself. That makes Gary effectively in charge. He's made an executive decision, which has got to stand."

"But, Pete…" I started.

"There's no point in getting upset." Pete was uncomfortable as he tried to argue me down.

"You're covering yourself, Pete."

"What do you mean?" exclaimed Pete, somewhat shocked.

"You know you've made a mistake in agreeing to appoint Adrian without going through the proper channels."

"No," he countered. "I know that…" He let out a defeated sigh. "You're right. I'll come clean. Yes, he was coming on stronger than I felt comfortable with but we're desperate to fill that position. And as Gary says, he's keen. Gary won't admit to his mistake, I know, so we'll have to let it stand."

"Well, just remember. There was another ferrety, power-hungry man with the same initials. Watch out for the 'Night of the Long Knives' repeating itself."

"Alright, Dave. I'm uncomfortable enough as it is. Look, I'll watch him. If he steps out of line or oversteps the mark, I'll sort him out. Now can we change the subject?"

I let it drop but was still seething, because I knew I had been right, while Gary had stamped, once again, over my feelings in an attempt to make himself look good. I was worried for the future of the Chorus, too, because something had changed. It was not the same comfortable, achieving Chorus that we were used to in previous weeks. I decided to watch Adrian myself. I did not trust his keenness at all.

I did not trust Adrian Hilton full stop.

PUPPET ON A STRING

CHAPTER 7

Gary told everyone, who was prepared to listen, how busy he was being kept by the change to the rehearsal schedule. To my mind, a reorganisation of the schedule to include Wednesdays was a couple of hours work, typing it up and getting prints, plus a couple of dozen 'phone calls to those resting members of the Chorus did not constitute anything like being busy. But I was becoming increasingly aware of Gary's truth-stretching as I took a more distanced and objective stand from him.

By the time we met again for rehearsals, Adrian Hilton had succeeded in turning the wardrobe nightmare into a regimented inventorial dream. To give him his due, he had done an excellent job in turning an area of complete disarray (such that finding anything was a long-term exploration, which required careful planning and signing up Sherpas for the mission) into something where it was instantaneously easy to find anything. If it could be kept in this state, no longer would we be required to perform with the wrong props or no props at all or borrow costumes from different operas. He had divided the floor-space into several sections, allocating areas according to the size of the opera's needs, to each opera. There were several trunks and free-standing, wardrobe-type boxes for all the props and clothing, respectively. Where these were left in untidy piles on the boxes before, Hilton had listed all the items, put them in the boxes, hung up the clothes, typed out a sheet of the contents, sizes, etc. and stapled the sheet on the outside of the boxes. Once all that was cleared up, he drew up a floor-plan, copies of which were posted all around the room, with 'You Are Here' markers on them to further assist the users in finding what they wanted. Finally, he had produced a defect list, so that these could be remedied, which was held in a folder by the door. By each item on the list was a box for a target completion date and another for the actual completion date. All of this was controlled by a list of 'Do's and 'Don't's, which is where I noted the genesis of his attempts at empire-building. Unfortunately for him, too, sorting out the basement meant that Adrian Hilton had done little private rehearsal. I thought it was going to be interesting to see how this was going to be handled by Bob, Pete, Gary and, ultimately, Sir Norman.

As I entered the foyer of the rehearsal halls, I glanced at the notice-board. There, between the committee list and Adrian's officious instructions regarding wardrobe and prop use, Gary had pinned up the review from *Le Monde*, which had originally held my photograph with Marie. Except that Gary had carefully performed surgery on it, so just the text of the review and nothing about my dalliance with Marie nor the photograph remained. In some ways, I was glad that Gary's biliousness had driven him to do that.

"Good review," said Pete from behind me, making me jump slightly.

"If you can understand French."

"True."

"I see that the surgeon-in-chief has been at this copy."

"Yes, indeed. He was so annoyed that you had achieved something that he has always wanted to do. Achieve momentary, if fleeting, fame and notoriety. Forget the music. He still is irritated, by the looks of things. Why don't you put up your copy?"

"No, I don't think so."

"Go on," Pete goaded, "a bit of sensationalism!"

"No, Pete. If I put it up there, I feel that I would be devaluing the relationship between Marie and myself – such as it is. I didn't want that photograph to be published but at least it stands as a testament to what happened. And it brings back good memories."

"But it would really get up Gary's nose."

"Forgive me but that would be petty. Anyway, when you're fond of someone – I mean, really fond of them – you don't want to broadcast it to the world. You want them to find out for themselves. I'm sure nothing will come of it and I need to lock those feelings and experiences away for the time being. Anyway, being on page thirteen is unlucky enough as it is."

"Yeah, point taken," said Pete and we made our way into the hall.

* * *

"For anyone who is interested," said Gary pompously at the rehearsal, reading from a clip-board, "there is a review of our Paris *Tosca* with

Visconti and Duvois on the notice-board in the foyer. It's from *Le Monde*, I think." He turned over a page quickly and then stroked the hair growing over his collar. "Er... other good news: we now have a new wardrobe manager –." A rousing cheer from everyone, thanking any passing deities that they would not be volunteered, at least for the short term. Gary pointed towards the tenor section: "Adrian Hilton, who, for those who have not been down there since the weekend, has done a marvellous job in the basement."

Adrian was preening himself in his own pungent cloud, as he pouted a little and received the imagined adulation for his efforts from the rest of the Chorus, even though it was a displaced relief and wrinkled noses from his immediate neighbours following his exertions and labours in the cellar. There were some minor discussions whispered around the sections as to why this person had been so quickly co-opted to the committee in such a short space of time between joining until now.

Gary put the clip-board under his arm and walked ostentatiously back to his seat next to Pete. Sir Norman stepped up to the podium, worry creasing his brow. His greeting was met with the accustomed tide of lethargy. "We have a lot of work to do," he said. "Tonight I would like to do the *Peasants' Dance* and *Chorus*."

Before he could start, Anthony Devlin – perhaps the most boring person in the Chorus; a person who could make anyone glaze over within two minutes of an opening sentence – stood up. He was an Oxford graduate, proud of it and was always flaunting the doctorate he had achieved in Ancient History, implying that he was of superior intelligence. A literary snob, if you were unlucky enough to be cornered by him, he would hold court on many subjects that were so far above your head that they would be in danger from oxygen-starvation. His nasal, monotonous voice, like a depressed fog-horn, intoned now: "Excuse me but can you tell us with whom we are doing this recording?"

Sir Norman looked at Devlin, nonchalantly, but with his jaw muscles tightening and releasing and a look of scorn battling for prominence on his features. He did not take these interruptions kindly. He leant over to his briefcase, opened it and removed a piece of paper, which he unfolded. "Mr. Devlin. May I remind you that in your assumed eloquence and the breadth and colourful range of the English language, you might wish to consider using the magical word 'please' more often." Norm's Gorms were off, just avoiding the likelihood of doing themselves an embarrassing mischief. Devlin sat down unruffled and Sir Norman addressed the Chorus in general.

"The orchestra is the München Philharmonische, conducted by Christoph Schmidt. The only singers I have details of here so far are the main leads. Matthew Wilson, Guido Estente, Mikhail Torchev and title role is to be sung by Marie Duvois, whom the gentlemen have already met recently in Paris."

My heart jumped into my throat, decided not to give up the ghost quite yet and resumed its normal position, thumping erratically. The pain in my chest eased off as I tried to calm down. Marie Duvois – Marie – was coming back into my life and so soon. Once again, optimism and pessimism were arm-wrestling and sweating profusely in the process at the forefront of my mind.

Sir Norman put the paper back into his briefcase, which he closed, picked up his baton to silence the inevitable conversation that had sprung up. "So, the *Peasants' Chorus*, please, on page one-fourteen. Christoph Schmidt wants the women to sing like innocent young girls – vestal-virgin style. This should give you ladies a lot of opportunity to show off your acting skills!"

Norm's Gorms responded predictably.

"And the men," continued Sir Norman, "to sing like old men – dirty old men. No opportunity for the men to show *their* acting skills, then!"

A veritable explosion in a greenhouse from Norm's Gorms.

Stunned, my concentration was not what it should have been. My mind raced forward to the end of May, concocting scenarios, quickly looking for flaws, discounting them and thinking up new ones.

> Marie Duvois
> *I've written about this evening already*
>   is a vestal virgin
> *Please relax and enjoy yourself*
>   and I
> *Give me your hand*
>   am a
> *See? Flesh and blood*
>   dirty old man!

* * *

Over the next two days, I could do little of anything: private rehearsal, sleeping, eating, nothing. It was difficult to tell whether I was excited, worried, upset, nostalgic or just plain foolish. I wanted to see her again and yet I did not. What would happen? What would we say? Where was her admirer? Gary would also be bothersome, sniffing around her like a dog around a lamp-post. I was going to have to do something. About Gary. And about Marie.

And fast.

PUPPET ON A STRING

CHAPTER 8

It was around this time that Amanda Beglow first came into my life. I could not be absolutely positive because I was too wrapped up in my fatuous mental pursuit of Marie Duvois to notice. She had joined (I later checked the records) shortly before our tour to France. She was a blonde, five feet, eight inches tall, with blue eyes, aged twenty-two, slender in figure and superficially slow-witted in mind. She was a member of the soprano section and she had witnessed my explosion in the pub during the Adrian Hilton episode.

She was in the Goat and Dramatist just before half past five on the Tuesday evening. After the initial politeness of meeting, she asked about the previous week's argument. Her voice was that of a manic-depressive, in that there was little inflection and everything she said had sounded negative, but her smile was radiant. I think that, in retrospect, was what attracted me to her. That and her eyes.

"Well, I agree with you," she said, sipping a Martini and regarding me, cow-like, over her glass. Those eyes seemed to go on forever; if the eyes are the windows to the soul, hers appeared to go just behind the soul and through the hidden door in the panelling. "Adrian Hilton shouldn't have been co-opted just like that so soon after he has joined. It seems a bit odd when no-one knows anything about him."

"Yeah," I opined moodily into my drink, which I was revolving distractedly in its own beery puddle on the bar. It had occurred to me that I ought not to be discussing the argument and my feelings with someone I had only just met – the irony of Amanda's postulation about not knowing Adrian Hilton was not entirely lost on me – but it was good to have someone sympathetic and empathetic listening to me. "Anyway, it's all in the past and, as Gary has pointed out, he has done a fantastic job in the basement. You wouldn't recognize it. So good luck to him, I guess." I changed the subject to the recording to lighten the conversation. I asked: "Are you around for it?"

"Yes. I'll be there. Really looking forward to it," she replied with as much enthusiasm as the lack of inflection in her voice would allow. "I never realized the Chorus worked so hard!"

"You'll get used to it. Even blasé about it. Trust me. It gets like that. When you first join, you're very nervous and think you can't possibly do all the work the Chorus has lined up and aren't all those singers and conductors wonderful. Then after a couple of years, you become acclimatized to the pressures and start saying things like: 'Oh, no! Not Malcolm Sargent *again!*' or: "Why can't we sing with Maria Callas for once?' For example, when we were in Paris, I met Marie Duvois and we –."

"So did I. Very nice woman. Very approachable." Damn him! I had not noticed Gary coming into the pub. "She gave me a personal autograph."

I knew that this was going to be dicey. Because of Gary's innate charm, he could inveigle himself into any relationship he wanted before they found out what sort of a person he really was – oleaginous and slimy. I felt I had little enough chance with Amanda as it was but all that would be blown out of the window if Gary went on to the charm offensive and his mouth charged on to the scene.

I had concluded that the only way to get Marie Duvois out of my head was to find a good, down-to-earth, attainable woman. Like Amanda Beglow. Gary, being almost obscenely jealous when his mates were successful with women, would try first and, if he failed or the relationship dried up, then you could pick up the pieces (if you could sustain the acid that he spat over you, like a hydrochloric puff-adder, in the process). Gary had been married twice before, both ending acrimoniously in the divorce courts on the grounds of incompatibility and mental cruelty – neither of which surprised me, since the cruelty was not just restricted to his marital partners and the only person Gary actually loved in any sense was himself. He frequently made light of his inability to hold his marriages together by making witty statements such as: "My wives didn't understand me. They both said I was a lousy lover, although how they came to that conclusion in twenty-three seconds, I'll never know." Right now, I sensed that he had targeted Amanda and my chances of forgetting Marie Duvois via this route were lessening the longer he was sniffing around.

* * *

Bob and Pete (who had arrived a little later, taking the pressure of Gary's lechery off Amanda), Gary, Amanda and I walked up to the rehearsal halls at about twenty-five past six. Although the danger had significantly reduced, Gary had immediately interposed a question of his own every time I had tried to start up a side conversation with Amanda. Such was my insecurity, I could not tell whether she was getting annoyed with him and laughing politely in the hope that he would disappear or if she preferred Gary's more ebullient company to mine. As we walked up the hill, he spoke animatedly about the things he had done, the work he had to do to hold the Chorus together, the famous people he knew, all the famous singers he had talked to and how altogether bloody marvellous he was. He was very callous in his approach to achieving the philosophical motto of his life: Look after Number One, regardless of how many people are trodden underfoot on the way.

He had reached the latest exaggeration on the story of obtaining Marie Duvois's autograph as we entered the hall (apparently it had *three kisses* on it and he had kissed her – embellishments I am certain he actually believed). Sir Norman was already there, as ever, by the piano, sorting through papers in his briefcase and he looked up and beckoned to Gary.

"Excuse me, Mandy dear. Business. Never ends for me. I'll see you for a drink afterwards," he said, not even awaiting a response, and self-importantly went to speak with Sir Norman.

"Gary. You remember our rule of re-auditioning every two years?" asked Sir Norman, neatening a pile of papers by tapping the end on the piano top.

"Yes," replied Gary suspiciously, worried that his days were numbered having been finally found out.

"I think we must enforce it more strongly. After three and a half years, I re-auditioned the Chairman." Sir Norman paused and turned to face Gary. "He's gone."

Gary relaxed visibly and smiled cruelly. "Excellent news," he said and rubbed his hands together subconsciously.

"Be that as it may, we need a replacement. And soon because we must not destabilize the Chorus before this recording. Please can you make the announcement for the requirement for a new Chairman?"

"Yes, ma'am," said Gary, still rubbing his hands. "When?"

"The platform is temporarily yours."

Gary then clapped his hands officiously together for silence and informed the Chorus of the Chairman's recent demise, the need for a new one, the requirements of the successful candidate, the democratic process surrounding the appointment of proposer and seconder and that the statutory fortnight required before the appointment was to begin.

While Gary was revelling in his own pomposity during the delivery of his pretentious speech, an idea struck me; an idea that would be perfect if I could make it happen. Secure my future and turn the tables deliciously on Gary. I did not have that many close friends in the Chorus but I was sure that I would have enough supporters. Amanda, should I get to her before Gary, could look after the women's sections; Pete and I could deal with the men.

* * *

After the rehearsal, I waited in the entrance hallway for Amanda. Edgy with excitement, plans burgeoning in my mind, I tapped Amanda on the shoulder and she awoke from her daze.

"Oh, hello, Dave," she said, smiling, the light of recognition switching on suddenly with an almost audible click. "Sorry, I was miles away."

"Obviously," I said and flashed what I hoped to be an engaging smile, then took her by the elbow and said: "Look, do you fancy getting something to eat?" I looked over her shoulder and saw that Gary was on his way out, talking to Sir Norman.

"Erm," she hesitated, "I already had something before I came to rehearsal."

Gary had reached the rehearsal room door.

"I don't mean a four-course meal. Something light. More of a snack."

Gary was through the door and I felt the whole thing slipping away.

"Well, I'd have trouble getting home. It's already late."

Gary had not yet noticed us in amongst the throng of others leaving the building, so deep in self-aggrandizing conversation was he.

Desperation wafted past me, stepped back and slapped my brain. "I'll give you a lift."

Gary looked over, noticing Amanda for the first time, and, patting the shoulder of his less than enthralled audience, he made his way towards us.

"Okay, then," she said eventually and I released my held breath.

"We're going to get something to eat," I called to Gary. "See you tomorrow."

Amanda and I almost ran out of the main door, leaving a startled and bemused Gary in our wake.

* * *

We went to a modest little bistro just outside South Mimms called La Trattoria. As one might expect, it specialized in Italian food and was one of the first such restaurants outside of central London. It was little more than a converted front room, but it was clean, warm and pleasant.

Over the meal of lasagne and garlic bread, I discussed with Amanda her part in my plan. "Look," I said, "I need some help."

"What's that?" she replied, flashing a smile.

"You remember Gary's announcement about the forthcoming election for Chairman?"

"Uh-huh."

"Well, I want to go for it."

"And you want me to enlist support from the female sections?"

I was a bit taken aback by the bluntness of her observation. Maybe I had misconstrued the level of scattiness about her. "Um…" I tried, "well, yes."

She smiled winningly. "I'd love to."

"Well, after that fiasco in the pub the other day, I feel that the likes of Gary and Adrian need to be reined in a bit. He shouldn't be making those arbitrary decisions."

"Too true. But I have to ask why you've chosen me. I don't know that many women. I've only been in the Chorus for a little over a month."

"Well," I countered, "you don't necessarily have to know them; just be on a nodding acquaintance with them. It's essential that I get all the views from each section of the Chorus to make sure that we move forward democratically. Something we have not been doing over the last year or two under Gary's covert direction."

"You really want this appointment, don't you?"

"Yes."

"To put Gary down?"

"Phew!" I was startled again by the second blunt observation. "You're a bit sharp!"

"Well is that the reason?"

"Partly."

"It's no reason to be running for the office of Chairman, though."

"No, no," I said quickly. "I want to stop the dictatorial methodology that Gary employs, true, but it's not to come out on top. That would be a little childish. No, there are lots of reasons: the main one being getting a democratically elected Committee to act in a democratic way. If I do get the position, I know there is a strong likelihood of huge personality clashes with Gary but I think it's something I am willing to work through and hope he is too."

Amanda was looking at me intently, drilling me with those soulful eyes, before saying: "Gary's an enigma."

"How do you mean?"

"On the one hand, he seems to have a very strange approach to people management, not seeming to care about people and then on the other, he can be quite charming."

"So I've witnessed. It's one of the things that needs to change in this Chorus. High morale means better output."

"But I also find him an arrogant bore. He appears to think that everyone is interested in him and him alone, hanging on every pearl of wisdom that he might drop."

"He is very conceited," I conceded, grabbing the opportunity to offload my feelings about him to a willing listener. "And you're right. He's very arrogant. I think he confuses that with charm. By telling people how wonderful he is, he feels that they will agree."

"I'm glad you dragged me here and away from him."

"I get frustrated with him, barging in and taking over. The charm offensive metamorphoses into drooling all over you like a salivating oil-slick."

"I thought you were great friends when I first joined. Was I wrong?"

"Not really," I replied. "We were great friends but I think the sands are shifting and he feels unsteady. He's losing control of things as I try to be more independent and less reliant on his friendship."

"That's quite sad, really," said Amanda, a couple of lines deepening on her forehead. "How does that make you feel?"

"Nostalgic for the good times," I agreed, "we had a lot of fun, but I think in the last month I've grown up or moved on. Gary hasn't and, looking back, I think our friendship was more a distraction than anything else. I was always doing his bidding and now that I'm refusing, he's hitting back." I just managed to stop myself from saying that it had been since the episode with Marie.

The conversation diverted inevitably to music and our ambitions. We were still at the table at half past eleven, with the waiters striding around the restaurant, impatiently removing cutlery, table decorations crockery and other detritus from our table, hinting less than subtly that we should perhaps think of leaving.

Amanda asked if I would like to go back to her flat for a nightcap. Stunned by the opportunity and still wanting her on my side for the upcoming election, I agreed a little too eagerly. Improper thoughts about Amanda and how jealous Gary would be when he found out about this whipped through my mind. I tried to tamp them down because this was inappropriate behaviour. We paid the bill and went out to my car. The restaurant door shut abruptly and locks and bolts turned and shot behind us.

In those days, I drove a relatively old Austin Mini and it was into this that we squeezed to go to Amanda's flat in Ware. Her living-room was tastefully furnished and the decoration was aesthetic to the eye; colourful and warm in shades of yellows and reds. The furniture was not modern and I later found out she had inherited it from her parents, who had died in an accident abroad some years previously. While she was in the kitchen, making the coffee, I browsed through her bookshelves built into the alcoves either side of the Yorkshire stone fireplace, looking at the spines. I have always been fascinated by the insight obtained from looking at what people read; it says a lot about their psychological make-up. However, in Amanda's library, there was little of interest, with all the books being saccharine-sweet, romantic fiction.

I went out into the kitchen, ostensibly to help, but actually to watch. I jumped up to sit on the work surface by the fridge, passing nightcap ingredients to her as she asked for them.

"You hate Gary, don't you?" she asked.

Again taken aback by the refreshing bluntness of her questioning, I responded meekly: "Yes. Well, 'hate' is a very emotive word. At the moment, I dislike him with an intensity."

"Why?" She spooned sugar into her coffee.

"Women, mainly," I let slip.

"Meaning?" She smiled encouragingly.

"Well, he treats them badly for one. He has a couple of failed marriages behind him to prove it. For me, personally, it's because he treats me like some kind of puppet on a string, moving in on any woman I have a conversation with, determined to have the first opportunity, expecting me to step aside for him to steam in. Thus, any potential romance is shot down in flames. That's the first part of my resentment towards him. The second is that he really gets under my skin because these women – most of them anyway – start fawning around him because of how wonderful he is. Or, rather, how wonderful he says he is. They seem to have difficulty seeing through him. Ninety percent of what he has to say is one hundred percent bullshit. He just winds me up."

Amanda had finished pouring the coffee and we returned to the living room. We sat on the sofa, where she removed her shoes and elegantly placed one foot underneath herself and stroked her hair with her free hand. She continued: "I know what you mean, I think. He was rather eager to move in on me, when I was talking to you before the rehearsal."

"Right. And that's a prime example of why I dislike him at the moment," I responded, spitting a little venom in the words. I relaxed and smiled: "I'm sorry. I shouldn't be laying this all on you."

"Not at all," she replied, stroking my arm for comfort, "it's cathartic to get these things off your chest. You're insecure – I've picked up on that – and you bottle things up, which is not good for you. Gary is also insecure and insecurity breeds more insecurity without a supporting strength. You are the stronger personality and have that necessary strength not to spiral out of control."

I blushed. "Thank you. The problem is that you can never tell what he's going to do. He's very unpredictable."

"In what way?"

"Again it's only over the last few weeks that I've noticed, but he is very two-faced."

"That's what I meant about him being caring and charming. Two sides of the same man with a massive chip balancing on the edges."

"I like that. That's good," I smiled. "What it makes me wonder is just what he has been saying and doing behind my back for the last couple of years. Now he's more overt in his prejudice towards me, threatening to chuck me out of the Chorus if I attempt to have success with a woman. Always using the situation to his advantage where he possibly can."

"He threatened to do that?" she asked, incredulity slapped across her face.

"Well, almost. I'm paraphrasing and embellishing a little. It's not quite that bad but almost."

"Surely he can't do that. That's another abuse of power."

"If he can appoint who he wants to the Committee, I'm sure he can oust me from the Chorus."

"True but what a bastard."

"So, now, when I find an attractive woman, he tries to muscle in and my insecurity allows me to think that I have lost her. No point in pursuing her further. You say I'm stronger than Gary but his character is almost overpowering."

"You've got it wrong. Can I tell you something?"

"What?"

"I've been looking at you in rehearsal for some time. Since I first saw you, I've wanted the opportunity to get to know you better. That's rather forward of me, I know, but I think you are far better and stronger in outlook and character than Gary will ever be." She took a deep breath and then added coyly: "And handsome."

"Thank you," I replied. Before I knew what was happening, we were kissing. I cannot remember if it was she or I who started it but, nevertheless, our passions rose unchecked. Her mouth tasted sweet, a hint of coffee still lingering as I ran my hands through her hair, eyes closed. My hand dropped to her shirt-front and I slipped a couple of buttons free. To my surprise, my hand rested on a silky-smooth breast, completely free and unfettered by a brassiere or other restrictive underwear. We stopped kissing momentarily; she drew away, took my hand and led me to her bedroom, breathing heavily and with eyes aflame.

She let go of my hand and pushed me lightly down on to the bed, which had white satin sheets and a continental duvet. Deftly removing her shirt to reveal a pair of pert, milky-tea-coloured breasts, she clambered on to the bed and straddled my lap to unbutton my shirt.

"My God!" she breathed hoarsely, "I *love* hairy chests!"

Flickering at the back of my mind were warning signals that this, perhaps, was not such a good idea but, as she ran her fingers through the hair on my chest, moaning softly, any such misgivings were shut off to be replaced by the more preternatural, carnal thoughts. I stroked her shoulders, her arms, her stomach and back to her breasts. Her body was toned without being too muscular and she had a natural all-over tan. The smoothness of her skin appeared to be an extension of the silk sheets – my brain melded the sensations together, increasing my heartbeat three- or fourfold.

"Take your clothes off," she ordered in a passionate whisper, pulling back the duvet to create more room.

I needed no second bidding and we were soon naked, lying on the bed, with clothes discarded like so much rubbish on the carpet. I kissed her breasts, neck and shoulders and sucked at her nipples. Then, turning her on to her back, I clambered on top and entered her. It did not last long; she dug her nails painfully into my back and wailed like a banshee. It was almost comical.

I rolled off her and pulled the duvet up to my neck. Reality bit hard as Amanda cuddled up to me, lying on my chest. With the reality of the post-coital depression came shame: we had not made love but had had sex. Love had had nothing to do with it – at least not for me. It had served to satisfy the primeval urge to reproduce and had helped to relieve some of the recent tension I had had stored up inside me. I did not really enjoy it beyond that. It is my belief, that you cannot truly enjoy it unless it is with someone you love.

I was ashamed because I felt I had taken advantage of her. Not only because she was warm, soft, great at cuddling and kissing, passionate and, above all, because she actually liked me and wanted me but also because I had wanted to keep her sweet since I needed her help. What worsened the shame was that during our coupling, I had closed my eyes and imagined that it was Marie Duvois's arms that I was stroking and picturing Marie's face. I was disgusted with myself for using Amanda in my fantasy, effectively using her as some kind of sexual toy but I had been unable to stop myself and she had been willing. What compounded things was my embarkation on a guilt trip because it felt as if I had committed an act of infidelity against Marie rather than Amanda. Falling into a restless sleep, confusion and depression raced and eddied unstintingly around my head.

PUPPET ON A STRING

CHAPTER 9

Pete dropped by my house the next day at lunch-time shortly after I had returned from Amanda's flat. I offered him some of my meagre repast but he suggested, with a look of disgust, that we go to the pub instead. This is one thing that is common in the creative world; a large amount of time is spent with your lips around the rim of a glass of some volatile liquid or other. It is mainly the social aspect, the desire to talk with like-minded people, but also some of the greatest performances and creations have come from self-confessed drunks. At that time, and I am not proud of the fact, I could happily drink two pints without even feeling it.

Pete had wanted to go to the Goat and Dramatist, through force of habit more than anything else, but I had a suspicion that Gary would be there and he was the last person I wanted to see at the moment. I suggested that we go to the Rose and Crown, a good pub just down the road from my house. Not the height of originality in the choice of name but it was a pleasant place, larger than the Goat and Dramatist with two bars, fake oak beams which were black-painted plaster shaped to look like wood (although failing badly, it has be said) and the beer was a penny cheaper. We sat in the lounge bar after I had purchased two pints of frothy bitter.

After the previous day's events, I was feeling exhausted and had wanted to get forty winks before starting private rehearsal on the policemen's chorus, when Pete had arrived. Through my inherent need to sleep, my conversation with Pete was rarely raised above the monosyllabic, as I sat in an armchair like a stuffed dummy, stroking my forehead in consternation.

At length, after repeated tries to get the conversation flowing, Pete observed: "Christ! You must have been at it all night!"

"At what all night?" I asked, not particularly interested.

"Well…you know," he encouraged, crooking his elbow and nudging the air.

"No, I don't."

"Ah, come on, Dave. Spill the beans. You can tell me, I'm a doctor."

I caught on to what he was saying and smiled weakly. "I'll ignore that with all the ignorance at my command."

Pete raised his eyebrows and put out an encouraging hand to indicate that he was still interested. "Well?"

I changed tack. "Pete, can I ask you a favour?"

His smile faltered and he replied, uncertainly and carefully: "Yes, if I can."

"I need your help on something."

"Always a catch," he said, still speaking warily. "All right, go on."

I outlined my plan for standing for the Chairman's position and told him that Amanda had been lined up to garner support from the women's sections. I repeated some of the thoughts I had had while discussing it with Amanda and was surprised and relieved that he needed little convincing.

"Well, that was easier than I thought it would be," I said, after drawing my manifesto to a close. "Please can you discuss it with Gary, though?"

"Shouldn't you speak to him yourself?"

"Yes, in an ideal world. But I'm not his favourite person at the moment. And I think I can accurately predict his reaction."

"Good point. It's not going to be the best reaction whatever his mood."

"Please don't let me down, Pete," I said, insecurity edging into the timbre of my voice.

"Why should I let you down, Dave?"

"Well, it's Gary. He's dead set against me and would explode if I told him I was standing." I shrugged. "I just thought…you know."

"Gary's too full of his own self-importance. Especially over the last couple of weeks and it's getting a bit tiresome. But I have a bit of a hold over him – not much, but enough. He'll see it my way even if I have to ram it down his throat with a pitchfork." He smiled. He tapped me on the knee and said: "Now, tell me about last night. I'm dying to find out all the salacious details."

"Not much to tell, really."

"That's what you said about a certain Marie Duvois, I seem to recall."

At the mention of her name, a heavy weight dropped on to my heart and settled there, dragging my mood down further. "To tell you the truth, Pete," I said, rubbing my face with the hand not holding the pint glass, "right now I could use a friend. A good friend."

"Why?" asked Pete, genuine concern replacing the lascivious leer. "What's wrong?"

"It's difficult to know where to begin." I looked up at the ceiling and stroked my chin and scratched at my throat.

Pete started singing a song from *Sound of Music*, in imperious tone: "Let's start at the very beginning; that's a very good place to start." He smiled and then his face straightened. "Sorry, Dave. Well, you can't have got her pregnant because it's too soon to know. So it can't be *that* serious. Must be some other kind of serious."

"Yeah. Maybe. Or maybe not." I rubbed the chin stubble, made up my mind and leant on the table. "It's got a lot to do with France."

"Somehow I thought it might," said Pete, getting up and picking up his empty glass. "This will be a long one, so I had better replenish them so I can't interrupt you. Drink up." He held his hand out for my glass.

It was over half-full with beer but, as I have said, it was like water with the effect it had on me for the first couple of pints. I drank the remainder in three swift gulps, belched with accustomed vulgarity and handed him my glass.

When he had returned with renewed drinks and had settled back into his chair, looking suitably earnest, I took a mouthful of beer and began my story. "When I went to Marie Duvois's room that evening in the Opera House, I expected little more than a cursory hello, a quick signature and a swifter goodbye. As it turned out, I had nothing to write with nor any paper to write on. I think it was my idea to use her lipstick on my handkerchief, which seemed to endear me to her in some way. Anyway, you remember the message she wrote?"

Pete nodded: "'Thanks for a wonderful evening'. Yes."

"Mmm," I agreed, "well, that was before the meal."

"Before?"

"Yes."

"Wow! I thought she had written it after dinner. You're one lucky boy; Gary had to almost force her at gunpoint to write what she wrote on that photograph."

"Did he? Well, I'm not surprised and it had occurred to me that the message was not Marie's style. From the short time we were together.

But then again, I got to thinking that I didn't know what her style was because her admirer had been present."

"Her admirer?"

"Yes. That chap, who was there when Gary got his autograph."

"Ah, yes. Her admirer. May I say that you are putting yourself down a little?"

"Maybe." I shrugged again. "Anyway, we talked for a while about her life and music, the fact that she had wanted to be an artist before taking up music, because it was not paying. Did you know she was under the tutelage of Pierre Croumeux?"

"Blimey!" exclaimed Pete, his eyes widening with awe in much the way I had done when Marie first told me. "No wonder she's so good."

"Indeed. She was also *found* by Sir Charles Minton, because a singer had fallen ill. She took over the part and became an overnight sensation."

"A real rags to riches story."

"Yes. Anyway, to get back to the point, *she* insisted that *I* take her out for supper."

"I told you that I wasn't the Queen of Sheba. Or anywhere else for that matter."

I laughed. "But when we were in the restaurant, she started opening up her heart a little, saying that she was frustrated that everyone treated her like a commodity, like a rag-doll, who is only brought out of her box for performances before being cast back in when the applause has died down. Well, that was the gist of it. Then, to prove that she was a delicate human being, she took my hand and rubbed it on her arm. I can tell you, I nearly fainted with desire. Or ecstasy. Or both."

"Sort of passive love-making," grinned Pete. His face fell as the comment was met with stony silence. "Sorry. Carry on."

"Well, the rest of the evening was taken up with talking about this and that, after which I walked her back to her hotel. No, before you say anything, nothing happened. She just left me and said that I should remember my handkerchief."

"Your handkerchief?" repeated Pete, confusion corrugating his forehead.

"'Thanks for the wonderful evening'?" I suggested.

"Oh, yes, of course. The autograph," said Pete and then paused in thought. "Maybe she had the evening already planned."

"No, I don't think so. There was too much spontaneity about it. Anyway, next day, I woke up and thought about what had gone on for a very long time, deciding that I had fallen for her heavily and that I needed to act. Maybe it was borne out of infatuation but I don't think so. So, that evening, I decided to ask her out again… for dinner. But Gary stopped me as I was following her back to her dressing-room, ostensibly to reprimand me about my attack of amnesia on stage but I know that he was deliberately stalling me from seeing Marie.

"He riled me badly and I was seething magnificently. I had to wait to calm down and, when I had, I retraced my steps to her room, only to see Gary coming out. Then, spitefully, he told me that she had another man in there – her admirer. I knew he was enjoying the disappointment and the effect his malice was having on me, at which point I decided to go and get steaming drunk."

"Which you did spectacularly, as I recall," said Pete, wincing at the memory. "And the rest is history, as they say?"

"Not really. That's the background to the story. My insecurity dictated that I was foolish to pursue a woman, who, as Gary so viciously points out, is way out of my league. But it was difficult (and still is) to get her out of my mind. I started to think that if I were to become interested in some other girl, I would become less infatuated with Marie. Which is where Amanda comes in. I asked her out with the determination to stop thoughts wandering in Marie's direction. Unfortunately, it hasn't worked out that way and I feel so incredibly guilty that it was probably done out of the selfish need to get support from the women in the Chorus for my ambitions to become Chairman. It feels an intolerable mess that I am finding difficult to dig myself out of."

"And how far did you go with Amanda?"

"Too far," I winced with the familiar guilt pangs. "I slept with her last night. And I am ashamed to say that, while we were…" – I groped for a suitable euphemism, my face reddening and sweat trickling from my brow with embarrassment – "…getting it together, so to speak, and, although Amanda is, how shall we say, erotic and everything I consider to be perfect in physical attraction, I could only really enjoy the…er…act by closing my eyes and imagining that it – she – was Marie. Isn't that appalling? In fact, I kept stroking Amanda's arms and remembering the desire I had felt in the restaurant. I'm surprised if Amanda did not think that I was behaving strangely – even perversely. I don't know." I looked up at Pete and wiped a bead of sweat from the side of my face. "What do you make of that muddle?"

Pete ruminated with a mouthful of beer and said: "I don't know, to be honest. Not immediately, anyway."

I let out an exasperated sigh, my voice rising in pitch as I laid bare my thoughts: "Am I really using Amanda? *I* think so and I'm appalled by it. Do I have even the remotest chance with Marie, given that I'm unlikely to see her again on a one-to-one basis? Will I lose both of them? I will if I can't stop thinking about one woman when I'm with another. Should I talk to Amanda about it? What if –?"

Pete put a restraining and comforting hand on my arm: "Dave, calm down. Look, I'll get another round in and cogitate on your position while I'm at the bar."

"Thanks, Pete," I sighed shakily and on the verge of tears. I had not expected the whole thing to affect me like this.

When Pete returned from the bar, he put the pints down, spilling some from his own as he knocked the table when taking his seat. He sat with furrowed brow and a fist against his cheek, leaning on the arm of his chair, like a parody of *The Thinker*. His quiet analysis allowed me to finish the last pint before embarking on the fresh one. Finally, he pursed his lips, leant forward with elbows on the table and sucked at his top lip with his teeth. "What I think is this: Gary, first of all, is totally wrong to screw you up like that. That so-called admirer of Marie Duvois's was her agent. When Gary told me, I thought he was particularly cheerful about what I thought then to be quite a dull fact. Like you, I'm only just starting to realize what a nasty individual he can be sometimes.

"Now, Marie. You know, given what you've told me, I reckon, Queen of Sheba or not, that you have a good chance to romance Marie Duvois in the future –."

"Yes, but what about Amanda?" I interrupted like an impatient and frustrated child.

"Just a moment," replied Pete, raising an admonishing hand, "I'm coming to that. From the way you talk about her and your feelings, I don't think you are infatuated with her and that something has clicked between you. So there is a good chance that you can exploit that next time you see her. My suggestion is that you talk to her when we do this *Carmen* recording. If she recognizes you and wants to talk to you, then you're made.

"However, I agree that Amanda is the problem. I know why you wanted to go out with her but if you are not emotionally attracted to her, you should stop the relationship before it goes any further. It's only fair on her. And you, come to that. Perhaps, you should suggest a cooling off period; let her down gently. Say that you want to be friends but that your feelings for her are never going to romantic. Be honest – most women appreciate that. She should soon get the message."

"But what about my plans for the Chairmanship and the support she would be getting from key areas of the Chorus?" I countered. Pete's advice appeared hopeful and sound until I overlaid the ambition to stand for that position.

"There are other ways of getting that support. Have the courage of your convictions. And you never know, Amanda might still be willing to support you even if you end your relationship."

"I'll talk to her. Thanks for listening Pete. I feel somewhat easier with my conscience."

"What are friends for?"

We continued drinking until closing time and were, as Pete joked, like trees having been carelessly sawn by an under-performing lumberjack – half cut. My sense of humour had returned by degrees and we were laughing as we left the Rose and Crown. Treading the road to hell confidently, the intention of joint private rehearsal in the afternoon was trashed by me falling asleep on Pete's couch.

I awoke with a fuzzy mind and Pete suggested adjourning to the Goat and Dramatist to wake us up a bit. Not exactly the design I had for the day, but I had established support for my venture from Pete and with him acting as my confidant had largely assuaged the nagging guilt.

PUPPET ON A STRING

CHAPTER 10

By the next rehearsal, I had done an inordinate amount of thinking through my predicament and hit upon what I considered to be the best way forward, which would impact my relationships and ambitions the least. And the answer was simple, I thought, entering the Goat and Dramatist and ordering a soft drink from a very surprised John, who entirely forgot to be gruff as a result. Most of my problems, went the reasoning, were attributable to my attitude, which was affected by my insecurity and paranoia, which, in turn, was a direct side-effect from the volumes of alcohol I had consumed too much and too often.

Pete came in, looking flustered and joined me at the bar. Force of habit meant that I also ordered a pint of bitter for myself, even though I was already holding a glass of lemonade. John was satisfied that normality had returned and whistled a painfully flat melody as he poured our beers.

Pete gulped a couple of mouthfuls, before burping surreptitiously into the back of his hand. He then said: "I spoke to Gary about your aspirations to become Chairman. As predicted he is not at all happy with you or me, because we are trying to ruin him apparently. He has similar ambitions. I thought I'd better warn you." He took a gentler sip of beer.

"Oh, dear." I rubbed my closed eyes with a forefinger and thumb. "But are you still behind me?"

"Yes, indeed. All the way," Pete replied, enthusiastically. "I listened to Gary's ideas and thoughts on the direction of the Chorus to give him a chance of a fair hearing. To be honest, I have never heard such ridiculous rubbish; basically, he wants to manage things in the sense that he will get other people to do things and take the credit. Not the best basis for a democracy as you pointed out the other day."

"Right," I said, decisively, "what we must –."

The quietness of the pub was suddenly broken by Gary's entrance.

He was wearing a false smile as he shook first my hand and then Pete's, saying: "Dave. Pete. Very nice to be working with you again. It must be, ooh, about…two? Three? Four days?" He gave a sickly leer. He was attempting to cover up what was eating at him by being amusing and, frankly, failing miserably.

"How are things going, Gary?" I asked, feeling nervous of him and his answer.

"Not too badly," he replied, just as nervously. It was like two cats arching their backs, fluffing up their tails and awaiting the first to make the move. But it had given him the opportunity to regain some composure because the immodest boasts started up: "I've been working hard on getting this recording off the ground. Very tiring, getting down to the nitty-gritty of what needs to be done."

I translated that as not doing very much at all but getting others to do the work of the donkey. Conversation was further foreshortened as Adrian Hilton joined us. His activities had been so low-key and my aspirations so far at the forefront of my mind, that I had almost forgotten about him. I was reminded that I did not enjoy his company, in the same way that a cat might not be first choice of companion for a mouse, as he greeted Pete and Gary but completely blindsided me.

"And how are you, Dave?" I muttered. If looks could kill, I would have been transformed into a smoking and smouldering pile of ashes.

"Hello, Adrian," responded Gary, visibly relieved to see someone who could be at his beck and call. "We were just talking about this *Carmen* recording thing. It'll be fantastic and I can't wait to see old Marie Duvois again." He looked at me momentarily, a steely glint in his eye; Gary was almost back to the normal Gary we had come to know and loathe. "I can't tell you how much work there is still to be done for it. It's a lot for one person to handle on top of everything else. To be honest, I don't know how I manage to find the time for rehearsal."

"Yes, it must be difficult to keep on top of something as big as this," replied Adrian. "Well, you know you can always use me to help out. You can always…you know."

"That's worth bearing in mind," said Gary.

"After all, I have done very well at being the Wardrobe Manager."

"You're not fishing for compliments, are you?" I asked.

Adrian glared at me as Gary said: "Careful, Dave. That was a bit unnecessary."

"It was intended to be a light-hearted riposte, but I'll retract it and won't say another word." I smiled sweetly.

Adrian turned back to Gary and said: "Let me know if you need me."

"I'll keep you in mind if anything comes up. Cheers, Adrian. Nice to have someone who is willing to look after the best interests of the Chorus." A sideways glance at me to emphasize what he was saying confirmed that our friendship, such as it was, was irrevocably damaged.

I remained quiet for the rest of the conversation. Although I had expressed joviality, anger was trying to get hold of my emotions again; anger with Gary for bleating on about the amount of work he had to do, when I knew it was neither true nor anything less than required for the position he held in the Chorus. I was made livid further by his continual attempts to upset me over Marie Duvois and his faith in the power-hungry Adrian Hilton. And I was very angry with Adrian Hilton just for being Adrian Hilton. It was increasingly obvious, now that our friendship was on its knees in supplication and I was able to view him from outside the cosy bubble we had been in, that Gary was an insecure but egotistical fool – not a happy psychological mix.

I was not particularly bothered by his conversation being aimed primarily at Adrian, a little at Pete and none at me. Just talking to him would make the red mist descend and I needed to avoid any such *contretemps*.

* * *

As we entered the rehearsal hall, slightly late, Sir Norman was by the piano, head in his briefcase as usual. He looked up from what he had been reading, beckoned and called Gary over. Gary strode over, his unctuous façade of confidence returning now that he could preen himself in front of the Chorus by having the ear of Sir Norman.

"Hello, Norm. How's your bum for love-bites?" he asked.

No reaction at all. "I've had a letter from America."

"Really? They haven't started conscripting us Brits into their damned war, have they?"

"Good God, no. No. It's from the New York Metropolitan Opera House. They were present at the Paris *Tosca* performances and want us to go over there to take part in *The Marriage of Figaro*, *Don Giovanni* and *Die Zauberflöte*."

"Mozart!"

"Accurate at least!" riposted Sir Norman, wryly, "Do you know any of them to sing?"

"Only a very little."

"And how much would be 'a very little'?"

"Not at all." Gary laughed.

"Hmm, just as I thought," replied Sir Norman, not even registering Gary's witticism. He cogitated for a moment. "Okay. Look, I think we'll accept this because it will increase our international standing. Unfortunately, we need the Chairman to sign on the dotted line."

"But we haven't got one," Gary pointed out.

"Spot on. Glad to see your pre-rehearsal imbibing has not impaired your logical faculties."

Gary was a bit taken aback and stung by this overt criticism but, for someone who did not believe he had a drink problem, he ignored his comment and let it wash over him. "Well, *I* could –."

"No," interrupted Sir Norman firmly. "It stipulates the Chairman. We need to act fast so I'm suggesting that we bring our referendum forward to the next rehearsal. We need the contract signed, sealed and delivered back to the States as soon as poss. The people who are running this festival have a huge interest in America, so we can't afford to sit around, waiting for another Chorus to pick it up from under us. Who are the nominees for the post?"

Gary sighed. "The first one is Anthony Devlin."

"Not that absolute bore?" Gary nodded. "Oh, dear, I hope the Chorus sees sense. And?"

"Dave Loughton."

"He's the chap who is a member of your clique with Pete, isn't he?"

Gary flinched a little before responding doubtfully: "Yes."

"Might be a good choice. Pete is a good judge of character. Okay. Any more?"

"And finally, myself."

"Oh, no. No, no, no," Sir Norman shook his head quickly. "That won't work. No, not at all."

"But –."

"No, Gary. I'm sorry if you feel I am unjustly over-riding your aspirations. But you are the Secretary of this outfit and have been since we started. No-one knows what you do and it would take too long to train someone else, if you were lucky enough to get the vote. It would mean, during an exceptionally busy time, change at the helm and that could risk our future. Any other time, of course, I would be grateful to have you as our Chairman. Who are your proposer and seconder?"

"Bob Holden and Jane Hoare. But I –."

"Well, that shouldn't be too difficult to withdraw from the race. Tell

them what I told you. About being busy and not having the time or
facilities to train someone else up at the moment. They'll understand,
I'm sure."

"But, Sir Norman, I wanted –."

"Gary!" said Sir Norman, tersely, patience slipping a little. "Please!
Not this time around. *I* want *you* as Secretary. For now, at any rate. Back
to the subject at hand – we need someone to sort out this New York
festival."

Petulant and forgetting his usual routine to make Sir Norman laugh,
Gary said sullenly: "Well, I can't because I've got to look after this –."

"This recording thing," finished Sir Norman, wearily as if he had
heard the same excuses trotted out several times before, which was
probably true. "Yes, I know. That's why I say that we need someone else
to do it. Now, is there anyone else who can, that you know of?"

"I don't think so."

"Well, there must be someone who can be trusted to do a good job.
What about your mate David Loughton? Might give him an
opportunity to show what he can do before these elections."

"No," said Gary quickly, alarm sparking in his eyes before he got
himself under control again. "I don't think that would be wise for just
that reason. It might provoke an outcry that the elections are being
rigged."

"Good point."

Gary mulled it over, stroking his moustache with a finger as he did
so. Excitement entered his features and he clicked his fingers: "I know, I
could ask Adrian Hilton."

"Our star Wardrobe Manager?"

"Well, he's keen. And at least he's willing to do some extracurricular
work for the Chorus, which is more than I can say for some of these
buggers. And I'm sure he'll do a good job. Besides, I can keep a tight rein
on him. When the recording is over, I'll probably take the New York
shindig off his hands."

"Hmm," said Sir Norman, doubtfully. "Okay. Please will you ask
him, then?"

"Will do."

"Any notices to give out before we start?"

"Only about the Chairmanship elections."

"Well, I'll do that after I tell them about America."

Gary nodded and withdrew to sit down, dejection still skittering
about him. Taking out a piece of paper from the briefcase and a pencil

from an inside jacket pocket, Sir Norman stepped up on the podium and raised his hands for silence.

"Ladies and gentlemen, I have some good news and perhaps some mundane news. First, the mundane news: the election of the new Chairman will be brought forward to next rehearsal, because of the position we find ourselves in, which I'll come on to in a minute. As you know, it's a secret ballot at the beginning of the rehearsal and, at the end, our erstwhile Secretary will announce the result. At present, we have only two nominees, Gary having stood down graciously to continue his burden as Secretary. And they are Anthony Devlin and David Loughton, both of whom hopefully you know. Because of the importance of the position, after today's break, I will ask each of them to provide an *ad hoc* speech on their manifesto and direction they see for the Chorus and what they aim to achieve in their term of office, should they reach that far. You can then go away from here tonight and cogitate on your choice until the next rehearsal, but please don't lose too much sleep over it.

"And now the good news: the *Coro di Londinium* has been asked to sing a number of operas in no less a place than the New York Opera House. That's in America, by the way."

Excited chatter broke out around the seated Chorus. With the bombshell of having less than two hours to prepare a major hustings speech for the elections, the nerves that were jittering and jangling were overcome by this piece of extraordinary good news.

"Sh. Sh. Sh. Please. Please," Sir Norman implored, waving the piece of paper up and down to signify silence. He continued when quiet was resumed. "Of course, it means that rehearsals with me are going to have to be increased if we are to meet the demands set by these operas."

Groans from each section. This was not necessarily dissatisfaction but, in Choruses everywhere, I have witnessed that the members tend to treat it as if it were a pantomime.

"I'm sorry but all will be much more exciting as we get near to that date. But more of that later. Who knows *The Marriage of Figaro*, *Don Giovanni* and *Die Zauberflöte*?"

A smattering of hands was raised.

"Hmm. About seventeen or eighteen. As I thought. Okay, we'll definitely do it but you'll have to work hard for your money." Sir Norman ticked something off on the paper and replaced it in his briefcase. "Right. We're now running about twenty minutes late. *Carmen*. I would like to run the whole thing from beginning to end and see if we've got it yet."

We launched into a vigorous rehearsal of the *Carmen* choruses.
Taking part remotely, I concentrated on the points to be made in my
electoral speech after the break. I had to think quickly of something
other than putting Gary firmly in his place as a reason for standing.
Although I knew that I was driven to stand by observations of how the
Chorus was being run and the direction it was being pointed in, those
thoughts needed to be crystallized into something more appropriate. By
the time the interval had arrived, several ideas had burgeoned in my
mind and I was feeling a lot more confident about the *ad hoc* speech and
the prospects in the election.

* * *

In some ways, I was fortunate that I disappeared to the pub at the
intervals, because the largest contingent of the Chorus ended up there
too for a refreshing tipple, the lively atmosphere or both and there I
could hold a pre-election hustings forum. Anthony Devlin, on the other
hand, rarely came into the Goat and Dramatist, preferring instead to go
with the other bores to the tea-shop opposite the rehearsal rooms. Being
a bit snide, Gary had suggested that he did not go near dens of alcohol
for fear that the very proximity would kill off an important brain cell,
one which stored a little-known but essential facet of information, with
no ability to replicate it. While that observation had been amusing and
chacun à son goût, it seemed to me that Anthony had missed a trick by
not going to the emporium which served the majority of the Chorus,
given that abstention in the elections was not an option.

In the Goat and Dramatist, I had greeted Amanda rather more
warmly than I had resolved or Pete had advised. However, as my
seconder, I found it difficult to ignore her, partly because it was rude and
mainly because I feared the impact such an action would have on my
ability to stand for Chairman. We had kissed lightly and, with each
poisoning gulp of beer, the two resolutions I had made about drinking
and Amanda elicited one more crack nearer shattering. I would sort it
out later, I told myself, knowing that this may be unlikely. Amanda was
too useful – was she not? – for my electioneering and it seemed foolish
to talk to her seriously, while this was going on and she had her arm
around my waist.

Pete was doing an excellent job as my public relations man,
expounding on the themes we had discussed briefly the week before.

While we were inveigling ourselves on the members who were undecided, Gary had taken Adrian to one side.

"Adrian," said Gary, with a furtive glance over his shoulder, "you know this American trip?"

"Yes," Adrian replied, eyes darting around the room following the direction of Gary's confidential glances.

"The problem is that I have so much on to organize this *Carmen* recording."

"Yes."

"Well, I wondered if you could possibly help me with the American tour?"

"I'd love to," Adrian responded eagerly, smiling magnificently and puffing out his chest.

Still furtive for no reason at all, Gary said: "I knew I could count on you."

Adrian started counting off on his fingers: "Right. I'll need names of the Chorus members who will be taking part. And I'll check out the airline companies for seat availability – see if I can get a group discount, maybe. And I'll need to think about travel once we're in the States." He was almost feverish with the elements of a plan coming faster in his brain than he could enunciate. "Oh, I'll also need all the rehearsal dates. Can you get those for me? And I want –."

"Whoa!" An increasingly alarmed look had taken over Gary's face and he interrupted Adrian's flow. "Hold the 'phone here. Don't get carried away. The contract hasn't even been signed yet!"

"Sorry, Gary," replied Adrian, calming. "I get excited by planning the detail of these sorts of things."

"Well, that's all well and good," frowned Gary. "You'd better keep me informed every step of the way."

"Of course."

"I mean it."

"Yes, I will!"

"I'm relying on you, Adrian."

"I know."

* * *

On the way back to the rehearsal, Amanda took hold of my hand and gave it a loving and encouraging squeeze. It took me by surprise and I turned towards her, smiling. She planted a kiss on my lips.

"I think you're going to win this," she said, giving my hand another squeeze and looking deep into my eyes before kissing me again.

"I hope so," I replied, troubled by the disappearance of the earlier resolution to end our relationship. Weak-willed, I procrastinated, telling myself that the deed would be done over the next couple of days. Right now, I had other things to worry about, such as my imminent speech.

"Gary looks put out. I think he was told to stand down by Sir Norman."

"Mmm," I agreed, "Pete said that he was requested to remove his nomination in no uncertain terms."

We had reached the door. She pulled me round gently to face her. "Are you ready? Your public awaits you."

"As I'll ever be."

She put her hands up to my face, stood on tip-toe and gave me a long, lingering kiss. Marie Duvois's face flashed into my mind. I pulled away as gently as I could.

"Now or never," I said and smiled.

"My hero," said Amanda crossing her hands over heart and laughed.

Everyone was seated by the time Sir Norman stepped back up on the podium and addressed them: "Right. Ladies and gentlemen. Ten minutes' exposé from Messrs. Devlin and Loughton each and then back to Act Three of *Carmen*. I think then we can go home earlier than usual."

This suggestion was greeted by a few cheers, to which Sir Norman raised his hands for quiet. He signalled to Anthony Devlin, who stood up. "Mr. Devlin, ladies and gentlemen."

Anthony cleared his throat and shuffled a sheaf of notes. "Well, I believe that –."

"Mr. Devlin," Sir Norman interrupted, "to avoid being rude to your fellow basses by keeping your back to them, you may wish to use the podium."

Norm's Gorms giggled behind hands. It was not obvious whether Sir Norman had singled Anthony Devlin out for personal ridicule or if he had more of the same lined up for me as a kind of test. Either way, Anthony made a real fuss of making his way to the podium, reshuffled his notes and began to speak. If his voice sounded normally like a depressed foghorn, it now took on the ponderous, lugubrious nature of a positively suicidal cruise liner docking in its berth at Southampton. Throughout his monologue, he leafed through his notes constantly, as if searching for a phrase of such subtle and piquant innuendo and nuance that would guarantee him the Chairmanship, and he did not make eye contact with anyone in the serried rows around him. "I think that the Chorus should team up with an orchestra of similar standing," he started. "Then we would be our own complete integral unit, therefore affording us the ability to take on more performances." He went into detail as to how that idea might be put into action and I observed several people stifling a yawn by opening their mouths slightly, breathing in and their eyes glazing over. I noted that my speech needed to be short, sweet and snappy to maintain their interest.

"Further," he continued, "I believe the recent choice of works which we have been performing has been pretty diabolical and there is a tendency to do too many of the simpler operas and we're losing sight of the original vision of the Chorus. I would like to see the Chorus being challenged more by doing pieces by Janáček and other more modern composers. If I were to be Chairman, I could make that change."

"With the sanction of the rest of the Committee, I hope," interjected Sir Norman.

"Well, yes," Anthony conceded, looking at his notes and pulling out one piece of paper. "I suppose I would have to. But I see the job of Chairman not as one of administration and execution but as one of leading by example. Therefore, the Chairman should have the right to veto any particular contracts which come in and, indeed, any particular decision made by the Committee." Sir Norman raised one eyebrow and checked his watch. Devlin was already in danger of over-running.

"This brings me on to my next point," he continued to drone. "The Committee, in general, don't do anything. At least nothing visible. They appear to be too keen on talking and nothing else. This must stop and I would personally see to it that things were made to happen by making executive decisions where we are not proceeding at the speed I expect. The last Chairman was not very effective, as we all know, preferring to act as some kind of figurehead, rather than doing anything to move the Chorus forward. I want to see the Committee do things and, if they don't, I would exercise the Chairman's right to sack them from the Committee to keep the current incumbents on their toes."

There were a couple of sharp intakes of breath as Sir Norman enquired: "And how would I be included in your grand scheme of things?"

"I don't believe you would be involved because it is a Committee decision and not a musical one." Another raised eyebrow from Sir Norman. "Finally, I think that this Chorus is overworked and we ought to be doing less. Continually, we are touring or doing recordings and have little time to rehearse or do other things."

"Surely, you don't have to do them?" questioned Sir Norman.

"I'm speaking for the Chorus as a whole. I'm sure everyone else feels we are overworked," Anthony countered. He looked around his audience for the first time and was met with glum, bored faces.

"I see," nodded Sir Norman, "but did you not say at the beginning of your oration that we should line up with an orchestra, in order to do more performances?"

"What I meant was that we should concentrate on a more varied repertoire, look to doing more live performances and fewer recordings and foreign tours."

"Well, thank you, Mr. Devlin, for that insight into how you would run this Chorus as Chairman. I suspect there will be many questions for you." Anthony left the podium and found his seat. "Now, Mr. Loughton, perhaps the Chorus will indulge you for a maximum of ten minutes, after which we can get back to the rehearsal."

I was pleased with Anthony's speech. He had shocked Sir Norman and members of the Committee – indeed, Gary was almost puce with rage at some of the comments, obviously aimed in his direction – and he had taken a wrong turning into a cul de sac, from which he could not recover. Overall, it sounded as if he had taken little time in his speech's construction and the monotonous delivery had switched many people off. Hoping that he had done himself sufficient damage to guarantee me the position, what I had to do now was to capitalize on it and keep my points light and clear.

Sir Norman quietened the discussion that had arisen by hissing dramatically likely an enraged rattlesnake. It cut through the cacophonous babble like an arrow through wet newspaper and brought everyone's attention to the fact that I was stepping up on the podium. Pete and Amanda had placed a few people to clap loudly in key positions, which prompted others to join in. When the applause had ebbed away and my heart reduced its beat to marathon-run speed, I started to speak.

"Good evening. First of all, for those of you who don't know me, my name is David Loughton and I am a member of the tenor section. Let me say, before I get into my speech proper, that the present Committee should be recognized for the work that they have done and will continue to do. I know that many had difficulty with Sydney Althorpe, the predecessor in this post, but I am sure that he led the Chorus with the best of his ability and intentions and should, perhaps, be thanked for that.

"Now, to the reasons as to why I'm standing and why I feel you should vote for me. I believe that a large organisation such as this can be improved by sorting out communication issues. I hope to create an environment where everyone feels comfortable enough to air their grievances and to share success. More importantly, to take action if necessary to resolve conflicts before they become deep-rooted. Now the Section Managers are responsible for the voice sections, so I would not impede them in their responsibilities but would support them and act as an objective ear should it be required.

"I have to observe that the Chorus occasionally appears to have very little 'get up and go.' I would push the Chorus forward, helping it to rise to new challenges and give everyone the fire in their eyes to go on achieving.

"All music decisions, just in case he's worried," I continued, briefly smiling towards Sir Norman, "would remain with Sir Norman and discussed with him in Committee."

Sir Norman nodded and smiled back at me.

"I would also like to publicize the continual need for more good voices. Our salaries are attractive – something I will be keeping an eye on to keep them that way – and the better the Chorus, the better the choice and class of engagements. I know, for instance, that we have this New York tour in the offing, but it is a 'one off'. We should not rest on our laurels, thinking that we have made it. Yes, we have made it – but for one night only. The challenge is that there are many other nights on which to make an impact. Therefore, we need to work towards such prestigious concerts on a regular basis. And continually improve ourselves. All of this can only be achieved if the standard of the musical output is high.

"Another area I think we should become increasingly involved in is in the recording arena. It's relatively new technology but I believe it will become the single-most important medium for music entertainment and we need to exploit that now. We have a barely used recording studio downstairs, which we ought to make more use of. I have a few ideas how we might develop a unique brand and sound and I am thinking we might want to consider starting up our own record label. In, say, twenty years' time in the nineteen-eighties, every Chorus is going to be at a premium and in high demand, so we need to prepare for that demand now. Hit it before the Christmas rush, so to speak.

"Finally, we ought to think about a patron. *I* would not choose the patron but would garner your views. After discussion at the Committee, I would then put it to our sponsor. If he agrees, I would persuade the chosen person to be our patron. It would be best were this person to be in an eminent position, either in music or in the political or Royal sphere. Publicising the presence of the patron at our performances will help increase ticket sales because a lot of the public will come to say that they had been in his or her company for an evening.

"I think that was all I had to say," I concluded, glancing at my watch. "Eight minutes. Not enough to say to fill the time but I've said all I wanted to. Thanks for your attention." I bowed a little as I stepped off the podium to spontaneous applause. Even Gary and Sir Norman were clapping.

As Sir Norman regained his place on the podium, I figured that it might all be sewn up. Eloquent though Anthony Devlin considered himself to be, I had not attempted to dictate or patronize. I had also been lucky to go on second. "Thank you, David," said Sir Norman, "most interesting. And thanks for keeping it interesting but nonetheless short. Right, enough of that."

As promised, we had ended the rehearsal earlier than anticipated. I was gasping.

* * *

In the pub afterwards, several people I had never spoken to made an effort to talk to me about the expressed views, wanting to know more and to help decide whether I had those convictions or had acted politically. Some of them bought me drinks so, by ten o'clock, I was practically on the floor talking to the table-legs. Amanda told me she thought I had done very well, bristling with pride, hugging and kissing me and putting her head fondly against my arm as yet another person discussed the points with me. It was interesting but not necessarily noteworthy, at that stage, that Adrian Hilton was conspicuous by his absence.

Completely against my resolution – weakened as it was by the corruption of the other resolution to reduce or cut out my alcoholic intake – naturally, I ended up back at Amanda's flat having given her my keys to drive. We had perfunctory and unsatisfactory sex, as well as I could muster under the circumstances. This time, I was relieved to note, Marie Duvois did not enter my head once. I did not so much fall asleep but pass out even when Amanda nuzzled into my neck, arm across my chest and uttered three terrifying words before oblivion took me.

She said passionately: "I love you."

PUPPET ON A STRING

CHAPTER 11

By the following week, what was left of my nerves had been completely shot to ribbons. I had valiantly tried to steer clear of the drink during those long days, breaking the vow once or twice when it all got too much for me to manage it. The problem was that I would castigate myself heavily, in much the same way as I had, while waiting for the boat at Boulogne. Essentially, I was using the alcohol as a crutch, although it was worth observing that I was trying hard and had actually drunk less than would usually have been the case. Being the Sixties too, any number of so-called recreational drugs were available, especially to creative types and the popular end of the music business, in particular. I was scared to even entertain the thought of taking these drugs with the rumours of their mind-bending and –altering 'qualities'. Although it can be argued that alcohol falls under the same category, I preferred to view the difference to be self-poisoning rather than affecting my brain permanently. Nonetheless, the alcohol dependency was beginning to worry me. It had also occurred to me that nicotine might be a suitable calming substitute. However, the effect on the breathing capacity of the lungs and on the purity of the larynx ensured that this was not pursued with any vigour. Besides which, I had noticed that the withdrawal symptoms from the lack of tobacco were exacerbated the more a person smoked. Gary was a case in point. In that long week, it became apparent that, not only had he taken up smoking again – the first time since Paris – but that he was smoking a lot of cigarettes. He appeared to be aggravating his sense of paranoia by so doing.

Unfortunately, I had spent a lot of time after the election speech in Amanda's company. The original determination to sort out my life had slipped several degrees because the advice Pete had given me was becoming more and more impossible to implement. The hole I was digging for myself was getting deeper and wider and there no longer seemed to be a way out. We slept together a couple of times, partly as a distraction or diversion from the tension in the lead-up to the elections but mainly because I felt that she was still necessary to the campaign and did not want to upset the apple-cart. It depressed me every time I thought of how she was being used by me and, even now several years later, I still feel pangs of contempt for myself. All of my life – certainly until I went to prison at any rate – people have been using me at one level or another, because of my relatively easy-going nature and that made me reasonably fair game for it. Some of it caused me little worry, because it helped me to reach a particular goal but mostly, the pulling of the puppet's strings and dancing to different tunes made me indignant at being used by people without any gratification, compensation or rewards. The way that I have dealt with it in the past is to bottle it up, explode on occasion and get back to normal; unfortunately, this means that those people reciprocate with more of the same. It frustrates me to be used so casually and yet that was precisely what I was doing to Amanda. In retrospect, and I am philosophical about it now, she had every right to start loathing me in the end.

* * *

On the day of the election, I arrived at the rehearsal halls early, forgoing the usual trip to the Goat and Dramatist, in order to take the opportunity to talk to people as they came in. For the reasons highlighted in my hustings speech, now embellished and better planned, obtaining the Chairmanship had become incredibly important to me. No longer was I pursuing this ambition to ensure Gary's nasal displacement. Alongside me was Amanda, greeting people as they came in, flirting outrageously with the men and warning them to remember that they only had one vote and to use it wisely. To anyone who cared to stop and talk, I asked a direct question as to what they envisaged to be the future of the Chorus, particularly in the light of my recent speech. It had the double-edged effect of creating an atmosphere to show that I genuinely cared for their views on our immediate world but also of being able to press home the points that I had been making, matching what they were remarking on with the manifesto.

Seated in the auditorium, when Sir Norman took the podium, I estimated that half the Chorus had been spoken to and roughly three-quarters of those had expressed their similar views and support. On each chair in the hall, a piece of paper had been placed, drawn up by Pete, with Anthony Devlin's and my names printed on it beside two boxes against which the voting cross was to be put. There were some minimal instructions as to what to do to complete the voting slip – how to fill it in, how to fold it and to await the Secretary to collect the completed ballots.

"Ladies and gentlemen," boomed Sir Norman's voice, to create silence, "please can you put your daubs on the voting papers? Gary will then pass among you to pick them up."

Everyone reached into their pockets, briefcases, handbags or wherever they kept their pens and pencils, crouched over the paper, made their marks and folded the slip for Gary to pick up. He moved along the rows quickly, and threw each of the voting slips into a cardboard box he was carrying, balanced on a hand like a waiter serving lunch. When all the voting slips had been collected, he strode purposefully to Sir Norman and muttered something. Sir Norman nodded, stood down from the platform and gesticulated with a sweep of his hand to Gary, who stepped on to the box, moving the music-stand down to the floor.

"First of all, ladies and gentlemen," he said imperiously, "I will go into the office and count these slips, with the help of someone to ensure fair play." He pointed at Adrian and cocked a thumb over his shoulder towards the office. "Adrian, please can you step out." Adrian stood up, puffed out his chest and walked ostentatiously to the back of the hall. Stabs of worry pricked my stomach momentarily as I was sure that they would try to rig the election in Anthony's favour, but could say nothing. "Secondly," he continued, "for the New York trip, our wardrobe manager will be handling the details initially. Ultimately, however, you are answerable to me." He shook his head slightly backwards as if with a twitch and stepped back off the podium towards Adrian, who opened the door and they disappeared together.

Conversation had sprung up about Gary's off-hand manner, why the wardrobe manager was being given such responsibility and a few salacious comments regarding Gary's and Adrian's relationship, all of which dulled as Sir Norman stepped up to the podium, replacing the music-stand to its position and took the rehearsal.

* * *

During the interval, I had decided to take the opportunity to discuss the elections with the increased number of patrons attending the Goat and Dramatist. Originally intending to stick to soft drinks, I felt obliged to drink the celebratory pint proffered by Amanda. Although the result had yet to be announced, she was convinced that I would be the successful candidate. Sipping her martini and scrutinizing me with a dolefully sweet gaze, like Bambi in a staring contest, over the rim of her glass, she asked me if I intended to go home with her that evening. I seized on the opportunity, before the effects of too much alcoholic ingestion kicked in, to straighten things out and hopefully let her down lightly, now that we were this side of the electioneering.

Despite all the planned and rehearsed soliloquies and platitudes, the eloquent arguments for breaking off our relationship and the optimistic view of the world post-break-up, all I could muster, in answer to her question, was a ridiculous and plaintive: "Well, I don't know."

"What does that mean?" Her sweet and doe-eyed demeanour had melted into a cautious frown.

Awkwardly, I looked at a fascinating corner of the ceiling, trying to remember my lines and failing dismally: "It means that I don't know whether to come back with you or go back to my house."

"Well, your house is nearer," she observed, brightening a little and smiling. Oh, those damned eyes!

"I meant going to my house alone," I countered, sipping at my beer, nervously wondering which direction this conversation would take.

Her face fell. "Why don't you want to be with me?" she asked in a very offended tone.

"I'm…I'm very tired," I tried, but with little conviction.

"Tired?" Little red patches were appearing on her cheeks and her eyes were on fire. "Tired? There is a perfectly good bed at my place, you know."

Several heads were turning towards us like meerkats. I waved a hand at her: "Okay, okay. Keep your voice down."

"Why should I?" she retorted loudly, before dropping to a conspiratorial whisper. "Well?"

"It depends."

"On what?" Her cheeks were very flushed now.

"I need to go home for a change of clothes and to write a couple of letters."

Still adamant, she jerked her heel down in a mild stamp and hissed: "You can wash your things at my place. And I have paper."

"I know, but –."

"Why don't you want to be with me?" she repeated. Her voice had now taken on an ugly whine.

"I do," I lied, in a desperate attempt to keep the peace.

"You said you loved me," she added, giving another little heel-stamp.

I was so taken aback because I had never said anything of the sort, my resolve slipped again and I said: "I…alright. I'll come back with you."

Now coy, she smiled and said: "You don't have to if you don't want to."

"I've said I'll come," I snapped back.

Sadness filled her face and I feared she would start to cry. "There's no need to be angry about it."

"I'm sorry," I said gently, holding out a placating hand. She took it and kissed the palm, before pulling my head towards her for a more lingering kiss. The last thing I wanted to do was to hurt her but I was starting to swim in this turbulent sea of weak-willed mess with no apparent way out or saviour to come to my rescue. I also knew that the longer it was left to make the final break, the more arduous and more hostile it would be to rectify things and the worse would be her hurt. Battling against those feelings was the recognition that she was becoming very cloying and was beginning to manipulate me; she made me feel very claustrophobic but I still found it increasingly painful and hard to take the necessary and humane actions.

* * *

I do not remember much of the remainder of the rehearsal – the nerves which were in ribbons before had been atomized by the *contretemps* in the pub with Amanda and the impending outcome of the election. Procrastination once again appeared to solve the relationship with Amanda temporarily and the end of the rehearsal would see the announcement of the results. Then, maybe, my nerves would settle a little. But there was another impending issue that surfaced now: Marie and how I was going to deal with meeting her again. After the words with Amanda, I had had great difficulty in maintaining my façade of everything being alright as others came to me to discuss the Chorus' future and it was now with bated breath and anticipation that I awaited the announcement, when Sir Norman had put his baton down. All thoughts of Amanda and Marie were banished *pro tem* to the back of my mind.

"Ladies and gentlemen," he said, quietly, almost with reverence. "That's about it. The only thing that I would ask you to concentrate on, gentlemen, is sounding much more woefully earthy towards the end of the chorus. Right, thank you, ladies and gentlemen. I will be behind a glass panel next week, should you wish to gesticulate at me for any reason. In the nicest way possible, of course."

A swollen stream of titters issued from Norm's Gorms, starting in the soprano section and liberally overflowing into the altos.

Sir Norman continued: "I won't actually be able to make it to Christoph Schmidt's piano rehearsal on Thursday due to other commitments. I'm sure, though, that Christoph will let you know exactly what he wants. The Chorus itself will be left in the capable hands of our new Chairman. On which subject – Gary?"

Gary rose to his feet and moved to stand by the podium, officiously referring to a clipboard every now and again and returning it under his arm like a sergeant-major's regimental baton. The frisson of anxiety surfaced again as I wondered what had gone on in the counting room between Gary and Adrian. I figured that it would not be in their interests to rig the elections away from my favour, because I might call for a recount to be carried out by other, more trustworthy people. Judging by the sour look on Gary's face, hope spurred me on a little that he was going to deliver what he would consider to be bad news.

"Alright," he said now. "It was a close-run contest." He forced a smile to add: "It says here." He continued by describing the process we had all been through, which was completely unnecessary.

Get on with it, Gary, I thought, frustrated that he was taking the floor in his own inimitable way.

"So," he said finally, "the results are…" He paused for dramatic effect. "Spoiled ballots: five; Anthony Devlin: twenty-three votes; David Loughton: one hundred and sixteen. Very close as you can see. Therefore, I hereby pronounce David Loughton to be our new Chairman."

The world seemed to lose its definition. For a moment, I had an out-of-body experience, as I appeared to be looking down on myself, slowly circling before everything snapped back into focus. Standing up a little shakily, and advancing to the podium, I acknowledged the polite applause. "Thank you. Thank you, ladies and gentlemen," I said, shocked not only at winning but at the size of the margin between Devlin's and my received votes. "I'd like to say that I won't be making a marathon Oscar-acceptance speech, you'll be glad to hear, but only that you'll be hearing from me. Or my lawyer!"

Surprisingly, a generous round of mirth issued from the various

echelons of the Chorus and particularly from Norm's Gorms. Sir
Norman stepped forward and shook my hand. Still feeling in a world of
disbelief and unreality, I remembered Gary was still behind me and
turned to offer him my hand. He was slumped morosely cataloguing the
parquet flooring and he looked at my proffered hand as if it were a week-
old kipper. Finally, he consented, shook it firmly once and stalked off to
the exit.

"Congratulations, David," said Sir Norman, after dismissing the
Chorus, and reached into his brief-case. "Your first duty as Chairman is
to put your name to these." He produced the American tour contract.
"It's the New York performances. In triplicate, I'm afraid."

He spread the sheets out for me to sign, which I did with an artistic
flourish. When I had completed those, Sir Norman provided details of
the Thursday rehearsal at which he would not be present and the
protocols for meeting and greeting the soloists and conductor. I did not
know whether to laugh or cry – I had been elevated from obscurity to
Chairman in a matter of days. Always knowing that if I were to apply
my mind to something, however difficult or complex, I could make it
happen and get on top of it. With this achievement in my virtual awards
cupboard, I knew that now a greater strength had germinated to attack
the other problems in my life with vigour and sort them out.

* * *

"Congratulations!" said Bob, forcing a pint of best bitter into my hand
and clapping me heavily between the shoulder-blades. Thanking him
and taking a gulp, I thought that this celebratory drink was deserved but
that would be only one to be drunk that evening. A righteous plan
indeed!

Several people, even Anthony Devlin, had congregated in the Goat
and Dramatist. Although I was used to driving the bar when it came to
getting rounds in, I was relieved that everyone else was buying the
drinks, despite it being three-deep at the small bar, serviced by a very
flustered and a gruffer than usual John.

I smiled quietly to myself – the adulation, such as it was, was
overwhelming. It was difficult to come to terms with being treated as a
celebrity and with it came one of the first resolutions made regarding the
future: I would not succumb to the trappings of the position and keep
my promise to become the chairman for the people rather than the
figurehead.

After an hour, I had two pints in my stomach, one in my hand and three pints slowly going flat on the window-sill. I had started to refuse the offers of drinks, aware that I would not be able to drink any more than those lined up. It was a slight nod, too, to my acknowledgment of the need to give up the booze for my own good.

Over on the other side of the bar, Gary had struck up an animated conversation with Adrian, running with two concurrent subjects. Adrian wanted to talk about the specifics of the American jaunt, while Gary had wanted to whimper in the corner, licking his (self-inflicted) wounds.

"Gary," started Adrian carefully, having interrupted his monotribe on just who did David Bloody Loughton think he was. "I need some dates for the airline company."

Gary sighed noisily, a pained expression on his face as he lit a new cigarette from the dying butt of a previous one. "I don't know. What do you think I am? A walking diary?" he said, clouding Adrian in tobacco fumes.

"Sorry, Gary," replied Adrian, trying not to cough.

Gary threw his arms up animatedly, scattering ash down the back of a girl's coat, but he scarcely noticed. "I'm sick and tired of having to hold the whole bloody Chorus on my shoulders."

"Look, Gary," said Adrian gently, "I –."

"It's like carrying them over a lake of water but the burden is getting so heavy now that I'm being pushed under." He drew heavily on the cigarette so that his cheeks hollowed. "I'm in fear of drowning here."

"Yes. I know that you –."

Gary was working himself up to a crescendo as he diverted back to his favourite current subject. "I tell you one thing, Adrian," he said, jabbing the cigarette between two fingers towards him, "anything on New York, you discuss with me and not the Chairman. I want Mr. David 'I'm the big noise now' Loughton kept out of this totally."

He was interrupted by Pete joining them, ducking away from an extravagant, punctuating elbow. He was carrying two pints of beer, one of which he gave to Gary. "What's going on?" he asked. "You seem a little overwrought."

"Nothing really," said Gary, snatching the glass and taking a large slug of beer. "Just our new Chairman."

"I think he'll do alright."

"Well, *you* would," responded Gary, spitefully prodding Pete in the chest. "*You* are on his payroll."

"I object to that," asserted Pete, carefully avoiding losing his temper and keeping it in check for the moment. "I support his views: yes. But I am not in his pocket. This may surprise you, Gary, but I do have the brains for independent and rational thought."

Gary relaxed a little, knowing that he was not in the right frame of mind for an argument or to come up with anything more coherent than petulant and childish observations. "Okay, okay," he said finally, by way of an apology, "I'll give him two months to prove that he's willing to support me and is not just wind and wee-wee. And that he hasn't got a personal vendetta out on me and then I'll decide what he's like." He dragged deeply on his cigarette and took a mouthful of beer without exhaling.

"Sounds to me like you've already reached one," rejoined Pete.

"I haven't," snorted Gary.

An impatient Adrian interrupted: "Gary, what should I do about the airline company?"

"Not now, Adrian," he replied, pained again. "Can't we discuss this some other time?"

Adrian's expression was one of frustration and consternation, but he knew when he was beaten. He nodded briefly and wandered over to talk to Anthony Devlin to give his commiserations. Anthony was expounding his theories on the musicology of *Carmen* and extolling the virtues of Bizet in his usual monotonous voice (one such delicious intellectual gem was: "I think you can't understand Bizet, until you really understand Bizet").

"That was a little rough on Adrian," said Pete, concerned.

Gary exhaled another lungful of smoke quickly and whined: "Oh, don't you start at me, Pete. Please. I've had a hard day, I don't earn any more money as Secretary, I come along to sing at a rehearsal and end up getting nothing but jibes from everybody. And not the least from our illustrious Chairman." He spat the adjective as if it were bile.

"Why? What has Dave said to you?"

"He doesn't have to *say* anything. Look at him over there. He's preening himself like a ruddy peacock." Another gulp of beer emptied the glass and he followed it down with two long drags on his cigarette, inhaling deeply as he did so. His right eyelid flickered to keep the smoke at bay, giving an overall impression that Gary's brain had gone into seizure.

Pete glanced behind him towards me. "He just looks like he's getting very drunk to me," he observed. "Let's hope he doesn't repeat the last night in Paris!"

"No," replied Gary, vehemence shaking ash from the cigarette tip between his lips. "He's telling everyone how marvellous he is and how he's going to take over." He sighed melodramatically and went to the bar to replenish his glass. Pete smiled pitifully, frowned and shook his head.

* * *

In fact, regardless of Gary's paranoid impressions, what I was trying to do was to restart the earlier conversation with Amanda and to summon up the courage to bring our relationship to a satisfactory conclusion; one, which would cause the least hurt. As a public relations person, she had served her purpose very well but it could not continue on those lines because of that one selfish reason. Unfortunately, the quantity of consumed beer had bleared my mind to the point that the strong arguments were just out of reach and consequently went unremembered. I could only revert to the questions relating directly to the immediate predicament.

"Do I *have* to come back with you?"

The flushes of pink flashed on to her cheeks again. "You said you would earlier."

"I know but I just want to get to bed and sleep off this alcohol."

"As I said before, my bed's perfectly qualified for that!"

"No, I mean alone."

"Why?" The fire was back in her eyes and she was breathing heavily, hands on hips.

"I need to adjust to the new circumstances and prepare for my first day of work tomorrow as Chairman." Good one, I thought to myself.

"And I can help you," she said more gently, reaching for my hands and squeezing them.

"Look, I'm tired," I tried again. "It's been a long week and I'm getting steadily drunk. Can't we talk about this tomorrow?"

"But I love you," she said miserably.

Slightly panicked, I said: "I don't want anything too emotional right now. We can talk about it tomorrow." The energy that I put into procrastination and putting off the inevitable was astonishing.

"You're the one that's emotional," she countered, tears brimming over her eyes. "What's wrong? I love you and you love me. Is there someone else?"

Momentarily confused and caught off-guard, I wished I was not so drunk. "Of course not," I said, pulling her towards me and hugged her. Good God! What was I doing?

"I love you," she repeated, wiping away a tear and kissing me.

Through the alcoholic haze, Marie's dimpled smile popped into my mind. "Oh, damn!" I almost whispered.

"What?" asked Amanda, pulling away warily.

"Nothing," I sighed. "Me. My life. Alcohol. Stuff. Come on. Let's go, then." I shouted what I hoped sounded like a cheery goodbye to those remaining patrons and we left.

My mind was spinning between half-truths, reality and perceived paranoiac delusions connected by the tenuous link of alcohol. When we reached Amanda's flat, I had sobered up considerably and had the beginnings of a hangover creeping into the edges of my brain. Still, nothing could be said because I had told myself that I was too tired and needed a clear head.

We went to bed and had, after being pestered by Amanda to the point of furious distraction, what can loosely be described as sex. I do not believe that either one of us enjoyed it. Deep down, it was evident that Amanda had figured that there was something wrong and that I was attempting to end it amicably. All that was fogged to obfuscation by her determination, possessiveness and jealousy. As I slipped into an uneasy sleep, breathing fast to counter the effects of the alcohol, I knew that, tomorrow, there would be no further pussy-footing or procrastination, no matter how hurt she was. I had to end it for the sake of my own sanity, if nothing else because I was beginning to feel suffocated and miserable by the affair with Amanda. The cold light of day would help me see the most appropriate path to investigate and follow.

PUPPET ON A STRING

CHAPTER 12

There were two dreams, which used to haunt me regularly. It was not only that they appeared on a regular basis but also that they were cyclical in nature. When the dreams finished, they would return to the beginning and off they would go again. It did not even matter, in the worst cases, if I got up in the middle of it all to get a drink of water or whatever; as I fell back to sleep, the dream would pick up from the same point.

The first dream was about my unexplained knowledge that a dead body had been carelessly buried in a gravel pit, which was in regular use. In the dream, it was unknown to me how the body had met its end, who it was, how I knew it was there or even if I had been involved in burying it. What made the dream scary and so distressing was that I knew that it would be located any time soon, that it would be disastrous were it uncovered, that a sloppy job had been done burying it and that I would be quickly implicated.

The second dream went back to my lawyer studies and university. Although it was based in present day, I would be carrying out my normal day-to-day activities and then have a panic attack that my finals were scheduled for the next day and could not remember doing any revision work for it.

The psychology seminars taken during my training told me that the first dream was about guilt and the second was about fretting that nothing in my life was ordered. It was quite simple to see the parallels.

During the night, I had both dreams running and segueing into each other. Even though I was dehydrated from the evening in the pub, I awoke with a start, sweat dripping down my face and back, the vestiges of the dream appearing real in the half-light of the bedroom. I buried my aching head in shaky hands and realized that today was the day to inaugurate the solutions to all the outstanding problems, regardless of the dull thud in my head.

The day was bright and sunny and extraordinarily sultry for early May. My head was aching still and I had been forced to take a dose of liver salts to reduce the general feeling of malaise in my stomach and liver. Staying awake after the dream, the rush of thoughts running through my head filled me with angst. I decided to get up at the crack of dawn to avoid a confrontation with Amanda and to be on my own for a while to gather my thoughts. Amanda had half woken as I pulled on my clothes and asked where I was going, to which I answered soothingly that I was going to the office to start the first official day of my Chairmanship. She had appeared satisfied, rolled over, cuddled the pillow and grunted her way back into sleepy oblivion.

In fact, although I had every intention of going to the office in the morning, I had first returned to my house, cowering in the glare and heat of the rising morning sunshine, like a vampire on overtime. This was a distance of some six or seven miles and, with the queasy feeling of still being slightly drunk and my tongue flicking dryly around my mouth, I breathed deep and embarked on the journey. Sobriety from the physical exertion and a full-scale hangover met me at the front door and I let myself in gingerly.

Popping a couple of aspirin and overdosing in orange juice to replace the vitamin C, I forced myself to think through my various predicaments once more to compose a coherent mitigation plan. I paced around the sitting-room, hands in pockets, brow deeply furrowed and literally kicking myself on the calf and ankle every time a home truth became too unbearable to accept.

First, there was Amanda. Her cloying, oppressive involvement with me was dragging me down and she had convinced herself that she was in love with me. Having used her so shamelessly to secure the position of Chairman, I needed to rectify the position. There was no point going back over what I had done because it could not be undone. However, I could take action to reverse an almost irreconcilable situation. I had observed before that the longer it went on for, the worse my general outlook would be and the more difficult it would be to end this amicably. It had often amused me that, on my bookshelves, I had a self-help book called *Overcoming Procrastination*, which I had never got around to reading. The situation now was not funny; the dilatory approach to the management of the problem had led me to increase the likelihood of hurting Amanda badly. Nevertheless, this was not a reason for further delay and our relationship needed to be confronted head on and soon, if not today. I decided that what had to be done was to state the situation as I saw it, not to try to sweeten the bitter pill in any way, end the relationship and provide support where and if possible.

Second, I had become Chairman mainly to prove something to myself – that I was no worse than Gary Adner. Running up to the election, passion had taken over and I still felt the vestiges of it even now. I needed to activate my election promises. Otherwise, I would feel very disappointed with myself. And the re-elections were scheduled within the next twelve months. If I was serious about making something of the role, the Chorus and myself I needed to draw up a plan of how to implement my ideas, the timescales we would be looking at and some kind of measure of success to see how much further work was required.

Third, my relationship with Gary had become increasingly frosty over the previous weeks. In order to make my manifesto effective, I needed as much support and drive from the other committee members as possible. I thought that the only way was to be firm with Gary but to try to be supportive as well. I could understand how his world suddenly appeared to be turned upside-down and, rather than be castigated for his reactions, he needed to be treated with empathy. When I made my appearance at the office, I would call him in for a meeting to work out how we could best work together. The risk was that he would fly off the handle and the situation would be ten times worse than currently. However, like the relationship with Amanda, it needed to be confronted and not be subject to further protractions awaiting the right moment. The right moment rarely, if ever, arrives.

Fourth, Marie Duvois! What did I really think my relationship was with her? She was present daily in my thoughts. She was the main focus whenever she was in my sight. To me, that meant that I had a deep attraction towards her and, thinking through our conversations, I believed she was attracted to me. Was I then treating her as a future lover who needed to be chased and conquered in some way? Or was I looking for a longer-term commitment? If so, would I not end up being thoroughly disappointed because she was so unattainable? Or was she? The relationship was the most confusing aspect of the issues facing me and, until I had had a chance to talk to her again, I would only be predicting, presuming and assuming the situation. The recording was scheduled over the next week and I knew there would be ample opportunity to talk with her and see how the land lay. The immediate problem on this issue was to suppress my optimism but balance it by ignoring the insidious pessimism.

Fifth and final problem: alcohol. I had an increasing dependence on it and it was sickening to me that I should plan my day around the next time I could cuddle a pint glass, destroy a few more brain cells, become morose and be visited by the latest bout of paranoia. If I could be strong-willed, life would be easier to cope with if I were to give it up. Not cut down, because that can lead to 'just one more and I'll start tomorrow' – as had been clearly evident over last few days. No. I had to cut it out entirely for a long period to detoxify my body and to be able to think clearly and get decent sleep at night. It had become increasingly apparent that I spent most of my days feeling subdued and unable to meet my potential.

Having spent the morning soul-searching and near self-immolation, exhaustion hit me. But it was an exhaustion that was easy to manage because important and concrete decisions had been made, rather than letting my life drift haphazardly any which way.

* * *

It was about ten to twelve when I entered the main building and walked up the stairs to the office. I was feeling a lot fresher, my headache had gone and I was feeling positive for the first time in ages. Thinking about how to deal with Gary and how to approach the telephone call to ask him to come in for a chat, it startled me to see him already sitting in front of a mountain of ash in the ashtray, feet crossed and on the edge of the desk, lounging back, a cigarette never more than two inches away from his mouth, gazing out of the window. As I entered, he jerked forward and began writing something in a book, which was correctly guessed to be the appointments diary.

"Morning, Gary," I said, as breezily as the tense and smoky atmosphere would allow. My mind raced as to the suitable opening gambits to sort out how we would operate together in the future.

Gary grunted what I assumed to be a greeting without looking up. I looked around the office, which was oblong and roughly the size of an average kitchen, and frowned at the stupendous mess. Along the two longer sides of the room were sets of fitted bookshelves, on which higgledy-piggledy piles of correspondence, contracts, reviews and other administrative paraphernalia wobbled precariously if you went near them. On the shorter back wall was a free-standing book-case, which housed all the conductor's scores for each opera in the Chorus' repertoire. By comparison, this was extremely neat and tidy and it was obvious that this was the preserve of Sir Norman. At each end of the room was a desk, positioned opposite one another so that, when occupied, the tenants faced each other. On each desk was a black sign with gold lettering. On one, the overspill from the shelves avalanched over the sign which proclaimed 'SECRETARY'. The other, at which Gary was seated, was clear apart from the one telephone, the appointments diary, a typewriter, the overflowing ashtray and a small pile of present correspondence. The sign on this desk signified 'CHAIRMAN'.

"Delusions of grandeur, eh?" I said, cheerily and smiled.

"What?" snapped Gary, looking up and far from amused.

"'CHAIRMAN'," I replied gently, pointing at the sign and smiled again.

"Oh, yeah," he said quietly and returned to the diary, pencil poised.

"Any correspondence for me, then?" I asked lightly, hoping to break up the iceberg, which was slowly nudging its way between us.

"No!" replied Gary, defensively, his hand straying to the top of the pile of papers.

"So what are you up to? Anything I can help with? You know, try and understand how this business runs?"

Suddenly, Gary grabbed the pile of papers, dropping the pencil, and stood up violently, sending the chair crashing against the wall. "Christ almighty!" he ejaculated unnecessarily and stubbed his cigarette into the ashtray, spilling grey tobacco ash on to the desk. "I've been doing this job since we began this outfit and now we get some wet-behind-the-ears Chairman, who wants to take over." His face had turned puce.

Holding my hands out palm forward in a calming gesture, I tried to placate him, somewhat alarmed by the vitriolic abuse: "Not at all. I just want to get into my role as Chairman. A team is what we are and I am the new leader. That doesn't mean I'm taking over but I do need to know what's going on. And I need your help to inveigle me into the mechanics of this organisation. I'm fair, Gary, not a dictator." This was not going well and I was trying to salvage something from my determination to make this work. However, Gary's attitude was not going to make it happen easily.

"Well," he said, pointing an accusing finger, "don't dictate to me is all I can say."

"Gary, calm down," I said in a conciliatory tone. "That's the last thing I want to do. I want you to help me to help you, if you see what I mean." I paused and added: "Would you like a coffee?"

After a moment's hesitation, he nodded briskly. As well as the main kitchen area, there was a tiny annexe just outside the office with space enough for a cupboard to hold the refreshment ingredients, a small fridge, a kettle and a sink. Zealous determination took hold of me as I waited for the water to boil. It was important to set a precedent of our working relationship from the outset. I needed to be strong and firm and I needed to try to get Gary on my side – first we had to clear up the divisions of responsibility.

"There you are," I said, pointedly placing his coffee cup on the desk marked 'SECRETARY'. "Please can I have my chair now?" I walked behind just in time to see him cover up 'To: The Chairman' on the top piece of correspondence with a hand. "And if you could leave any correspondence for the Chairman on my desk."

He stood up quickly, his head almost connecting with my chin, and gathered up all the papers. I sat in the vacated Chairman's seat and watched as Gary sighed and deliberately made a meal of moving the papers on the Secretary's desk on to the floor, puffing and panting as he did so. The top of the piles toppled and slid into the centre of the room, although Gary ignored this. When he had sat down, facing me, I leaned back in the chair, lacing my fingers across my stomach, and said: "Please can I have all the correspondence for the Chairman?"

"What correspondence?" he asked hotly.

"Gary, I know there was at least one piece in that pile."

"Rubbish," he scoffed and leaned forward to write on a pad of notepaper he had taken out of a drawer.

Standing up, I tipped out the ashtray into the bin, made my precarious way to his desk and put the ashtray on his desk. Gary put his hand over the paper pile once again and glared at me ferociously, much as a lion might to a hyena trying to steal meat from the kill, his jaw muscles flexing.

"I don't have to take this from you," he spat. "I coped perfectly well all the time Sydney Althorpe was Chairman. Don't you dare try to take over!"

"Well," I said, good-naturedly, "my name is David Loughton, not Sydney Althorpe. *I* am now Chairman and I will be an *effective* Chairman. It is true that you had to act as back-stop for Sydney but that is now changing. In order to be effective, however, I need co-operation and not the least from you."

"You see," replied Gary, shaking his head viciously. "You're trying to step in and take over all the hard work that I've done. You want to claim all the perks for yourself and take all the glory. You want to steal my thunder."

"I'm sorry, Gary," I said firmly, "but you're wrong there. I want us to have a cogent working relationship together. In the meantime, please may I have the correspondence? While we sit here arguing, nothing is getting done." I held out my hand.

Gary stared ahead at nothing in particular, his breath-rate increasing until he was wheezing and his face was bright red. Finally, he stood up, scooped the papers in his hand and threw them violently into my face. "There you go," he said through gritted teeth, "if you're so bloody marvellous. I wash my hands of the whole business."

"Gary," I tried appealing to his better nature. Unfortunately, at that moment, he was bereft of one. "All I want is to work together with a little mutual co-operation."

"Well, see how you cope with that lot without me to spoon-feed you, you bastard!"

"Gary!" I said more firmly, because this had gone far enough. "I've tried to be understanding and lenient. I know that you feel that you have had to bear this Chorus single-handedly on your shoulders and that is why I want to try and assist you. But you do not seem to be able to see that. In fact, you are being quite insulting but I'll overlook that for now. You are not talking to me as a friend or a colleague. You are talking to me as Secretary to Chairman and, if you want me to pull rank, I will."

"Christ!" he scoffed. "Talk about ungracious."

I was confused; it felt as if we were having two different conversations in parallel universes. "Let me tell you something. The Chairman is not a figurehead; he is a doer, a mediator and a delegator. I have now been elected to that role and I will try to do it to the best of my ability. That includes dealing with correspondence addressed to the Chairman and I will delegate it to you as and when I see fit to do so. Is that clear? I don't want any one person shouldering total responsibility."

Gary's eyes were bulging as he lit another cigarette and dragged deeply on it, his shoulders slumping forward. "Are you giving me the sack to add insult to injury?"

"Gary, I have not said anything about sacking. Where did that come from? I am, as I keep saying, asking for your co-operation. This is our new regime."

"And you're nothing but a niggling little dictator."

"Gary –."

"Oh, shut up, will you? Get on with *your* work. *I'm* going to the pub."

With that, he yanked the door open, stalked briskly through it and melodramatically slammed it, the effect lessened by the door being caught on the piles of paper on the floor. I stared at the door for a while, shrugged to no-one in particular and set about picking up and glancing through the scattered, disputed mail.

PUPPET ON A STRING

CHAPTER 13

On Thursday, although the weather was fairly sombre and overcast in comparison to the previous day, I awoke feeling refreshed and better than I had done for ages, mortified to realize and admit that it was the first time in years that I had not consumed alcohol the night before. This dawning realisation spurred me on to achieve the fifth resolution. I could think more clearly and my imagination was sparkier than I could ever recall – the liberation was really quite illuminating.

I had stayed at the office until about half past six the previous evening, before thinking I ought to return home. The sun had lingered on the horizon and it was only turning on the light that made me look at the time. The pile of correspondence had eventually been sorted through and the overflowing piles on the floor and the shelves had been categorized and organized into appropriate areas on the shelves for consistency and the whole place had been almost spring-cleaned. I was satisfied with my efforts and felt that it was a good day's work. As my grandmother had always said: "Tidy room; tidy mind" and I think, for the first time, it was obvious what she had been getting at by trotting out this old adage. The tidiness in the office allowed for more coherent thought on establishing the way forward for the Chorus. Because I knew where to lay hands on anything in the office, it was comforting.

So, on the Thursday morning, I was able to find out a little more to do with the internal workings of the Chorus, the future dates, the rehearsals, the material and so on. The letter, which Gary had coveted like a jealous child, was from the management of the Paris Opéra. So impressed, they said, were they by the success of the *Tosca* performances, that they wanted us to return the next year with a view to consider making it an annual event. Their suggestion was to double up the *Tosca* performances with other operas, which would change each year. Perhaps *Don Giovanni* might be an appropriate choice for the next spring.

Checking the dates in the diary, there was no clash with anything we were slated to do at that time, so the appointment was pencilled in against the proposed dates and I made a note on my 'To Do' list to inform Sir Norman so that rehearsals could be set. There were also a few invoices from various clothing manufacturers and from our primary props maker addressed to Adrian Hilton, which I left to one side for him to deal with.

It was at that point that I wondered why the Chorus did not have its own Treasurer to deal with payment of invoices and the like. Instead, each year, we paid large sums of money to a firm of accountants to highlight discrepancies after the fact. I added a note to the list to discuss with the Committee the opportunity of finding a member of the Chorus, preferably with some sort of accounting background, to fulfil that role and handle our outgoings and income.

Looking through the diary, I was astonished to see how much Gary had kept the Chorus in the dark about upcoming engagements. There were some wonderfully prestigious events coming up, plus the possibility of recording the entire *Ring Cycle* in September. I typed out a sheet, giving the details of confirmed bookings and those, which had yet to be finalized, because the information would help the Chorus members to organize their lives and holiday plans around the schedule.

As I pulled the paper out of the typewriter, the telephone rang.

Picking up the receiver, I said in as professional a voice as I could muster: "*Coro di Londinium*, good morning. How can I help you?"

"Is that Gary Adner?" came a thin voice across the crackling connection. There was a lot of activity in the background.

"I'm afraid Mr. Adner is unavailable at present. My name is David Loughton. I'm the Chairman of this organisation. Can I take a message or help at all?"

"Yes. This is the Western General Hospital. We have been asked to let you know that we have admitted a Mr. Robert Holden after a stroke."

My eyes widened with alarm. "My God! How is he? Is it serious?"

"As yet we don't know," came the reply. "We're running tests at the moment. But he did ask me to 'phone his office as there is no available next of kin."

"Well, thank you for telling me. Please pass on our best wishes to him for a speedy recovery."

"I will."

"Thanks," I said and slowly put the handset back on its cradle. I sat musing for a while, fingers templed up to my lips before deciding to go down to the Goat and Dramatist for a spot of lunch.

I saw Gary talking with Pete in a corner, gesticulating wildly and relating a story with much energy and vigour. I could guess what that was about. Pete was leaning back, one arm across his belly and the other hand playing idly with a beer-mat on the table. I went to the bar, ordered a round of cheese and pickle sandwiches and an orange juice. John, the barman, regarded me suspiciously for a while, hands on hips, but I nodded and he scuttled off. Because he had his back to the door, Gary had not seen me come in. When I joined them at the table, Gary's face fell and he stuttered: "And s-so...er...I thought that was the...erm...b-best thing to do." It was as if he were reading badly from a script, obviously in an attempt to cover up that he was talking about me.

"Good afternoon," I said as I sat down, ignoring his pantomime, "how are we all today?" I took a bite out of the doorstep sandwich.

"Fine, thanks," replied Gary hurriedly and looked at his watch, adding lamely: "Oh, dear. Is that the time? I must go, I've got work to do." He smiled weakly, although it was not reflected in his bloodshot eyes, picked up his briefcase and shot through the door, leaving a barely touched pint of bitter on the table.

I watched him leave and shook my head slightly, turning back to Pete. "Something I said, do you think? He's not a happy soul at the moment."

"No," agreed Pete. "And he's been giving me a lot of mouth about you and what you said to him yesterday."

"I'm afraid it was justified. Gary is treating it in a very immature light. What has he been saying?"

"That you almost sacked him but knew that you would struggle without him. So you recanted. And that you have big ideas about stealing all the glory from him."

"And what do you think?"

"I think he wants someone to complain to. I get the feeling he's running scared because we now have a Chairman who appears willing to do something instead of insinuating that they are doing something. And I think he fears being found out. I kept telling him that I thought that, if you put your mind to it, you would do a fantastic job."

"Thank you very much," I said, raising my glass to him.

"Here!" exclaimed Pete, astonished. "Is that orange juice?"

"Orange juice, indeed," I confirmed. "Orange juice totally untainted by anything other than a couple of ice cubes."

"You've jumped on the wagon, then?" He still sounded incredulous.

"Yes, I have. And not before time. Alcohol has done enough damage to my brain and I don't want to destroy any more of it. I tell you, I had nothing yesterday and I woke up feeling better than I have in years. I put that down to being the first time in ages that I went to bed without alcohol knocking me off-balance."

"Is it a permanent thing?"

"Not for all time but I'm moderating my intake. Special occasions. That sort of thing."

"Well, good luck to you," replied Pete dubiously.

"Another thing. Look at Gary. He drinks like a fish and look at the paranoid state he's in. I believe it's a direct cause because I felt myself slipping down that path."

"Hmm, maybe," said Pete quietly, worriedly looking at his own glass, which remained half-full and permanently undrunk.

I sipped my orange juice, put down the empty plate and brushed my hands together. I said: "Change of subject: I had a 'phone call about half an hour ago."

"Ooh, that's nice," said Pete camply and laughed.

"Not really. It was from the hospital about Bob."

Pete's face dropped and he leaned forward urgently. "You're joking. What's wrong with him?"

"He's had a stroke. They can't confirm its intensity until they've completed their tests."

"Poor old Bob. Mind you, he is getting on."

"He is and he's done well so far. Dear! Hark at us! That sounds like we've consigned him to the scrapheap already! Anyway, do you think you could buy a 'Get Well Soon' card and we'll sign it from the whole Chorus? I'll get it sent up to the hospital. If I've got time, I might go and see him and take it with me."

"Yes. I'll probably drop in on him too. See how the old goat is. But I'll get the card either after the rehearsal or tomorrow morning."

"Excellent." I looked at the clock on the wall and checked it against my own watch. "If you've finished, shall we depart for the hall?"

"Sure thing, baby. I've finished. You've put me right off that stuff."

"Good thing too," I said pompously and laughed.

* * *

My heart increased its pace as we neared the halls and slowed again when I realized that neither Amanda nor Marie had appeared yet. Those were the two remaining problems that had not yet been tackled and I was determined to do something today. Nonetheless, the relief was palpable when I could not see either of them. I popped up to the office and, as I opened the door, Gary jerked guiltily out of my chair and moved over to the Secretary's desk.

He stabbed a mottled cigarette in my direction as he said: "What's the big idea of putting that notice up on the board?"

"I thought it about time that the Chorus were enlightened as to what we have in the pipeline."

"Why?" he asked sniffily.

"To help them co-ordinate their personal lives a little better. Besides they are paid to do this job and it is only fair to let them know what they are being paid for rather than leaving it to the last minute. Bad information networks and communication leads to bad and complacent workers." I sat down at my desk and noticed that Gary had picked up that day's correspondence again.

"Look, Loughton," replied Gary, shaking a little, "I haven't told people in the past because I happen to think that it would make them sloppy. They would pick and choose performances."

I got up and walked over to his desk, hands in pockets. He protectively covered the letters, before resignedly relinquishing them to me. I said: "That is their contractual prerogative but no performance equals no money. Simple economics. That shouldn't make them sloppy. Besides, it might generate excitement and more involvement if they were aware of it before it becomes too late to change their plans."

Gary stood up, dragged on his cigarette and stubbed it hard into the ashtray as if squashing a recalcitrant bug. "The way I have done it has never had any ill-effect."

"No, but it hasn't had a positive effect either."

"Why do you have to change it? If it ain't broken, don't mend it. I am good at what I do and I don't need some poncy, jumped-up little bastard like you –."

"THAT – IS – E – NOUGH!" I shouted, punctuating each syllable with a prod of a finger on Gary's chest. It took him completely by surprise and he looked a little scared and bemused. Before he could come back at me, I continued more gently but still firmly: "I don't have to take that kind of insulting bullshit from anyone – as Chairman or as a human being. I have jurisdiction over this Chorus and I am going to make it work and improve it. Rightly or wrongly, in your eyes, it was a democratic decision and will not change until at least the next election campaign." Our faces were a couple of inches apart. Gary was flinching with each aspirate and fricative syllable and backed off with me following him. "I've tried to be pleasant and co-operative," I continued, "and I've tried to be understanding. But it's not working because you are not willing to help me. Now, any more rudeness from you, Adner, and I will consider making moves to ensure it is taken to a higher authority. Maybe our sponsor would be interested to see how you carry on. Now get out to that rehearsal, sit down and sing. That, after all, is what we are here for, not to have destructive, petty, jealous conversations about who does what?"

I was breathing hard as Gary glared at me with real hatred. I thought he was going to continue his vilification but he decided against it, turned on his heels and marched out of the room, this time successfully slamming the now unencumbered door. I breathed a sigh of relief – this was not what I had in mind when dealing with Gary but at least the position had been made clear. If we could not work together, I would have to find another way to make it work. I abhor unnecessarily tense atmospheres and had hoped our *tête-à-tête* had gone some way to clearing the air, although I suspected not. I knew that in future dealings with Gary, it would be I, who had to keep the temper in check.

From the office window, I saw a large, black, chauffeur-driven car draw up and predicted that this must be Herr Schmidt and his assistant. Taking the stairs two at a time, I breezed swiftly through the rehearsal hall, ignoring Amanda's puzzled waving and looked towards the soloists, resting momentarily on the face of the wonderful Marie Duvois, my heart skipping a few beats. She was talking with Guido Estente, turned slightly away from me. I moved on quickly so that it was not obvious that I was gawping ungallantly at her. As I reached the doors, Christoph Schmidt stepped out of the car, thanking the chauffeur who was holding the door open for him. Herr Schmidt was a tall, thin man, looking younger than his forty-eight years. His hair was still dark, had not receded and wafted carelessly in the breeze.

"Guten Nachmittag," I ventured, holding out my hand to him, "Willkommen an London. Kommen Sie herein, bitte." I had been practising barely remembered schoolboy German at odd moments in the morning and felt that I had mastered the simple phrases of welcome.

However, after he had shaken my hand, he smiled warmly and said in near-perfect English: "Thank you for your trouble. But I think, if I may be so rude, that it would be best for all of us if we spoke in English."

I reciprocated his smile: "Not at all. That's actually a great relief. Please come in."

I showed him into the hall, avoiding direct eye-contact with Marie, and up to the podium. He produced his score and a baton case from a thin document bag. While he unzipped the top of the case and removed a prospective baton, I clapped my hands together and looked around the Chorus for silence.

"Ladies and gentlemen," I called, rising to my role, "please will you give a warm welcome to the maestro, Herr Christoph Schmidt." I gesticulated towards the podium, while the Chorus and soloists applauded.

Christoph Schmidt raised his hands in modest appreciation. "Thank you, ladies and gentlemen, danke sehr."

I turned to sit down and, in so doing, happened to glance at the soloists and my heart jumped once more. My eyes met Marie's and held for a second, locked. She smiled and there was that slight wink she was so good at. I returned her smile and sat down, optimism now winning hands down.

"So, ladies and gentlemen," continued Christoph Schmidt, "before we go any further, may I take the pleasure to introduce a few of the soloists for our recording?" As he announced their names, Torchev and Estente stood up and bowed briefly and self-consciously. But Marie's introduction was met with applause and one or two wolf-whistles.

"Popular lady, huh?" asked Christoph Schmidt, looking directly at the bass section. A couple of them, including Pete, cheered in reply. Marie had blushed prettily. I just could not wait for the interval to take the opportunity to be close to her again.

* * *

Just before the rehearsal interval, I informed the Chorus that a thirty-minute break was the maximum. Off to one side, I invited Christoph Schmidt and the soloists to the pub. There was general agreement that, while it sounded like a superb idea, the smokiness of the atmosphere and the noise of the pub might be excessive and that a cup of good English tea would be more palatable.

At the tea-house, which was normally inhabited by Anthony and his cronies, we settled down at a table in the corner. I spoke with the waitress ordering Assam tea and home-made Madeira cake and settled down in the remaining seat, between Mikhail Torchev on one side and Christoph Schmidt on the end of the table and diagonally opposite Marie. Guido Estente sat opposite me. The conversation was a little strained, because they all seemed to be nervous of each other, although Marie and Estente appeared comfortable with each other. Personally, I find it very difficult to do small-talk. However, I did initiate several conversational topics relating to the common theme of music. Discussions about the weather and personal health feel insincere and uninterested, so I was desperately hoping someone else would take the lead. I was feeling faintly embarrassed that they were visiting me (us) and that the conversation was so stilted.

When all other conversation had dried to a trickle, I turned to Christoph Schmidt and asked, almost desperately: "Which opera do you think is the best to conduct?"

"*Otello*, I think," he ruminated, "but every opera has its moments. I used to sing, you know." I nodded. I owned a number of his fine recordings. "Yes," he continued, "but when one reaches beyond the age of forty-five or fifty, it becomes more difficult to produce the same quality as ten or fifteen years previously. Perhaps one should be sitting in front of a roaring fire in a pair of slippers with a meerschaum pipe, no?" We laughed. "So then, I thought I would take a different direction in music, although I had been conducting on and off for years. Mainly Festivals. So, *Otello* to conduct but I think, to sing? Perhaps Puccini's *Turandot*. I particularly enjoyed singing the *Nessun Dorma* aria. It never failed to get spontaneous applause when one ends on those high notes."

"I think," rumbled Torchev in the clipped Russian way of removing the articles, apparently turning each word over in his mouth before speaking it, "that *Don Giovanni* is very fine opera. It is also first opera I sing professionally."

"And what do you think, Signor Estente?" I asked, feeling more relaxed now the conversation was flowing once again. Marie had the same expression of amusement in her eyes as at the time of the wine-tasting in the restaurant. I smiled at her and she raised an eyebrow, eyes twinkling. The fact that this tacit conversation was taking place at all raised my hopes enormously.

Estente replied in the rhythmic sing-song voice that all Italians seem to possess: "I particularly like the opera we are doing now. *Carmen*. And especially *The Flower Song* is a beautiful aria." He turned to Marie. "And what about you, Signorina Duvois?"

"Ask Mr. Loughton," she replied playfully. "We've had this conversation before. Let's see if he remembers." She rested her head on an upturned hand, elbow on the table and drumming her fingers against her lips. She stared wickedly and directly at me.

I tried in vain not to go crimson and utterly failed. "Ah, yes," I blustered, "I seem to recall that it was *Carmen* and *Il Trovatore*. In that order."

"Very good," she said, smiling, "well remembered. But what about you, David? What is your favourite opera?"

A smile winched itself up on one side of my face and gleam came into my eyes. "Mine," I said, looking from one to the other of the gathered company, "is little-known. In fact, it has only been performed the once and that was in Mademoiselle Duvois's home ground of the Paris Opéra House. And it's called" –I looked directly at Marie – "*The Little White Handkerchief.*"

Marie burst out laughing and clapped a couple of times. As I have mentioned before, Marie's laughter was infectious and beautiful. It was like that of a teenage schoolgirl's, full of innocence but nonetheless lethal. It was enough to start all of us laughing, although the other three men could not have possibly understood what it was all about.

* * *

Over the road and around the corner, Pete and Gary were sucking thirstily at their pints. In a repeat performance, Gary was winding himself up into a real lather. He was windmilling his non-drinking arm violently to illustrate his points and exhibiting a rising anxiety, spilling ash carelessly over everything and everyone in his vicinity.

"The Goat and Dramatist's too good for him now, I suppose," he said, his voice rising in pitch. "Doesn't want the stars to mix with the plebs." He dragged shakily on his cigarette, the glowing tip racing towards his yellow-stained fingers, and swallowed a large whisky he had lined up to complement the pint. He took out another cigarette and lit it from the glowing butt of the first, which he squashed in the ashtray, wisps of smoke still curling up from the dying embers.

"Gary," said Pete, exasperatedly, "why are you getting yourself so worked up?"

"Me getting myself worked up?" Gary shook his head in defiance and sucked the cigarette to the filter in one long drag before stubbing the burning foam out in the ashtray and coughing out a huge cloud of blue smoke. "Do you know what that son of a bitch said to me earlier? Eh? Eh? He said that I was a useless shit and he's taking over from me. I think that's a dreadful way to carry on. If –."

"I'm sure that if he said that he didn't mean it in the way you've taken it," Pete butted in. "Is that really what he said?"

Gary scoffed loudly and said: "I'm reading between the lines, mate, but he might as well have said it." His eyes were bulging as he nodded to underline his thoughts and took a large swallow of beer he had bought to chase the previous pint. "No, I'm going to do something about him, mark my words."

"Come on, Gary. You just said that he didn't say what you're accusing him of. He's only trying to form a team – a team we haven't had up until now."

"Oh, no. He doesn't want a team. He wants a dictatorship."

"That's a little strong. I mean –."

"Just because you're all buddy-buddy with him doesn't mean he's right."

"Yes, but Dave is the kind of person –."

Pete's flow was interrupted by Adrian appearing at Gary's elbow and butting in: "Hello. Sorry to jump in but have you got the dates for New York yet?"

Gary turned viciously on him. "Adrian, can't you see I'm talking?"

Adrian flinched and apologized timidly before returning to the bar to order a drink. He glanced back over his shoulder as Gary lit yet another cigarette using his battered lighter. The soloists' assumption that the pub would be too smoky was proven correct and was almost single-handedly generated by Gary.

"That was a bit unnecessary," said Pete crossly and put his hands in his pockets.

"Well, for God's sake, why should I have to bear everything in this Chorus? I'm sick and tired of it. Why can't Adrian Hilton use his initiative for once?"

"But you still shouldn't snap like that. Anyway, that's just what Dave is doing really. Using his initiative."

"Well, that's different," replied Gary, tipping his head back, opening his throat and quaffing the remaining three-quarters of his pint in one go.

"Look, I don't want to talk about this any more. You're working yourself up for no reason. What I wanted to mention was Bob."

"Bob?" Gary was quizzical, just about to respond to Pete's comment about working himself up but the complete change of conversational tack had caught him off-guard.

"He's had a stroke."

Gary was a little concerned. "How is he? I mean how serious?"

"They don't know. I'm getting a card this afternoon. Dave wanted to send it from –."

"You see? You see!?" exploded Gary, shrugging his shoulders wildly and waving his hands in the air, "that's just what I mean!" On which cryptic note, he stormed out of the pub back to the rehearsal room.

* * *

By the time we left the tea-house, everyone was getting on like a house on fire. That is, they were getting on very well with each other, the ice having been broken. I have never understood why houses being on fire should be considered to be something to be attained and good. The distress and impact should surely create the opposite emotion.

I still had not come to terms with the fact that I was treating these world-class singers and conductor like mates down the pub. Torchev had taken to clapping me between the shoulder-blades as if I were choking every time I uttered something reasonably amusing. Three weeks ago, I would not have considered this situation to be remotely possible, let alone actually to happen. The tea-house had rung out regularly with vocally well-trained laughter, usually started by Marie's silvery giggles and it continued on the way back to the rehearsal. With the ice broken so well, the recording would be a joy. It is often difficult to work with someone you have not worked with before and any light-heartedness brought to bear on the proceedings creates a friendly atmosphere. That then becomes apparent in the recording. It is similar to the sexual chemistry that is often obvious between the lead actors in Hollywood films.

I held the door open for everyone to make their way back into the hall. Bringing up the rear was Marie, who looked at me, gave me one of her winks and patted me on the shoulder gently before sliding her hand quickly down my arm. She wandered over to her seat, leaving me wide-mouthed and light-headed. I could not believe what had just happened and Pete returning from the pub interrupted my reverie.

He wore a querulous look and said: "Eh, bien je jamais!"

"Pardon?" I almost squeaked and cleared my throat.

"It's French. You might have to learn it. It means 'Well, I never'. Quite literally."

I thought momentarily, quickly got the trans-Channel pun and laughed. I took him by the elbow. "Actually, Pete, can I have a quick word?"

"Un mot rapide, eh? About Gary?"

"Shrewd, Pete, very shrewd."

* * *

The second half of the rehearsal felt particularly gruelling because the brief discussion with Pete and the curious sensation of Marie's warm touch had left me in a highly anticipatory mood. Having thanked the soloists and Christoph Schmidt publicly, I reminded the Chorus of the schedule for the Sunday. I knew I had to talk to Marie and say what had to be said but the butterflies in my stomach and war brewing in my head were telling me to do otherwise. As I was walking away, someone grabbed my shoulder. I had expected it to be Gary and was fearful, as I was in no mood for an argument with him this evening.

"Oh, hello, Pete," I said, somewhat relieved.

"Do it, Dave," he said, releasing me from his grip.

"What?"

Pete smiled knowingly, and gave a sideways nod towards Marie, who was putting on her coat and collecting her bits and pieces from under the chair. Although feeling doubtful, I nodded and returned Pete's smile, took a deep breath, almost hearing my heart clicking in my throat, and made my way over to her.

Marie looked up as I neared her. "Pretty tiring, huh?" she said, letting her face drop in mock exhaustion and then giving me a winning smile.

"Oh, you get used to it after a while," I said in a deliberately condescending manner and smiled.

She laughed: "Of course, only an old hand like you would know things like that."

I smiled again, took a breath and tried: "Look, do you fancy going for a meal somewhere? On me?"

"What? Everybody?"

"Well, if you like," I replied, disappointed, "but I was thinking just you and me."

"Oh, David, that is a lovely offer but please forgive me. I'm very tired. I was in the Frankfurt Opera last night and had to get up very early this morning to arrive here on time. I need to find my hotel, so perhaps we can make it another time?"

I was taken aback. Normally, you expect the worst in these situations but always with the underlying hope that you will receive the best. When the worst or the best does not materialize, it comes as a complete surprise and is not something that has necessarily been catered for. As in this case.

"I'm sorry," she said, noticing the crestfallen expression. "I would really love to but I am so tired I really would not be good company this evening." She took my hand and gently squeezed it. "I'd be a bore, honestly. Let's talk more on Sunday."

I pointed at her and winked. "You've got it," I said, "it's a date." I felt so much happier but still frissons of disappointment used my stomach as a punch-bag. In some ways, it did not appear to be a rejection but in other ways it did. But at least I had an appointment for a conversation with her. "See you on Sunday, then."

"I'll look forward to it. Have a good weekend." And with that, she left the building for the waiting taxi.

Estente and Torchev interrupted any further thoughts I had by patting me heavily on the back and vigorously shaking my hand, both men cupping it with two hands. On reflection, they could have been brothers: the two men were large, heavily set, with receding hairlines, closely cropped beards and a fearsome grip when shaking your hand.

I bade them and Christoph Schmidt farewell, absconded to the office and considered what the next few days might bring me. Everything seemed to be slotting nicely into place; some things, though, needed a final nudge and my life would be perfect.

* * *

Back in the Goat and Dramatist, Pete had cornered Gary before he could order any further drinks.

"Gary," said Pete in a business-like tone, which made Gary wary, "please can we have a word about your reactions to Dave Loughton becoming Chairman?"

"Oh, no," said Gary in a pained way, cigarette waggling between his lips, and swept the air with his hand as if to demonstrate that he did not wish to enter the conversation. "Do we have to? I'm not going to take any more hassle from anyone about him. I'll sort him out in my own way." He bent forward to light the cigarette and puffed at it.

"Okay. As you wish," continued Pete, still businessman-like, "but I'd like to say three or four things to you and then I'll leave it. First of all, most of what I have to say is in Dave's words and not mine."

"Oh, I told you," he whined, breathing smoke through his nostrils like an angry dragon and then pointed at Pete. "You're becoming his lap-dog. You see, I knew you –."

"Shut up and listen for once, Gary," interrupted Pete firmly. "I knew you were going to say that and that brings me to my second point. I agree with every word he says, otherwise I wouldn't be saying it. So please give me some credit."

"But –."

"Quiet!" ordered Pete, but still keeping the tone civilized. "Think about this: politics in general and Chorus politics specifically are very intense subjects. One disagreement can break up friendships."

"I don't think so," scoffed Gary. "What –."

"Shut up and listen!" insisted Pete. "I haven't finished. We – that is, you, me and Dave – used to have a good laugh together. Now look at us. I'm playing piggy-in-the-middle between you and you're at Dave's throat all the time. Dave isn't without his faults but at least he is making an effort to patch things up. Threatening to 'sort him out' won't help anything.

"And when did all of this begin? Well, if you think about it – back in the Paris Opéra, when you didn't like the idea of Dave getting on with Marie Duvois."

Gary looked incredulous. "Well, she's way out of his league."

"*That*, my friend, is not something for you or I to judge and should only be between them. Because of your jealousy over the Chairmanship and Marie Duvois, you are wrecking our friendship and it's becoming almost impossible to work or drink alongside you at the moment."

"But –."

Pete put a hand up quickly and Gary stopped immediately, cigarette stopped in mid-transit to his lips. "Thirdly – or is it fourthly? – I am fed up to the back teeth with hearing about how David Loughton is trying to take over, because he most certainly is not. Just give him a chance. He's only been doing the job for a few days and seems to have made a difference – a positive difference – already."

At this point, Adrian Hilton tried to join them, was on the verge of saying something before Pete put a firm hand up once again and turned to him.

"I'm afraid we're talking private business at the moment, Adrian," he said, a dangerous glint in his eye, "please can you come back later and you can have all the information you want."

"Okay," said Adrian, frowning and shrugged as he walked away.

"Where was I?" continued Pete, turning back to Gary, "Oh, yes. I don't want you to give me any more ear-hole abuse. It doesn't sound any different each time and, frankly, I'm getting very bored with it."

"But –."

"But nothing, Gary. Either you change your attitude and try working as part of the team Dave is trying to set up or continue the way that you are, alienating yourself. Because you aren't going to talk to me about it."

Gary puffed quickly on his cigarette, letting it out before he had drawn it into his lungs. Finally, he said venomously: "He's taught you well, hasn't he?"

"No, Gary. This is my brain that I have used to say this. Yes, I talked it through with Dave but he felt he was getting nowhere and I agreed that I would try. I'm no puppet on a string, Gary. I have the ability for independent thought and action. You, of all people, should know that, Gary."

"I'm going home," said Gary, hotly, and picked up his coat and briefcase. "I don't have to take this sort of thing from anyone. I come here to sing. I am the Secretary. I don't get paid for it but does anyone take any notice? And then all I get is 'yap, yap, yap' about what I should or shouldn't do. Well, I've had enough."

"Well," said Pete, calming a little, "I'm sorry you feel like that."

"Yes, of course you do," rejoined Gary, and then spat: "Like hell!" With that, he stormed from the pub, cigarette clamped between his teeth, and pushed the door open violently, as I was coming in. He stopped and glared at me as if I had just accused his grandmother of sexual misadventure. His gaze held, and then broke off and he was gone. I read into it that if Pete had spoken to him, it had not gone well. If that were the case, obviously it was down to Gary to sort himself out because I had taken it as far as it could go.

I stared out into the encroaching dusk watching his retreating shadow, resisting the urge to tut. I turned and, just in time, balletically avoided completely spilling a drink that Amanda was holding up at my elbow. She stepped back smartly to avoid the slight spillage hitting her shoes.

"I bought this for you," she said, quietly. "I knew you'd come down here."

"Hello, Mandy," I said, jumpily. I had prepared myself to talk to her this evening but not quite so quickly upon entering the pub. I had wanted to catch up with Pete first. I took the jug and put it down on a nearby table. "Thanks but, unfortunately, I'm off that stuff for the time being. Give it to someone else." I subconsciously wiped my hands together.

"That's a bit ungrateful," she said, looking at the pint on the table.

"I'm sorry," I tried again, more gently this time, "I've decided to go on the wagon for a while. You know. Dry the brain out."

She stopped me trying to get further into the pub with a hand on my chest and said: "Why did you ignore me when you came into the rehearsal today?"

"I didn't even see you," I lied, aware that the final resolution was slipping away if I continued in this way.

"Hardly surprising," she responded, nostrils flaring a little. "You were staring at that Duvois woman all rehearsal."

"That's unfair," I argued, although I had to admit to having given her fleeting and occasional glances. Amanda must have been watching me all the time. "You probably saw me at a point when I happened to be looking at her."

"What? Like the whole second half?" Indignant fire sparked in her eyes and the now familiar rose blushes appeared on her cheeks. If I did not rescue this soon, the chance would be lost.

"Look, Amanda," I said, firmly, "today has been tough and it wasn't my intention to completely ignore you. I was concentrating on my duties and I apologize if I appeared to give you the cold shoulder. Right now, I really want a drink and that's making me hate myself even more. Please don't make this hard for me because I really need to talk to you without you flying off the handle."

"I suppose that means you won't be coming home with me?" she asked, defiantly.

"Yes, Amanda, it means exactly that. I'm trying to take control of my life and that includes looking at our relationship. You must know that it's not working out between us, despite both of us trying hard. There is no easy way to do this; I should have done it before but I've been too weak and didn't want to hurt you. And it's only made it worse for which I am deeply sorry."

"You ungrateful bastard," she spat, hate sparking from her eyes and trying to burn holes through mine and into the brain.

I put a hand out in warmth. "Please, Mandy, I knew it would be like this. Please don't make a scene. I know you are feeling extremely hurt and I wish it could be different but I cannot see our relationship going anywhere."

"Christ!" she said, breathing hard and raising her voice. The pub meerkats had starting looking in our direction. "You're a selfish bastard!"

"Please, Amanda," I started, wanting to extend a hand of friendship, but was completely startled when her hand, full-palmed, slapped me across the face with such force that the next morning I would wake up with mild whiplash. Before I could recover from that and regain my senses, she caught me across the other side of the face with her other hand and with greater force.

She pointed an accusatory finger at me, breathing hard as I staggered to regain my composure, touching my cheeks gingerly with surprise. "Don't you ever come near me again!" she screamed. "I've served my usefulness now, have I?" She picked up her coat and bag and, trying to stop the tears, she stopped on her way to the door and, with reddened, maddened features, enunciated carefully: "I – hate – you!" She left.

"Well, that went well," said Pete, reaching me as the door banged shut and put a caring hand on my shoulder, which I shrugged off.

I had deserved to be hit, certainly, maybe even deserved the public humiliation too, much as I would have wished otherwise, and tried to regain my composure and self-esteem under the prying eyes of the bar. Slowly, they returned to their conversations after it became apparent that the spectacle was now over. Amanda had been avenged for the way that I had behaved and I hoped that that would be end of the matter.

PUPPET ON A STRING

CHAPTER 14

On Friday, the sky was a misty blue, the temperature had risen to the upper seventies and the tabloid newspapers had made front-page news of the fact. It felt like a new beginning as I walked the short distance to the office. The jumper I had decided to wear was tied around my waist knotting the arms loosely and shirtsleeves were rolled up to the elbow by the time I arrived. During the walk, I had taken the opportunity to cogitate on the state of my five resolutions. In general, it felt like I was making a lot of headway but there were still some unknowns.

First, Amanda: it had not gone anywhere near as well as I had hoped but at least the relationship had been broken off. Now the subsidiary task was to provide Amanda some space to work out her anger but also to create the circumstances by which we could hopefully remain friends. Given her reaction in the pub last night, that might be a tall order but I wanted to make it up to her in some way for the shoddy way she had been treated.

Second, the Chairmanship: this appeared to be going very well. I had already instigated a number of the points from the election manifesto and it was clear that it would be hard work but not impossible to implement. Not only had the office been sorted out, but I had also started creating the important environment for those with grievances to come and talk to me and had established regular sessions with each of the Section Managers. I had also talked at length with Sir Norman about the setting up of the Chorus' own record label and how the recording studio in the basement might be better used – the number of ideas I had for a new sound and approach to recording were exciting and I wanted to try them out. There was still the review of the best way to get good and better voices outstanding and I had given some consideration to the patron idea. All in all, it appeared to be going exactly as intended and planned.

Third, Gary: that, correspondingly, had not gone well, although I was less surprised at that result than I had been with the development with Amanda. Being as arrogant as Gary was about Chorus matters, his pretensions were now being found out and he was consequently worried that his façade was crumbling. Having been able to take all the glory before, his reactions were now highly defensive. It was true that he was trying to throw mud at me but it would no longer stick because I was unwilling to accept that attitude, as had been the case in the past, when cultivation of his friendship was paramount. This compounded the situation. With Pete fighting in my corner, too, it was my guess that Gary was suddenly feeling very vulnerable. However, there was no helping him because he did not believe he had any problems to resolve – they all lay with other people. Until that could be reversed, the relationship was going to continue to be hard. I was prepared to give him a little leeway but vowed to remain firm.

Fourth, Marie: well, I was confused. The last conversation had fuelled further what had already been going on in my head with the ongoing battle between pessimism and optimism. She had turned me down flatly but had suggested getting together on Sunday. For the moment, the glass would remain half-full until Sunday was over, when the situation would be reviewed.

Fifth, alcohol: I had succeeded in conquering this. It was easier than I had anticipated and it was willpower, which was the chief ingredient. I had had several temptations but by waiting for each successive five minutes to go by, it became easier. This was excellent, because I was thinking clearly continuously and was surprised that I was enjoying the new-found freedom.

By the time I let myself into the side entrance to the office, I was confident that everything was under control and that things looked rosy. Picking up the mail, I went through, opening some as I approached the desk. Scarcely having the chance to read any of it, I jumped almost guiltily when Amanda appeared silently at the door and spoke. I had not even been aware that she was around, nor had I heard her come up the stairs and it was very unsettling. She stood in front of the desk, looking very pale, tired and miserable, her bottom lip pouting.

"Dave," she said gently, "I'm sorry about last night."

"I'm not really," I replied, putting the correspondence into the in-tray at the edge of the desk. I would read it later because the chance to activate the support for Amanda had presented itself earlier than expected. "I deserved it."

"No," she said, tears brimming in her eyes, "I behaved like an immature schoolgirl."

"Well, I think you had every right. I've been carrying on appallingly. Last night was a good point to stop it."

"And I didn't mean what I said about never seeing you again."

"Obviously," I tried a stab at humour, "you're standing in front of me now."

"Please don't be sarcastic," she said, bottom lip trembling and I feared she was about to break down.

"Sorry, Amanda – Mandy – I was trying to lighten a horrible situation."

"You're angry with me, aren't you?"

"No," I responded. It was the truth. "I'm angry with myself. I wanted to make our relationship work. Really I did. But it was doomed from the start. The problem is that I think I used you – it might appear that I did – to obtain this Chairmanship. And that makes me feel really terrible."

"You don't have to feel bad," she replied, dabbing at her eyes with a handkerchief, and laughed humourlessly. "I had this big speech prepared but what it comes down to is that I love you. I really, really love you."

My wariness increased. "I'm sorry, Mandy. It just won't work. Please can't we just be friends?"

"But I love you," she insisted as if that would change my mind.

"I think you think you love me. We had only been together for a few weeks."

"That's enough for me."

I took a deep breath and tried again. This was going to hurt to the quick. "The problem with that is that I don't love you. I did try but I just couldn't make it work."

"Oh, that's nice!" Her simpering had stopped and there was a dangerous edge to her voice.

"Please, Mandy. I didn't intend to hurt you and I should have had the balls to do something about this earlier but I didn't. But now I'm trying to do the best thing by both of us. I would really like our parting to be amicable and for us to remain friends."

She sneered and let out a held breath. Her hands were now defiantly on her hips. "I didn't offer you my bed and body just to be friends."

"I know you didn't. And that makes me feel even more ashamed. It makes this whole situation so much worse. At the time, I was very unsure of myself, you were there and…it happened. And I'm sorry if you think I used you."

"Used me?" she bellowed. "Used me? Too bloody right you used me."

"Please, Mandy," I said, putting up a hand in a calming gesture. "There is no need to shout. Let's talk about this rationally. Please?"

"We have got on our high horse, haven't we?" she said childishly. She pointed at me and screwed her face up in hatred. "That's ever since you became Chairman."

"No, it's not a high horse," I tried to reason with her. "I'm trying to tell you that our relationship is over but I want to remain friends, if at all possible. You and I, as a couple, are over."

She leaned on the edge of the desk with her knuckles and the dark look in her eyes scared me. She spat: "You mean you just slept with me for kicks?"

"No, I didn't. What I –."

"So you didn't enjoy it?"

I opened my mouth to say something but I was not sure what. I closed it again to give myself time to think. The conversation was teetering dangerously out of control. Finally, I said: "To be truthful, and that is what I intend to be from now on, I did enjoy it on a physical level but not on a spiritual or emotional level. That sounds absolutely dreadful, I know, and it is. Which is why I want to end it now, before I continue hurting you. I mean, I have never said I loved you but I do like you. I think you're a wonderful person, I respect you and –."

"Respect me? Huh!" Her eyes were wide with anger and hatred, her cheeks blossoming red, her eyes spilling tears down her cheeks. "*You* respect *me*? Don't make me laugh. You sleep with a girl then say that you didn't really like it, drop her unceremoniously and finally say you respect her. You used me like a prostitute."

"Look, you're complicating things out of hand and skewing what I'm saying. I respect you enough to try to end our non-starting relationship amicably." I stood up and walked to the window for inspiration. The trees were rustling idly in the hot May sunshine. I decided that, as truth was what I had started out to say, I would give her everything. Feeling dreadful that her perception of me and that her suggestion that our relationship could be reduced to one of tart and customer, I needed to come completely clean. For the sake of my soul, if for nothing else.

"Mandy," I started, "this is turning into such a mess. But I will be completely honest with you and maybe we can pick up from there. At the time I met you, I was almost infatuated with Marie Duvois, having met her in Paris. I didn't think anything would come of it, although I felt that it was something deeper than infatuation. So when you came on the scene, it gave me a chance to climb down from such aspirations and to try and forget her. I never meant to use you sexually – that was never my purpose. It just happened and I really wanted to make our relationship work and hoped that the purposefulness of the electioneering would help us bond. I tried hard but it never worked because Marie Duvois was always on my mind somewhere. Now, seeing her again, the same feelings have come back. It's only fair on you that we stop our relationship before I hurt you more than I have already done. I think you knew that I tried to end it last week, but I was too lily-livered. Too weak. I'm sorry I had to –."

A sharp blow hit me between the shoulder-blades, winding me, followed by several more. Amanda was pummelling with her fists and then she kicked out wildly, her fashionably-pointed shoes connecting frequently with poorly-covered ankle-bone. I was shocked. With the same quietness as when she had entered the room, she had moved swiftly around the desk. A fist caught my chin as I tried to get hold of her wrists and I managed to turn my body sideways before her knee could incur damage to my groin. Another couple of kicks and a punch to my ear, causing a startled buzzing, and I had managed to get hold of her manically pumping arms and I pushed her away forcibly. She stumbled against the edge of the Secretary's desk and she fell, banging her head painfully on one of the shelves on the way down. She crumpled on the floor, her face creasing with pain and she yelped.

I pointed a finger at her, rubbing my ear with the other palm. "You, young lady, can take a month's unpaid leave, effective immediately. A: for attacking the Chairman at office and, B: to go away and sort yourself out. I deserved the slapping in front of our colleagues last night and the humiliation that came with it but I don't deserve to be attacked as if you're practising for a heavyweight boxing title. Remember where you are. And who you are." I stretched my shoulders gingerly. There would be bruises there tomorrow. "Now get out!"

She picked herself up from the heap she had fallen in and shouted back: "I know who I am. But you're someone different from who you think you are!" She massaged the bump on the side of her skull just forward and above her temple. It was already turning grey with angry purple edges and a thin beading of blood surfacing along the centre. She slumped a little and said: "That hurt."

I felt a little guilty but felt that, overall, I had come off worse. "I'm sorry about that but I had to calm you down."

She stood up, wincing slightly, still massaging the bump. Her normal temperament had reappeared, I was relieved to see, until she said: "I love you, Dave. You can't change that."

"Mandy, dear –."

The switch had been flicked. She stopped rubbing her head and glared at me. "Don't patronize me!"

I put my hands up in surrender and said: "I'm not patronizing you. I'm trying to end this with both our dignities intact. Look, I'm fond of you –."

"Oh, yes," she spat, "fond enough to abuse my body."

She had recognized that this was the main point of many over which I was giving myself a tough time and suddenly it was clear that she was trying to manipulate me. "Look," I said again, "I've told you the truth. There were several things going on and I was confused. Very confused. I knew then that I was using you but I am not proud of that. I'm not in love with you. You're great fun to be with but I love someone else. This is only fair to tell you."

Suddenly, she lashed out again, her nails penetrating the skin on my neck. She punched at my face and I managed to parry the blow. Her knee jerked up again and I moved back instinctively but was caught full on the solar plexus. I crouched, arms folded across my chest, wheezing and winded.

"Get out," I gasped with as much authority as I could muster.

She moved towards me, as the calmer Amanda switched back on. Her face showed concern and she said: "Dave, I'm sorry."

I stood up, staggering against the desk and clutching my stomach. I pointed at her and said: "Don't you dare come near me. Now get out. You have a month to cool down."

Something akin to fear crossed Amanda's face and then, defiantly, hands on hips, she said: "All right. I'm pregnant. What's your answer to that?"

Another ploy. "It's too early to tell. Come back in eight or nine months and we can discuss it."

"You bastard!" she screamed, swinging at me again. This time I was ready, caught her fist, turned her around and pushed her arm up her back. Feeling the tendons of her shoulders stretching under my savage grip, I pushed her away as she cried out.

"Get out! Get out!" I shouted, shaking uncontrollably, losing my temper to a degree I had never witnessed before and never hoped to again.

She turned back to me and I thought she was coming for another attack. I tensed, prepared for it, but she screamed back at me: "I'll kill you! I'LL BLOODY KILL YOU, YOU SELFISH BASTARD!" She turned on her heel and ran out the door, slamming the door violently behind her.

I sat down, shakily, put my head in my hands and struggled to get myself under control again. I breathed a heavy sigh of relief, the pain in my ankles throbbing dully, as they swelled up from the recent onslaught from Amanda's shoes. My head was pounding from her punches and I was still wheezing from the deft knee she had placed in my chest. That was not how I had planned the morning to go but hoped that Amanda had now finally got the message.

PUPPET ON A STRING

CHAPTER 15

The next day, Saturday, was similar in heat and the tabloids were now predicting a long, hot summer, which would probably put the kiss of death on it. The remainder of the previous day had been spent working through a few things to do with the future of the Chorus, planning the approach for the recording label and getting a patron for subsequent Committee discussion. However, my heart was not totally in it. Amanda's attack and the associated kerfuffle and fall-out had shocked, upset and agitated me. Having thought that I had everything under control, it appeared that I had seriously misconstrued the signs. Although I was happy with the direction the Chorus was taking, I was concerned about the attitudes and reactions of three people: Gary, Adrian and, of course, Amanda.

As is so often the case with insecure people, I started with the premise that I was basically at fault and worked my way up (or, rather, down) to the philosophy that all the blame lay with me and had had several moments where I had reached for the 'phone to talk to all of them, apologize and give in. However, my new and burgeoning inner strength countered the temptation. That direction would be an easy one to take and was the pathway of cowardice. With tremendous resolve, I decided to continue the battle.

So, it was on the Saturday morning, with renewed vigour, I activated the next step of my plan for the Chairmanship – the face of caring – by visiting Bob in hospital. I also knew that I needed to talk to Pete, as my confidant, about the current situation because I felt seriously undermined.

The Western General is to the north of St. Albans and I set off in my Mini at lunch-time to catch the afternoon visiting hours. I found my way through the maze-like corridors with unhelpful signs to Bob's ward, where he was dozing quietly, lying on his back, looking grey in the face and one cheek slightly dropped from the stroke. I considered leaving

him alone to rest and was about to walk away when his eyes opened and
he smiled.

"Dave!" he croaked and cleared his throat. He struggled to get into a
semi-seated position leaning against his pillows. "How are you?"

Despite Bob being the closest thing I had to a father, I decided not
burden him with my problems right now, so simply responded: "I'm
fine. More importantly, how are you?"

"Oh, I'm alright as far as it goes."

I gave him the bag of grapes and that month's copy of *Gramophone* I
had brought with me, for which he was grateful. I noticed with some
sadness that there were only two 'Get Well Soon' cards on the cupboard
by his bed, one of which was the generic well-wishing from the Chorus,
which Pete had bought and circulated. If I had been more sensitive, I
would have picked up on the nurse's comment about the apparent lack
of next of kin and organized individual cards from those who knew him
best rather than the relative facelessness of the combined card.

"Thanks for the card, by the way," he said, seeing me looking at it.
"Most unexpected."

"No problem. So what's the prognosis?"

"Well, I've been prodded, tapped, had various fluids removed and
loads of other tests. They confirm it was a minor stroke. They had hoped
that it would be a temporary aberration but it's permanent. I haven't lost
complete feeling down my left side. The edge of my hand feels tingly
and I can't quite get my cheek muscles to work properly, but otherwise
I'm fine."

"That's great news."

"I'll be there for the recording on Monday."

"Er..." I began, wondering about the wisdom of coming back to
work so quickly.

"It's alright," soothed Bob, "I know you're worried but, as I said, it
was a minor stroke and I have the all-clear from the doctors. I'm fed up
with this place, to be honest. They are just sorting out an ambulance to
take me home this afternoon. And then I can get on with some personal
rehearsal." A look of concern came over his face and he added quickly:
"If it's alright with you for me to do it." He placed a pleading hand on
my arm.

I was dubious that it was the right thing to do but reasoned that it
would cause him more stress not to do it than doing it would create,
potentially causing more problems if I were to refuse. "Well, if you're

sure," I said cautiously, "I wouldn't want you to overdo it. Let's take it a day at a time and review it."

He removed his hand from my arm and said: "That's very good of you, Dave. If I start feeling unwell, I'll let you know. And if I don't know the music well enough, I'll keep quiet until we get to the bits that I do." He smiled gratefully.

It occurred to me at that point just how important music was to Bob. It was the right decision. To deny him the chance to be involved would be more detrimental than allowing him to take part. I made a mental note to ask Pete to help me keep an eye on him nonetheless. "So, how have they been treating you in here?" I asked to change the subject.

"You know me," he said in response, "hate lying around doing absolutely nothing. And the worst thing is the number of sick people in here." He grinned.

I laughed. "Yes, hospitals would be so much better if it weren't for the ill people."

"The saving grace, of course, is being tended to by such lovely, young nurses." He winked at me.

"I think I'll suddenly find an illness so that I need incarceration!"

"Yes," agreed Bob, smiling, "but nothing contagious or they'll be dressed up in masks and whatnot."

I clicked my fingers. "I've just thought. You don't need to wait for an ambulance. I can drive you back."

"That would be very kind."

I scuttled off to organize that with the nurse station. An auburn-haired, pretty nurse came to help Bob get ready for his journey home. Wrapped up in an overcoat and a scarf, despite the warmth of the day, Bob steadied himself against me as I helped him out of the hospital and across the car park to my car. To my mind, he was very unwell and I was nervous about releasing him from the hospital. Bob, however, being the headstrong man he was, not wanting to make a fuss, simply wanted to get out of there because he hated hospitals.

On the drive back to his house, after a momentary silence, he said: "So, are you going to tell me the story of that bruise on the side of your face?"

The question surprised me. Looking in the mirror earlier that morning, I had convinced myself that the bruising was superficial and barely noticeable. I had obviously been deluding myself. "All part of the job that I have foolishly put myself up for."

"Meaning?" asked Bob, turning to me.

I related the story of the dying moments of my relationship with Amanda, sighing as I finished: "It was not what I intended at all. I had wanted to do the best thing by her but she's so damned unpredictable."

"If it means anything," said Bob, as we pulled into his driveway, "I think you acted correctly. She does sound unpredictable and wild, too."

I smiled in thanks as I switched the engine off and got out to help Bob from the small passenger seat. He fumbled with his keys before finding the right one for his door. Putting the suitcase by the hall table, I helped him off with his hat, coat and scarf and followed him into his living-room. Expecting him to sink into an armchair, I watched him wander through the connecting archway to the dining-room and to his obvious pride and joy: the baby grand piano, placed by the French windows and looking out on an immaculate garden, although the grass was in need of a cut. On the right hand side, halfway down was an apple tree with massive boughs reaching into the garden, under which was a small bench and a table. I could imagine Bob, in the warmer weather, taking an ice-cool drink to the bench and reading through operatic manuscripts. I turned back to him and saw him weeping, tenderly rubbing a couple of fingers over the wooden lid of the piano, before sitting on the stool, lifting the lid and repeating the exercise over the ivory keys.

"Are you feeling alright?" I asked him gently.

"Yes," he replied with a nod and pulled himself together. "Yes. Thank you, Dave. I missed the old girl was all."

Offering to cut his grass, which he accepted, I left him playing Chopin preludes and Beethoven's *Für Elise*. By the time I had cut the grass, stacked up the cuttings at the bottom corner of the garden and put the lawn-mower away in the shed, sweat was trickling off me in rivulets. Bob fixed up a cold drink, registering surprise at my refusal of a beer, after which I left for home. Confirming that I would see him at the orchestral rehearsal the next day, I exhorted him to look after himself and to give me a ring if he needed anything. He was flattered and overwhelmed with the attention but gracefully declined it.

When I got home, I called Pete to let him know Bob was out of hospital, that we would need to keep a collective eye on him and that I would like to meet him in the office before the rehearsal the next day.

* * *

As is usually my practice, I picked up the Sunday papers on my way to the office. Intrigued, my eye was caught by a picture of Marie Duvois on the front of *The Investigator*. Flicking through to page nine as directed, I found a small piece on her and the suggestion that she had picked up a new paramour. Not only that but they were rumoured to have met again in London recently. The piece was attached to a beautiful studio picture of Marie and another of her at London Airport, on her way to the rehearsal. Smiling wishfully at the report, lifted from the Parisian newspapers' story some weeks previously, I bought the less than cerebral rag for the pictures alone.

When Pete and I were safely ensconced in the chairs in the office, with hands wrapped around mugs of coffee, I talked through what I had said to Bob, my fears for his health and so on. Pete readily agreed to keep an eye on him. In the meantime, we thought that we would need a temporary Section Manager to take some of the pressure off Bob. Pete offered to talk that through with Bob and I added it to the growing list of items for discussion at the next Committee meeting.

"To be honest, Pete," I said, putting my pen down and taking a sip of coffee, "I think we're going to have to bring the Committee meeting forward. There's too much which needs discussion and decision to delay it."

"I think you're right. What about one of the recording days when the Chorus is not required?"

"Good idea," I nodded and made another note.

"Now," said Pete, putting his mug down on to a caffeine-encrusted coaster on the desk, "tell me how you got that bruise on your face."

Instinctively, I raised a hand to touch it gingerly. I had thought of providing a cover story but, having talked it through with Bob plus my decision for complete honesty, I thought better of it. "You remember Amanda slapping me around the face on Thursday night?"

"Bloody hell, I didn't think it was that hard. I mean, it must have hurt but..."

"Surprising amount of power in one so petite," I said and winced. "No, it wasn't that. I deserved that slapping for the shoddy way I treated her but had figured that that was it. Anyway, on Friday, she came into the office, tail between legs, begging forgiveness, could we continue where we had left off and telling me that she loved me."

"I hope you didn't agree to any of that!" said Pete, alarmed.

"No, of course not. I had an iron resolve that I did not want to retreat from. Still have. Anyway, I told her the complete truth, bared my soul, including my feelings for Marie and why, therefore, it would be kinder to her to end it there and then. I apologized profusely for the way that I had treated her. And I really meant it. I asked her if there was any way that we could be friends. I enjoy her company, you see, but there are no feelings of the required deep emotional attachment. Just being friends is quite a hackneyed phrase, I suppose, and I was feeling deeply remorseful. That's when she attacked me."

"What?" exclaimed Pete incredulously.

"Yes, punching, slapping, kicking. That's how I got this bruise." I pointed at my face. "I have more bruises on my swollen ankles and a tender spot on my abdomen where her knee connected. And of course, this." I pulled the neck of my shirt away to show three small, healing scabs from where her nails had dug in.

"Bloody hell!" exclaimed Pete again. "You're better off without her. Absolutely no excuse for that kind of behaviour regardless of the circumstances."

"Unfortunately, I feel even worse about it, because I threw her against those bookshelves." I grimaced with the memory. "She went down hard and banged her head. To add injury to my earlier insult, I think she was quite badly shaken and hurt. *Her* bruise will be far more obvious."

"So what?" countered Pete, defiantly. "You were being rational and she wasn't. As I say, no excuse for that behaviour whatever the provocation. Think about it, you were only protecting yourself."

"I know, I know. But I don't like hurting anybody. My upbringing tells me that it is a worse offence if the recipient is of the feminine gender. The upshot of it all was that I told her to take an unpaid sabbatical for a month to sort herself out and for attacking the Chairman."

"You should have sacked her outright, in my view." Pete was still indignant, which brought me some relief.

"The final ignominy was that she accused me of making her pregnant."

"It just gets worse," said Pete, vicariously winding himself up. "That bloody woman. I hope you realize that that was just a manipulative ploy on her part."

"Of course," I said, quietly, "but I did work myself up into a lather and you would not believe the number of times I had to restrain myself from picking up the 'phone, apologizing to her and suggesting getting back together, contacting Gary and apologizing to him. I was getting into a bit of a mess on Friday afternoon. I think I'm better now though."

"Good," said Pete, "but just for the record: you were absolutely right to give her a cooling-off period. Personally, I would have gone further but that's your decision. As for Gary, I had strong words with him as you know. His selfishness and drive for glory for himself means that the changes that have been enforced in the last few days are highlighting exactly the type of person he is. To be honest, I have little time for him any more and, having always considered myself to be a good judge of character, I'm surprised that I have never seen just what a fickle, self-centred swine he is. But better late than never, I guess. And, anyway, he can't see when he is trying to be helped. For him, 'grateful' is a unit for measuring of warmth-radiating fossil fuel."

I laughed without humour. "Yes, indeed. I also think we will have similar issues with Adrian Hilton."

"I agree. You're quite right. I wish I had listened to you at the beginning when Gary decided to appoint him. With the twenty-twenty vision of hindsight, it is patently obvious what his ambitions are and I wish I had seen it then. Not such a good judge of character at all, really." He harrumphed slightly and looked out of the window.

"Don't forget that I didn't see Gary for what he really was until the Paris trip. It was only with that knowledge that I was able to be objective about Adrian. If Gary hadn't stopped me seeing Marie that night, I might have fallen for their collective ambitions myself."

"Possibly," agreed Pete, nodding slowly and then brightened, sitting back. "And, if you're at all worried about Marie, which I know you are, you're definitely on course. I've seen you two talking together. I've succeeded in steering Gary away from you two so that he can't spoil anything. She is absolutely taken with you in exactly the same way as you are with her. If you two don't make it, I'll eat a whole milliner's shop!"

"I hope so," I said and smile. "We're due to do something after today's rehearsal, so…fingers crossed. And thanks for your confidence on the other matters. It makes the job of sorting it all out a little easier."

"No problem," he replied. "Sometimes, it takes two to see that you are even in a wood, let alone starting to consider whether there are trees present."

I glanced at my watch. "Fancy a spot of lunch before this afternoon's rigours?"

"Indeed. But please can we avoid the Goat and Dramatist. I'm not really in the mood for another discussion with the one they call Gary."

* * *

Entering the hall for the afternoon's rehearsal, I noted that nearly all the Chorus and orchestra had assembled, as had the seven soloists. The cacophony that greeted us was incredible, with people chatting at increased volume to be heard over the random melodies being played by different parts of the orchestra. The three soloists, with whom I had shared tea and cake on Thursday, observed my entry and waved, which I returned before looking for Sir Norman. He was standing at the back of the hall, beside a tall chair and table, on which his ever-present briefcase was placed. He glanced up from leafing through his notes as I approached him and smiled.

"Sir Norman," I said, shaking his hand, "good news, I think."

"What's that then?" his brow still furrowed in concentration, more intent on establishing the recording production schedule than listening to me. I did not mind.

"Paris Opéra have written to me asking if we can do *Tosca* again next year, with a possibility of making it an annual event."

He looked up from his notes. "Excellent. We need something concrete on our schedule. It'll stop the onset of my stomach ulcer. Although we might want to consider broadening the repertoire to include the female voices."

"That's precisely what I thought."

"So what's the latest on it?"

"I've already written back to them, with the suggestion that we might wish to broaden it to a more appropriate set of operas, maybe extending it to a week, if that is acceptable. But I have agreed in principle to the suggestion."

"Splendid. I might tell the Chorus when I tell them about the rehearsal schedules for New York. Changing the subject, how are things for you in your new role?"

"Great. I think we're on the brink of great things."

"I noticed your renovation of the office. I scarcely recognized it. I'm impressed."

"Thank you. My grandmother always used to go on about a tidy office being a tidy mind. Besides which, I would have been embarrassed taking anyone up there, like Christoph Scmidt."

"Absolutely right. Incidentally, he told me that he enjoyed his rehearsal on Thursday and said that you did an excellent job in looking after them. Should make for a good recording. An atmosphere of *bon humeur* does wonders. Well done!"

"Thanks again!" Embarrassed by the plaudit, inside I was puffing up with pride. With this kind of feedback, I knew that I was starting to make a difference.

He glanced at his watch. "I think we ought to get this ball rolling," he said, patted my shoulder and made his way to the podium. "Good afternoon, ladies and gentlemen," he said, booming through the racket and swiftly getting silence. He pointed to the soloists. "Please will you welcome our full complement of soloists, a few of whom you will have met on Thursday."

Applause met this request as they stood up and took a small bow.

"And, of course, our orchestra, the Münchener Philharmonische."

More applause.

"Now," he said, looking into a small diary, "if they will bear with me for a moment or two, I have some Chorus business. This New York tour in four weeks' time: since there is a vast amount to do for the three operas we will be performing, rehearsals will have to be stepped up." He found his place in the diary and flicked over each page as he said: "So after this *Carmen* recording, the first Monday is a music rehearsal, Tuesday is an acting rehearsal. Then Wednesday is a private rehearsal day. The Thursday and Friday are acting *and* music rehearsals. The following week, Monday and Wednesday are music rehearsals and Friday and Saturday are acting rehearsals, then there is another rehearsal on the Monday for music…and the same for Tuesday and Wednesday. Er…and Thursday. Then a dress rehearsal on Friday and Saturday, flying out on the Sunday. Any questions?"

"Yes," called Pete, hand up. "Pardon?"

Norm's Gorms giggled a little, joined by the orchestra. The kind of semi-vicious laughter associated with a barbed put-down in the school playground.

Sir Norman smiled and waved down his hands for quiet. "Alright, alright. I see your point, Pete. Okay, I'll ask Gary to print up the schedule and post it on the notice-board." Sir Norman looked further around the bass section and asked: "Anyone seen Gary?"

Any response was obliterated by a loud crash and clatter at the back of the hall. The main doors, closed normally for rehearsals in deference to the neighbours' need for noise abatement, had flown open with great force, knocked into half a dozen or so chairs stacked immediately behind and pushed the stack over. Silhouetted in the bright glare of the sun shining through the door and on to the polished parquet flooring was Gary, supporting one door by the handle and almost genuflecting in the effort to stand up. The interruption had forced everyone to whirl around in surprise and now they stared in amazed silence as Gary struggled to pick himself up gradually and stride as purposefully as he could in the rough direction of his seat; the silence only broken by his progress, righting a knocked-down music stand and its music here, bumping into an alarmed orchestral-player there and raising an apologetic hand everywhere. His attempted air of self-importance was impeded by the fact that he was obviously very, very drunk. Imbued with the ostentatious carefulness that a person in that state exudes, he reached the bass section and sat down unsteadily, almost falling off his chair. Blearily, he looked around as if nothing of importance had just happened.

"Bang on cue," said Sir Norman finally to Gary's obliviousness.

Norm's Gorms tittered again but more out of nervousness for what they had witnessed than for any attempted ingratiation at Sir Norman's witty remark.

Sir Norman raised his eyebrows in resignation and continued: "Good of you to turn up. Thank you. Okay, enough of that. I see that Herr Schmidt has arrived, so I will hand over control to him."

More applause. It was not surprising, in the circumstances, that he had forgotten to mention the Paris annual event.

* * *

Orchestral rehearsals are particularly gruelling and none more so than the final rehearsal before a performance or recording. It is at this rehearsal that the final problems are acknowledged and resolved. It was, however, very satisfying because we were getting good results and it was auguring well for the recording over the week.

Gary had spent the entire afternoon with his chin on his chest, occasionally mumbling and breathing heavily. Whether he was actually asleep or simply trying to contend with the volume of alcohol swilling around his body and restricting oxygen to his brain was not obvious from where I had been sitting but I decided to have a word with him. As I neared him, I saw that his eyes were very bloodshot, his nose very red and his face had an ashen, sallow complexion. His hair was greasy and unkempt and it was quite blatant that he was in need of a bath, because there was a force-field of stale body odour under the wafts of alcohol emanating from him. He looked like pictures I had seen in the Sunday supplements of a cancer victim in the terminal stages.

"Gary," I said gently, putting a hand on his shoulder.

He turned towards me unsteadily, his eyes swivelling in their sockets in their attempt to focus on me. "Oh, get off my back," he slurred when he had finally recognized me through his whisky-induced fog.

"I'm not getting *on* your back, Gary. But, let me say this, I will get on your back if you turn up drunk to the recording sessions and repeat the dreadful exhibition you made of yourself today. I'd hate to think what our visitors thought of it. I've already had to banish one member and I don't particularly want to have to repeat it. But I will, regardless of your position in this Chorus, if you do this again and don't pull yourself together. Take that as a warning and not a threat."

"Right little Hitler, aren't we?" he mispronounced, head shaking unsteadily on his neck.

"Because you're drunk, I'll ignore that remark."

"Very magnam...magnurse...magnamus of you," he said, spitting with the effort of enunciation. "I don't mean it but I'll say I'm sorry, if that will get rid of you."

"I suggest you go and sleep it off, Gary."

"You can suggest all you want. I want a drink," he said, getting up falteringly, leaving his stuff behind and lurching towards the door.

I caught Pete looking at me, hands apart as if to say, 'you can't do any more' and I shrugged in agreement and resignation.

                                    *   *   *

At the back of the hall, Adrian Hilton had found Sir Norman and was talking furtively, occasionally glancing over his shoulder to ensure they were still alone.

"I need the times and dates of rehearsals for the American tour," he said, pulling a notebook from his pocket. "I've got to inform the coach-hire company. I think we'll be using the Greyhounds private hire, incidentally."

Sir Norman was irritated but tried to cover it. He smoothed his hair down over his head as he said: "Look, shouldn't Gary be handling this?"

"Er...Gary is not that interested at the moment," replied Adrian, quickly.

"Doesn't sound like Gary. Mind you, he is acting a little oddly at the moment. Well, what about the Chairman?"

"No!" said Adrian sharply and then forced himself back to furtive discussion. "I...mean, I don't think we should bother him at the moment. He must have a lot on his plate what with becoming Chairman and all the hassle that that entails."

"Hmm," agreed Sir Norman dubiously, "maybe you're right. Let's go up to the office so that we can work out the details. Maybe you can type up the schedule and let everyone have a copy?"

Adrian nodded vigorously, a sly grin appearing on his face.

"Come with me, then," said Sir Norman, still irritated with the intrusion.

Adrian followed like a willing sheep.

* * *

Having watched Gary make his uncertain way out of the building, I noticed with mild annoyance that Adrian was monopolizing Sir Norman and had taken him away from the duty of looking after our visitors. Adrian needed to be taken in hand to find out what was going on with the American trip. But that would have to await the following day. For now, I had more important and pressing things to look after and contend with.

Marie was talking in a group with Estente and Torchev as I approached them. Torchev greeted me with a full-palmed but friendly pat on the back. I managed not to wince with the slight pain from where Amanda had beaten me a few days before and to avoid the much-needed but nonetheless rude cough.

"Come, Mister Loughton," he boomed in a rich, deep voice. "Let us all be going to dinner."

"Er..." I started, almost panicked by the carefully defined plan slipping away, glancing at Marie and then back at him. The missed opportunity was whistling its merry tune and was now sitting on its suitcase trying to get it closed, with the taxi blowing its horn impatiently outside waiting to take it on its holidays.

"No," said Marie gently and smiled.

Torchev's face momentarily faltered and broke up. Estente looked quizzically from Marie to Torchev and back again.

"I'm sorry, Mikhail," she continued and patted his arm. "I don't mean to be rude but I have already promised Mr. Loughton that we would dine alone."

The look of confusion on Torchev's face cracked into a broad grin and he threw his head back with a roar of laughter. "Oh, I see," he said and nodded once or twice.

"But," continued Marie, "you'd both be most welcome should you want to join us."

"Oh, no, no," replied Torchev, waggling a negative finger at her, "I couldn't possibly spoil your evening."

Estente regarded me and winked. "Be careful, she's a very pretty lady."

He laughed raucously, joined by Torchev and they bade us farewell. I turned to Marie and mouthed the words, "Thank you."

We awaited Sir Norman's return from the office to ensure the remaining soloists were looked after for the evening, before slipping away.

*   *   *

I had suggested going to La Trattoria but Marie insisted that we try somewhere in the city. Besides, she was not a great fan of Italian food. We boarded the overground train at South Mimms to Euston, took the Northern Line to Leicester Square and walked out into the deepening dusk of a city closing down for the day. It had not occurred to me that, being Sunday, it might not be easy to find anywhere open but we eventually came across a steak house just off the Charing Cross Road.

The steak house, which was relatively comfortable compared with some of the dives around the area, was an American monstrosity going under the name of Buffalo Steaks Inc., a foretaste of the onrush of foul, fast-food emporia in the Seventies (fortunately, something I would not witness first hand). But we were severely limited for choice and agreed we would try it. Inside, the lighting was soft to the point of extinction and the twangy guitars of the piped country music were too loud not to be unobtrusive but quiet enough to allow us to remain in the building. The burgundy, mock-leather seats were divided into small booths arranged around a central bar area. Giving an air of secrecy and privacy, it became apparent that that was an illusion, since we could hear the conversation between a couple seated two tables away. An overly effusive waiter with a very obvious toupee, which did not match his normal hair-colour and looked like a drunken, long-haired, ginger guinea-pig had been dropped on his head, showed us to our seats and produced menus from behind his back.

Given the enormity of their size, I wondered silently where they had been stored before he had given them to us. They were huge and subsequently antisocial, because it was impossible to have any discourse over them, under them or even around them without appearing foolish. They were hand-written, plastic-coated, near illegible pieces of card with the prices written unintelligibly in smudged, felt-tip pen on top of the plastic to avoid reprinting when the prices were hiked up. Each item did have a cipherable number associated with the individual entries, which might as well have been written in the Cyrillic alphabet for all the use it was to us. The menu also appeared to be divided into sections which might have been starters, main course and dessert or, of course, the author might have simply decided to leave a couple of blank lines. I could see Marie was struggling.

"I tell you what," I said. "Shall I order for the both of us?"

"Would you?" she replied, grateful that the onus was off her to understand what was on the menu let alone what she might fancy. "I can't understand this menu at all."

I signalled to the waiter, who almost trotted over, bent fawningly towards me with his notebook and pencil at the ready and gave me an insincere smile. "Sir?"

"Er...let me see. Two number threes, one with lots of tomato sauce. Then the lady will have a number twenty-seven, while I will have a number thirty-four with German mustard. No make that horse-radish sauce and a side salad. And to drink?" I turned the menu over to where pictures of beer bottles and wines were drawn. The same incomprehensible ordering system was in use for these too. "A bottle of the number fifty-seven," I plumped.

I gathered Marie's menu and handed them to the waiter, who regarded me with flabbergasted uncertainty. I smiled in encouragement and nodded. He glanced worriedly at Marie, who smiled impassively back and then he returned another incredulous, questioning look at me. I nodded seriously, knotting my eyebrows and he began writing the order on his pad. One more worried glance and then he scuttled off, retreating rapidly to the relative sanity of the kitchen, shaking his head.

Marie leaned forward and cocked her head to one side a little. "What did you order, then?"

I shrugged. "You know, I haven't the faintest idea."

Marie burst out laughing, covering her mouth with a hand as she did so. "I love it. That's wonderful."

"Thank you." I leaned forward on my elbows. "So what have you been doing since I last saw you in Paris?"

"Resting mainly," she said, more soberly, the twinkle still in her eyes. "Two *Tosca*s are enough for anyone."

"That's true."

"I had a performance of *Semiramide* in Frankfurt last week and I've also been rehearsing this *Carmen* for the recording. I had not realized how much of it I had forgotten."

"It's usually the way but it's like riding a bike," I said and grimaced in thought as I struggled to think of something witty. "Actually, it's nothing like riding a bike, is it?"

Her laugh tinkled again. "You did warn me that you are apt to say strange things."

The waiter, who had returned with a bottle he was drying with a towel, interrupted us. That's good, I thought, something cool. Perhaps champagne or a crisp Chardonnay. Nervously, the waiter said: "It was a bottle of the number fifty-seven which you wanted, wasn't it, sir?"

"Yes, it was," I replied.

The waiter finished drying the bottle and I glimpsed part of the Coca-Cola legend on the side. He set down two glasses on the table. Marie's eyes were watering with the effort to stop laughing out loud. He started pouring and I put a restraining hand on his sleeve.

"Please, I learned how to do this just recently. Let me taste it first."

The waiter stepped back, uncomfortable with the way I was acting. I picked the glass up, looked through the liquid into the light, swirled it around, sniffed loudly, took a sip and noisily sloshed the acrid liquid around my mouth. Marie had her face half-buried in her serviette, drying her eyes.

"Very good," I acknowledge. "You may pour."

"Yes, sir," said the poor waiter, who continued pouring the Coke into our glasses. He took the empty bottle and disappeared, again shaking his head in bewilderment.

Marie then let free reign to her laughter. "Oh, the poor man. You're dreadful," she said in mock admonishment.

"Well, they should write more neatly on the menus."

She dried her eyes on the serviette. "I cannot wait to see what you have ordered for food."

"After that, neither can I!"

"Anyway, we were talking about what we'd done. What have you done since Paris?"

"Not much."

"Not much! You're the Chairman. That can only be recent."

"Yes it is. In fact, about nine or ten days."

"I seem to recall that you said you didn't want to get involved in Chorus politics."

"Good memory. Well, I decided that I didn't like the way that the Chorus was being run and wanted to do something about it other than complain and wait for someone else to take the action. And you know what they say about a committee?"

"Something about camels, wasn't it?"

I smiled and nodded. "They also say that a committee is a group of people who individually can do nothing, but as a group decide nothing can be done. I want to ensure that that isn't the case with my Chorus."

The waiter returned with smoked salmon pâté and Melba toasts, which he put down almost gingerly in front of us. "Your pâté, madame...sir." He reached across to another table, where he had set down his large, round tray and produced a mini-tureen with a spoon in it. "And your tomato sauce. Bon appetit." And then he hurried away.

Marie was laughing again and I joined her. I raised my eyebrows: "We're doing well so far. Please. Help yourself to sauce."

During the first course, I gave Marie edited highlights of the election and glamorized Amanda's attack on me (steering clear of the reasons behind it). Marie touched the side of my face when I showed her the fading bruise, concern etching her face. I almost heard my pupils dilating with her touch.

"What on earth got into her?" she asked, putting her knife and fork together on the plate.

"Oh," I said, carelessly, as I popped the last forkful into my mouth, "I think she had some legitimate concerns but wasn't handling them very well. She vented her frustration on me as I happened to be the nearest thing to hand at the time." Although I had taken to being completely honest, it would have been uncomfortable providing Marie with the full detail. Ostensibly what I had said had been the truth although I had not given her the full story.

The waiter interrupted us again and replaced our starter crockery with the main course of Marie's pork steaks and my fisherman's pie with, naturally, the requested horse-radish sauce. Again, Marie could not contain her amusement, much to the annoyance and chagrin of the waiter. He must have thought we were drunk.

We talked about the recording, how Torchev and Estente reminded me of Tweedledum and Tweedledee, which made Marie laugh again and the forthcoming American trip.

"The problem is," I concluded, "I don't know what's going on with it and we are now less than four weeks away. But the good news is that I heard yesterday from the Paris Opéra earlier in the week inviting us to do an annual opera starting with a revisit of *Tosca* next Spring."

"Excellent!" said Marie, delightedly. "I'll have to come and watch you."

The waiter cleared the remnants of our completed dinner and asked if we wanted desserts or coffees. I did not dare consider ordering anything else and, when Marie had paid the bill and tipped him handsomely, we stepped out in the neon twilight of a London Sunday night. I was now aware that we were coming to the point where we should part and I was trying to think of something suitable to say.

"Please come back to my hotel," said Marie suddenly, as I opened my mouth to say I know not what. My heart stopped for an eternity and thumped back into action. "Just a small night-cap?"

I shut my mouth with an audible teeth-clunk. "Love to," I said, simply, quelling the thoughts tripping over themselves to enter my head.

*   *   *

Marie's hotel was almost into the West End. It was a huge, modern building, several storeys high and architecturally simple with juxtaposed angles and darkened glass, built in the early Sixties in an attempt to look modern but with a small nod to its more picturesque and gothic surroundings; a brave attempt indeed and something which it completely failed to carry off. The revolving entrance doors seemed to be roughly the same size as the front of a small, semi-detached house, while the foyer appeared to go on forever in every direction. To the left of the entrance, there was a long, built-in desk, panelled in mock oak, behind which buzzed over-busy men in pin-striped suits. Along the wooden-panelled wall behind them were serried rows of pigeon-holes with a hook to bear each key when not in use. On the right of the entrance was a series of eight lifts, with several clock-watching potential passengers waiting for them, and a hallway, which led to an entertainments area and gymnasium. The floor was of highly polished marble, reflecting every single light many times over. Scattered, apparently randomly, across it were several very comfortable-looking sofas, chairs and footstools, upholstered in a tasteful pastel blue to complement the general décor of pastel lemon and white. It was only by stepping into the centre of this vast room and looking up that you realized there was no ceiling until you hit the roof twenty-four floors up. Each landing had a cursory hand-rail to stop people falling, with the hotel rooms and suites around the edge. Looking up past each floor to the roof reminded me of a picture I had seen of the Beatles at EMI's Manchester Square headquarters, leaning over one of those rails, or of one of those pictures of a man holding a picture of himself, holding a picture of himself and so on *ad infinitum*. The thought made me feel decidedly giddy and I quickly followed Marie to a small bar off to the side of one of the elevators, she having picked up her key and confirmed that there were no messages.

"The very thought," said Marie hotly, as she lifted herself daintily on to a bar-stool, spreading out her skirt underneath her legs to avoid creases. Her face was a little flushed and her eyes sparkled with indignation.

"What's happened?" I asked.

"That clerk at the desk," she said and frowned. "He had the nerve to ask me if I were cognizant to the hotel rules regarding male visitors in female rooms."

Any lustful pre-occupations I might have had dissipated almost immediately. What I had read into her comment was not only that such a thing could be presumed of her but that it could be presumed of her with me. Such was my insecurity.

"I informed the prude that we only going for a drink at the bar."

A French-looking gentleman in evening dress manned the bar. The size of the bar reminded me of the one at the back of the Royal Festival Hall. Big but not too big – at least in comparison with the hotel foyer – and well-lit. There was one elderly man with a handlebar moustache sitting in one corner, wiping the port, which had dribbled from the corner of his mouth, with a handkerchief and in the other, a middle-aged, nervous man with thick, black-rimmed glasses sipping frequently from his beer glass. Other than that we were alone.

The barman came over and took Marie's order of two vodka martinis. I was on the verge of protesting that I wanted a non-alcoholic drink but decided my recently self-induced depression needed an alcoholic kick.

The cocktails arrived and Marie raised her glass towards me. "So. Cheers," she said and smiled.

I clinked her glass with mine and said: "Derrières en haut."

She took a sip and looked thoughtful. Then she laughed. "Ah! Bottoms up!"

I took a small drop and my tongue and throat responded to the relative unfamiliarity of the fiery liquid.

After a pause, she frowned a little and took a deep breath, saying: "You know, I've been thinking about you a lot recently."

"That's good."

"That's what I wanted to talk to you about."

Oh, God! Here comes the rejection

"That restaurant wasn't really private enough," she continued, looking around at the other two occupants and back at me. "I like you, but..."

I knew it!

"No," she said crossly. "I don't mean that. What am I trying to say?"

That you don't want me

"Oh, dear!" Consternation furrowed her pretty brow. "I'm tying myself up in knots here!"

Just say that you don't want me

"I don't want to hurt... No! I don't want to *be* hurt, but... I...Oh, this is so difficult."

You don't want me. There! Easy!

"I don't want... No! The time we would need... Right! We would need... I... Oh! Please forgive me, David. I thought I had it all planned what I was going to say. I am having difficulty getting my thoughts together. Please forget I said anything." She closed her eyes, drew in a breath and then sighed, blowing her tousled fringe from her flustered face in the process. "I'm sorry."

"Forgotten already." I smiled what I hoped looked like a genuine smile and glanced at my watch. "Well, I ought to get back home for my beauty sleep."

"So soon?" She grimaced, quickly put out a hand and retracted it, but I scarcely noticed.

"I need lots of it. Well, it's an early start tomorrow." I could feel myself doing the downtrodden martyr bit and tried to stop myself.

She put a hand on my arm, started to say something and decided better of it. She finished her drink and stood up. "Yes, of course. I'm tired as well. Thank you for accompanying me this evening. I really enjoyed the meal. It was...different." She gave a skewed smile but I registered sadness in her eyes, which I read to be sympathy for me being let down so gently.

She put down her empty glass and signed the chit, as I pushed my almost untouched drink away. She walked me to the door and said: "Thank you again."

"Not at all. Thank you."

She paused, looking at the floor and then said softly: "David?"

"Yes?"

She looked up into my eyes and then replied: "Nothing, really." She turned away and then added, almost inaudibly: "Just sorry."

I stood for a while, searching for something to say, something witty, something droll, but nothing came. Instead, I bade her goodnight, pushed at the revolving door, shunting myself through into the cool night. I turned and stopped midway through raising my hand to wave goodbye. Marie was gone.

Marie was fortunate: she could go to bed without a care in the world. I, on the other hand, was left with my over-active, insecure mind calculating the worst in the situation. Why had she said she was sorry? Why had she bought me the meal and the cocktail? Why the rebuff? Why had I been so quick to latch on to it and end the evening so peremptorily? What was I going to do in my confusion?

Obviously, another restless night was on the cards.

PUPPET ON A STRING

CHAPTER 16

There is something very different and exciting about a recording studio in comparison to other performance venues. The whole room is dead and every sound made appears to stop about six inches in front of the mouth, however loud it is. Yet someone speaking normally from the other side of the studio could be standing right next to you. It is a very curious aural illusion.

Most of the orchestral recordings for EMI were made in Studio One at Abbey Road in St. John's Wood. Occasionally the smaller Studios Two and Three were used for recordings of chamber orchestras or small groups, although Studio Two had been almost exclusively given over to the use of the Beatles since their enormous success in the previous four or five years. Studio One is a large room in the basement, at the back of the Abbey Road complex and is roughly the size of a large village hall. At one end, there is a raised platform on which a choir can stand or sit and a fire exit that leads through the bowels of the EMI heating conduits and low-slung central-heating pipes along the outside of the studio. At the opposite end is the main entrance and exit to the artists' bar. From the corner of that end to about halfway along the wall was a glass partition, separating the studio from the control room, a partition of such shiny proportions that it was almost impossible to see anything going on behind it through the reflected light. Along each of the side walls were positioned several proud, hardboard 'cupboards', which help absorb the sound echoes. Suspended from the ceiling on twenty or so iron scaffolding bars parallel to each other were thick, calico sheets, which served to deaden the sound as well – hence the close atmosphere once in the studio. In the middle of each wall was a red light to indicate that recording was in progress when switched on and a small speaker for the communication from the control room.

The orchestra for our recording of *Carmen* was laid out in a rough semi-circular shape around the conductor's rostrum, which was

positioned about three-quarters of the way down the studio from the
Chorus. Along the raised platform at the back were four or five rows of
chairs for the Chorus and at the front of them, on an extended rostrum
just behind the orchestra, were placed seven more chairs for the soloists.
In the infancy of stereo and the number of tracks able to be recorded at
once, there were fewer microphones than would be seen today. On each
side of the studio just to the front of the orchestra were two huge,
cumbersome, lozenge-shaped microphones pushed into the air on long,
steel booms, the microphone lead wrapped carefully along the length of
the boom and disappearing to a control panel in front of the booth.
Another microphone was suspended from the ceiling above the rostrum
and a further three could be seen positioned in front of the soloists. All
the leads from these microphones were stuck to the floor with brightly-
coloured, electric gaffer tape to avoid accidents. I drank all this in and
parked it in the folder marked 'New Approach to Recordings'.

When I arrived – I always arrive early to recordings: one of my many
inexplicable insecurities was that I had to prove to no-one in particular
other than myself that I was present at the recording and, to do that, I
had to be as near to the microphones as possible by sitting in the front
row. No-one, of course, would challenge the fact because they knew
what I did for a living but there it is – when I arrived, a few of the
orchestra were already squeaking or rumbling their atonal melodies on
their instruments to tighten their embouchure, limber up the fingers or
whatever they needed to do to ensure a good performance. The
timpanist was bent over the drums, bonging one occasionally and
tightening or loosening the keys to stretch or relax the drum-skin. Only
two other Chorus members were there and I nodded a civil greeting to
them before sitting down as far left as the tenor section was allocated and
in the front seat. I had not wanted to talk to anyone, preferring to
wallow in my insipient melancholy brought on by the events of the
previous evening and exacerbated by the lack of good sleep, and so hid
myself behind the late edition of Monday's *The Times*.

My concentration on the printed stories was very weak, with my
mind running over the various options presented to me as I had been
doing ever since leaving London the night before. I was eventually aware
that someone had come to sit down beside me. Thinking it was Pete, I
lowered the paper to make some ribald comment and met Marie's eyes.

She gave an uncertain smile. "Hello, David," she said quietly, eyes
never leaving mine, holding the gaze. She was wearing a red- and white-

striped, lambs' wool jumper, white cotton trousers and open-toed sandals. Her hair bubbled gently around her shoulders as she moved.

"Hello," I replied, grateful that she had come to see me. I folded the paper and put it on the chair beside me.

"About last night," she said, a worried look crossing her brow. She pulled the sleeves of her jumper up to the elbows and looked down to the floor. "I'm sorry."

This was one of the things that I had been tossing around my head all night. She had said she was sorry when I left her hotel and I had not understood why. "What's there to be sorry about?" I asked, gently.

"Oh, I could have kicked myself," she said, angrily and brought a fist down on her thigh. "I said all the wrong things."

"What do you mean?" I put a reassuring hand on her knee and then removed it gently.

"What I said came out as if I didn't want to see you again." She clasped her hands together and subconsciously wringed them. "At least," she added, "that's what I read on your face."

I reddened a little at being so transparent, in spite of the perceived Oscar-winning performance. She was looking down at her moving hands in her lap and I leaned down and peered up into her eyes and asked: "So what did you mean to say?"

"David," she started, looking up to meet my eyes again and then back down at her lap. "I'm very fond of you," she said finally, her cheeks becoming rosier by degrees as she said the words.

"Oh, that's a relief," I said and smiled.

"And I think," she said and paused, searching for the thought. "No, I'd *like* to think that you're very fond of me."

"That Oi be," I replied in a ridiculous attempt at a Somerset accent, reverting to the protection of tomfoolery.

She looked up again and smiled with a little relief. "I've been wrestling with this for the entire night. I haven't had much sleep worrying about this."

"What's the problem?"

She looked into my eyes, smiled a little, the corners of her eyes creasing and the twinkle was back. "You'll probably think that I am being incredibly stupid and maybe I am."

"I'm sure I won't."

"Well," she said and paused again. She took a deep breath and she blurted: "Oh, just say it, woman! I wondered if there was any chance of

you and me getting together." She took shallow breaths awaiting my
response.

"I…," was all I could manage. I was completely astounded. All this
time, I had been so insular about how I was feeling, how insecure I was
and here was Marie telling me that she was suffering the same mental
trauma. I took her hands in one of mine and smiled. "Yes, there is. I
cannot tell you what a relief it is to me to hear you ask that question."

She looked a lot more at ease and then became quizzical. "Why are
you relieved?"

I laughed. "You will not believe the agonies I have put myself
through in the past few days, worrying about what I viewed to be
unrequited love and how I could change that, trying to understand how
I could change it to my advantage. And my natural reserve probably
didn't help either! It never occurred to me that you were being troubled
by exactly the same thing. If you've been a fool, I have been a bigger one
and it's my turn to say sorry."

"Go on, then," she said, a mischievous dimple on her cheek.

"I'm sorry," I said, laughing and squeezing her hand.

"What a pair we make," she said, clasping my hand in one of hers
and stroking it with the other. What a delicious and sensual feeling that
was. "I totally misread some of the signs. I wanted to ask what I just
asked last night but I was worried that you might be scared off by a
number of things: my forwardness, me, my apparent musical standing.
What I took as you being flippant, was actually you being disappointed.
What you took for being off-hand was me being disappointed too. Then
I got so flustered that I thought I had literally lost all chance and had
frightened you off anyway."

"And then I appeared to have given up by ending the evening early."
I tutted and smiled at her. "I am indescribably happy that we have sorted
it out, finally," I said and lifted her hands to plant a small kiss. She
giggled girlishly. "Now that we have things straight," I continued, "will
you join me for lunch after this morning's recording?"

"Oh, I can't," she said, disappointment spreading across her face.
"I've already agreed to go out with Guido, Beth and the others. How
about this evening?"

The intercom clumped on and an estranged voice boomed: "Please
could David Loughton come to the control room? David Loughton.
Thank you."

I squeezed Marie's hand gently and said: "Duty calls. Let's get
together after this afternoon's rehearsal, then."

Pete arrived and put his things on top of my newspaper next to me and raised his eyebrows appreciatively as he looked from Marie to me and back again.

"I'll see you later," I said to Marie and she got up to find her seat. I turned to Pete, was about to say something, when the intercom clicked back on and relayed the same message as before. I looked heavenward and raised a hand as if testing for rain.

"The day of judgment hath come upon thee," said Pete in his best 'fire and brimstone preacher' voice.

"No rest for the wicked," I agreed, getting up from the chair, separating my belongings from Pete's and, asking him to guard them, stepped off the raised platform, making my way through the forest of music stands, chairs and dormant double basses and 'cellos to the control room. My spirits had lifted enormously and I exonerated myself for worrying about our relationship because I had wanted to make something of it. I felt a bit of a cad for the introspection I had displayed but was relieved that Marie had felt the same way as I had, torturing herself about misplaced expectations, hopes, wishes and dreams. The only view now was forward and not backward. As I opened the door to the control room, I felt an almost physical thump of a curtain coming down on my old life: perhaps it was a tragedy or a comedy. It did not matter now. A completely new script was being written for me and it was exciting and filled with nervous trepidation.

"Ah, finally," said Sir Norman, looking up from the recording notes clipped to the mixing desk at which he sat on a swivel chair with arms. The type-written notes had red technical markings and straight lines ending in arrows all over them. This kind of thing intrigued me, which is why I wanted to develop the Chorus' own label. The control room was a long, oblong-shaped room. Skirting the room were several machines, which served the purpose of key electronic wizardry for the recording and three reel-to-reel tape players. At one of these stood the recording engineer, Bruce Carlton – now *Sir* Bruce Carlton in the latest New Year's Honours list – loading a spool of brown tape, clipping the free end through the heads on the machine, pressing buttons, running the tape at high speed backwards and forwards, once it had been linked to the other empty spool, producing a weird Pinky and Perky gabble as it did so. He picked up the clipboard from the top of the machine and ticked off a couple of boxes before repeating the procedure with the other tape machines. Monopolizing the centre of the room was the huge mixing desk, with its slanted top. Knobs, sliders, levers, lights, numbers and gauges covered its impressive surface. The desk overlooked the studio via the glass panel and was connected to the wall-flower machines and two massive speakers either side of the desk by a spaghetti of umbilical electrical leads, neatly bundled and tied together at eighteen-inch intervals. Above the desk, in front of Sir Norman, was a small microphone winding out on curved metal, for the intercom communication with the studio. Behind the desk were placed two chairs: one for the producer, Sir Norman, the other for the engineer, Bruce.

"Ah, finally," he had said and smiled. "Attractive woman."

"Indeed," I replied, forcing myself not to blush, a dopey grin locked in place.

"Okay," he said and laughed. "I won't ask for any details." He leaned forward and picked up a type-written sheet, which he passed to me. "This is how the week looks for us. This morning, we'll have a warm-up, a bit of a rehearsal to acclimatize ourselves to the deadness of the studio and get the balance checked. Then we'll go for a take of the *Peasant's Chorus*."

* * *

Closing the control room door carefully behind me, I read through the essence of the schedule and stepped up on to the rostrum, shaking hands with Christoph Schmidt as I did so. I asked his permission to address the swelled ranks of the orchestra and Chorus, called for quiet and ran briefly down the week's itinerary, before making my way back to the seat that Pete was jealously guarding for me.

"You're really getting into this, aren't you?"

"Yeah," I said airily, spreading my fingers out and then looking at the nails as if to manicure them. "You've either got it or you haven't."

"On which subject. You probably ought to know that someone who hasn't got what he wants is trying to muscle in on Marie."

"Gary?"

"I'm afraid so. I saw him in the bar just now."

"God!" I exclaimed. "Isn't there anything I can do without him snooping around?"

"Doesn't look like it. He was boasting to anyone who would listen that he was going to endeavour to ask her out for a drink."

I tutted. "Thanks, Pete. Maybe I'll try to have a friendly word at lunch-time. Although, given his present state of mind, I don't know how much good that will do."

"True," admitted Pete. He bent forward to me conspiratorially: "How's it going with her then? I saw you holding hands."

"Well, I really think I have it cracked. We're having dinner tonight."

"Again?"

"Ho, yuss, I should say so," I responded in imitation of a Goon voice. "I've wasted so much time worrying about whether it was all practical only to find it was totally unnecessary. It's…great. It's…wonderful." I grimaced in thought. "I can't think of an adequate superlative."

"Well, I want to be informed of all the details, remember!" said Pete, lasciviously smiling. I laughed, stifling its ferocity with my hand. A few meerkats turned around to see who was trying to impersonate a seal and I transformed the laughter into a cough.

Christoph Schmidt calling for silence interrupted our conversation. "Good morning, ladies and gentlemen." He introduced the soloists and the orchestra to the Chorus again and the Chorus to the orchestra and soloists. "As you know, we are going for a take on the *Peasant's Chorus*. During recording, please make every effort to be completely motionless and without sound, except when playing or singing at the appropriate junctures. First a rehearsal and a check for stereophonic balance."

The orchestra tuned up and we launched into rehearsal. The resonance in the studio was practically nil from where I was standing and it took some time to adjust to the deadness of the place. It was exceptionally hard to stay on a note because the natural tendency in those circumstances is to pull the whole thing flat. This is due to missing the mutual feed from each other in the normal ensemble of singers and players, when the acoustics allowed it. It is therefore critical to watch the conductor and take the direction from him, more so than in a performance in an acoustically accommodating auditorium. Only a couple of times did Christoph point ceilingwards to indicate that our notes needed to be sharpened.

Marie was standing in front and to the right of me. Being in the front row now had an additional advantage as I had a completely clear view of her. Every time I looked at her, my heart raced. A string of melody from the Beatles' hit *And I Love Her* over-rode the music coming from the studio. I *was* in love; it was not boyish infatuation and neither was it simply a friendship. This was the real thing.

I drew myself temporarily back to reality as the rehearsal ended, the intercom confirmed that the balances were correct on all the microphones and that we were ready for the first take. Christoph Schmidt raised his baton in readiness and for silence. The studio grew silent, even down to the creaks of the boards as people shifted their feet to a more comfortable position for being immobile and the shuffling of manuscripts. The red lights around the studio flickered on to indicate that the tapes were reeling and we were ready to go for the first take.

It is incredible listening to a recording of people who are relatively unused to the medium. Standing in front of the microphone seems to be more nerve-wracking than talking to a room full of people. Unfortunately, the microphone displays little discrimination and picks up every mistake, which means that even a minor slip can ruin a complete take. Some of the individual *Carmen* pieces were put 'in the can' very quickly; others appeared to drag on. By lunch-time, after the first session was complete, everybody was tired, being unused to keeping still and silent for so long, with enhanced concentration to achieve the perfect recording take. I was parched and had left the studio with Pete to go to the subsidized bar, not noticing a furtive Adrian hanging around the control room door for when Sir Norman eventually came out.

"Sir Norman?" ventured Adrian, when he appeared, looking harried but pleased. Adrian was wide-eyed and looking around like a spooked bush-baby.

"Yes, Mr. Hilton. What can I do you for?"

"Er…" Adrian started and looked around the studio once more to ensure they were alone in their conversation. "The New York Met. has asked me for a list of administration and Chorus personnel for the official programmes."

"So?" said Sir Norman, irritably smoothing his hair down over the temples. "Surely the Section Managers can give you the details? And you know who administers the Chorus. At least, you should. Why don't you ask Gary? He's supposed to be looking after this."

"Yes, I know, but I thought you might want a say in how the details are laid out."

In his drive to be furtive, Adrian had not noticed Gary drawing near to this clandestine group. Gary glared furiously at Adrian, who agitatedly covered the clipboard he was carrying. "Oh," concluded Sir Norman, with a dismissive wave of a hand, "look at what we normally do and copy that." He looked at Gary, welcoming the slight diversion. "Gary?"

"Hello," said Gary, looking at Adrian sideways and frowned. "What's going on? My ears are burning. Have you been talking about me?"

"No," assured Sir Norman, "just a question about the New York programme layout."

"Right," said Adrian, hurriedly, and cleared his throat. "I'll get on with it." He tried to brush past Gary, who put a restraining hand on his chest.

"And keep me informed," said Gary. "I haven't heard anything about recent developments."

"I will," said Adrian, a dead smile flickering nervously around his mouth and scuttled off like a persecuted shrew in the shadow of a cat.

"Er…" said Gary, turning to Sir Norman. "Can I talk to you about something? Or rather someone? It's a rather big and delicate problem and I need your advice. Maybe over lunch?"

"I'm sorry, Gary," replied Sir Norman, starting to walk away from the control booth, indicating that Gary should follow. "I'm entertaining the soloists today. It's the only day they are here together for lunch. Is it really important?"

"No," admitted Gary, somewhat crestfallen. "I'm sure it can wait until some other time."

"Gary, contact my assistant and make an appointment will you? There are a few things I would like to discuss with you too."

Gary nodded and was left standing in the middle of the emptying studio, blinking and staring into the middle distance, mouth slightly open. He seemed to make his mind up, thrust his hands into his pockets and stalked out of the studio.

* * *

The bar in the Abbey Road studio complex is small enough for a large chamber orchestra and large enough for a small symphony orchestra. Squeeze a large Chorus in with that symphony orchestra and it was tested to the limit and over. It sold a small variety of beers, spirits and soft drinks, all of which were cheap and cheerful. Or, as Pete pointed out, they were cheap and, as a consequence, we were cheerful. Being the first two out, racing out of the back fire exit, bent double to avoid the overhanging pipes connecting with skulls, we had run into the bar and commandeered two high wicker-weaved stools and were now earnestly indulging in therapeutic gulps of cool liquid. It was surprisingly easy now to order orange juice or lemonade without the desire for something stronger. I had opted for a tall glass of orange squash with ice cubes. Pete stuck resolutely to a pint of bitter.

"Thirsty work, this being famous lark," I said, licking my lips and gasping with the prolonged drink I had taken.

"Well, you don't have to do this for a living, you know," replied Pete, sucking beer foam from his top lip.

"That's true, but what else could I do?" I pondered. "Atomic physicist, perhaps? No, that sounds too dangerous and cerebral."

"Astronaut?" suggested Pete.

"Now that," I agreed, pointing a finger at him, "would be out of this world. Ha!"

Pete grimaced and then suggested: "Prostitute?"

"No," I scowled, "I want to make a living, not donate to charity."

"Dustman?"

"No, I'd get all smelly," I grimaced and then added quickly with an admonishing finger: "And don't even think about saying anything."

Pete closed his mouth, frowned and then smiled. "I wouldn't dream of saying anything, he says, trying to look the epitome of innocence. Okay, how about becoming an accountant or going back to being a lawyer, with a sideline in macramé dish-cloths, origami animals or box-girder bridges built entirely out of matches?"

"You're weird," I warned. "And I'll have you know that I'm a black belt in origami."

"Wow, I'm really impressed," he said sardonically.

"Yeah, so be warned. Any trouble from you and I'll fold your leg into a frog."

Pete laughed. "Okay, okay. Don't threaten me! Anyway, why are you so happy? A certain French miss?"

"Could be."

"Well?"

"Well, we're going out this evening as I said."

"And?"

"We'll have to see but it just feels so right. No-one else will be as right or as perfect as Marie is for me."

Pete rolled his eyes and said: "I was going to have another pint, but I think I'll need a bucket if you get any more slushy." He smiled.

"Seems weird me talking like this, doesn't it?"

"It does but I'm glad you're getting along with her. Have you decided what you're going to say to Gary?"

"No, I haven't."

"Talking of whom, The Tempest has just walked in."

I twisted around and watched Gary slump on his elbows at the only available space at the bar. I slipped off my stool, patted Pete on the shoulder and meandered casually over to Gary. I tapped him lightly on the shoulder to attract his attention.

He turned around wearily. "Oh, now what am I supposed to have done?" he asked, in a very pained way.

"Nothing. I just thought I'd better let you know that I'm hooking up with Marie Duvois."

His face fell and his jaw dropped a little. His ordered drink arrived and he handed over a pound note to the barman.

"Just so you don't make a fool of yourself," I added.

"You're talking out of your arse," he said and quaffed half a pint of beer in one go. "I told you you're way out of her league."

"No it's true," I protested and then decided to try a different tack, before we went headlong down a well-trodden path. "Look. Can't we bury the hatchet?"

"No."

I was taken a little by surprise. "Why not?"

"I'm perfectly happy. It's you who has a problem."

"With what?"

"Wanting to take over. Stealing my thunder. Pretending you're better than me by saying you're going out with people who couldn't possibly be interested in you." He finished his pint quickly and signalled for another two to be poured.

"It's alright, Gary, I've got one waiting over there."

"It's not for you," he said, turning his back on me slightly as he waited for his drinks to be supplied.

I was unsure how to respond to that one. I folded my arms and tried to say amicably: "I'm not trying to steal your thunder, neither am I trying to be someone I'm not."

"Could have fooled me," he retorted over his shoulder.

"Gary, please can you drop this attitude?"

"Why?"

"Because it's petty and we've been over this before." I paused in thought. "Okay, let's approach it differently. What is it about me that you are not fond of?"

"You want me to tell you?" he replied after taking a long draft from one of his beer-glasses.

"I do. Yes please."

He turned, still leaning on the bar, forcing him to look imperiously down his nose at me. "You're officious. You're impolite. You want too much from other people. And you disturb good people trying to have a quiet drink."

I reflected momentarily and unfolded my arms, putting my hands in my pockets. "I'm not getting through to you at all, am I?"

"No. And you probably never will." He had started on his third drink already.

"Okay. I'm in danger of talking to a brick wall but I'm willing to give it one more go. This is the way I see the direction of the Chorus going. We need to be pushier. We need to put ourselves on a pedestal, head and shoulders above the competition. To do that, we need to work as a team, and particularly you, me and Adrian. That isn't happening at the moment and I'm mystified as to what else I can do. Before I came to the Chairmanship, you were doing it on your own or getting others to do it for you. That's too much of a burden for anyone to carry, especially if we are stepping up to the oche to get extra work. I need you to work in the same division as me. Not against me. Can't you see what I'm saying?"

"No," he replied, his back now completely to me. "Now bugger off." He had half a pint left of his second drink but signalled for two more.

"You ought to ease off on that stuff, too. It can't be doing you any good." It was meant as a piece of friendly advice but I knew as I was saying it that it would be taken as criticism.

"Sanctimonious git!" he said almost to himself and polished off the remainder of his beer as two fresh glasses appeared.

"Okay, I'm sorry, I didn't mean it like that."

"Yeah," he said, irritated, as he pocketed his change.

"Gary, please can you answer me a straight question about business?"

"What?" he replied, hotly.

"How's America?"

"Still there. Has been ever since Columbus stepped ashore in the West Indies. No reason to assume it has gone anywhere." He chuckled to himself at his witticism.

"Yes," I said, trying to smile and folding my arms again. "I should have seen that one coming." The smile was cut down by a suddenly stony glare, put on the endangered species list and then forced it into extinction. I tried again: "Okay, Gary, what I really meant to ask was how the arrangements are going for the American trip?"

"Fine." Another half-pint of beer disappeared quickly. I waited for him to continue but the silence became oppressively embarrassing.

"Just fine?"

"Yes."

"We've got a Committee meeting coming up this week, which I'm thinking of bringing forward. One of the agenda items is America colon progress and report. How do you think the minutes of the meeting will look with just the word 'Fine' written by it?"

"Not my problem." He took another mouthful of beer.

"It is your problem. Are you going to answer my question?"

"No," he replied, coolly. "Are you going to leave me with my drink in peace?"

"I will, Gary. But you are going to have to come up with something better than that for the meeting. But think on what I have said. This childishness cannot continue and let's cut it dead here. Turn over a new leaf."

Gary stared levelly at me and drained his fourth pint, picking up the next one, and chain-drinking.

"I'll leave you with a couple of points to mull over, Gary. If I really wanted to steal your thunder and take over as you keep saying I do, I would have had you sacked. Remember that!"

A small facial tic was activated but he still said nothing.

"And, for information, Marie Duvois is certainly not out of my league nor I out of hers and I am taking her to dinner."

Gary harrumphed a patronizing scoff and turned back to the bar to be with his remaining pint.

I left him alone, shaking my head in consternation and regained my seat next to Pete, to relay the strange conversation.

* * *

The afternoon recording session went very well as everyone had relaxed into it and become acclimatized to the studio, its surroundings and atmosphere. Sir Norman and Christoph Schmidt were more than happy with the results on the playbacks.

As I packed up my score and other musical accoutrements, Bob made his slow way over to Pete and me, offering to purchase drinks to thank us for our thoughtfulness during his recent illness. I was still dubious about Bob's involvement in this recording, but underneath the tired and gaunt look, I could see he was happy to be here.

"I'm more than happy to take up the offer," said Pete, cheerfully, "but our man Dave is like a train-guard, dreaming away on top of the ticket-hall roof."

Bob shook his head quizzically.

"Bob," said Pete, putting an arm around his shoulder, "I'm afraid Dave apparently has ideas above his station."

I joined in his laughter and said: "That's so contrived! And I warned you. Any trouble and I'll fold your leg into a frog."

More laughter and more confused looks from Bob.

"Sorry, Bob," said Pete.

"Yeah," I added. "Don't worry, we're not completely loopy. Pete will tell you all about it over that drink. I must go."

"Where are you going?" asked Bob, still a bit confused.

Pete patted his shoulder again and said, as he picked up his belongings: "I'll tell you all about that too. Lots of juicy gossip."

I pointed a warning finger at him. "Be careful. I'll see you guys tomorrow."

Pete waved me away with an insouciant hand, as I jumped down to the soloists' platform. "Good recording, do you think?" I asked, coming up to Marie.

"I think it's wonderful," she enthused. "But I do feel a little hoarse."

"You mean a foal," I said wittily and instantly wanted to retract it.

"I'm sorry?" she frowned.

"A foal…is a little…horse."

Her brow creased momentarily and then her face crinkled into a laugh. She had deep dimples every time she smiled which just melted me every time she produced them. "Forgive me but I am slow on English word jokes."

"No, it is I who should apologize. My infantile sense of humour keeps rearing its ugly head. Anyway, what do you fancy to eat this evening? Should be more restaurants open than last night."

Her eyes lit with mock alarm. "Oh, I don't think my nerves are quite up to another meal with you, just yet!" She smiled. "But, I would love to go to the theatre. What do you suggest?"

"Well," I tried to think. I lived near London but rarely frequented such places. "There's a lot on. A revival musical at Drury Lane. A Cole Porter thing, as far as I can remember."

"Oh, no. Enough music for today, I think."

"I'm inclined to agree with you. Erm… there's a comedy at the Palace Theatre. Or would you prefer something in the line of thrillers?"

"A thriller? Yes," she almost jumped up and down with excitement at the prospect. "I love thrillers. Ian Fleming, Agatha Christie –."

"Agatha Christie?" I interrupted. "There's *The Mousetrap* at St. Martin's. Quite near your hotel too. Do you fancy seeing that?"

"That would be lovely. Let me just say goodbye and we can go."

Marie briefly said goodbye to the remaining soloists, we gathered our gear and made our way back into Central London to the St. Martin's Theatre.

* * *

It was a good play and an inspired choice. At the most dramatic and thrilling parts, Marie had squeezed my hand and, at one point, to relieve the angst built up within the story had buried her head in my shoulder. It was a closeness that I could not have enjoyed more as I smelt her hair and felt the soft skin of her hands against mine. It was an unimaginable sensation and one that I never wanted to lose hold of experiencing.

After the play had finished, we stepped out into the mild but cooling London night air. I casually draped my jacket over my arm as we battled our slow and impeded way through the heaving morass of humanity that seems to cling to all places of public entertainment. Marie had her hand on the crook of my other arm.

"That was marvellous," said Marie, as we sauntered unhurriedly towards Cambridge Circus.

I looked back at her. "Believe it or not, even though it's been running for over fifteen years or so, I have never seen it."

"Really?" she replied. "Fifteen years? That's a long time in the theatre."

"So what did you make of the story?"

"Wonderful," she said and smiled at me. "I love the tangled webs that Christie weaves and the suspicion she derives against each of the characters. And when he murdered –."

"Ssh," I put a finger to my mouth and whispered: "The plot's supposed to be secret."

"Why?" she whispered back.

"Because…" I said, still whispering. I returned to my normal voice, realizing that I did not know why I was being secretive. "I'm not sure. But, if you don't tip the taxi-driver enough on arrival, he tells you who did it. In fact, none of the papers has ever printed the plot and it differs from the book. And, what's more, I have no idea whether anything I just said is remotely true!"

"You English are so weird."

"Why, thank you," I said, giving a slight bow.

She smiled and stopped, turning me towards her. "I would love to ask you back to my hotel for a drink but I'm worn out by the recording and want to just go to bed. Would that be awful of me?"

"Of course not," I said, returning her smile. "I'm a bit whacked myself."

"Maybe we can do something a bit more boisterous tomorrow night?"

"Yes, please," I replied my smile broadening further.

"I suspect that both of us will be getting a much better night's sleep than last night." She gave a half smile and winked.

I put up a hand to hail a passing taxi. As it drew up by the kerb, I said: "Thank you for yet another lovely evening." My heart was hammering as I was uncertain what I should say or do next.

Marie appeared to read this, the dimples dented her cheeks and the twinkle appeared in her eyes as she put her hands around my neck, drew me towards her and said: "Come here." She gave me a long, lingering kiss on the lips, as I enfolded her body in my arms, closing my eyes as I did so. All sorts of emotions were rampaging through me, struggling for prominence, as fireworks appeared to go off behind my eyes, rapt as I was with the pressure of her lips against mine, her body held against me, her hands stroking my neck. We parted and I felt momentarily drunk. We looked at each other and both started to say something at the same time and stopped. She motioned me to speak.

"I don't know," I started, melting into those dark brown pools, "I was going to say –."

"C'mon, lady," said the taxi-driver, leaning over to the passenger window.

She waved quickly to him and put a finger against my lips. "Let me say it. Thank you for not giving up on me. It's been a lovely evening and I really enjoyed your company tonight." She kissed me again. "I'll see you tomorrow."

I relinquished my embrace slightly, kissed her forehead ardently and then stepped away to open the taxi door for her. "See you tomorrow," I said, gently, waiting until the last possible moment to release her hand.

The taxi tore away from the roadside and I held my hand up as I watched Marie's wave disappear into the distance. After the tail-lights had completely disappeared, I stood cemented to the spot, hands in pockets. What I really wanted to do was jump up and down and holler loudly. Which is what I did.

I ran to the nearest lamp-post, stepped up on its ornate lower bulge and swung round on it, waving my jacket in the air and shouting incomprehensibly before jumping down into the steadying hands of a policeman.

"Thank you, sir," he said, eyebrows raised querulously. "It is a little late for that sort of thing."

"I'm sorry," I said, breathlessly, "but she kissed me."

PUPPET ON A STRING

CHAPTER 17

As Marie had predicted, I had an excellent night's sleep, completely uninterrupted by worries about our relationship primarily or anything else secondarily. Indeed, as I finally came to, stretching gloriously in the expanse of the double bed, with the sun streaming in through chinks in the light curtains, an inane grin was permanently etched on my face.

The weather on that Tuesday morning perfectly reflected my mood. It was sunny and bright, dry without being stiflingly hot and there was just a hint of wind, picking up leaves and flowers every now and again and gently returning them back to the ground. Birds were twittering their errands in the tree- and roof-tops, the peace only momentarily shattered by one frightened into flight. A light soughing came through the poplars fingering the sky with their secret election, as they whispered discreetly between each other. It was a typical late spring day and everything seemed alright with the world.

As I sauntered along to the Chorus office, the grin still on my face, I could not honestly believe that there was a stupid war raging in Asia or that Africa was becoming so deeply poverty-stricken. It seemed impossible that I was enjoying this day, the best day of my life so far, when so many others around the globe were suffering so badly. Everybody should drop everything, sit on a hillside somewhere, hugging their knees and cloud-dream in true Winnie the Pooh style.

Such romantic notions were replaced by harsh reality upon opening the office door and a wave of hostility from the office swept over me. Adrian Hilton was at the Secretary's desk and his face contorted into a grimace as I entered. But nothing could mar the beauty of the day or my inherent ebullience, not even Adrian's dark scowls.

"Morning, Adrian," I said breezily as I gained my seat behind the Chairman's desk, throwing the letters I had picked up on the way into the tray for later perusal.

Adrian grunted morosely without even looking up, preferring to concentrate on a number of diagrams that he had laid out across the desk.

"How are you today?" I asked and leaned back in the chair, lacing my fingers together on top of my head.

He growled something and then sighed deeply, focusing more intently on a corner of one of his diagrams.

"So, as you are so communicative today," I continued, "perhaps you can tell me what's happening about America?"

He looked up, his lip curling up and trembling: "Gary said that you would try and muscle in."

I leaned forward on my elbows and looked him directly in the eyes. "I'm not muscling in. It was a perfectly reasonable question, Adrian."

"He also said that you wouldn't drop it until I said something in anger."

I was flabbergasted with this reaction. I was dealing with two very similar people and I had visions of going over exactly the same ground with Adrian that had been covered with Gary and could not bear the thought of the wasted energy. Still, I was coming from a position of fortitude and decided not to respond to his accusations. "Straight question, Adrian. All I want is a straight answer. What is happening about America?"

He seemed disappointed that I was not playing his game. He sneered: "Not much."

"I hope it's a lot more than 'not much'. It's only three of four weeks away. How's everything going?"

"Okay," he responded defiantly, looking up briefly. I smiled broadly at him and he returned to his diagrams.

"Just 'okay'?"

"Yes."

"Can you expand on that at all?"

"No."

"Why?"

"Because."

"Good grief!" I exclaimed, slightly amused. "It's like listening to someone leafing through a dictionary and saying the first word he sees on the page."

He mumbled something in response and the corners of his mouth flickered downwards as if he were on the verge of tears for being told off by the headmaster. I almost expected him to say "Sir" in low tones, as if he were awaiting a caning, such was his regression into childhood and monosyllabic answers.

"Adrian?" I asked, almost exasperated.

He looked up sharply, his eyes narrowing. "What?" he spat.

"Calm down," I said, putting up a hand. "Now that I have your undivided attention, tell me about America."

"What about it?" Spittle flew out of his mouth with the vehemence of the words.

I rubbed my forehead. "It's like trying to get blood from the proverbial stone." I stood up and sat on the edge of the other side of my desk, folding my arms. "I don't know, Adrian. You tell me. Travel? Accommodation? Er…wardrobe? Visas? Itinerary? Rehearsal schedule when we're out there?"

He glared at me. I was astounded to notice that he had developed the same facial tic as Gary when put under pressure. After a pause, he said non-committally: "They're okay."

"Adrian?" I said, exasperation showing in my voice as I put out a begging hand. "I need to know the details. Tell me."

He stood up suddenly, chair crashing into the music director's bookcase behind it, which made me jump a little in surprise. His face darkened and his lip curled up again, quivering. "Why the hell do you have to know?" he said, his voice strangulated.

"For information, apart from anything else. So that I know that everything is running smoothly. So that I know if I need to do anything. So that I can tell Sir Norman –."

"*I* will tell Sir Norman anything he needs to know." His right leg was shaking with indignant petulance.

"Ah," I replied, folding my arms again, "so if I were to ask Sir Norman, he could provide the details of what I need to know."

His sneer faltered and he said: "Well, even he doesn't need to know everything."

"That's as maybe, Adrian, but I do."

Adrian's eyes narrowed and his upper lip curled right back to bare his teeth. Red flushes appeared on his cheeks and on his neck. A vein pulsed in the middle of his forehead. "Just who do you think you are, lording it over people?"

"Um. The Chairman," I patronized and smiled.

"And you think that makes you special?"

"Adrian, please calm down. You're going to do yourself a mischief," I said as the vein bobbed with increasing speed. "It doesn't make me special at all. It makes me the Chairman of this Chorus and I would like to know more detail about one of our appointments."

"Well, I'm not going to tell you," he replied impetuously.

"All right, Adrian," I said, getting up from the desk and making my way back to the chair. "As you wish. But you'll have to tell the Committee something at the meeting. I've decided to bring it forward to today, as we are not in the recording studio this morning. Ten o'clock. My place. I hope you have something more inspirational to tell everyone then."

Adrian opened his mouth to say something, decided better of it and shut it with a 'glub' sound. His lips turned impossibly downward with disgust, his eyes bulging with hatred and he said: "Gary was right about you, you self-important, bastard nobody. I don't have to listen to this rubbish." He picked up his diagrams, hastily and carelessly stuffed them into his briefcase and turned back to me. "Bloody dictator. Gary was right about that, too. I'm going to tell him about this conversation!" With that, he swept to the door, yanked it open, stalked through it and slammed the door shut.

I smiled to myself that his attitude was becoming more playground and wondered if the door-frame could take much more battering. That was the third hefty slam it had had to endure in the past few days from various people. However, there was a serious undercurrent that I needed to grab hold of. I had no idea how progress was going on the American trip and I had picked up on a rumour that the President might be in attendance when we got there. There were two problems with that: first, we needed to present ourselves as a competent organisation with a united front; second, if the rumour were true, I could see that that was why both Gary and Adrian were being protective of the details and that it would potentially engender further problems when it came off. I hoped that a more concrete and adult approach could be adopted following the Committee meeting.

I picked up the 'phone and contacted all the members of the Committee apart from Gary, to inform them of the change in meeting date, time and venue, all of whom accepted it. It was only after the third cup of brown caffeine and carcinogens that I summoned up the courage to call Gary. Gingerly, I picked up the receiver and started to dial.

After a click on the line, I heard Gary say tersely: "Yes?"

"Gary, it's Dave."

Silence. And then, more quietly: "What do you want?"

"Committee meeting. Today. Ten o'clock. My house."

"What's wrong with the office?" he shouted so loudly that the line crackled. He was slurring his words a little and I glanced at the clock. Five-and-twenty past nine, I observed, refraining from tutting. Maybe it was the hangover from the previous night's indulgence.

"The office is really far too cramped to accommodate all of us. Besides, I can offer a few more creature comforts at home. One of the items is a discussion of your efforts on the American jaunt."

"You're really going too far!" I held the receiver away from my ear and gingerly returned it, wondering if the outburst was complete.

"I'll...er...see you at ten then."

An expletive and the 'phone was slammed down. I replaced my handset gently and considered what my options were.

* * *

My house was in a quiet, horse-chestnut- and cherry-tree-lined avenue about halfway between South Mimms and St. Albans, as the crow flies. Force the crow into a car or on foot, then the distance could be trebled or quadrupled. It was a detached, three-storey building set in an attractive, green, large lump of Hertfordshire. Left to me by my father, who died of heartbreak and loneliness shortly after my mother succumbed to her protracted illness, with the mortgage paid off, at the beginning of the Sixties, it had changed little. It was what I liked to describe as hygienically messy. The only other occupant rattling around such a large space was a lame, overweight, feline, tabby marshmallow, also inherited from my parents. She was lame following an altercation with an over-protective mother vixen and had come out of the battle the worst, with a large, deep gash on her back leg. Unfortunately, it turned nasty quickly and the only option was to have it amputated. My parents had called her Trixie – a name, which to my mind was only marginally better than Tibbles. After her punch-up and operation, I had toyed with the idea of renaming her Tripod, before settling on the more subtle Isla (as in 'Isla Man', after the island's symbol). Besides, the story broke the ice at the infrequent parties I held.

As I banished Isla, protesting half-heartedly from her favourite position in the middle of the dining-room table from which she could observe the whole of the back garden, I wondered vaguely what Marie would make of her and vice versa. Isla and the toppling stacks of books, magazines and other higgledy-piggledy paraphernalia accumulated over recent months transplanted to other rooms in the house, a bit of dusting and vacuuming and I was ready to receive my Committee guests.

As everyone arrived, they took a seat at the table, read the agenda I had printed at the office and chatted amongst themselves. Five minutes after the scheduled start of the meeting, neither Gary nor Adrian had turned up. Assuming this to be some form of protest, I opted to start the meeting, when the door-bell rang.

Ushering Gary and Adrian into the room quickly, nervousness descended across everyone and sliced through the conversation, stopping it dead. I shivered involuntarily with the perceived drop in temperature. There was one remaining seat at the head of the table and another between Bob and Pete. Spotting the 'important' seat, they raced each other to the end of the table, both launching themselves at it. It rocked violently and, with the unfamiliar pressure brought to bear on it, it collapsed beneath them, amidst bitter acrimony from both towards my furniture and each other.

I tried to steady my temper. The dining suite was an heirloom from my grandparents and was actually an antique. I have no idea of the monetary value and cared even less but this was a monstrous abuse of my ancestry. Directing Pete to pick up the shards of broken wood and take them outside, I went to a spare bedroom to get another chair, which Gary promptly took and sat on at the head of the table. Adrian stamped his foot in defeat and pouted in defiance before reluctantly taking the remaining seat. Pete returned, wiping his hands together, and gave me a questioning glance. I shook my head slightly. Gary had picked up the agenda, his brow furrowing as he worked his way down and slammed the paper down with a heavy sigh, looking around the room for something more fascinating to focus on.

The atmosphere was becoming oppressive as I took a deep breath and opened my first official Committee meeting, nominating Jane Hoare to take the minutes, a secretarial job that Gary contemptuously refused to do, considering it to be beneath him. The first two agenda items on the subject of a proposed Treasurer and a nominal patron for the Chorus were relatively unimportant and required minimal discussion. While these were being discussed, Adrian pushed his chair back and continually crossed his legs one way and then the other, folded his arms and stared vehemently out of the windows into the garden, the vein I had seen throbbing earlier making another appearance. Gary sat sideways on his chair, staring at the mantelpiece, sighing heavily and unnecessarily, while drumming his fingers irritatingly on the table-top, giving the impression that he had far more important things on his schedule and mind.

I could not let it go. I stopped the discussion and said: "Gary, what's the matter? Don't you want to discuss these items?"

"Of course I don't," he scoffed. "I have been working damned hard on this *Carmen* recording and this American gig and all you want to talk about is who we can hand out free tickets to." Adrian smirked but I ignored that. "And we don't need a Treasurer either. I have covered that position since we started."

"Gary, I recognize the importance of the American –."

He scoffed loudly again. "Yeah, I'm sure," he sneered, this time relishing the supportive smirk, as if he were playing to an audience solely of Adrian.

"I assure you I do," I countered, gently but firmly. "The reason I put the agenda in this order was to discuss the less important items without losing sight of them so that we could devote the remainder of our time on the important discussions, such as America."

He scoffed once more, as Adrian shook his head, arms folded tightly across himself. Gary reached into his pocket and brought out a packet of cigarettes.

"I'd rather you didn't smoke in my house, Gary," I said, realizing too late that this would be taken as another rebuke. "If you want to smoke, please can you do it in the garden."

Gary sighed heavily and slammed the box on the table with the flat of his hand, muttering some blasphemous imprecation.

I needed to speed this up before it got further out of hand. "So," I continued, returning to the discussion, "I think we've taken the treasurer and patron proposals as far as we can for now. There is general agreement that they should be pursued but I won't make a move until I have spoken with our sponsor."

June White raised a finger and chipped in: "And don't forget all the contacts that Sir Norman has. Some quite influential people. He knows the Master of the Rolls personally."

Gary sighed again, rasping the breath deliberately in his throat to show that he was unhappy and tapping the cigarette packet on the table and resuming his mantelpiece vigil.

"Thanks, June, I won't and a good point," I said quickly, hoping to draw the discussion to a close to diffuse the situation from becoming ugly. "Perhaps you could put me down to chat to Sir Norman as soon as possible, Jane." Jane nodded and wrote a few words for the minutes.

"Er…" I continued gracefully, "so, item three on the agenda is a discussion on progress and outstanding issues for the American trip. Perhaps we can ask Gary to enlighten us on the subject but, before we do that, I would like to express my gratitude and ask for a vote of thanks for all the work that Gary and Adrian have put in so far."

There was a general hum of agreement from the assembly, which was met by stony silence from both Gary and Adrian. Gary leaned forward on his forearms head down as if studying the minute detail of the intricate carving on the table.

"So, Gary," I took up after the silence began to feel very uncomfortable. "America. The floor is yours. How's it all shaping up?"

"It's all right," he murmured without looking up.

"Are you sure?"

"Why shouldn't it be?" he looked up, caught Adrian's eye and winked slightly. Adrian returned it with a knowing smile.

"Well," I tried desperately, "I was hoping for a run down on what's been happening and any issues you're aware of."

Red rag. Bull. Here, Toro! Gary exploded: "Why? Because you want to take the whole lot over, take the glory after I've worked so damned hard on it."

Adrian looked up from his trance and added: "And me!"

A kind of shocked, loud and discomforting silence fell upon the room, broken only by the steady ticking of the pendulum in the grandfather's clock standing in the hallway. It was the first time that he had had such an outburst to me about me in public. His face had turned red with fury.

"No," I replied slowly. "What I meant was to find out whether you needed any help –."

"No!" exclaimed Adrian, standing up and knocking the chair over, which was deftly caught by Pete before it hit the hearth. "No help."

"But, surely," I countered, "an operation as massive as this –."

"No!" Adrian slammed his hand on the table with a loud crack, making everyone else jump in unison. An alarmed astonishment crept over everybody and the room perceptibly darkened.

"Okay," I said finally. "If no-one else has anything to add or say, any other business, then I'll call this meeting to a close." I pointing quickly around the table but everyone shook their heads – they did not dare to say anything after those outbursts. Adrian was breathing heavily through his nose, mouth twitching and looked at the hand that had brought the meeting to such an abrupt end and sat down again slowly. Gary was noisily clenching his teeth together as if he were trying to chew through tough gristle. "Thank you, ladies and gentlemen. If everybody would like to adjourn to the front room, Pete will organize wine or other drinks you might like. You know where everything is, Pete." He nodded briskly and guided them from the room. "Gary, Adrian," I said, authoritatively as they joined the back of the queue, "please can you stay for a moment?"

They sank back into the nearest seats at the opposite end of the table from me, Gary shaking his head and Adrian quivering his lip. Both had synchronized facial tics. I closed the door softly behind Bob and waited until I heard everyone in the next room. Then I looked from Gary to Adrian and back again as I resumed my seat.

"Well!" snapped Gary finally. He restarted the irritating tapping of his cigarette packet.

I leaned across and brought my hand down firmly on his to stop him. "What the hell was the meaning of all that?" I asked, my anger rising.

"All what?" said Adrian innocently and cast a smirked aside to Gary.

"Slamming your hand on the table, all that petulant and unnecessary sighing, ignoring everyone present. All that!" I took my hand back.

"Don't get angry with us," retorted Gary, nudging Adrian with an elbow. "You're the one who wanted to discuss minor issues. Don't you think that tours are more important than –?"

"Gary?" I interrupted, fiercely. "Do you think that I am reasonably intelligent for my age?"

"Eh?" He was bewildered by the question and it caught him a broadside he was not expecting. "S'pose so."

"Well, talk to me like an adult and not a bloody five-year-old!"

Gary thought for a moment, divining a suitable response, before plumping with: "You're the one that's being petty, if that's what you're getting at." He waggled his head slightly and mimicked: "'I would rather you didn't smoke in my house'."

"You have been to my house dozens of times, Gary, and you know that I cannot abide cigarette smoke." I had correctly guessed that he had taken the request as a slight.

"So?"

"So don't tell me that it is I who is being petty!"

"Sorry," he said, sarcastically. Another smirk from Adrian as he licked his lip briefly.

"Now," I continued. "You have the gall to sit through one of my

Committee meetings, making life generally uncomfortable and unpleasant for all and sundry and then refuse to talk about the very subject you wanted to bring forward in the agenda. Now, why is that? Choose your answer carefully because I am losing what little patience and temper I have left."

"I have the gall, *Mister* Chairman, *Sir*, because the topic is important," Gary sneered.

"I gave you ample opportunity to talk about it but all I got was monosyllabic answers. 'Fine', 'all right' and 'okay' were just some of them. I warned you both that you would have to do better than that at this meeting."

"The more you know, your *Majesty*, the less likely we are to get the credit. You'll put your name up in lights, I'm sure of that."

"Yeah," added Adrian, supportively.

"Listen, you two. This is old ground and I am not covering it again."

"What right have you to talk to us like this?" whimpered Adrian, as Gary took in a deep breath for further vilification.

"I am your democratically-elected Chairman. And, so help me God, if you dare make a scene like the one this morning, I'll make sure it's taken further. As it is, you will both receive a bill for the repair of my antique chair."

"Ha!" they said in unison.

"I will not have the Committee run like a football terrace. We are intelligent people and I will not accept the kind of behaviour you exhibited today. It was a disgrace!"

"Are you threatening us?" said Gary, clenching his teeth and standing up.

"No, I am laying down the regulations of this Chorus."

"You can't get rid of us," said Adrian, standing at Gary's elbow, "we're too useful."

"No-one is indispensable. Including me."

"How dare you?! How dare you after all the work I've done?" Gary's eyes were wide with anger and fear.

"And I've done," added Adrian, weakly.

"Adrian, Gary?" I said, trying to calm everything down a little. "What can I do to help this problem to a satisfactory conclusion?"

"Resign," snivelled Adrian and it was Gary's turn to give a supporting smirk.

"Adrian, calm down. I'm only trying to nip this problem in the bud

before it worsens beyond redemption. But I will say this: buck your
ideas up or neither of you will be in the Chorus this time next month."

There was a sudden and angry silence, broken by Gary breathing
hard. He clenched and unclenched his fists. Adrian's lip resumed its
quivering as Gary said finally: "I'm not staying here to be insulted.
Come on Adrian, we're going to the pub."

They left swiftly slamming the doors on the way. Pete peered around
the door as I sat slowly back in the chair. "Not going well, is it?"

"No," I agreed. "What else can I do apart from sack them?"

"Nothing, as long as Gary is in a position of authority and Adrian is
there to wipe his arse."

"I can't keep on at them; it's tantamount to victimisation."

"Just let them cool. Maybe they'll see the sense in your words. Come
on, let me get you a richly deserved drink." He added quickly with a
wink. "Orange juice only, of course."

PUPPET ON A STRING

CHAPTER 18

I arrived at the Abbey Road Studios at about a quarter past one, in plenty of time for the afternoon session. A few other anti-tardiness junkies were hanging around, snatching a few moments of solitude before the intense onslaught of the afternoon's recording session. I positioned myself in exactly the same seat as the day before and placed my music score and largely-unread newspaper, purchased at the station on the way to the studio, on Pete's chair. I had not been able to read it in any great detail because my thoughts kept wandering to what I had come to call 'The Situation' but had made a few notes in the blank margins. I was still considering other options to pursue, when two hands came down on my shoulders from behind.

"Boo!" said Marie, stepping over the chairs to sit next to me. "Bet that scared you!"

I feigned shock by holding a hand to my chest and the other to my forehead. "Oh, don't do that. Don't you know that I have a weak heart?"

Marie smiled, her eyes twinkling. "How are you?"

"All the better for seeing you, sugar-plum."

Marie wrinkled her nose in disgust. "Sugar-plum?"

"Sorry. First thing I could think of."

"I'd hate to think what the *last* thing would be, then."

I looked up to the ceiling for inspiration. "Let me see. Pussy-cat? Star of my night sky? Pearl of my oyster?"

Marie grimaced again, showing her dimples and poked her tongue out quickly. "I think 'Marie' will do. For now, at any rate, until you can think of something better."

"Okay. I promise to think of something better. How was your night?"

"I slept wonderfully. I didn't want it to stop."

"I was exactly the same. First time I've had such a good sleep in ages. And that is thanks to you." I put my hand momentarily on her knee and she smiled. I saw Sir Norman arrive in the studio and signalled to him, to which he responded with a wave. I turned back to Marie. I had a number of things to discuss with Sir Norman but my preference was to stare at Marie's loveliness a little longer.

"Do you need to talk to him?" asked Marie, gesticulating towards the control room.

"Yes I do."

"You'd better go then," she replied, putting her hand on mine. "Problems?"

"Nothing a two-ton demolition ball couldn't solve."

"A?" asked Marie querulously.

"Doesn't matter," I smiled, "just me being colourful with my grasp of the English language. I'll tell you about it later. That is, if you want to meet up."

"Well, that was going to be my question before you sidetracked me by calling me names." She grinned. "What do you want to do?"

"I'll leave it to you, petal."

She screwed her nose up and shook her head a little. "I'll think of something and keep working on those names!"

"I'll speak to you afterwards," I said, taking her hand surreptitiously, wallowing in the extraordinary softness of her touch. I got up from the chair.

"Of course," she responded, giving my hand a little squeeze. "I'll come and find you after the session."

* * *

Sir Norman was behind the mixing desk in the control booth, leaning back with a cup of tea in one hand, spectacles perched precariously on his forehead, and massaging his closed eyes with the thumb and forefinger of the other hand. He stopped, winced once or twice, sighed and then, seeing me, sat abruptly forward.

"Oh, sorry, David. Just having a quick stretch."

I pointed to the door and said: "I can come back later if you like. I don't want to disturb you."

"No, no," he said and smiled wearily. "I've had my half hour rest. What can I do you for?"

I produced a piece of paper from my jacket pocket and handed it to Sir Norman. "We received this this morning. This is your copy."

He opened it up, put his spectacles back on his nose and peered down at what I had just given him. "Paris Opéra," he said, quietly. "Superb."

"I've filed the contract. It's signed, sealed and delivered."

"Marvellous," he said, putting the paper into his briefcase. He looked up again, taking his spectacles off and putting them on the desk. "Hopefully, we can get a similar residency at the New York Met. You never know!"

"That would be fantastic! Do you know how the tour's shaping up, by the way? Have you heard anything?"

"No. No, I haven't," he replied, furrows of concern spreading across his brow. "I'm worried if you don't know anything and I don't either."

"My thoughts exactly," I said, a little exasperated. To top it all, Adrian had been lying to me about keeping Sir Norman up to date, as if I had not guessed that already. I put my hands on my hips. "I've been thinking whether I should tell you this or not but I think I have no option."

"About Gary?"

"Yes, and Adrian."

"They do seem to be in a very strange mood these days. And as for that spectacle Gary made at Sunday's rehearsal, I was appalled. Do you know what's got into them?"

"I think I do and I've used up what options I thought I had and they are now bringing pressure to bear on getting it sorted out. They are both wearing down my patience. I don't think it's going to change any time soon."

"Meaning?"

I gave Sir Norman a précis of my discussions with Gary and Adrian and what had transpired at the morning's Committee meeting. Alarm slowly spread across Sir Norman's features as I retold the elements of the story.

"That is very shoddy, especially from two people in the positions they hold in the Chorus. I had no idea that Gary felt this way. Mind you, he has always struck me as a rather irrational character. And quite insecure. Would you like me to have a word with him?"

I put my hands into my jeans pockets. "Might not be a bad idea. I've taken it as far as I can. Maybe he'll listen to you more than me. I don't think he has taken kindly to me obtaining the Chairmanship and still views me as his personal puppet. So, if you wouldn't mind?"

"Not at all," said Sir Norman and scribbled something in the margin of his recording schedule. "Leave it with me. Gary has been trying to schedule some time with me anyway. Now I know what that is likely to be, I'll get in first." He shrugged slightly.

"Thanks. Except that it might be an idea to pretend that we never had this conversation. He might view it as taking sides and we need to take the advantage of your position of authority."

"Good point."

"Thanks," I said gratefully. "I have so little detail provided that I don't even know what the festival is about."

"As far as I know, it's being regarded as a festive last rites kind of thing. Say goodbye to the old Opera House and hello to the new one. If I've understood it correctly, we will be performing two operas one day, then after a short ceremony and then we'll do the remaining two the next day. We'll be augmented by a few other Choruses; such is the scale of this thing. Much more than that I don't know, which is what makes me worried about Gary's attitude."

"That's interesting. While they are covering things up, and without the necessary detail to hand, the arrangements could be a complete shambles."

"Yes," said Sir Norman, getting up and pulling up his waistband to a more comfortable position. "You're absolutely and worryingly right. I'll make sure I talk to Gary as soon as possible. I'm less worried about Adrian because he appears to be following Gary rather than architecting any of this mess himself. I might be wrong and I'd be willing to talk to him too, if things are not improving. David, please can you keep a close eye on things and let me know if I can help further."

"Of course."

"Such a prestigious event with the media attention cannot afford to be messed up for the sake of a couple of ego trips!"

"Exactly. My thoughts entirely," I agreed, stepping out of the control room. "I'll keep you posted."

*   *   *

The afternoon session went well and we were released early, much to my joy because of the extra time afforded me to be with Marie. As I gathered my belongings, Pete tapped me on the shoulder. He mimicked drinking with a flick of the wrist and asked: "You going for a quick one? Or are you going elsewhere?" He winked.

"Elsewhere, I'm afraid. I hope you don't mind me..." I waved my hand vaguely.

"Don't be stupid. Gary's the jealous one, remember."

"No, I meant that I don't want you to think that I'm forgetting my friends."

Pete waved the concern aside. "Of course not," he said. "Besides which: I'll be here at the weekend and she won't."

"Good point," I conceded. "Let's go for a drink on Sunday, then."

"Fine," he agreed and then raised an eyebrow. "On to more important things. Have you...?"

"Held hands? Yes." I laughed. "I tell you Pete, she is one girl in a million. My mother would have loved her. She's witty, she's bright, she's intelligent, she's...well, wonderful." I shrugged.

"Yes, forget about that," Pete forged on, smiling and then began winking grotesquely. "Have you...you know?"

"Put my arm around her?"

Pete slumped a little and said: "I suppose that will have to do. You're not giving me any of the details, are you? So, have you put your arm around her?" He asked the last question as if reading mechanically from a script.

"Yes, I have. Eventually. But last night was wonderful. We really clicked. And she kissed me."

Pete frowned. "Congratulations, Dave. Really. I'd better go and leave you two lovebirds to it, before my stomach revolts against all this lovesick slushiness."

I grinned. "Now I know how to get rid of you. I'll bring a bucket in tomorrow."

"You do that," he rejoined and smiled as he jumped off the platform. "Don't you two do anything I wouldn't know how to."

"That's impossible," I laughed, returning his wave and wandered over to Marie, who was giggling with Beth Jackson and Guido Estente. As I came up by her side, she took my arm gently and we said our goodbyes.

"How are you?" she asked.

"I'm fine. Never felt better," I grinned. "Now. There's a restaurant –."

"No," she butted in decisively. "You are going to be my guest to dinner at the hotel."

"Suits me perfectly," I nodded.

* * *

We walked leisurely to Marie's hotel from the Underground station. We had been talking about the day's sessions, when we turned to where we lived. Marie had an apartment in one of the southern *arrondissements* of Paris and gîte on the outskirts of Bordeaux. I talked about my somewhat untidy homestead and did my best to describe the resident furry lump that was Isla.

"I'd love to meet her," she said, amusement twinkling around her eyes, "she sounds quite a character."

"She is. Very inquisitive too. That's how she got her injury, of course. I suppose that's the origin of the expression 'curiosity killed the cat'. Never thought of that before."

"Well, you must introduce me," she said.

"In which case, you must come and visit me."

"I'd very much like to do that." She put on a serious look. "But let's talk about now."

"What do you mean?" I said, somewhat befuddled.

"Oh, you English are so reticent. Look!" She deliberately took my right hand, placed it in her left and closed the fingers and smiled. "There," she said finally, "is that not better?"

"Much," I agreed and smiled shyly.

"You should smile more often. It really suits you."

"Thank you, but smiles are like eyelashes: a brief flicker and you can tell whether they are fake." I paused and pondered. "Actually, I have no idea why smiles are like eyelashes and, indeed, why I even said that!"

We laughed and continued walking wordlessly but comfortably to her hotel. Inside, I was feeling blossoming happiness; happiness not felt for years, if ever. This felt so right and I thought that I would not change anything, given the opportunity, other than making the move earlier and not getting so bogged down in paranoid worry and personal persecution. But all that heartache was largely forgotten because I was with Marie now.

At the hotel, she notified the desk clerk that she was entertaining a guest for dinner and to put all orders from the bar and restaurant on her room bill and we entered the bar. The same portly gentleman was sitting in the corner and a couple of suited businessmen were discussing earnestly the documents spread out on the table in front of them and pausing occasionally to slurp their coffee.

Marie stopped me as I delved into my pocket for change out of habit. "No," she said gently. "This evening is being paid for by me. You have been more than generous on our outings."

"You're the boss," I said, sitting down on a vacant bar-stool while she ordered. When she had them, we made our way to the dining-room. Incredibly, it was very similar in décor to the one in the Boulevard de la Madeleine, where we had first had dinner together. This one was, as befitted everything else in the hotel, on a larger scale than the Parisian version but the similarities were nonetheless astonishing. The lights were very subdued and, on our table almost hidden amongst the decorative décolletage of foliage huddled round it, was a large red candle, the flame flickering slightly every now and again. Our table was one of the few designed to allow only two to eat in comfort.

"I know what you're thinking," she said, as we sat down, the waiter pushing Marie's chair in for her.

"And what's that?" I asked, accepting the velveteen-covered menu.

"It's the same as the first restaurant we went to."

"Staggering, isn't it?" I confirmed.

"That's why I wanted to come here tonight. A special occasion needed to have something a bit special." Marie winked and looked down the menu.

Over dinner, we reminisced about Paris, I described my feelings the following day, the joy of seeing the photograph of me with Marie in the Parisian papers, the loathing I felt for Gary for stopping me seeing her in the corridor underneath the stage and the heart-stopping moment when I had seen her with another man, whom Gary had made me believe was more than just a friend.

"He doesn't sound a very nice man," she said simply, as she put her knife and fork together on her plate.

"Oh, he's OK," I bluffed and then added ruefully: "But only in small doses. And those doses are needing to be smaller by the day."

"When I saw you talking to him outside my door, my heart leapt into my mouth because I was desperate to see you again."

"Were you?" I asked, almost incredulously.

"Oh, yes. I was almost unable to breathe because my dream seemed to be coming true."

"What a missed opportunity!"

"Although I had my agent with me, I wanted to stop and talk, but he was running out of time. I think I said something like I was in a hurry. The look on your face."

"I'm sorry," I said, leaning on elbows and taking her hands in mine. "If only I had known."

"I thought that I had really destroyed any chance of a relationship with you."

"Likewise but because of my actions. However, I was not exactly happy because of Gary's treatment of me."

"And when I learned of this recording with your Chorus, I spent ages trying to work out what the week would be like, whether you would talk to me and whether we would actually get together."

I bent forward and kissed her knuckles. "And here we are!"

"But it feels so…." She struggled for the right word. "Meant. Do you know what I mean?"

"I do. I was thinking exactly the same as we were walking to this hotel. I am so glad that we got over our stupidity and we are here together."

We sat back as the waiter cleared our plates and we declined the offer of coffee. When he was out of earshot, Marie leaned forward and said conspiratorially: "I have a bottle of champagne up in my room – a present from Christoph – do you want to share it with me?"

"I can think of nothing more pleasurable," I replied in similarly hushed tones, glad of the reprieve from the arduous and lonely journey home.

"Unfortunately," she continued, smiling, "Madame is very cognisant of the rules about male guests in female bedrooms after lights out, so we'll have to devise a way of getting you up there."

I cogitated and then clicked my fingers in inspiration. "I know. Pretend you're ill and I'll tell them that you've got to be carried up there."

Marie giggled and put a hand in front of her mouth. "I couldn't keep a straight face."

"No, bad idea." I thought for a moment. Another inspirational click of the fingers. "There's only the one desk clerk on duty at this time of night, isn't there?"

"Yes."

"Well, I tell you what, I'll stay here until you get to the desk. Go to the front door end so that he's facing away. Then while you're talking to him, I'll sneak up the emergency stairs. What do you think?"

"It'll be easier than you carrying me up there," she conceded, smiling again.

"What room number is it?"

"One-four-three. What shall I talk to him about? Something convincing."

"Oh…er. I know. Say that you don't want to be disturbed and that an early morning call should be given to you at, say, half past eight. But drag it out to give me more time. Make out that you're having difficulty with the language."

"All right," she whispered excitedly and stifled another giggle. "You haven't done this sort of thing before, have you?"

I shook my head with a mischievous grin and then nodded encouragement as she went to the door. She looked back to me, nodded briefly to confirm the coast was clear, put on her best smile and went out to the desk clerk. I made my way over to the doorway and surreptitiously peered around the jamb to pick the right moment. While she was talking to him, pointing vaguely at the large clock behind the desk, forcing the clerk to look in that direction, I took my chance and crept across the foyer to the emergency stairs door. My first impressions of the size of the hotel were as nothing to the wide expanse this illegal tenant was now confronted with in this unpopulated and massive reception hall, desperately trying to go fast enough to reach the other side quickly but slowly enough not to make a noise. I was glad that I had decided to wear rubber-soled shoes that morning; I remembered considering wearing something more stylish but with a wooden heel. I heard Marie milking the 'bemused and befuddled foreigner' act for all it was worth as I reached the door to the emergency stairs. I brought myself up short and stared at it, knowing that it would squeak. I tested it very gently and felt the resistance of the hinges.

It appeared that I had been foiled at the final hurdle, when a bell-boy appeared in the glass panel inset in the door coming the other way. I waited until the timing would be perfect. I pushed the door open, quickly went through it, as the hinges squealed their opposition to being put to work. The bell-boy tipped his cap up in a gesture of 'goodnight' and I waved a cursory hand at him, trying to look as if I had every reason and right to be there. The desk clerk would have been curious because of the hinges' protest and would have glanced at the door. All he would have seen would have been the bell-boy. I was not taking any chances, though and took the stairs two at a time until I arrived at the first floor landing. Fortunately, the first-floor emergency exit and room one-four-three were hidden from the desk-clerk, being on the same side of the hotel. All the rooms on the other side would have been clearly visible because of the balcony-style arrangement. I thanked my lucky stars because I had not considered that potential problem, as I crouched down beside the bedroom door.

I was laughing silently to myself from the nervous energy expelled, as the lift pinged, the doors opened and Marie came out. She started giggling when she saw me and, after much mutual shushing, she fumbled the key in the lock. Her hands were shaking both with the urgency to get into the room and the suppression of laughter. As each attempt failed, the giggling became harder to contain, which made the efforts at entry even more difficult to achieve. Hushing and giggling like ten-year-olds, the key finally seated itself, Marie turned it and we burst in and shut the door quickly, still shushing each other noisily. We fell on the couch in the reception part of the suite, laughing for what seemed an age; every time one of us stopped, we would look at the other and it would set us off again.

The suite was very plush and lived up to the façade presented by the entrance foyer and restaurant. High-ceilinged in keeping with the unnecessary size of the rest of the hotel, it had an air of a hospital or doctor's waiting-room about it, because nearly everything was white or off-white-cum-cream colour; the chairs, the sofa, curtains, cushions, the walls and ceiling. Those things that were not white were made from a dark, mahogany-like wood. In the corner of this lounge was a latest model of television beside a broad mini-bar, propping up one side of a writing desk. At the other side of the desk was a set of drawers. Hotel stationery, a blotter and writing implements were all provided, as was a telephone. Halfway along the longer wall and opposite the front door was the doorway to Marie's bedroom and *en suite* bathroom.

Managing to contain myself finally, I stood up to ease the pain of the stitch that had formed from so much laughing on top of a rich dinner. Tears were etching their way down my cheeks. I turned to Marie to ask her if she was alright, but burst out laughing again, having to crouch down to stop myself falling over. She, too, had tears in her eyes and was desperately trying to keep a straight face, which is what set me off again. Her addictive giggling made me worse and I went over on my back, knees bobbling above my chest.

Struggling to breathe properly, I avoided Marie's gaze until she gasped: "Oh, dear!" I watched her rubbing the tears away with her palms. "I'm sure the man at the desk suspected something."

I dried my tears with the cuff of my shirt and slowed my rasping breathing. "Well, he can't do anything," I finally managed. "You've asked not to be disturbed. But just to be sure." I got up from my prone position, turned the key in the lock from the inside and sat down again next to Marie.

"Right," said Marie, wiping the last wetness from her prettily flushed cheeks, "champagne!" She got up and went into her bedroom, returning with two tooth-glasses and the bottle. "Ridiculous, isn't it?" she said apologetically. "An hotel this snazzy ought to be able to provide decent champagne flutes."

"No matter," I said, taking them from her, setting the glasses down on the edge of the long table positioned by the couch. "Would Madame like to sniff the cork?" I asked, taking the wire cage from the bottle-top and easing the cork out. Suddenly, with a loud 'pop!' it shot out of the bottle, bounced on the ceiling, leaving a small dent, and passed over Marie's head and into the bedroom. Then, the liquid began foaming out of the bottle and over my shaking hand, frothing on to the carpet. "Oh, God!" I exclaimed, beginning to laugh again. "Quick!"

Marie rushed forward and placed one of the glasses tremblingly under the champagne Niagara, trying to follow my laugh-induced oscillations and then repeated it with the other glass. We fell back on the couch laughing again and were suddenly shocked into silence by a sharp knock on the door. I slapped a hand over my mouth and the other over Marie's until we had composed ourselves. The sharp tap came again.

"Who is it?" she asked, her voice trembling from the effort of composure, holding my wrist.

"Desk clerk, madam," came the response and a slight pause. "Is everything all right?"

Marie looked at me and gave a slight nervous giggle. I pointed at the television in the corner. "Yes," she said. "I'm terribly sorry, I turned the television on too loudly."

There was a pregnant silence from the other side of the door and then: "Alright, madam. Good night!"

"Good night!" called Marie, suppressing the urge to laugh again.

We sat on the couch in excited silence, listening to the voices of our irate neighbours outside their door, remonstrating with the desk clerk, until the footsteps receded and the next room's door banged shut. We waited a bit longer just for safety.

"That was close," I observed, sobered slightly by the experience.

"Speak in whispers," said Marie hoarsely.

I filled the glasses up once the foam had bubbled itself out to nothing, passing one to Marie. I raised mine to hers, clinked slightly and sipped. The strange effect of champagne is that it feels wonderfully smooth on the way down but once in the stomach, the bubbles become mischievous.

"Wow!" I said, avoiding a garrulous burp and shook my head.

"It's nice," she said, taking another sip and smiled. "I love champagne." Her face softened and she paused. "Thank you for coming out tonight."

"No. Thank *you*. I've really enjoyed myself. In fact, I've enjoyed the whole week, including creeping around a hotel like a trainee burglar."

Marie laughed and she put down her glass next to mine on the table. Once again her face became serious as she looked deeply into my eyes. Maybe it was the champagne but I felt as I had when holidaying in Swanage one year as a child, standing in impressive waves, feeling the fresh, cool foam bouncing around me and then the strength of the undertow as the waves receded to try again; I was being drawn into those beautiful brown eyes. My head moved towards hers, as she put her arms around my neck and then brushed my lips lightly with hers. Her tongue flicked and explored them and then ventured into my mouth, her passion rising as she ruffled my hair. I took her by the shoulder and stroked her slender arm, tasting the sweetness of her mouth, wallowing in the softness of her that I wanted so badly. She drew away, breathing   · quickly.

She asked simply: "David, please will you stay the night?"

My heart missed a couple of beats and resumed its now familiar, erratic course when I was anywhere near Marie. "Yes," I responded, equally simply.

She stood up gently, taking my hand and led me to the bedroom. Kicking off her shoes, she sat down on the edge of the massive double-bed and pulled me down beside her.

I do not believe that I have ever felt such a burning passion for anyone; passion mixed with lust, desire, love and the need to be close to her. My heart was beating incredibly fast as we continued to kiss and touch each other. Nervously, I reached out to unbutton her shirt, pausing at the bottom, in case I had misread the signs and she wanted me to go no further and to retract her earlier offer. Gently, she took my hand, as if reading my thoughts, and placed it on a brassiere-covered breast, which seemed to fit the size of my hand perfectly. Stroking the cloth slowly, while Marie deftly unbuttoned my shirt, I felt her nipple harden under my touch. She ran a hand across my chest and fireworks of delight went off in my head, such was the pleasure of her caresses of my naked flesh. The feeling was a wonderful, unique sensation and I wanted more. With relatively unaccustomed ease, I unclasped her brassiere with one hand and moved back to her soft breasts again, savouring the soft curves. Marie murmured softly and our lips parted.

She gave me three pecks in quick succession, looking at me intently in between each one.

Breathing heavily, she stood up, loosening the skirt and removed the remainder of her clothes. Taking her lead, I took mine off, both sets left where they had landed. When we were both naked, I hugged her, still standing, taking in a shaky, sharp breath with the new excitement of her exquisitely soft and adorable skin against mine and kissed her urgently, my tongue linking with hers, exploring her mouth; the passion was almost as unbearable as it was intense. My nerve centres were being bombarded with the new experiences: the taste of her mouth and lips; her breasts against my chest; her stomach pressed firmly to mine; thighs and feet rubbing together; her silky arms, shoulders and back. The facial freckles extended to a starburst across the top of her chest, shoulders and arms and I wanted to kiss every one. Sitting her gently on the bed and laying her down, I knelt and bent over her neck, giving her butterfly kisses, moving over her nipples, back to her neck, across to her shoulder and up to her lips. Moving into position on top of her, I gasped with the excruciating ecstasy of entering her and continued kissing her lips, cheeks and neck. Marie stroked my back and buttocks, kissing my head and ruffling my hair as her passion continued to rise.

Locking my elbows, I stopped moving, looked into her eyes and then down her body, her breasts, her flat stomach, her shoulders, her arms and her legs arcing around my thighs. Looking straight back into her eyes, stinging pain reached my eyes as the onset of the climax took hold of me and grunted to its conclusion as Marie suddenly and urgently pulled me further into her, bear-hugging me, gasping and bucking as she reached the zenith of her climax simultaneously.

It had only lasted a few seconds but it was the most powerful sexual experience I had ever had. It was very beautiful, it was meant and we had momentarily become one. I now felt whole as I had never felt before and was encountering a previously unknown satisfying peace.

We lay silently in a cowl of mutual perspiration, she leaning on and stroking my chest and I on my back, one arm protectively and firmly around her, the other hand stroking her arm and shoulder.

"Marie?" I asked, eventually.

"Mmm," she responded lazily.

"Can I ask you a question?"

"Yes."

"How come you can speak English so well?"

She raised herself up on one elbow and looked at me. "That's a strange question to ask now. I thought you were going to ask whether I had enjoyed our lovemaking or whether I had any regrets." She smiled.

"And?"

"What?" she teased. "The lovemaking or speaking English?"

"Which do you want to answer?"

She settled back down, nuzzling tightly into my side. "The English question. Why did you ask me now? I'm curious."

"If I'd asked you that within the first five minutes, it would be regarded as small talk and therefore worthless. By asking you now, it shows that I am interested in you and that I care about you."

She moved comfortably against me. "That's beautiful. Well, I knew the basics but it wasn't until Uncle Charles took me under his wing that I really started to learn it. Plus I lived in England for a long while."

I nodded and squeezed her arm. "And the next question, being the strange person that I am, was going to be about your levels of enjoyment."

She looked up again and returned my smile. "Mr. Loughton. What can I say?"

"I do know how you felt." I cuddled her to me.

"I know you do. But just for the record, I have never experienced such fantastic love ever. It felt so right and it was as if we had somehow become the same person momentarily."

"That is precisely how I felt, too." She reached up and kissed my lips, holding on to my neck. "You know," I started, feeling myself being pulled in by her undertow as I stared into those beautiful, deep, brown eyes, "I thought this would be very difficult for me to say this to any girl, but –."

She gently placed a finger on my mouth and said: "Then let me say it first. I love you, Mr. Loughton."

"And I," I replied, reaching to kiss her forehead. "And I love you too, Mademoiselle Duvois." We kissed again. "But I have a major problem."

"What?" she asked, slightly concerned.

"I only have to look at you and I want to ravish you."

She giggled as she moved on top to straddle me. "That's good," she said, taking me inside her again, "because I have exactly the same problem with you. We are going to have to work hard at sorting this out, aren't we?"

She leaned forward into my arms, as we made love more languorously but no less passionately. I stroked her back, her arms, her thighs, touching her all over to experience the exquisite joy of her perfect flesh. The joyous sting in my eyes returned as, again, we reached a simultaneous climax.

I kissed her urgently, holding her head and cuddling her forcefully. "I *do* love you, Marie," I said.

"I've never really been in doubt since I first met you," she responded, cheeks flushed and panting lightly, as we lay cuddled together for a few moments. "I knew you were the one from the moment you entered my dressing-room in Paris."

I kissed her. "You haven't been out of my thoughts since, either."

"I don't know about you," she added, giggling and rolling over and pulling me on top of her, "but my problem is still there!" Even her giggles had the electric effect, as I eagerly confirmed that the problem had not abated in the slightest.

PUPPET ON A STRING

CHAPTER 19

Whenever I sleep anywhere other than my own bed, frustratingly I always wake with the first light or even before it. Not frustrating now, the following morning, as the sun shone strongly through the plain, beige curtains, bathing the room in a soft, orangey glow. I was awake and tired from the exercise we had had the night before, but I felt completely fulfilled. A large gap in my life had been suddenly and wondrously filled by a bundle of warm, beautiful, cuddly girlish giggles. I was amazed by the strength and depth of feeling that Marie and I shared in so short a space of time and I knew that she was my destiny and I hers – a destiny preordained by fate forcing me to join the *Coro di Londinium* and she to pursue a solo career, culminating in my strange hobby of collecting autographs from the chief performers and landing the trip to Paris. One slight change in that sequence would have meant that our paths would have diverged and it was something that was too terrible to contemplate now that I was lying next to her softly sleeping form.

Marie was lying with her back to me, one arm over the bed-clothes, the other hidden under the pillow. Her hair spread delicately over the linen pillow-case, her chest rose and fell slowly with her sleepy breathing. Resting my head on my hand, I spent a long time fascinated by and drinking in her features: the way the colour of her hair contrasted superbly with her skin tones; the shape of her shoulders hunched round in sleep; the athletic configuration of the muscles in her back and arms; the contours of her body; the intricate patterns formed by her freckles; the healthy sheen to her skin reflecting the gauzy sunlight coming into the room. I reached out and stroked her arm and shoulder gently with the back of two fingers, tracing the freckles. She stirred slightly and I bent to kiss her shoulder.

She rolled on her back and with half-open, sleep-filled eyes, said drowsily: "What a lovely way to be woken up."

I put my arms around her gently, settling back into the pillow and kissed her lips. "Good morning," I said and smiled. Those limpid eyes were drawing me in again and I was aroused by the contrasting heat of our bodies pressed together. The coolness of her skin against the high temperature of mine was highly erotic.

"Come here," she said and giggled, pulling me on top of her.

I kissed her lips, chin and neck, passion rising. Marie responded by hugging me tightly and rubbing her hands up and down my back in her growing excitement, moaning softly as she did so. Soon, with pulses returning to a normal rate, we kissed and nuzzled in the post-coital afterglow.

"Ooh, I *do* love you," she said, as if there had been some doubt, and, to confirm it, she put her arms around my back and squeezed tightly. We rolled over so that she was on top of me and she folded her arms just below my neck, resting her chin on her hands. "Well?" she said, a mischievous twinkle in her eyes.

"Well what?" I teased, stroking her arm.

She moved away from my hand, smiled impishly and said: "There'll be no more of that until you say what you're supposed to say in return. Well?"

"Er..." I ruminated, scraping my chin.

"Oooh," she squealed and began poking my ribs until I was begging her for mercy.

"All right, all right! I love you too!"

She folded her arms again and said in mock hurt: "Hmm, so I should think too."

I looked into her eyes and she held my gaze. The look on her face said more than she needed to vocalize and I knew that this was the woman I wanted to spend the rest of my life with. Her face told me that she felt the same way about me. I leaned forward and kissed her nose. Stroking her arms and feeling aroused again, I said: "You have a wonderful effect on me."

"So I can feel," she responded, a lop-sided grin on her mouth and the mischievous twinkle in her eyes. "And you have a similar result on me. It feels like I could do this forever and never get tired of it."

I smiled and kissed her forehead. "Me too. I could think of nothing more pleasurable than spending the day in bed, but I guess we ought to think about getting up before you get me so excited that I can't."

She sighed, resignedly, and replied: "You're right, of course. I must have a bath. I'm all clammy." She got off me and sat at the edge of the bed, hands on knees, looking back coyly over her shoulder, adding: "Not that I'd have it any other way!"

"Nor me," I agreed.

"I'll run the bath," said Marie, standing up. Her body was just so painfully beautiful, well-proportioned, slender limbs, athletically slim legs and back and breasts to die for. "Would sir like to join Madame?" she asked, the same coquettish look on her face.

I swung out of bed eagerly. "Sir would very much enjoy joining Madame!"

The telephone rang and Marie bent to pick up the receiver, putting a finger to her lips, listened momentarily and replaced it on its cradle. "Apparently, it's half past eight." Another mischievous smile, as she crooked a finger to beckon and slinked towards the bathroom. "So, if sir would follow Madame, he might find something to his advantage."

"I think I already have," I said and grinned, following her graceful nakedness into the bathroom.

The size of the bath was in proportion with everything else in the hotel. It was huge and took a long time to fill. "I'll do a few lengths before we go," I quipped. But at least it could accommodate two people very comfortably. While it was filling up with steaming hot water, Marie cleaned her teeth and offered me her spare toothbrush.

Eventually, the bath was full enough and I sat at one end, with Marie nestled between my legs, her back to me, the water at lower chest level. I picked up the bar of soap and began washing the foamy suds over her shoulders, arms, breasts and stomach. Another extraordinarily wonderful and new thrill of our slippery and wet bodies sliding against each other.

"I think you like me," said Marie, a little breathlessly, reaching behind her back.

"Does it show?" I asked innocently, passions rising as my arms slid against her breasts and arms, my chest against her back.

"Just a little," acknowledged Marie. "We ought to do something about this."

She raised herself slightly, bracing her weight by using the edges of the bath and gasped as I filled her again. Continuing to soap her back, front and arms and myself, I hugged her to me, slippery against her back and nuzzled her neck and shoulders as I moved my arms and hands around her stomach and breasts, tweaking her nipples.

"Oh, mon Dieu!" she gasped, shuddering in my grasp moments before I too finished, holding her tight. "I love you, I love you, I love you," she exploded, sliding against my bear-hug. She leaned heavily against me, panting.

"Not as much as I love you," I countered, equally breathless.

"Where did you learn to be so good?" she asked, when her breathing had slowed. Her eyes were almost closed and she had a permanent grin on her face. It mirrored my own.

"I didn't," I replied, "it must be you. Where did you learn to be so good?"

"May be we just know what each other wants," she said and moved to the other end of the bath and turned around, splashing water on herself to remove the suds. "If we want to get out of here today, then we ought not to touch each other because look what happens!"

"You're right," I said, disappointed. I wanted more of her but this was not getting the potatoes peeled. I watched her suppleness as she washed herself and added: "And I ought not to look at you either because you have the strangest impact on me!"

We finished bathing and I dressed quickly resisting the temptation to touch or stroke her again. We discussed ways that I could get out of the hotel without arousing suspicion or to provide sufficient evidence for the hotel management to put two and two together. I hit upon an idea and talked through the detail with Marie.

"I'll see you in a minute," I said, dropping back into the clandestine gait and surreptitious whispers of the previous evening, and kissed her forehead. I opened the door slightly, and peeked through the crack, confirmed that there was no-one in the corridor and that no-one could see me above the balcony from the foyer and slipped guiltily out, shutting the door gently. Stepping over the detritus of half-eaten breakfasts on trays outside the rooms, I crept to the emergency stairwell, fearing that someone would notice me at any minute. I ran down the stairs and reached the door to the foyer. Taking some time to smarten my appearance and straighten out some of the creases in my shirt and trousers from their overnight sojourn on Marie's bedroom floor, I glanced through the glass panel in the door. The foyer was empty apart from an elderly couple sitting in the central seats, looking disconsolately in different directions, surrounded by several suitcases and plastic bags from London's main tourist traps. Two staff were on duty behind the desk, one looking into the registration book and the other out of the front windows into the street. Now was as good a chance as I would get.

I eased the door open to limit its squealing protest and squeezed through the minimum gap I could allow myself and walked swiftly over to the front desk as both men turned in my direction. I raised a finger as I reached the desk and said: "Ah, there you are." The one who was about to talk closed his mouth again. "Where have you been?"

He looked uncertain, gave a sideways glance to his colleague and stuttered: "I –."

"No, no," I stated in a deep voice, further bemusing him as I had intended, and waved the potential answer aside, frowning. "Doesn't matter. I'm not interested. You're here now." Both men looked at each other with the anticipated effect I was having on them. "Now, where is Mademoiselle Duvois? I was supposed to meet her half an hour ago but she hasn't turned up." They were looking at each other, searching for something to say but only managing inadequate goldfish impressions. "So I've come here," I added helpfully.

With relief, they saw the lift doors open and Marie rush out to greet me. "Oh, Mr. Loughton," she said, pretending to be distressed but I could see the wicked twinkle in her eyes, "I'm so sorry, I overslept."

"Oh, dear," I said, trying to sound officious and glanced irritated at my watch. I sighed: "Well, if we leave now, we'll be on time."

"Of course, of course," she replied, pretending to pacify me and I could hear the tremor of a giggle in her voice. I had to get her out of there before she broke down.

She was saved by one of the clerks coming to his senses. "Oh, madam," he said, snapping back to reality. "There's a message for you. I would have put it through to your room, but you expressly asked not –."

"No, no, that's alright," she said putting the note in the pocket of her slim-fit red jeans.

We managed to get to the other side of the revolving doors before Marie could contain her giggling no longer. "Oh, the poor man, " she said, "what must he have thought?"

I joined her giggles unable to help myself. "You should have seen his face, when I first approached the desk! It was like he'd seen his worst vision. He kept looking at the revolving doors which weren't moving."

"I'll make sure I leave a suitable tip this weekend."

I looked up and down the street. "If we don't get a move on, we really will be late." I took her hand and we walked swiftly down towards the Strand, on the look out for a passing taxi. I saw one with the yellow light of availability switched on and raised my free hand. He shot past without even recognizing my hail. Marie pointed out another free taxi coming in the opposite direction. That cab, too, shot past with similar lack of recognition. "Am I invisible? What do I have to do to get a taxi?"

"Stand in front of one?" suggested Marie, pointing out another one turning the corner towards us.

I stepped into the road, hand raised but the driver leaned on his horn and veered melodramatically around us, making a few choice remarks and gestures as he did so. "Obviously not!" I observed, jumping back on to the pavement. "What a colourful chap! And it's not true what he said about my parents' marital status. Come on."

Marie giggled as I took her hand again and we ran towards Trafalgar Square tube station. The ticket concourse was fairly empty with a tramp nestled down in one corner, gruffly making observations to himself, a group of schoolchildren excitedly babbling about the day's planned excursion and a queue of six people waiting to buy tickets and the ticket inspector standing by the barrier. Two out-of-breath people running into the booking hall, making a brief survey of the time it would take to buy a ticket and running for the barrier shattered the peace.

"We're in a hurry," I said, helpfully indicating to Marie, as the inspector put up a hand to stop us going further. "She's pregnant." Marie stifled a giggle.

"Oh, yes, sir?" replied the inspector doubtfully.

"Okay, no not really. But we are in a hurry. We're late for recording sessions in St. John's Wood. Please can we pay at the other end?" I waved at the ticket office, the queue at which had been extended by two more people. The person at the front of the queue was paying by cheque and the frustration was setting into the people behind him, as they stuffed hands in pockets and shifted from foot to foot, muttering under their breath in the way that only the English do. "The queue will make us even later."

"You need to buy a ticket before travelling, sir, madam," the inspector responded bluntly. He looked at Marie. My secret weapon!

She put her head slightly on one side, flashed her best smile and said: "Please. We will pay at the other end. You can 'phone ahead to them to make sure we do." She knitted her eyebrows together a little.

The inspector let out a held breath and relaxed. "Okay," he relented and opened the gate for us to go through.

"Thanks," I said as we passed through, patting him on the arm. We ran for the escalator and I turned. "St. John's Wood," I called but he smiled and waved us on our way.

We took the steps two at a time, landing loudly at the bottom of the moving staircase and sprinted on to the northbound platform just as the stationary train's doors began closing. I caught one of the doors, struggling with it before I managed to force them open. The guard barked a warning from the other end of the platform. Marie jumped in and I forced myself through, releasing the door with bang, catching my shoulder slightly. We collapsed into two adjacent seats, puffing, rasping air through our throats.

"I didn't think we were going to make it," said Marie eventually, after getting some breath back, pointing out the black marks on my hands.

"That makes two of us," I gasped and tried to wipe the oily, grimy muck obtained from the doors from my hands with a tissue I had in my pocket. I sighed noisily and sank back in the seat, placing a hand, which she covered with one of hers, on Marie's thigh.

The train appeared to acknowledge the need for speed as it rushed through the black, dank tunnels, the lights flickering off and on occasionally as the electricity momentarily failed its connection to the live rail underneath. It stopped only briefly at all the stations and few people embarked or got off it, the doors slammed shut and off we went again screaming through the tunnels.

We arrived at the Abbey Road studios with barely five minutes to spare, before the session was due to begin. We ignored a group of photographers and journalists, asking for some of Marie's time, bustled in the entrance and stood in the foyer having signed in at the small security post to the left. We took some time to gain our breaths and to prepare the look of nonchalance on our faces. Marie gave me a peck on the cheek, grinned and winked and we took the steps down to the studio quickly and acquired our respective positions more sedately.

"Business," I said, as I reached the seat that Pete had reserved for me, and frowned with one eyebrow in a pretence at seriousness.

"Business, eh?" he asked knowingly. "And that business includes staying away overnight does it?"

I was genuinely surprised. "How did you know?"

"I tried ringing you. It was a bit of a give-away that you didn't answer."

"I might have just been ignoring the 'phone," I suggested.

"The other give-away, of course, was when you came in just now."

"How do you mean?" I asked, knowing that he had me cornered.

"Well, you and Marie came in together."

"We might have arrived at the same time and it's just co-incidence," I replied, amused by Pete's interrogation.

"Yes, that's a possibility," he conceded, "except for one thing."

"Which is?"

"How long have I known you?"

"Years….and years," I responded forlornly.

"And in all that time, I have noticed one thing."

"Yes?"

"Marie came in wearing something different from yesterday. You, on the other hand, are wearing exactly what you were wearing yesterday."

"Um," I tried, providing time for thinking of a suitable response. I clicked my fingers and grinned. "Saves on washing."

"That is also true. You can't get away from it though. In all the time I've known you, you have never worn the same thing twice in a row. Always been fastidious about such things. And you haven't shaved!"

"Ah!"

"'Ah!' indeed! So I needn't ask how it's going then?"

"No, you needn't," I replied and grinned again.

"But I will. You look like the cat, who's got the *crème de la crème*! How's it going? And I warn you, no slushy stuff."

"Oh, *comme ci, comme ça*," I replied, deliberately non-committal. "Well, more *ci* than *ça*."

"Are you officially an item, then?"

"As I say, more *ci* than *ça*! What did you ring me about?"

"Quick change of subject. Okay. I understand," he grinned and winked grotesquely, which made me laugh. "It was nothing really. Just a few ideas I had about Gary was all."

"Oh, God!" I exclaimed. With the excellence of the past few hours, I had pushed all thoughts of Gary, Adrian and Chorus business to the back of my mind. Now Pete had reminded me of the stark reality of my responsibilities. "Right, I'll talk to you about it later."

"Fine," he said and looked down at the floor and then back at me, an evil glint in his eyes. "And then you can tell me all the gory details." Another wink and we laughed.

"Fat chance, mate," I replied and patted him on the shoulder.

* * *

The whole of the second Act of *Carmen* was recorded in two or three extended takes, with only a few small patches here and there. I had taken every opportunity during the recording to observe Marie singing, when I was not required to concentrate on singing myself. I loved her more then than earlier that morning and I knew that I had fallen madly, deeply, obsessively, passionately, achingly, beautifully, heart-poundingly in love with her. Each time she was required to sing, she stood and stepped up to her music-stand, placing a hand in each of the back pockets of her jeans, only removing them to express subconsciously the music and words she was singing, before returning them, accentuating her pert bottom. She was wearing a red and white striped tee-shirt, which was simple but so sexy worn by her. Once or twice, she caught my gaze as she returned to her seat and grinned warmly in response to my surreptitious half-wink.

As a result of the success of the recording session, we were released three-quarters of an hour early, much to my relief. Because of all the frenetic activity with Marie, the tiredness was creeping up on me and it was not helping concentration. But, every time I looked at Marie, standing at the microphone, singing so beautifully, drinking her in, her stance, her neck, her hair, her bare arms, the graceful fingers, the shapely legs beneath the red material of her trousers, the tiredness dissipated. Nevertheless, I was glad to get out of the recording studio.

I turned to Pete once sufficient people had dispersed so that the conversation would not be overheard. "So what were these thoughts on Gary?"

"Well, it occurred to me that the root of his problem is that he feels you're taking something away from him, something he has traditionally assumed to be solely his domain. A bit like cocking your leg in another dog's territory."

"True enough."

"So why not give him something to do as proof of the opposite?"

"Like?"

"I don't know. That's the problem. I mean: you can't get much bigger than this American shindig."

"Yes," I said distantly, lost in thought and pointing a finger at Pete. "I like it. Give him something to do, the more prestigious the better and he'll back off."

"Exactly."

"I think you've got something there. I was thinking about how I could get this record label exercise off the ground. Maybe I could give that to Gary. What do you think?"

"Won't you feel a bit frustrated, though? He'll take all the credit."

"It was one of my election pledges, remember, so he'll have difficulty doing that."

"I think it would be perfect, then."

"Good. Search your grey matter for any issues we might come up against, so that they may be mitigated before they happen."

"Will do," he said and then started winking as if he had a large piece of grit in his eye. "Now, about the details of…you know?"

"Sorry, Pete," I replied, half-smiling, and patted his arm, "must talk to Bob."

Pete clicked his fingers in mock disappointment and quivered his bottom lip as if he were about to cry.

"Maybe at the weekend, then," I said and laughed.

"You're on!" he said brightening and grinning. "Seriously, Dave. Good luck with it all."

I thanked him and went over to Bob, who was looking very pale and wan a couple of rows behind me. His face lit up a little as I approached him.

"David, my boy, sit down, sit down," he said and indicated the chair next to him. "I see that you have made your mark."

"I'm sorry?" I responded quizzically, sitting down.

"A very beautiful, French singer?"

I was astounded. "Is it that obvious?"

"To me, yes," he smiled. "I was watching the stolen glances between you during the recording. You have a very fine lady there. Very beautiful. And she has a fine man in you. Look after each other."

My cheeks had reddened a little and I stuttered my assurance that we would. Marie joined us at that moment, perfectly timed and I introduced her to Bob. The colour had returned to his gaunt and sallow cheeks as he shook her hand.

"I was just saying to young David here that he has a lovely lady in you," he said to Marie and smiled.

"Why, thank you, Mr. Holden," she replied shyly.

"Bob. Please."

"Thank you, Bob," she repeated and pretty flushes coloured her cheeks.

"You must come to lunch one day, if it would not be too much trouble," he invited.

"Bob! That would be fantastic. How about Friday?" I suggested, receiving a nod of agreement and approval from Marie.

"Done," said Bob and stood up, using the edge of his music folder for balance on an adjacent chair and let out an old man's sigh.

"Are you alright, Bob?" I asked concerned.

"I am, my dear boy, thanks for your concern. Just too long sat down in these small chairs. See you both tomorrow."

"I look forward to it, Bob," said Marie and flashed a pretty smile.

Bob responded with a chuckle and tottered along between the rows of chairs to the exit.

"What a nice man," observed Marie.

"He is. A true gentleman. And absolutely obsessed with music. He's the one I told you about who had a stroke last week. Wild horses would not stop him being involved."

"He certainly seems to be struggling physically. Still, if the voice is there."

"Exactly. And he's got a fantastic voice. I envy him."

"You'll have to let me listen to yours some time."

I nodded with slight alarm. "Bob's been my mentor in this business and I feel obliged…no, obliged is the wrong word. It's my desired duty to keep an eye on him."

"And you are a gentleman, too, for doing that," she said, taking my hand in hers.

"You'll love his house. Fantastic views across the greenery of Hertfordshire, massive garden and a baby grand piano in the huge dining room."

Torchev and Estente drew up and interrupted us. Torchev clapped me on the shoulder and said: "We would very much like to be taking you to having dinner this evening, both you and Marie."

"Lovely," said Marie.

"Have you anywhere in particular in mind?" I asked.

"No," replied Estente, brow furrowing, "we are hoping you could suggest somewhere."

"No problem," I said and then realized it was an issue because I did not really know where to suggest.

"What about that steak place?" giggled Marie, as we left the studio.

Estente patted his stomach to indicate that steak would be delicious. I waved a hand and said: "I think we'd be thrown out before we even sat down."

"Why is that?" asked Torchev, his eyebrows dancing.

Marie told the story of our last visit and they roared with laughter, spurred on and infected by Marie's giggles.

Torchev clapped me on the shoulder and said: "You are very great man. You do not take life too seriously."

"Thank you," I responded and walked on ahead with Marie to avoid further dislocation of my shoulder.

* * *

Over dinner, the four of us swapped many anecdotes about our careers to date. Some of them – either because of the accents or poor grasp of sentence construction and English idioms – seemed funnier because of the unintentional incomprehensibility of the story. Torchev apologized for his knowledge of English.

"No, please," I said, embarrassed that he thought I was poking fun at him. "You speak English well; you get your points across. If the roles were reversed, I would flounder with Russian or Italian."

"No offence was taken," he rejoined.

"Good," I responded. "Actually, it reminds me of a story of just how difficult it is not to offend the person in whose tongue you are trying to speak, even if you think you are fairly fluent. I went to Austria once and stayed with a nice family on a remote farm. Now they couldn't speak that much English, so I was forced to speak in German."

"And could you speak it?" asked Marie, the impish glint in her eyes, the dimple on her cheek.

"Yes, but not all the colloquialisms, of course or the finer points of grammar. On my last day, the farmer's wife made a real effort with the breakfast, wanting to make the traditional full English breakfast. It's strange but it tasted nothing like it but it was good enough and I was thankful for the effort made. The farmer then told me everything on the plate was home-grown produce, from the bacon to the home-made bread for the fried slices. It was then that I thought I'd praise him on the quality of it, because it was good. So, I tried: 'Ich liebe deine Eier' wanting to say 'I love your eggs'. I worked it through and could see nothing wrong with the sentence: 'ich', 'I'; 'liebe', 'love or like'; 'deine', 'your plural'; 'Eier' 'eggs plural'. So I said it and the farmer exploded with laughter slapping the table with the joy of what I had said. His wife was grinning too, somewhat red-faced."

"Oh, my God!" exclaimed Marie, her hands fluttering in front of her mouth, expecting a shock, "What had you said?"

"Well, after the farmer had calmed down a bit, finishing his coughing and spluttering after the effort of laughing so hard, he said: 'Ich liebe *die* Eier'. Well, I looked at him quizzically. I could understand that the sentence construction might have been incorrect but not why it was so funny. I asked him what had sent him into such paroxysms and he told me that the eggs were not directly his and the comment was generic to the eggs on the table. But by using the word 'deine' – thinking 'your' – instead of 'die', I had stumbled over a colloquial euphemism for testicles. I had complimented him on his testicles!"

Estente and Torchev looked a little shocked for a moment and then roared with laughter in unison. Marie was hiding her mouth behind her hands, giggling with her eyes wide open in mild shock.

"So, if I can make such an apparently rudimentary mistake, please don't worry about your use of English. It's even harder than German."

"But, don't worry," said Marie, patting Torchev's small hand, "we'll tell you as soon as you insult us." She giggled and Torchev's frame shuddered as he joined in.

In one quiet moment to ourselves, while the other two were arguing about the intricacies of Beethoven's work as an operatic composer against that as a choral composer, I thanked Marie for the previous evening. She blushed a little and said covertly: "I bet I enjoyed it more than you did." She smiled.

"Absolutely impossible!" I retorted in similarly hushed tones and smiled back, stroking her thigh under the table. "So what about tonight?"

"Oh, David," she said, putting a fist to her forehead, consternation etched into her face, "I forgot to tell you. That note I picked up at the hotel was from my agent. He's flying in from Lyon to give me a contract to sign and talk other important business. It's deathly dull and Michel insists on doing business alone, because he doesn't like to discuss the finer detail with others present. Then he's insisted on taking me out for a meal."

"Well," I replied, trying not to look too disappointed, "business is business."

"I tell you what," she said, placing a hand on my leg, "I'll come and find you tomorrow."

"I've got to wait that long?" I smiled. "How will I last?"

"I'll make it worth your while," she replied, raising a seductive eyebrow.

"Okay, okay," I said, looking heavenward, "just roll on tomorrow!"

Marie squeezed my thigh and looked at her watch, saying: "We had better get back."

I held Marie's hand all the way to the station and made sure they got on to the correct train for St. John's Wood rather than heading for

Watford Junction. Standing on the platform and Marie on the train, I pulled her gently to me with a finger on the neck of her shirt and kissed her lips. She placed a hand gently on my chest. We parted from our kiss and she said: "Your heart's beating very fast."

"You have this effect on me, especially when you're kissing me."

"Sweet," she said and kissed me deeply, pushing her tongue between my lips, parting from me as the doors began to shut. She stroked my cheek and pulled her arm in as the doors banged shut. Marie mouthed 'I love you' to me and pouted seductively. I pointed first to my chest and then to her, nodding energetically, a stupid grin on my face. I blew her a kiss as the train jolted into motion and watched it disappear into the dusty tunnel and then made my own way home.

By King's Cross, I was really missing her and was feeling quite low by the time I reached my front door. It was incredible the speed at which things had taken place and that I had been in her company almost exclusively for twenty-four hours. It was hardly surprising that I was starting to feel lost.

The melancholic feelings were dispersed by a 'phone call at eleven o'clock. "I love you," came a voice, when I answered it.

"I love you too."

"I'm really missing you. When I look at the bed where you were lying last night, I feel emotional. So I thought I'd ring you to say goodnight."

I was almost skipping to bed after the call was ended. Such a simple device of hearing her voice had cheered me up no end and I fell into a deep and peaceful sleep.

PUPPET ON A STRING

CHAPTER 20

I awoke on Thursday morning with the same stupid grin on my face. Normally, I hate lying around in bed because of all the other things I could be doing: once I'm awake, I have to get up. But this morning was different. I had had a wonderfully refreshing sleep and did not feel tired but I wanted to relish the events of the past few days, to remember minute details vividly, such as the pattern of freckles across Marie's nose or on the tops of her shoulders, the silky smoothness of her skin under my touch, the exact colour of her eyes and eyelashes, the muscles in her back as she moved, the daintiness of her small feet, the timbre of her girlish giggles and the breathtaking sensation that swept over me every time she was near, the tingle she gave me when she kissed me, making love to her, bathing her and the fun we had had getting into and out of her suite.

I still had to pinch myself to ensure it was not a dream and that it was real. Though it was very definitely real and happening, it was like waking from a pleasurable dream after a very long succession of terrifying nightmares. Marie was mine and she loved me; she was the first woman for whom I felt anything deeper than lust. The very few girls I had known – socially and sexually – had done very little for me. Almost literally. They had been nonentities, superfluous, who began to irritate quickly – so much fluff in my cluttered world. That was almost entirely down to me and to the laziness with which I had approached previous relationships. But now everything was happy and simplified, so full of hope and all down to this one perfect woman. I knew that this was completely different from everything else I had experienced. I had been just as lazy but fate had worked hard to throw us together.

At the back of my mind was the nagging acknowledgment that tomorrow – Friday – would see us parting for an extended time. Previously, at the beginning of the week, my insecurity would have told me that the relationship was doomed to failure but I now had an inner strength borne from my deepening love for Marie Duvois.

Reluctantly, I pushed away all the stored memories and decided to get up.

* * *

As I walked to the Chorus' office, wearing a cotton short-sleeve shirt to combat the heat, jeans and deck shoes, hands thrust into pockets, I worked through some of the details for the idea to bring Gary along with Pete and me and ensuring we all faced in the same direction. Setting up our own record label was relatively simple, because it was like setting up any business. The difficulty was getting a distributor for the records once made. Also, we needed to have professional recording staff on the base – although Sir Norman would probably take over the production duties, we needed other studio staff, including engineers for the recording and studio set-up. I thought that both facets of the record label would be suitably high profile for Gary to get his teeth into and, because it was originally my idea, relinquishing some of the control to him would hopefully stop the antagonistic paranoia that he felt towards me. The idea made sense and I was grateful to Pete for the suggestion. I was hopeful that it would drag Gary and, therefore, Adrian out of the well of stupidity into which they had fallen.

When I arrived, the building was locked and empty. I let myself in and picked up the delivered mail, carried it up to the office and made myself a cup of tea in the annexe. I sat down at the Chairman's desk, having opened all the mail and pulled up a fresh piece of paper and a pen. On it, I wrote headings of things for consideration and actions to be taken in order to get the record label off the ground.

I had been working on it for about forty-five minutes with two sheets covered with lists of tasks to be done with headings and arrows linking each list together to show interdependencies. My concentration was broken by a soft knock at the door. I noted with amusement that my tea remained undrunk and was now undrinkable in its tepidity. "Come in," I said, standing up. All other thoughts dropped out of my head or were filed under 'Pending'. A surge of mixed emotions gripped me, causing my skin to prickle and unhinging my jaw.

Marie smiled, her eyes sparkling. "Well, don't I get a kiss, then?" she asked, closing her eyes and pouting her lips in readiness and leaning forward. I almost ran around the desk, put my arms around her, pecked her lips and squeezed her to me. She was wearing a halter-neck vest and a small skirt, which reached just above her knees.

"What are you doing here so early?" I asked finally, holding her away by her arms and looking into her eyes.

"The recording schedules have been changed around because of the success of recording yesterday and I thought I'd come and see my favouritest person."

She kissed me again and put a hand on my chest. "Just checking," she said, giggling, "it's beating very fast again!"

"Come on in," I said, pulling up the spare chair for her from the Secretary's desk. "Did you find the place all right?"

"No," she said and frowned a little. "I was a bit ruffled as well because I was trying to avoid a persistent journalist who insisted on following me in to the station. He wouldn't leave me alone. I got on the wrong train and ended up in somewhere called Stalbans."

"St. Albans."

"Oh! Yes, that's the one. Then I got a taxi here. Is this your desk?" I nodded and she walked around it to sit in my chair. She sat in it and leaned back, swivelling it slightly. "Very comfortable," she said, leaning on the arm-rests and arching her fingers together.

"Well I'm glad you made it here. I've missed you."

"I've missed you too, which is probably another reason why I got on the wrong train. I was thinking about you too much!"

"Coffee?"

I picked up my cooling tea, took it out to the annexe and flicked the switch on the kettle. I mused over how happy it made me to see her, earlier than expected. It had been a bit of a struggle to convince myself to do some work and now here was the perfect opportunity to avoid it. Marie was reading the binder, which held our most recent critiques and articles, as I returned with our drinks.

She took the mug from me and I sat in the spare chair. "I was just reading the one on *Tosca*," she said, taking a sip and licking her lips. "I haven't had the chance before. They seemed to like it."

"Sure did, hunny-bunny," I responded.

She wrinkled her nose. "You still haven't got a good name, have you? Still 'Marie' then." She smiled. "Why has the picture been cut off?"

"That's a long story," I replied, eyes widening in warning.

"Ah," she said, looking up excitedly, and tapping the *Tosca* review, "I didn't tell you last night, did I?"

"What about it?"

"The reason my agent rushed over here was the time limit on the new contract. It's with the Paris Opéra. The same as your Chorus."

"Excellent!" I went over and crouched beside her, hand on her thigh, and leaned up to kiss her nose, adding ruefully: "At least I'll get to see you once a year."

"And that's something else I want to discuss," she said, stroking my forearm. "England and France are so near, yet so far. What do you –?"

The conversation was interrupted by the door-handle being rattled. The door opened and in walked a cheerful Gary.

"Hello, Gary," I said, standing up with a complaining crack from my knee.

"Hello, Dave," he returned breezily, shutting the door with a carefree flourish and placed the documents he was carrying on the Secretary's desk. His mood had obviously changed and he had improved upon his most recent and frequent appearance – that of a drunken slob. In fact, he looked a lot better than the last time I had seen him a couple of days previously in the Abbey Road bar. Turning to Marie, eyes crawling over her body, he said: "And Marie. May I call you Marie? So much less formal." He squeezed past me to take Marie's hand and bent to kiss it. Patting it, he continued: "And may I say what a pleasure it is to be working with you again. I think you have a lovely voice." His eyes flashed down to Marie's chest and back to her face, as if expecting the action would go unnoticed.

"Well, thank you very much," replied Marie, smiling coyly. I was astonished: was this the Gary Adner we had come to know and not like very much? I could see what Gary was trying to do and wondered what Marie was making of it all.

"Well, this is where it all happens," Gary said, relinquishing Marie's hand and making a sweeping gesture with a careless hand at the rest of the room over his shoulder. His eyes never left Marie's figure. "No doubt David here has been telling you all about the Chorus. I run a tight ship here."

Incredulity opened my mouth but nothing came out for a moment. "Er...yes, I have. Gary, I need to have a word with you some time."

"Anything interesting?" he asked, fixated on Marie's knees.

"Only an idea or two I've had to take the record label forward."

"I'm sure I'll be able to manage," he replied and smiled at Marie, hooking a thumb over his shoulder at me. "David always gives me the difficult things because he knows I'll be able to do them effortlessly with all my experience."

"Okay," I said and went over to the other side of the desk as a protective action for Marie. "I'll catch you some other time and give you the full run-down of my thoughts so far."

"Fine," he replied and looked at his watch. "Look, I've got to go. No rest for the wicked. I've got so much to do for our American tour in a couple of weeks. Has David told you about our American trip?"

"I think he might have mentioned it," said Marie, amusement lines crinkled at the edges of her eyes.

"Well," said Gary, self-importantly, "I'm organizing it so I'm sure it will go swimmingly." He raised his eyebrows and added: "Maybe we could go for a drink tomorrow some time?"

"Maybe," replied Marie and looked at me. A stab of misplaced jealousy hit me.

"I'll see you then," he said and smiled. He patted me on the shoulder on his way out and gently closed the door behind him.

I turned to Marie. "Well, I don't know quite what to make of all that."

Marie smiled and her eyes glinted mischievously. "Is he always like that?"

"No," I confirmed, shaking my head a little in bewilderment. "I'm lost for words, to be honest. Never has my gast been so flabbered nor my ox so flummed."

Marie smiled and frowned simultaneously. "Another use of colourful English words?"

I laughed. "Yes." I crouched down beside her again and asked with disbelief: "You're not seriously thinking of taking him up on his offer of a drink tomorrow are you?"

Marie stood up and, holding the fingers of one hand with the fist of other behind her back, she walked balletically on tip-toe around the desk, occasionally glancing at me over her shoulder, tongue poking into her cheek. "What if I am?"

I opened my mouth to say something and shut it with alarm. I thought momentarily and then said: "Well, apart from the fact that I would rather enjoy that favour, he's only after you for one thing."

"So?" She stopped in front of me, smiling.

"You're not serious?" I asked, eyebrows shooting upwards with scepticism.

"Why, Mr. Loughton, I do believe you're jealous," she observed, kissed me quickly and continued her coquettish walk the other way around the desk.

"No," I retorted and scratched my head. "Well, yes, I suppose I am. But you don't know what he's like."

"Oh, I do," she smiled. "He is a creep. All that slobbering over me and looking at parts of my body only reserved for a special person and telling me how marvellous he is and putting you down." She was getting cross. "He's horrible. Very shallow."

"So you *are* a good judge of character, but –."

She stopped her walk in front of me, her hands still behind her back. "I'm glad you're jealous. It shows that I've made a great impact on you and you don't want to lose me."

"As if you needed to find out."

"True!" She kissed my cheek, put a hand on my chest, giggled and then said: "Don't worry. I want to be with you tomorrow being the last day. Do the recording, be together, have lunch with Bob. Why would I waste my time with a twit like him when I can be with you and get this response from you." She put her finger-tips over my heart.

"Come here then," I ordered.

"Gladly," she said and pressed her body against mine, her hands returned behind her back.

"Now kiss me," I added. She stood on the tips of her toes and pecked my lips. "Alright," I conceded, "I'll let you off!"

Marie put her arms around me and said, "Now, let's get back to the more serious matter of the width of *La Manche*."

"*La Manche?*"

"The English Channel is what you English so arrogantly call it. We French prefer to call it a sleeve for some strange reason."

"Good idea. But let's do it in the comfort of my house so that Gary doesn't disturb us again. I'll introduce you to Isla."

* * *

Isla took to Marie very quickly. Normally, she runs and hides from strangers but, as soon as Marie sat down, Isla jumped – or rather staggered – on to her lap. Marie grimaced slightly at the ton and a half of feline landing on her but Isla quickly settled and spread her enormous mass into a mutually comfortable position.

"She's lovely," said Marie, putting her face to Isla's head and stroking her under the chin. Isla seemed to purr more loudly at the compliment, closing her eyes in contentment, her paws stretching and closing in the ecstasy of the attention she was receiving.

"So what do you want to do for the rest of the day," I said, sitting beside Marie and stroked the top of Isla's head.

"Cuddle," she replied and gave a lopsided grin.

"Sounds good to me."

"Without our clothes on."

"Sounds even better." My heart had begun to race again.

I hoisted a mildly protesting Isla gently from Marie's lap, and settled her on a cushion on the sofa. Taking Marie's hand, I led her upstairs to the bedroom. She said: "At least I don't have to creep around trying to get to your room."

I laughed as I pushed the door to my bedroom open, showed her in and then took her in my arms for a kiss. The closeness of our bodies and the ardour it created had not diminished since the very first time.

Lying in each other's arms in post-coital bliss and peace, with the curtains shutting out the world, we tried to address the problem of our native distances. It was obvious that my career was centred primarily around London, while Marie's work was internationally based. We talked ourselves round and round in circles but could not establish any real solution that spurred agreement.

Instead, we spent the afternoon making wonderful love and being close, making each other laugh with observations on our life and the events of the previous week and simply being together. Marie had taken to putting a hand on my chest to check my heart-beat whenever I kissed her; a touching gesture and one, which I loved from the uniqueness and affectionate quality of it.

PUPPET ON A STRING

CHAPTER 21

Beth Jackson was a pretty, tall, slim, dark-haired, doe-eyed mezzo-soprano, who, since they were fellow students under Pierre Croumeux, was a close friend and *confidante* of Marie. They had been witnessed having girly huddles occasionally during rehearsals and the recording. Beth had a beautiful voice that blended perfectly with Marie's soprano and some of the best moments of the *Carmen* recording were the aria duets they sang together. She had a less physically expressive way of singing than Marie but she purveyed a similar emotion in the way that she used facial expressions. It was while Marie and I were lying in bed, the first light of dawn breaking in through the window and putting sharp edges on the black shadows around the room that she mentioned Beth's name.

"Oh, I forgot to tell you," she said suddenly and urgently, propping herself up on one elbow and slapping my chest lightly. "You know Beth Jackson?"

"Yes."

"Of course you do," she admonished herself, and then a cheeky grin came to her face as she regarded me impishly. "Well, I know something you don't."

"Which is?" I asked, raising one eyebrow.

She lay back down on the bed, staring at the ceiling, and smiled. "I'm not going to tell you."

"Right!" I said and began tickling her ribs and belly until she was shouting for mercy.

"All right! All right!" she said, hunching herself up, arms and hands in front of her body to ward off the onslaught.

"Well?" I asked, hand poised menacingly near her chest, waiting to restart the torture.

She glanced at my hand pleadingly and said: "You know your friend

Pete," she started and then, as I pretended to start tickling her again, she put out a hand to stop me and giggled: "No!"

"Yes, I know Pete. Vaguely," I grinned, hand still poised.

"They're going out together," said Marie and my hand dropped in astonishment.

"Since when?"

"Since Wednesday. Apparently, they got talking because both of them were looking for each of us and they hit it off."

Marie unhunched herself and got back into a warm embrace. "Well, I'm blowed," I said. I had recently been so wrapped up in my little world – my *big* world – that I had completely failed to notice. Even when I had been talking to him about my initial trials and tribulations and then my success with Marie, he had not mentioned anything. "This should be interesting because he doesn't know I know."

"I thought you would be intrigued," said Marie and lifted her head to kiss me, placing her hand gently in the middle of my chest. "Still working. You still like me," she said quietly and grinned.

"No, I don't," I replied and returned her grin.

She pouted and said: "You don't?"

"No, I love you," I said, planting a kiss on her nose, my ardour rising.

"Good," she responded, pulling me on top of her.

*   *   *

While I was making breakfast, Marie was in my living room, looking through my extensive record collection in one bookcase and my musical scores in the one next to it. I had a purpose-built 'music centre', which housed the latest stereophonic turntable, radio tuner and a brand new cassette tape player. She picked out a recording of *Die Fledermaus*, took the vinyl out of its dust-jacket, took the static duster, wiping it carefully around the playing surface and placed the record gently on the turntable. As the first strains of the orchestral melody wafted around the room, she put her hands on her hips, closed her eyes and took a deep breath. I placed the breakfast tray on the table and came up behind her, slipping my arms around her chest and butterfly-kissed her neck. She raised a hand to my head and murmured softly.

"I love you," she said for the fortieth time that morning and turned to kiss me, hands either side of my face and then dropped one to my chest and smiled distantly. "I'm going to miss this."

"As will I," I agreed. "So let's make the most of today. I won't go anywhere near the office this morning. We can have fun instead. Then we'll go to Bob's for lunch. On to the recording and then out for the evening."

"And then?" she asked mischievously.

"And then, we'll make love until dawn," I replied, winking.

"Until Dawn does what? Who is this Dawn woman?" she pursed her lips, frowning and broke into fluttering giggles.

I pointed at her and she responded similarly so our fingers met at the tips. "Hey! You're learning the mystical art of punnery!"

We ate breakfast, listening to Mozart, and decided to go for a walk in the mild morning air with the intention of coming back via Bob's house, just to be completely together. While I washed up, Marie put the record away and jumped a little when I cuddled her from behind. She was just putting the score for *Die Zauberflöte* back in the book-case.

"Why so jumpy?" I asked, one eyebrow raised.

"No reason," she replied, a dimple appearing on her cheek, "you'll find out."

"Intriguing," I said and kissed her. "Before we go out, I'll just give Bob a ring. See if there's anything we can bring over for him." I went into the hall and picked up the receiver, dialling Bob's number from memory and waiting as my call request clunked its way through the exchange. I let it ring twenty times but it remained unanswered. A sinking feeling plumbed the depths of my stomach, as I pressed the cut-off and dialled again. This time, with a sense of foreboding growing more intense, I let it ring thirty times, counting each ring under my breath.

Marie had sensed my concern and had put an arm around me as I gently replaced the handset in the cradle. "What's wrong?" she asked, her eyebrows knitted together with worry for me.

"I don't know," I said distantly, "there's no answer."

"He might be in the garden," she suggested, although she did not really believe it.

"I think we'll have to go round there," I said, decisively and then turned to Marie. "If that's okay with you?"

Marie smiled and hugged me. "Of course it is. You're obviously worried about him. Anyway, it's nice to see you looking after your friends."

Ten minutes later, my Mini was spewing up the gravel on Bob's driveway as I brought the car to a speedy and abrupt halt. Opening the door, I suggested to Marie that she might want to stay by the car and that I was sure that there was nothing to worry about, belied by my frown and rapid speech. She got out of her side of the car, closed the door gently and folded her arms, leaning against the front wing as she watched me knock on the door.

"Bob!" I shouted through the letter-box, when there was no answer. I rang the door-bell and knocked more frantically. I shrugged to Marie as I stepped on to the flower-bed, cupped my eyes to reduce the glare and tried to see through the net curtains at the window. "I'm going around the back," I called over my shoulder as I went round the corner of the house. I jumped up at the side-gate, hanging over it by my arms and jiggled the bolt loose to let myself through. I raced to the back-garden, shielding my eyes from the sun and called his name again, looking down the garden. It was empty. Standing on the small patio, with dread, I turned to look through the French windows and saw Bob slumped over his piano, hands on the keyboard, head resting on the music-stand. He looked as if he had fallen asleep playing the piano but I knew it was more serious than that. I pounded on the doors with a fist, shouting his name again with no response. Stepping away, I looked around for an open window or an easy access point – there was none. Taking a deep breath, I picked up a large stick from the garden and went to the back door. Shielding my eyes and face with an arm, I swung the wood gently at the window beside the door. It bounced off. I tried harder and the glass gave way, tinkling to the window ledge and floor. Tapping at the dangerous shards of glass left in the window-frame so as not to cut myself, I reached in and turned the key to unlock the door and pulled the handle down to open it. Marie had heard the commotion and had come round to see what was going on.

"He's in there but I can't raise him," I said in a determined voice, dropping the stick to the side of the alleyway.

"Come on," she urged and took my hand.

The pervasive smell of death hit us as we entered the room and I felt like gagging. Marie was wide-eyed with shock and she put a hand to her mouth. "Oh, David," she whispered.

"You don't have to do this, Marie," I said gently.

"No, I want to. He was kind to me and I know what he meant to you."

I quelled the gag reflex and approached to the piano tentatively. I could see now that he had been dead for some time, the blood pooling in the points of gravity and darkening under the skin. I gently lifted Bob from the piano to lay him on the floor, *rigor mortis* keeping him in the same position. Marie returned with a blanket to cover him and, seeing a tear drop from my eye, put a gentle and reassuring hand on my shoulder. Her eyes too were watery. Patting her hand, I stood up to go to the telephone and turned back: "Thanks, Marie."

"I didn't really do anything," she replied, a lip quivering.

"You did. Just by being here."

A tear rolled down her cheek and we embraced. I could hold back no longer and my body was wracked with sobs. A full ten minutes later, looking over at Bob's blanket-covered body, I said: "I must make that 'phone call." I looked back at Marie, her face pretty with the tears and added: "I'm sorry, I've messed up your T-shirt."

She glanced at the damp patch on her shoulder and smiled forlornly. "That doesn't matter. The point is that you needed to do that. You are more important than a silly old shirt. Do you feel okay?"

"I do. Thank you, my darling. You are a tower of strength." I kissed her nose and then said decisively: "Right. Let's get this sorted out. I'll 'phone the police."

Ten minutes later, blue lights strobed the front of the house. Police panda cars, an ambulance and a funeral director's van were jostled haphazardly on Bob's driveway. The detective in a dirty, brown raincoat asked me a few questions as to how I had come across the body and I showed him the back door, with the side panel of glass broken and also told him that Bob had been in Western General with a stroke the week before and that he had been of ill-health for several years. Any possible hint of suspicion he might have had fell from his questions as this information was imparted. Marie and I watched the proceedings numbly, she hugging my waist with her head on my shoulder and I with my arms around her slightly trembling shoulders. We saw Bob's body-bag-covered body brought out on a stretcher and put into the funeral director's van and we bowed in silent contemplation. The ambulance switched off its lights and backed down the driveway empty. It was as if the whole process had taken on an unreal, gauzy quality about it. We stayed until the funeral director had left and had been given clearance to do so by the police. Tears were brimming in my eyes again and I saw that Marie had been crying softly too.

* * *

We arrived at St. John's Wood later than anticipated and were met at the foot of the Abbey Road steps by popping flashguns and an inarticulate reporter, asking impertinent questions about our relationship. In no mood to ride this out because of what we had just experienced, I pushed through and waved them tersely aside and guided Marie up the steps to the relative security of the entrance hall.

"Are you alright?" I asked gently, lifting her chin with a finger.

"I'm fine, David. I'm more worried about you." A tear rolled down her cheek.

Taking out a handkerchief and dabbing her cheek, I replied: "I'm okay. Honestly. I think I'm over the shock now. I'm sure grief will hit me at some point but I have a job to do. I need to let Sir Norman know." I kissed her forehead and she hugged me. Marie left me to find her place as we entered the studio. I diverted to the control booth.

"David!" exclaimed Sir Norman, "you look as if you have seen a ghost!"

"Not quite," I replied, tight-lipped with effort of covering up my latter propensity to break down.

"Whatever's the matter?" he asked, concerned and got up.

I gestured for him to sit down again, which he did slowly. "It's Bob Holden. I'm afraid he died last night."

Sir Norman frowned and slumped a little, shaking his head. "Oh, poor sod."

I was surprised – I had never heard Sir Norman use any colourful language before. "Heart attack, they reckon. I had to break in this morning and found him slumped over the piano, rehearsing for today's session."

"You poor boy. At the risk of sounding cliché, it is the way that he would have wanted to go."

"That's what Marie said, too. She was with me."

Sir Norman smiled for the first time and said: "You've got a good woman there."

"I wouldn't want any other," I replied, attempting to smile. The nervous energy expended in the past couple of hours had left me feeling suddenly drained. "Anyway, I do feel partly to blame because I agreed that he could take part in this."

"I should think that he would have known what he was doing. He was a surprisingly lonely man, given his sunny nature and friendliness. Music was really his only joy. That and his beloved garden, of course. He would have done himself much more harm if you had barred him from coming along. It was the right decision." Sir Norman mused momentarily before continuing: "It's amazing how quickly one lapses into the past tense, isn't it? Anyway, don't worry. I'm convinced that you did right by him."

"Hmm," I responded doubtfully and paused. "On a business footing, however, we need to find a new section manager to replace Bob. But, for now, I'll find someone to stand in temporarily – Mike Shedson maybe – and hold the election at a later date."

"Good." Sir Norman nodded his approval.

"And I'd like to send a wreath to Bob's funeral from the Chorus."

"Are you going to attend?"

"I am."

Sir Norman, puffed his cheeks out in a sigh, straightened up and took a deep breath. "On a lighter note, courtesy of Christoph Schmidt, since we have been so successful in getting the whole opera in the can in a shorter time than planned, the Chorus committee, the soloists and I are invited to a slap-up feast tonight."

"Excellent!" I brightened a little. "Anywhere in particular?"

"He suggested that Chinese restaurant in Leicester Square. It's got quite a good critique in the Good Food Guide."

"Wonderful."

There was another long pause, Sir Norman reflecting on what I had told him. He looked up quickly and said: "Oh, and by the way, I've had that long overdue chat with Gary. I think, because he couldn't back-chat me, he's promised to mend the error of his ways."

"So that's why he seemed so different yesterday. You can't believe what a relief that is on top of everything else going on. Thanks."

"No problem. And let me know if he still tries any strong arm tactics again and I'll endeavour to sort him out."

"Thank you, Sir Norman," I said, opening the door and bowing a little in reverence and gratitude, "I'll see you at the meal."

As I made my way to my seat, I noticed Marie and Beth talking and was relieved to hear her laughing a little. After the heightened emotions earlier in the week, the sudden roller-coaster ride to the other end of the spectrum worried me with the effect it might have on her. Of course, she was inwardly strong and had shown that she could take these things in her stride. She turned as I sidled past a dead double-bass and I waved, smiling. She waggled her fingers just once and returned a warm smile, one eyebrow raised. I nodded that I was alright and she relaxed.

Pete stood up as I attained my seat. "Dave, what's this Beth and Marie tell me about Bob?" His eyebrows were pressed together tightly in concern. "Is it true?"

"I'm afraid it is Pete. I had to break in and found him at the piano. He had obviously been there for a long time."

"Poor old Bob," said Pete sitting slowly and looked at the floor.

"I've just spoken with Sir Norman. He said that, a bit of a cliché, but he went out the way he would have wanted. I just hope he wasn't in too much pain or scared with no-one there with him."

"He invited me and Beth to lunch there tomorrow." He shook his head in disbelief and paused in reflection.

"Which reminds me," I said, lightening a little. "You're a dark horse!"

"Anna Sewell!" said Pete, pointing and smiling.

I frowned and then tutted and laughed. "Yep. Black Beauty. I get it."

"Why do you say that anyway?" Pete sat on his hands and raised his eyebrows knowingly.

"You and Beth! When did that happen?"

"Well, I was getting so heartily ill from your lovesick nonsense that it obviously rubbed off in some way on me." He grinned. "It was Tuesday, I think. I was looking for you and she was looking for Marie. Anyway, we fell to talking about how you two were crowding us out" – he winked – "and it just kind of happened. We realized we had a lot in common, I asked her out for a meal and it went on from there."

"And have you...?" I asked, finger across lips, mimicking his questioning stance back in Paris the morning after the meal out with Marie.

"I'm too much of a gentleman to tell you," he replied, blushing.

"No you're not," I grinned. "So you have then."

Pete raised his eyes heavenwards and resolutely refused to say anything, a smirk appearing on his lips.

"Maybe when Marie's back in this country again, Beth and you can join us and we can go out on the town."

"What? Foursome?"

"Only if we have to but I'd prefer it to be voluntary."

Pete thought for a moment and then let out a wild laugh, clamping his hand over his mouth as the studio meerkats swung their heads in our direction.

"I've told you about that before," I admonished, pointing a finger and then frowned. "Or was that me?"

* * *

While I had been dealing with Bob's body and the practicalities of the inevitable funeral that lunch-time, Gary, with his new-found professionalism after his talk with Sir Norman (his words and not mine), decided that he needed to find out more details about the American tour. I was glad, when Pete told me what follows, that Gary had bucked his ideas up and wanted to wrest control of the tour back from Adrian. However, I am certain that the descriptions he gave Pete might have been embellished so I have toned it down a little, where I think that exaggeration has happened. I include it here to assist the narrative and to help the reader understand how things might have reached the head they did. There is also the slight discrepancy of the change of attitude since I had last witnessed Gary and Adrian together, although the newfound lease of life in Gary could possibly mean that the blinkers were off.

I do not believe, either, that he regretted the actions of the past couple of weeks but, whatever Sir Norman had said to him, he had obviously taken the criticism and was now charged with a little more energy. At that point, I was willing not to dwell on some of the issues and let bygones be bygones, let sleeping dogs lie and other appropriate platitudes, provided he continued his renewed approach to the Chorus with the same vigour.

Gary had found Adrian in the studio bar, sitting on his own in the corner, staring into space and taking melancholic sips from his glass of lemonade. Adrian was a very proficient and efficient worker but he lacked the personality and leadership qualities to tell someone else to sling their hook, if his toes were being stepped on. The same applied to Gary to a lesser extent, which goes some way to explaining why their conversations so often degenerated into childish name-calling and mud-slinging. Adrian's way of dealing with this was to draw everything ever closer to his chest; Gary's method was to hit out verbally and physically at the nearest thing.

"How's America, Adrian?" Gary asked, silently walking up to Adrian's table, and folded his arms as he sat down.

Adrian jumped, startled out of his reverie. "Why?" he asked, carefully putting his drink down on the table.

"Because," said Gary, condescendingly, "it might have escaped your notice but I'm supposed to be managing the tour. Remember?"

"Where does that leave me, then?"

"Oh, you're co-ordinating the logistics but I'm controlling it. There's a subtle difference."

"Which is that you want to be in a position to take all the credit," Adrian sneered, folding his arms defensively and pouted.

"God, Adrian," patronized Gary, "you can be so petty sometimes." He had started talking quickly, which was an indication that he was on the verge of losing his temper. "Dave Loughton was right about you."

Adrian looked up sharply. "What does that mean? What did he say?"

"He says that you're nothing but a baby when you can't get your own way and that he is getting to the end of his tether with your petty attitude and that he might consider banning you from the Tour." Cruelly, Gary had latched on to his sensitivity and was sticking knives into the very heart of what Adrian cared about and was twisting them.

Adrian's bottom lip quivered a little and he stammered: "But, he can't." He unfolded his arms and leaned forward.

"He can and he will if you're not careful. So, just tell me what's happening."

Adrian regarded Gary carefully before slumping back in his seat with a petulant frown. "It's going all right. Not much to tell really."

"Come on," said Gary, animatedly waving his hand around. "It's being staged in three weeks and you're telling me nothing's happened?" Gary flicked open his packet of cigarettes and jabbed one between his lips without lighting it, imploring Adrian to answer him.

"No," countered Adrian, "of course not. I didn't say that at all. Loads of things have happened."

"Ah! Like what?" The cigarette was dancing as he spoke.

"Just things that you don't..." Adrian broke off and rounded viciously on Gary, hissing: "Look, why can't you and bloody Loughton leave me to get on with things in peace and in my own way?"

"No way. I've been far too lax with you. I've had so much to do with this bloody recording that I haven't had a chance to check up on you."

"It's all in hand," said Adrian finally and stared fixedly at a point on the floor, breathing heavily.

"Adrian!" Gary was raising his voice, losing a battle to keep what was left of his temper. "I am going to give you one last chance. Now, I'm not going to ask you the question again. Would you like me to leave you at the mercy of Loughton?"

"All right," snapped back Adrian. He began counting off each item on his fingers as if he were talking to someone who was having difficulty understanding the English language. "I've sorted out the travel. I've sorted out the visas. I've made sure that everyone has a valid passport. I've crated up the wardrobe contents. I've organized its shipment and

I've ordered a few extra props. Now I'm organizing the rehearsals for next week with Sir Norman."

Gary pursed his lips, became aware that the unlit cigarette dangling from them probably looked stupid and removed it. "Now, that wasn't too hard, was it? So, what about the programmes? I seem to remember you mentioning that in one of your cosy chats with Norm."

Adrian looked a little taken off-guard and responded quickly, eyes darting around the bar but not looking at Gary at all. "Still being sorted out."

"Anything else you feel you ought to tell me?" The cigarette was back between Gary's lips, and he cocked his head, closing one eye to avoid the smoke as he lit it up. He snapped the cigarette lighter shut, took a deep drag and sat back folding his legs, squinting at Adrian.

"No," said Adrian finally.

"Are you sure?"

"Yes," replied Adrian, some of his composure settling back in. "Now get off my back."

"All right, all right," surrendered Gary, holding his hands out to ward off Adrian's evil spirits. "I was only asking." He leaned forward, tapping ash from the tip into an ash-tray and looked Adrian directly in the eye, holding his gaze. "But from now on, I want you to tell me everything as it happens."

"Of course."

"And no more sly talks to Norm. You come through me from now on, now that I've got more time."

"Why?" said Adrian suddenly and guiltily. "Why should I?"

"Because I don't want you to ingratiate yourself with him any more than you have already. It's not healthy."

"I hate you," spat Adrian.

Gary stood up, picking up his cigarettes and lighter, and pointed an admonishing finger at Adrian. "Now, now, be a good boy or I won't hold Loughton back from sacking you outright. He's just looking for an opportunity."

Before he could respond, Gary stalked away, a manic grin etched on his features, leaving Adrian to fume in his seat, breathing heavily and clenching his jaws together in perturbation.

* * *

The first part of the session sounded very ropey. Maybe it was because my heart was not totally in it or that I was unable to concentrate as much as would normally be expected. I was relieved to watch the clock hands inch their way up to the designated break time. As soon as we had been released, Adrian scuttled off to the control booth like a rat down a sewer. Pete was the first to notice and pointed the fact out to Gary.

Gary screwed up his face as if in deep pain. "Oh, no!" he said wearily. "Now where's he going? I told him to do things through me from now on."

"Calm down," I said, testing the waters, "your stomach ulcer is not scheduled for another ten years."

To my relief, Gary returned my smile and said: "True. Ah, well. Suppose I'd better see what the old goat is up to." He sighed heavily and dropped sullenly from the platform, made his way past Marie, pausing to stoop and kiss her hand – I smiled as she turned to me, stuck her tongue out, grimaced and shook her hand as if something dirty had latched itself on to it – and meandered to the control booth.

Sir Norman was none too pleased with Adrian's interruption either, judging from the way that he was massaging his head while leaning on an elbow against the desk. Sir Norman had confided to me that, while Adrian was useful, at the same time, he was also sometimes exceptionally annoying and tiresome.

Adrian had handed Sir Norman a sheaf of papers from an envelope. "So what do you want me to do with these, Adrian?" said Sir Norman, leafing through them, scarcely hiding his irritation.

"These are the proofs of the personnel pages of the New York Met. programme. The colour is going to be burgundy, by the way. I need to ensure that everyone's name has been spelled correctly and I need it by next rehearsal."

"And why can't you do it?"

"I won't be there."

"Chorus business, I hope."

"Er...no. Not entirely."

"What about the Chairman? Or Gary?"

Adrian faltered for a second, his crafty eyes darting around again. "Er... I don't think they want to be tied down by such mediocrities."

"And you think I do?"

"I'm sorry, Sir Norman, I didn't mean it like that." He paused momentarily. "Basically, Gary asked me to ask you." Adrian was triumphant in his lie.

"Did he?" Sir Norman's eyebrows rippled in surprise and thought, rubbing his chin. "All right. I'll do it."

"Thanks, Sir Norman," said Adrian, gratefully and relaxed. "Now, I wondered whether I should start up attendance registers to monitor who is and who isn't doing the rehearsals."

"Surely, Gary has his attendance sheets. Will we gain anything having another system operating?"

Adrian thought quickly. "Gary's sheets are really to ascertain who should be paid what. These registers would be used to ensure enough time is spent on such a prestigious performance."

Sir Norman sighed and waved the discussion away. "Whatever you say." He paused, considering whether to continue. "Adrian, you seem to me to be a very thorough and keen sort of a chap. Particularly on the administrative side."

Adrian nodded on receipt of such high praise and smiled, puffing out his chest.

"Unfortunately, Bob Holden died last night. Did you know?"

"No, I didn't," replied Adrian, still smiling, guessing what was coming next. "Poor old Bob." Insincerity oozed out of every pore.

"So, we need a replacement. David is going to ask Mike Shedson to stand in, as he is the deputy until the elections can be organized. Now, I think that you could probably stand and would be good in that job. Would you have enough capacity to take on that role as well as the wardrobe manager, do you think?"

"Yes, I'd love to."

Sir Norman put up a warning finger. "Now, don't jump the gun. I'm not appointing you. There will be an election. And if you are lucky enough to get the rôle, it might just stop the infighting that has been going on between you two. The only reason I'm asking you to stand is that I think it is ridiculous with you and Gary duplicating so many tasks, when he is quite capable of doing it himself."

"Oh!" Adrian came up short, surprised by Sir Norman's explanation and frowned. "Well, what about America."

Sir Norman waved that aside, irritated. "Oh, finish that. We won't be having an election until we get back anyway. So, can you tell the other tenors – see who else would like to stand?"

"Of course," replied Adrian, eyes ferreting the control booth again.

"Has David told you about this evening's shindig?"

"Yes."

"I'll see you there, then," replied Sir Norman, firmly, returning to his recording notes, effectively dismissing Adrian.

Adrian retreated at exactly the point when Gary came in. Their eyes locked momentarily, before Adrian broke off to leave. Gary interrupted Sir Norman. "What's he been up to? He looks like a guilty weasel."

"Oh, something to do with the programme proofs for the New York Met.," Sir Norman sighed, indicating the sheaf of papers on the mixing desk with a carefree wave. "He wanted me to sort them out as he won't be there at the next rehearsal."

Gary squinted a little in confusion. "Can I have them? The proofs?"

"Gladly," said Sir Norman as Gary picked them up. "But I do not want it to lead to any arguments. Understood. Remember what I said the other day?"

"No, of course not," replied Gary, piqued at the very suggestion.

"I can already see something brewing because he told me you asked him to give those to me. You end it here. Is that understood?"

"Yes," responded Gary meekly.

"Right," nodded Sir Norman, taking out a handkerchief and unfolding it. "In an attempt to alleviate this problem you two have, I've asked him to stand as tenor section manager."

"Have you now?"

"Yes," Sir Norman said firmly, glancing up at Gary. "I have. And I've also asked him to inform the other tenors. I want it to have some pretence at democracy." He blew his nose sharply and dabbed at it with the bunched handkerchief, while he peered over the top of his glasses at his notes.

Summarily dismissed, Gary turned on his heel and muttered: "Maybe that will get him off my case."

* * *

While Gary wandered back from the control booth, I suggested to Pete that we talk to Marie and Beth and work out how we were going to get together as a group. Pete was just about to step down, when Gary caught him by the arm, refusing to let go, until I was out of earshot. Pete suggested that he would catch me up and I nodded warily.

Talking very quickly but earnestly at as low a volume as he could muster, Gary said: "I don't believe that bloody Adrian." He wafted the programme proofs angrily.

"Adrian?" asked Pete, hands on hips. "Why? What's Adrian done now?"

Gary's eyes bulged on the point of apoplexy. "Adrian...Adrian bloody Hilton has... Well look at this." He thrust the papers at Pete.

"'Chairman: David Loughton'," read Pete. "'Chorus Master: Sir Norman Pettinger; Secretary:...'" He looked up at Gary and shook his head. "Oh, dear! Oh, dear, oh dear! He has gone a little too far, hasn't he?"

"What bloody right...?" exploded Gary as quietly as he could, although several people were already looking in his direction. "I'm not having this. He needs sorting out."

"He certainly does remind me of a tin-pot general. Slowly but surely, he appears to be staging a military coup. But Gary –."

"Stalin had nothing on this guy," spat Gary, taking a red pen from his inside jacket pocket and obliterated Adrian's name after 'Secretary:' with several deep lines, cutting through the paper and substituted it with his own. He paused on writing the word 'assistant' and scrubbed that out too. "And I'm not even going to put his name in. How dare he?"

"So what you are going to do?"

"No idea. Yet. If bloody Loughton" – Pete raised his eyes in mild exasperation – "hadn't spent so much energy trying to subvert what I've been trying to achieve, I might have had a better chance at keeping Hilton under control. Did you know that Sir Norman has asked him to stand as Tenor Section Manager?"

"You're joking!" exclaimed Pete, wary that this might be one of Gary's fishing trips and he did not want to get hooked. "Gary, just be careful with what you're doing. Remember what Sir Norman said to you."

"How did you know about that?" Gary whirled around on Pete, danger flashing in his eyes.

Pete held out a placatory hand. "You told me about it in the pub the other night. Several times. You were very drunk."

"I was not drunk. I...had a cold coming on, that was all." Gary shrugged the lie on and felt that it fitted his version of the truth well. "Anyway, I only hope Norm isn't going senile. He'd better know what he's doing. And I'll bet Hilton doesn't tell the other tenors."

"Well, we can at least sort that out. Let's discuss it over a drink after the session. Right now, I need to talk to Beth."

"Oh, no," whined Gary, screwing up his face as if in pain. "Not another one with ideas above his station."

Pete was not smiling and simply raised one eyebrow. After a pause, he said: "Get used to it!"

* * *

The remainder of the session was a struggle but, nevertheless, we completed within the time necessary. Still, my heart was not in it. Not only had I lost a mentor today but, tomorrow, I would also be losing a significant part of my life to the other side of the English Channel.

The soloists, Sir Norman, the Chairman and the other dignitaries of the orchestra, Christoph Schmidt and the members of the *Coro di Londinium* committee made their way to Leicester Square for the celebratory meal nonetheless. The sombre mood was lifting slightly as we were shown to our seats. Each table was a huge circular affair, with a smaller circular raised surface in the middle, which revolved – the idea was to place the ordered food on to this surface and turn it so that the distant dinner companions on the other side of the table could partake without passing it from hand to hand. Given the number of dishes and the size of the table, this was a very efficient idea.

Gary had organized the seating plan and, as directed to do so, Marie and Beth sat down at chairs separated by one empty chair. As he was dictating where others should sit (Sir Norman to the left of Marie, Pete to the right of Beth and me over the other side of the table), I took my opportunity and placed myself between Marie and Beth, winking slightly at Pete.

"Dave!" whined Gary, "I'm supposed to be sitting there."

"Ah, not to worry, Gary," chipped in Marie. "Maybe another time."

Gary opened his mouth and shut it again quickly. Marie gave him one of her best smiles and he stalked off to take the seat originally intended for me, scowling at me over the large menu.

"Are you sure you wouldn't have preferred to sit next to your ardent admirer?" I asked, sticking my tongue out slightly.

"I am," she replied, taking my hand under the table and pecking my cheek. She placed a quick hand on my chest and nodded.

Gary's scowl had turned to frustrated jealousy and he folded his arms sulkily. By the time the first courses had arrived, he had quaffed sufficient quantities of free beer and wine for it no longer to bother him. Adrian, on the other hand, seated between Christoph Schmidt and Sir Norman, tried to engage Sir Norman in conversation several times but was met with polite but short answers, since Sir Norman had been talking effusively with Marie every time he interrupted. Eventually, Adrian, too, slipped into a sullen silence, leaning on the table and looking into the Chinese spicy sauce slick on his plate, his food largely untouched.

Beth turned to me and asked: "Pete tells me that you suggested getting together, the four of us?"

"I did at that," I acknowledged and smiled. "I thought it might be nice as we are all friends. Enjoy more of each other's company and the like. What do you think?"

"A great idea. But probably not before Marie goes back to France tomorrow. We wouldn't want to get in your way."

"If you know what we mean!" added Pete, raising his eyebrows quickly in Groucho Marx style.

Marie and I laughed. Pink flushes rose on her cheeks. "That's very considerate. So any suggestions?" I looked at Marie and then back to Beth and Pete.

Pete snapped his fingers. "Hey, just thought. Why don't we arrange a holiday together? Get away from this madness."

I looked at Marie. "You up for it?"

Marie's eyes sparkled with a sense of fun. "Of course."

I slapped the table lightly. "Gone. Sold to the delectable ladies in the Chinese restaurant."

The conversation turned to Marie's return journey home. I was desperately trying to fight the melancholy before Marie left the next day. Beth asked: "How are you two going to manage to get to see each other. I mean, it's easy for Pete and me as we live near other."

"Well, 'near' in the sense that we are the opposite sides of London," added Pete, which earned a smiling frown and a light slap on his arm from Beth. He pretended to be in great pain as Beth deliberately turned away from him, still smiling. I could see that the two of them were enjoying a similarly passionate love affair as us.

"It's something we need to sort out," I replied and looked at Marie, who linked her arm through mine and rested her head on my shoulder momentarily.

"And soon," she added, wistfully. She rested her elbows on the table, lacing her fingers and continued: "But don't let us think about that now. Where will we go for this holiday?"

The four of us carried on talking about the holiday and swapping anecdotes, now almost completely oblivious of the rest of the table.

Steaming dishes of Chinese cuisine flashed past us on the Lazy Susan and returned almost empty, the glasses in front of us remained half-drunk. I completely failed to notice the flashes of hatred, jealousy anger and retribution from both Gary and Adrian and, at that moment, I would have cared even less were I aware of them. As far as I was concerned, Sir Norman had had them both under control and would exert his influence as necessary to keep it that way.

PUPPET ON A STRING

CHAPTER 22

At the end of the meal, the four of us had got up together. I shook hands with Torchev, Estente and Christoph Schmidt and worked my way around Sir Norman and the members of the Committee. I stopped at Adrian, proffering my hand. His response was to sneer, resolutely sticking his hands deep into his jacket pockets. I shrugged with the out-held hand and said: "Good night, then, Adrian."

"You have no power over me!" he said quietly. His features contorted momentarily in disgust before he ignored me with a dismissive hand to talk to Sir Norman.

I looked at Pete and raised a questioning eyebrow. He shrugged a little and then indicated that he would update me later. I tried the same with Gary, who was a bit more civil, taking my hand quickly, shaking it once. He then moved off to Beth and Marie, showering them with oleaginous effluent, leaning into them as he spoke. It was quite amusing to watch both of them recoil slightly, resisting the temptation to back off a few paces to regain their comfort space. "What do you think he's saying to them?" I asked Pete quietly.

Pete had a worried look on his face that I had not seen before. "I don't know. I just hope that Gary doesn't try to take Beth away from me. I know she wouldn't go with him but it's the jealousy thing. You know what he's like."

I held his shoulder. "Only too well! I wouldn't worry, Pete. I went through the same with Marie. But, look, she can barely disguise her discomfort with his treatment."

Pete laughed a little in an embarrassed and reassured way. "You're right. It's just that I think I've found my soul-mate. Beth is…perfect."

"I hate to tell you that she isn't, Pete."

The worried look was back. "Why? What do you mean?"

"Well, look at it this way. Marie is perfect and Beth standing next to her, you must be able to see it. Almost perfect."

Pete's face softened and he punched me playfully on the shoulder. "My Dad's bigger than your Dad."

I laughed and folded my arms, looking back towards Gary and our girlfriends: "So, what do you think he's saying?"

Pete frowned and put his hands in his back trouser pockets. "I am absolutely wonderful," he suggested, adding the slight 'cheeky chappy' Cockney accent that Gary liked to employ. "You are wasting time with those two losers. I can take you both on at the same time."

I was a little shocked and laughed out loud, causing Gary to turn around, which made my attempts not to laugh even more difficult. "I asked what he was saying not what your impression of him was!"

"What's the matter?" asked Gary, returning back to us. It was obvious that we had been talking about him and that I was laughing at him.

Pete came to my rescue. "We were just talking about Adrian and his attempts at taking over."

I looked sharply at Pete but left it there. "Yes. I hadn't thought that he could be so underhand," I guessed correctly.

"Yeah. Bastard!" retorted Gary, before adding quickly with a sickly leer: "But I'm sure you'll take him in hand."

"Yes, I will," I agreed keeping the timbre of my voice somewhat jocular. "Now, we must go," I said, turning to Pete, "see you tomorrow Gary."

The four of us walked together to the station, Pete and Beth behind Marie and me. They departed for Beth's house in the leafy Surrey suburb of Cobham. I shook Pete's hand and kissed Beth's cheek. Marie and Beth embraced and gave each other a Gallic kiss. Holding hands, Beth said to Marie: "You must tell us when you're next back in this country, so that we can get together. Plan the holiday."

"I will, Beth," said Marie. "I want to get our living arrangements sorted out soon, too, so we can get together more regularly." I raised my eyebrows and Marie added: "David and I are talking about that later." She took my arm.

We arrived back at my house at ten o'clock and I checked around the side of the house. We had arranged for all of Marie's luggage to be sent on, principally so that we had as much time together as possible in the next few hours but also to avoid the growing paparazoid group camping outside the hotel just to get a glimpse of her.

Moments later, we were in my bedroom, naked and making love with an urgency that we had not experienced since the first night we had slept together. The exquisite climactic joy swept over me followed quickly by Marie gasping in orgasm. We rolled on to our sides and she placed a hand over the trip-hammer in my chest and smiled sweetly. "I seem to have had an even bigger impact on you tonight."

I smiled and cuddled her closer to me, her soft skin pressing against mine, knowing that soon I would be lying in this bed alone with none of these lovely sensations available to me. The nervous energy expended during the day, especially with the aftershock of finding Bob turning the day upside down and then getting back on with life had meant that we both had some very strong emotions to manage – I think this was why we had so passionately and frenetically enjoyed our coupling.

Very soon, we were making love a lot more slowly, drinking in the pleasure and ecstasy of our closeness. With Marie on top of me, I stroked her supple body, almost in tears at her beauty and my inherent physical and emotional need for her.

"I'll miss this," said Marie, nestling into my neck afterwards.

"I will too," I responded quietly, stroking the arm lying across my chest.

"You make me feel complete, Mr. Loughton. I love you."

"I love you, Marie."

She looked up. "I like it when you use my name."

"What do you mean?"

"I think it's nice when someone uses your name occasionally, rather than leaving it off or replacing it with some other term of endearment."

"Which reminds me: I still haven't come up with a suitable love-name, have I?"

Her eyes twinkled again as she pointed a finger towards my ribs. "Just be careful."

"How about 'angel bum'?" I yelped as a finger dug in. "'Passion-flower'? Ah! 'Hot sex goddess'?" Her eyes widened and her mouth opened and she began tickling me until I was begging for mercy. "Okay, okay. No more."

"Well?"

"How about 'sweetheart'?"

The poised finger dropped and she nodded. "Actually, I quite like that one."

"I'm relieved."

She repositioned herself cuddling into my neck and said: "Where do you think we ought to live."

"Pardon?" I was a bit taken aback.

"I hope you don't think this is too forward of me but, rather than look for a separate house or houses nearer to each other, why don't we just buy a house together?"

With no warning, a tear came to my eye and for a moment I could not speak, with the secret knowledge of what I had planned for the next day and how I was going to engineer it. This was perfectly in line with my aspiration but the reason why I was so choked at that moment was because the suggestion had come from Marie.

Marie got up on one elbow and was really worried. "David? I haven't said the wrong thing, have I? I didn't mean to take this too quickly, if that's what you are worried about."

I simply placed her hand on my chest and kissed her forehead. My heart was up to marathon speed again. "You are not taking this too quickly, Marie. I love you more than I can express…as you can tell from what you have done to my pulse-rate."

"I don't understand," said Marie, a little relieved but still confused.

"I have something I want to talk to you about tomorrow but, to answer your question, I think it's a fantastic idea. It's something I wanted to raise but was concerned that you might not be so…" I floundered to find the right words.

"Up for it?" suggested Marie, mimicking a Cockney accent à la Dick van Dyke, and we laughed.

"That's it. So, where does that leave us?"

"I've given this quite a bit of thought. Given that I can speak English fluently and given that your career is currently located around London mainly, it makes sense that we buy a house in this country. I can keep my Parisian apartment for when I have engagements there. What do you think?"

"I think it's marvellous. You really are a sweetheart!" I kissed her on the lips and looked into those achingly beautiful eyes. "On Sunday, I'll do some investigation on properties."

"I love you, Mr. Loughton," said Marie, kissing me fervently on the chin, lips and chest. Before long, we were making love again and, afterwards, we dropped into a very deep and restful sleep.

* * *

The concern that I had felt prior to the night before had trickled away following our discussion. I knew that she was serious about our relationship to the point of joint-owning a property and I loved her even more for making that decision rather than waiting for me to skirt around the question, as was my wont.

We lay in bed until mid-morning, before Marie got up to shower and get ready for the flight back to Paris. She was wearing the same blue dress that she had worn all those days ago back in Paris when all I was expecting of her was an autograph. I drove her to London Airport, parking in the short stay car park to see her to her gate. Although I was sad to see her go, I was already looking forward even more to her return.

Checking in her bags, she turned to me and said: "I thought you said you wanted to talk to me about something."

"Did I?" I smiled in pretence of innocence.

"Well, I've been waiting all morning and, while we talked a little more about houses and seeing each other next, there was nothing." She suddenly looked worried. "Unless that was it. When we were going to see each other."

I smiled and said quietly: "No." I took her gently by the arms and stroked her shoulders.

She relaxed and said: "So what was it?"

We were on the concourse, making our way to the departure gate. Strangely, for once, there were no pressmen following Marie. Several travellers were milling around, rushing for their gates or to the check-in desks, others were sitting bored on the provided chairs. I reached into a pocket and with fist closed and held out, I dropped to one knee in front of Marie. She let out a small exclamation, covering her mouth with her right hand and I took hold of the other gently.

"Marie, I love you dearly," I said, looking up into her eyes and unfurling my hand to reveal a gold ring, with three diamonds at the top, the central one slightly larger than its neighbours. "And while we have only known each other for a relatively short period of time," I continued, watching a tear appearing in her eye, "I would like to ask you to do me the great honour of becoming my wife."

Marie let out a couple of sobs, still covering her mouth. Shakily, she extended the fingers of her left hand for me to place the ring on it. "Yes," she said simply, tears rolling down her cheeks. "Oh, yes!"

There was a round of applause from several travellers who had stopped to watch this spectacle, as I placed the perfectly fitting ring on her trembling ring finger. I stood up and she embraced me hard, jumping up and down a little on the spot. "I love you. I love you. I love you." We parted and she looked at the ring. "It's gorgeous. How did you know my size?"

"I didn't," I conceded. "It's my mother's and I always promised that I would give it to the girl I wanted to marry. I'm glad it fits."

She looked in my eyes and then kissed me on the kips passionately, standing on tip-toes. "Mrs. David Loughton," she said dreamily and, sniffing a little, she smiled. "I think I can get very used to that."

Our audience had moved on as we held each other. At length, we agreed that Marie needed to get to her gate. Having obtained her boarding-pass, we embraced and kissed again. Tears were rolling down her face again, although she had a permanent grin too, that pretty dimple showing in her cheek. "I'll see you again soon," she said, "husband-in-waiting!"

It felt like I had just walked painlessly into a brick wall! I had not thought of my proposal in that way and a warm feeling rippled down my spine, etching a greater smile on my face than before. She released my hand and turned a couple of times as she made her way down the gantry towards the plane.

Through the long expanse of window in the terminal, looking out over the departure gates and runways, I watched her board the flight, saw the plane take off and continued looking into the blue sky long after it had disappeared to a feint dot.

* * *

Later on, although worried about listlessness brought on by the reduced proximity of my fiancée – my fiancée! – I had found that her acceptance of my betrothal had given me an unexpected burst of energy. Instead of moping around the house, I had telephoned Pete to suggest a lunch date next day and that I had something important to tell him. The rest of the day would be given over to private practice of the Mozart for the upcoming American trip.

Taking out *Die Zauberflöte* from the musical score bookshelf, I opened it and an envelope fluttered out, with my name on the front written in Marie's handwriting.

My dearest David,

Thank you very much for the best week of my life (so far!). In fact, whenever I think of the waiter in that steak restaurant or the desk-clerk in the hotel, I will think of you and the laughter that we shared.

I will be missing you so much and I will keep thinking of you. I will miss the softness of your skin against mine as we cuddle up at night and the immense passion you bring out in me and that we share and I know that I will not sleep as well without you.

You are the first man (of the few) that I have gone out with, who actually cares and wants me for me and not just to go to bed with me (and this week has taught me just what I have been missing!). It is very rare to feel so protected as you protect me; to feel so loved as you love me; to feel so safe as I do with you.

I just wanted to give you something to help you when you are feeling lonely. I know we'll meet up soon but it's not the same when we are apart.

You are a truly wonderful man and I want to spend the rest of my life with you. That may be a little forward but I hope that we will have agreed that we will at least live near each other by the time you read this.

I spoke with Uncle Charles (sorry, 'Sir Charles Minton', as you prefer to call him) about you the other night and he is very keen to meet the wonderful man who has (literally!) swept me off my feet; the man of my dreams. (I also told him about your interest in singing solo and he agreed to hear you some time!)

This week has truly been a whirlwind of emotions (all good ones) and I thank you for persevering with me, when I appeared to try to turn you off. I'm glad you saw me through that – the last few days have been so special.

All my love and more,
Marie
x x x x x

P.S. I want you to imagine me pressing my hand against your chest when receiving the above kisses.

PUPPET ON A STRING

CHAPTER 23

On the Sunday, I awoke in agitation and feeling disconcerted. The old adage of feeling as if a limb has been removed when someone very close is no longer present did not quite describe the empty but nonetheless full feeling I had. The emptiness, of course, was due to Marie not cuddling with me on waking up and that we could not have a conversation; the fullness was owed to the experiences of the last few days – in a sequence of just five days, I had moved from agonizing with paranoia to having a fiancée. An extraordinary shift and some would say too quick but the feelings I had for Marie were so very strong, I knew it was nowhere near a whirlwind romance. Another old adage of marrying in haste and repenting at leisure was completely inaccurate for us. The strength of emotion and the bond between us was as powerful if not more so than when we had finally stumbled together at Marie's hotel. The battling emotions of grief with her absence against the unbounded joy of her agreement to become my wife continued to jostle for prominence as I sauntered down to the newsagents to pick up the *Sunday Times*.

My focus, previously blurred by the insular emotional maelstrom raging in my head, was now brought suddenly into sharp clarity as the front page of *The Investigator* stunned me. Right across the page in slanted 'shouty' red letters was the question: *Is he after her money, her body, her lifestyle or all three???* The picture was the one taken outside the Abbey Road Studios after our morning shaken by finding Bob's body. Marie's tear-stained face was broken by a worried frown, apparently being pushed forward by a very grim-faced man – me!

Staring at it, I shakily turned the page to see what else was in the rag of a paper. Sure enough, they had grainy pictures taken with a long lens, which must have been photographed at various times during the week. Accurately, they pointed out, with the photograph in *Le Monde* that they had also published the previous week, as an inset, that we had got together in Paris. The other photographs had been taken during the week in London: one of me looking forlorn outside Marie's hotel when I had been considering whether she was letting me down lightly; another of Marie at Heathrow, looking tired after her jaunt from Germany to come to the rehearsals; several more of the ambush outside Abbey Road and another one of Marie in tears, dabbing at her eyes with a handkerchief, at London Airport on her return journey. So they had been there but were now hiding!

The story, such as it was, accompanying the pictures was little more than salacious and libellous gossip. A 'source close to Loughton', as the paper referred to me, had suggested that I had callously planned this relationship to take advantage of her jet-set and celebrity lifestyle (it was mooted that I was adamant that I should meet Sir Charles Minton, 'Miss Duvois's mentor', as a way to get a foothold to becoming famous myself), that, since Marie was a well-paid diva in the operatic world, I was probably looking to exploit Marie's generosity and be showered with expensive gifts and, in an almost gynaecological description of her, that the most obvious temptation was her erotic beauty. Hurtful though all that was, I could have laughed it off as typical of the rubbish that this paper printed were it not for the editorial attached to the story. What brought me up short, with anger throbbing at my temples, was the additional and sensational second-rate journalese, which implied that we were not happy and that I was obviously being mean-spirited towards her. This was upsetting her, and they had the alleged proof in the pictures – her tears at the airport and outside the studios, the heart-rendingly sad frown and my grim, pushy appearance added credence to what they had written.

Sauntering lackadaisically down to the shop, I was now running back home, newspapers lodged under my arm, as fast as I could go. I did not want Marie to hear this libellous claptrap from anyone but me. Shakily, I placed the key in the lock, pushed the door open, keys still clinking against the panel, dumped the papers in the stairwell and picked up the telephone, panting crazily.

The operator started the long process of linking telephones with France as I sat on the step above the stairwell, controlling my breathing and kicking the paper with a shoe impatiently. A final click and the world seemed sunny again as Marie's voice came on the crackling line: "David, how lovely."

"I'm glad I got through to you, sweetheart," I said, trying to sound as carefree and untroubled as I could.

"David?" Her voice now had a worried edge to it. "What's the matter?"

"I thought," I started, wondering how to pick this up with her. I cleared my throat and continued, forehead in hand, brushing my thinning fringe: "I thought I'd better let you know that one of our more lurid Sunday publications has written some more hurtful things. It's about me this time."

"About you?"

"Well, about me and our relationship." I gave her a précis of what was written and described some of the pictures.

Marie was silent for a while, which worried me a little. Eventually, she responded gently: "David, are you alright?"

The question was unexpected. "Marie, I'm fine. I'm worried about you and this... this.... this utter crap that has been written."

"Good. I was a little concerned that you might think that I believed it."

It had crossed my mind. "No, I'm not paranoid about us any more." I was lightening up from just talking with her. "But I guess I'm not used to having this kind of focus."

"I've never had anything quite so horrible printed about me either but I am a little more used to the publicity factor, I guess. Are you sure you're OK?"

I had calmed down considerably. If Marie was unconcerned by the publication then I was becoming less so too. "I'm fine, sweetheart. Truthfully. I was just a little shocked to see myself splashed across the front page with untruths being printed about something I feel is so precious."

"Are you going to do anything?"

"I don't know. If I go to a lawyer or write to them countering the claims, they might think that there is no smoke without fire and hound me – and, more importantly, you – further. I'm more inclined to let it go. What do you think?"

A pause. "Honestly? I think there is some truth written in that article."

My heart leapt into my mouth. "Truth? What –?"

"You are after my body. Several times as I recall."

"Right! Start prodding your ribs because you deserve a tickling. You had me going there!"

Marie giggled prettily and then said: "If you do decide to do anything – and I think you're right that it might make it more difficult if you did so – you must know that you have my full support."

I thanked her and, now desperate to change the subject, we talked about lighter matters, including her lovely letter. "It was such a surprise. Needless to say, I spent the afternoon re-reading it and sniffing your perfume on it, rather than doing rehearsal."

"I had no idea when I wrote it that you were going to propose to me. I just thought that we were getting on so very well, we'd fallen so deeply for each other, that all we would do is live together in sin."

"Sin being a small suburb of Peking?"

She giggled. "And I love your humour, as well, of course! Had you planned that?"

"Yes and no. I fell to thinking on Thursday night how much I was going to be missing you and that I hadn't felt that way really since the anniversary of my mother's death. That's not intended to sound as funereal as it might have done. It was when we were dozing off, cuddling closely and a thought came into my head – Marie Loughton. Simultaneously, I had a vision of my mother kissing you, welcoming you into the family and that led on to the engagement ring. It sounds silly but it was like I had my mother's approval and it provided me with the impetus to propose to you."

"That's lovely," replied Marie.

"And I'm glad I did it. All the way to the airport, I had to grip the steering wheel tightly to stop my hands shaking. But as soon as I started asking you, I knew you would say 'yes' and my nerves fell away. In retrospect I might have felt different about it, given that it was on the terminal concourse." A thought sprung into my head. "Now why could they not have taken a photograph of that instead of the one of you at the gate?"

"Maybe they did."

I was suddenly struck dumb. Marie was right; they were obviously following us around and had probably taken one of my betrothal speech but had decided not to print it because it would have taken the shine off their campaign. "I think I won't make any moves. See how it pans out. You never know, the Beatles might say something exciting and be front page news next week!"

"Ever the optimist!"

We finished our telephone call and agreed to talk later on Monday. Right now, I had a lunch appointment with Pete to get to. There was an important question that I needed answered.

Pete was already seated in the corner of the Rose and Crown, an almost full pint of bitter in front of him, elbow on table, leaning over the pages of *The Observer*. He looked up as I brought my drink over and shook my hand. "So, how's it like to be famous?" he asked, grimacing slightly. Obviously, he had seen my picture in *The Investigator*.

"I would prefer to achieve any such distinction on more glowing terms," I admitted. I shrugged and let my hands fall heavily into my lap. "It's not so much that they've published that shit but the hurtful inferences they've made."

"What are you going to do?"

"Nothing. Hope it will blow over. It's like dealing with bullies at school – show them you're unfazed and they soon run after someone else."

"Good strategy."

"I spoke to Marie this morning to make sure she was OK with it all – she is and is actually more worried about me. Anyway, enough of such seediness. Tell me about Beth."

"First of all, you can't have the word 'seediness' in the same sentence as 'Beth'!" Pete grinned a little. "You remember the conversations we've had about you and Marie?"

"I do."

"And how I criticized you for making me feel sick with all your cutesie feelings?"

"Yes, I do."

"Well, I think I know how you felt!"

"It's going well then?"

"Beth is fantastic. She is witty, caring, pretty, wonderfully intelligent and great at cuddling and…other things."

I rested my chin in my hand, covering an amused smile with fingers. "I seem to recall saying something similar about Marie. I can quite see how I made you feel like reaching for a bucket. When are you seeing her again?"

"This evening. She's coming round to my place." He looked furtively around and confided in me: "Spent the whole morning cleaning the flat up."

"Excellent! And I can't wait for this holiday."

"Neither can I," Pete agreed. "Should be fun."

"Pete, do you mind if I ask you a question?" I had been getting nervously itchy and could not keep my joy in any more.

He raised his eyebrows and shook his head a little. "Go ahead."

"Will you do me the service of being my best man?"

He shrugged his shoulders a little and began speaking and stopped abruptly, a smile spreading across his face as he realized what I had said. "You haven't?" he asked, semi-incredulously.

"I have and Marie's agreed."

Pete stood up, shook my hand enthusiastically. "Of course I will, Dave. It would give me great pleasure. Stay there." Pete went to the bar and returned with two flute glasses and a bottle of champagne. "I know you're not drinking but there is only one way to celebrate!" He ripped off the foil and manhandled the cage, pulling the cork out with a loud popping sound and tipped the bubbling liquid into the glasses.

I decided that Pete was right about the celebration and clinked my glass to his. "Cheers!"

"Congratulations, mate!"

I described the moment that I had proposed to Marie and Pete laughed at the unnaturally unself-conscious way I had done it. "It must be love," he agreed. "You wouldn't have done that if you weren't so besotted."

I took another sip. "I'd like to make a toast. What shall we drink to?"

"Excess?" suggested Pete.

We clinked glasses and said in unison: "To excess!"

"No. I would like to toast you, Pete, for being a good friend to me, seeing me through the dark days of the last few weeks, helping me see the light with Marie, for agreeing to be my best man and to wish you all the happiness and as much joy with Beth as Marie and I share with each other."

Pete's jocular expression turned into something of a cross between embarrassment and modesty. Putting a strong hand on my arm and patting it, he said, simply: "Thanks, Dave." We clinked glasses again and sipped.

By the time lunch-time closing came around at a half past two, I had a real champagne buzz in my head but it was pleasant enough. However, I resolved not to continue drinking. This was a celebratory one-off – the next time would be a special occasion or our marriage.

* * *

Over the next few days, I buried myself in Chorus business. There was Bob's funeral and representing not only myself but also the *Coro do Londinium*, organizing a temporary stand-in for Bob as Section

Manager, moving forward on the record label and the patron ideas and
to ensure that the uneasy truce between me and Gary and Adrian
remained in place. I knew the growing antagonism between me and
Adrian (nearly all one-sided) was driven by Gary's encouragement and
exploitation of Adrian's insecurities. It was one of the frustrations that
Pete had expressed to me that, despite all our efforts to dampen down
the fires sparked by these two, they still sprang up, diverting attention
away from our normal day-jobs. But he was particularly perturbed at the
growing undercurrent of unrest emanating from Adrian. I sought to
understand where the antagonism was rooted and, with the help of Pete
and perhaps Sir Norman, I could eradicate it before it became deep-
seated and pernicious to the Chorus.

Bob's funeral was a small affair. There were fewer than twenty people
present, including the priest. Sir Norman, Pete, Jane Hoare and I
represented the Chorus, while the remainder were people I did not
know. After the coffin had been laid in the ground and everyone had
paid their last respects, Pete and I laid a large wreath from the *Coro di
Londinium* at the side of the grave, stood back, hands folded in front of
us and bowed again. Other wreaths were laid by the funeral director's
men and I smiled inwardly, a little shiver of pride running over my body,
when I saw a small, delicate, rose-petal arrangement with a small note,
handwritten on it:

Bob,
You were a very gentle and good man.
May you rest in peace.
Marie x

It was only after the service, at which I had provided a eulogy to my
mentor, that I found out Bob had had a daughter. It occurred to me then
that I had not even been aware that he had married. Thinking back to
my hospital visit with Bob, she could have been the sender of the only
other card, but I had not inspected it closely at the time.

She was a pretty woman, losing the beauty of youth but blossoming
gracefully into middle age. I could see Bob in her facial features and
guessed that at one time he must have had similarly sandy-coloured hair.
She swept the errant, curly hair off her face with a hand, as she held out
the other in greeting, which I shook. "Thank you very much for your
kind words," she said, smiling sadly. "I'm Pippa Furzebrook, by the way.
Bob's daughter."

"Very nice to meet you," I responded, "I'm Dave Loughton, the Chorus Chairman and this is Pete Phillips, a friend and colleague, also from the Chorus."

She shook Pete's hand. "Very nice to meet you." She looked back at me. "You must be wondering why you've never met me."

A little flustered, I tried to make excuses. "Bob was a very private man. His only overt passion was his music. But I didn't know he had any family certainly."

Pippa looked down at her fingers, considered what to say and looked up at us. "Will you walk with me?"

Pete and I flanked her as we walked from the graveside towards her car. "You're absolutely right, Mr. Loughton. My father was a very private man. He was very gentle and considerate too, as you said in your eulogy, and would do anything he could to help people out. I knew he was in failing health but that has been the case for some time since Mum died. They had had an argument – something petty as couples sometimes do – and Mum had left the house in anger. Unfortunately, a man who had fallen asleep at the wheel knocked her down on a crossing. Anyway, she banged her head badly in the process and never regained consciousness. My Dad berated himself from that point on because the last words they had had together were harsh and unfriendly. I think he tore himself apart and perhaps even blamed himself for her death. Shortly after that, ten years ago, I had to take up a job in Bahrain, which is why I have not been around. But I called him religiously every Thursday night. The last time, the night he died, he seemed very cheerful and mentioned that he was entertaining Marie Duvois and her young man for lunch the next day. He said: 'It'll be nice to get back to the old days and have discussions about music with great singers. Like I used to do with your Mum and her friends.' I know that man was you, so I'd also like to thank you for making him happy on the day he died, even if you didn't know you had."

"It is good to know that he was happy and peaceful when he died," I said in hushed tones.

"Thank you," said Pippa. "I just felt you ought to know."

Since she was not resident nearby nor had she time to organize it, there was no wake but I suspected that Bob would not have wanted all the fuss that that would have entailed. The small group disbanded from the graveside and Pippa turned to Pete and me once more. "Thank you for coming."

"It was our pleasure," replied Pete, shaking her hand.

"It was good to meet you, at last," I agreed, taking her hand in both of mine and kissed her cheek.

As Pete and I walked away, I let out a sigh of relief. "I hate funerals."

"You'd be quite strange if you enjoyed them."

"That's true. No, I mean, it's the finality of it all. It forces you to look at mortality full in the face."

Pete nodded as we trudged on in silence.

Finally, I said: "If Marie and I ever argue, I am not going to let her out of my sight until we have it resolved properly."

* * *

Back in the Chorus offices, I made a quick telephone call to Mike Shedson to make sure he was still happy to act as Section Manager until the elections after the American trip. He was a bit reluctant, saying dubiously that he had never enjoyed positions of authority but would, for Bob's sake, step in temporarily.

As I put the telephone down, the door banged open and in walked Adrian, his face like thunder. He stopped when he saw me, eyes burning holes through my face, turned and stomped back out, slamming the door behind him.

"Now what the hell was that all about?" I asked myself quietly. Shaking my head, I collected the folder with all the papers, diagrams and doodles regarding the record label and left the office for Gary's house. If this apparently new-found respect he had for me was going to continue, I needed to ensure that I played all my cards face up to him.

Gary's house was a ramshackle, early Georgian monstrosity on the outskirts of South Mimms. The front garden was unkempt, with long grass turning to seed and a rotting tree, long since dead, dropping its small branches as the dead weight no longer held. Somewhere in the corner, by the dilapidated wall with chunks of mortared bricks fallen into the garden, was, allegedly, a rockery but I had never seen it. A side gate hung desperately on one hinge in between the house itself and the single garage, with the dark green paint peeling alarmingly from its doors and the wood underneath rotting and buckling. It felt as if a machete should be employed to get up to the front door, because of the thick overgrowth on the pathway. The house itself had dormer windows in the rooms on either side of the entrance porch, with a sunken back section on the first floor. All the windows were in bad need of repair and a lick of paint. Behind each one were yellowing net curtains, sagging in the middle. The house looked as if it were about to let out a long and heavy sigh, such was the air of despondency about it. I poised a finger at the doorbell and saw a naked wire uncovered on the side. The light behind indicated that it had power going to it but I did not want to take any chances and knocked instead, using the rusting metal attached to the letter-box.

The door opened eventually and Gary's face appeared around the side of it. "What do you want?" he said gruffly.

I put on a cheery smile. "I thought I'd come and talk to you about this record label. Remember we discussed it briefly that day Marie was in the office."

He stared at me non-committally for a moment before opening the door wider for me to come in. He was wearing a food-stained vest and khaki shorts, which had seen better days. His white, varicosed legs hung, knock-kneed, underneath them. Closing the door behind me, I wrinkled my nose at the acrid stench of a smoker's house. It was very gloomy in the hall; the walls were painted a glossy, dark-chocolate brown and all the doors off it were closed. Gary opened one of them – the kitchen-cum-breakfast-room – and dank, brown sunlight forced its way through the nicotine-stained net curtains at the grimy, smeared window. The room was a fugue of blue smoke swirling around and I wished I had remembered his penchant for chain-smoking before embarking on this jaunt. On the table, two overflowing ashtrays, one with a crumpled cigarette packet in it, balanced sullenly dropping grey ash on the table. There were several dented beer cans dotted around the table and the work surfaces – he had obviously drunk them, squeezed them, thrown them and left them where they landed. Piles of paper teetered on the remaining surfaces, threatening to avalanche at the slightest stirring wind. A fruit-bowl nestled forgotten behind one of them and the browning fruit within it festered quietly. That was the most memorable thing about Gary's house – everything from the décor to the fruit was brown!

Gary slumped into his seat, picked up one of the ashtrays and threw the contents in the vague direction of the waste bin, failing to get anything into it because the bin itself was vomiting its degrading contents around its base. He placed the ash-tray back in the small clear circle already created in the overflow, flipped open a packet and took out a cigarette to light it. "Well, what do you want?" he asked, without asking me to sit down.

Gingerly, I took one of the chairs and surreptitiously tipped it forward to drop any detritus that might be on it and sat down in one flourish. Resisting the urge to sweep the table clear before putting the folder down on it, I opened it and took the papers out, resting them on the folder. "I thought that, now we have the recording out of the way and before we gear up to the rehearsals for the American trip, you might want to talk about this opportunity."

"Sorry, Dave," replied Gary, looking at me for the first time, leaning forward on the table with his elbows, and exhaling a plume of blue smoke, which ballooned up to the ceiling. "I'm up to my eyes with this American gig."

"I thought Adrian was looking after all of those details?"

"No!" said Gary sharply, before softening the tone a little. "No, he's not. He's co-ordinating some of the time-consuming bits and pieces but, now that the *Carmen* recording is out of the way, I'm picking it back up again."

"Does he know?"

Gary looked at me conspiratorially. "I tell you what. He's getting to be a bit of a pain in the arse."

"A bit?" I responded.

Gary smiled for the first time since I had come in. "Exactly. Anyway, he's been trying to push himself into the public eye a little bit too much."

"What do you mean?"

"You remember those programme proofs?"

"Yes."

"Well, the only reason he asked Norm to look after them was because he had replaced my name with his as Secretary."

"You're joking!"

"I'm not. So, as a result of that, I've decided that I need to wrestle control from him before he gets up to any more high-jinks."

I was suspicious of Gary's motives but he was right on that point: Adrian needed to be controlled as he was getting out of hand. Eventually, I nodded in agreement. "Okay, Gary, do what you need to do but please be careful. I don't want a turf war on my hands."

A momentary stony glance softened into a smile. "Naturally. I don't want to give him any more rope than he needs to hang himself. He can't go around playing the big 'I am' all the time, slowing down our progress."

Gary's use of the plural pronouns aroused my suspicions further but

I thought that Gary would be able to handle Adrian a lot more effectively than I could. "So how are you going to handle it?"

Gary gazed out of the window, breathing smoke out slowly. He turned to me. "You know, I think what he needs is a guiding hand rather than all this rough stuff."

Exactly what I wanted to hear, which was why I was still suspicious. "And what does that mean?"

Gary's eyes darted to me and quickly away again. He dragged deeply and, as he spoke, the aspirate syllables were punctuated with a small puff of smoke. "I'm not going to take anything away from him. I'll try to help him understand how he makes others feel. How he gets their gander up." He stubbed out his cigarette and produced a fresh one, bending into the lighter flame. "I'll talk to him this afternoon."

"Good," I said, packing up the papers into the folder. "Let me know how you get on." I stood up to leave but it was obvious Gary was not going to see me off the premises. "I'll let myself out," I said finally and made my way to the door, shutting it quietly behind me. Wracked with coughs from the passive smoking, I stepped into the fresh air and decided to go home to change my clothes. The stench of Gary's kitchen was ingrained in those I was wearing.

* * *

Later that morning, in fresh clothes on a bathed body, I called Bruce Carlton to meet me at the Chorus offices and returned there to flesh out my recording plans and put them in motion. Actually, I was secretly relieved that Gary had turned the opportunity down because I had a vision of the record label in my mind and wanted to ensure it would work technically before pursuing it further. Bruce had agreed to meet me later in the week, so I busied myself designing what I wanted to be the ideal position.

Several hours later, with many pieces of paper strewn across the desk, dotted with diagrams, lists and underlined words, and balled up paper in the rough proximity of the waste-paper basket, I dropped the pen to the desk and rubbed my eyes with fatigue, glancing at my watch. I had been working away for three hours straight. The cup of coffee on the coaster had long since turned cold and there was a film appearing in the grey-brown liquid as the cream separated from the milk.

I decided to do one more hour before returning home but was interrupted by Adrian Hilton appearing at the door, opening it with the

flat of his hand so that it crunched into the book-case behind it. There
were rosettes of anger on his cheeks, his eyes shiny with indignation and
he was breathing heavily through flared nostrils, his teeth working away
at the inside of his lip as he chewed nervously.

"Adrian!" I said pleasantly, after getting over the initial shock. "How
are you?"

"Just who the hell do you think you are?" he fumed, his eyes almost
popping out of their sockets. His hand was still on the door.

I knew what this was likely to be about; Gary had had his words with
him. As yet, I could not determine exactly what had happened between
them because Adrian was in no mood to listen to me. "Adrian, please sit
–."

"You are a complete and utter bastard!" he shouted, hand still on the
door and breathing heavily. Childish name-calling was one of his
specialities.

"Adrian, why don't you –?"

"How dare you?"

I stood up. "Sit! Down!" I said firmly and pointed to the visitor's
chair.

Adrian was shocked out of his temper tantrum. He looked at the
chair for a moment and relaxed slightly, his shoulders slumping. He
took a deep breath and sat sulkily in the chair.

I sat back down carefully, watching him and catching occasional
wafts of stale body odour. "So, Adrian," I said, finally, gathering up the
record label papers into a neat pile. It was unlikely that I would be
getting any more of that work done today. I continued: "What was that
outburst all about?"

He jabbed a finger at me. "You can't treat me like this."

I was flummoxed. "Treat you like what? I don't understand. Do you
want to start from the beginning?"

"Don't patronize me, you git!"

I put up a resigned hand and sat back. "Not my intention. Okay, tell
me what's going on."

Adrian appeared to be sucking a toffee as he ruminated on what to
say. He knew that I would not listen to any angry outbursts. Eventually,
he leaned forward, still jabbing the finger at me but said with strained
control: "I have worked damned hard on this project and you can't treat
me like this."

"No-one is saying you haven't done a bad job or haven't worked hard.
I still don't understand where you're coming from?"

"Gary told me what you said. I can't believe you have the audacity. And, what's worse, you send him round to do your dirty work."

Gary! I should have stuck with my reservations and handled this myself. I put out a placatory hand and said: "Okay. Remind me what I told Gary to say to you? I can't remember the details."

Adrian scoffed. His eyes were darting around the room, shining and flashing with hurt pride, anger and frustration. "Oh, come off it! Don't play that game with me!"

"Adrian," I replied calmly, "I'm not playing any games. Please tell me what Gary said and I'll see if I can straighten it out."

He sighed and began counting off on his fingers. "That I'm useless. That I should be taken off this American project and Gary take over. That you are looking for an excuse to sack me. That you are watching me closely for the slightest mistake. Does that about cover it?" He was turning apoplectic with rage. "It's jobs for the boys, isn't it? You look after yourself by surrounding yourself with cronies. Unbelievable."

"Adrian –."

"And you don't recognize just what I have achieved since I've been here. Just look at the wardrobe department. And if I hadn't done what I'd done for the American tour, it would not be taking place."

He had run out of steam a little and was giving me a sidelong glance, while he drummed his lips with his fingers. I let the silence continue for a while, watching him carefully. He was far from inscrutable and I knew that anything I said to placate him in any way would be met with further vilification. When Adrian began shifting uncomfortably, about to say something again, I said carefully: "What do you want out of the *Coro di Londinium*, Adrian?"

He was about to open his mouth but stopped and frowned. He was unprepared for a question apparently unconnected with his tirade. "What do you mean?"

"Why did you join?"

"Are you trying to get rid of me?" A tic was jumping in one cheek.

"No, I'm not. That's ludicrous and you know it." I ploughed on before he could jump in. "I'm just interested to know what drove you to apply to join this Chorus."

He looked surprised and ruminated again. "I don't know," he said eventually, "I just enjoy planning and managing projects, I suppose."

"Planning and managing projects," I repeated quietly, as I wrote it down. "And where do you think you excel in that area?" I looked up at him.

He shifted a little uncomfortably. I was well aware that he had not been expecting this as a result of his hot-headed entrance and would have preferred a stand-up slanging match that he could boast about to Gary. His lips were moving soundlessly as he searched for something to say. "Control," he said finally.

"Control," I repeated, again writing it down. "And what aspects of control do you particularly like?"

"Erm," he said, drumming his fingers on his lips again, the tic working overtime. "I just like to be in control of what I do."

A typical answer for a control-freak to make. By controlling as much as he could, he felt more comfortable with himself and his life, not wanting anything to be left to chance. "What about the efficiency side of it? You've worked wonders in the basement."

"Yes," he replied with a glimmer of a smile. "I'm good at that, too. Tidy mind. Everything in its place." He made chopping movements with his hand.

"And what about the arrangements for America?" I wrote the word 'anally retentive' in the margin.

He stiffened again. Obviously not quite ready to give me any details, I thought. "What about them?" he asked cagily.

"I presume the same level of efficiency and neatness has been applied to them?"

"Oh," he said with relief. "Of course."

"What about communication?"

"What about it?"

"Would you posit that you are a good communicator, a mediocre one or bad?"

"Well," he started, searching for an answer again. "I think I'm very good. What do you think?" There was a sniff of anger rising in his voice. I changed tack.

"What about the music?"

"Eh?"

"Well, you say that you joined the Chorus to manage projects because you enjoy the need to be in control. I would have thought that the primary answer would have been for the love of the music. What's your view?"

He was completely floored with the question. He stuttered, opened and shut his mouth and flailed a hand around. "Well, of course I enjoy the music!" he blustered after a minute or two in introspection.

"In what way?"

More flustered bluster. "I don't understand," he tried.

"What is it about the music that you enjoy?"

"I can sing."

"Of course you can. Otherwise you would have failed the audition."

"I still don't understand then."

"Well, some people would choose artistry, others the fulfilment of performing or seeing the enjoyment in the audience, others the spine-tingle from beautiful music. Me, personally, I enjoy the adrenalin of a recording or live performance, coupled with the beauty of harmonies."

"No, it's the organisation required for each performance," he replied after some thought. I wrote that down. "All the various bits coming together."

"What about the glamour side of it?"

"Glamour?"

"Yes. It seems to me that you could get all of what you've identified out of working for an insurance conglomerate or a bank. So it must be the glamour connected with it."

"No, I don't think so." He was not letting anything else out.

"I think that you might then be interested in maintaining a high profile in this organisation because of the types of people from all fields with whom you might come into contact. Would that be true?"

"Yes," he said, then added quickly: "No. I mean –."

"You accused me of a number of things over the past few days but especially today, which just are not true."

"I didn't!" He protested.

This time it was my turn to count on my fingers. "I'm looking to find a way to get you out of the Chorus. I'm getting Gary to do my dirty work; that I am protecting myself with cronies; that I instructed Gary to take control of the American trip. Does *that* about cover it, Adrian?"

"I –," he started but was lost for an answer.

"Let me put you right on a few things. Gary was not instructed to say those things to you" – Adrian scoffed – "I am not looking for ways to sack you. And I am certainly not surrounding myself with people who nod at everything I say. I want people who make things happen – who have fire in their eyes."

Adrian pursed his lips but said nothing.

"I'll tell you what I've observed, though. You are very efficient at organizing things but you do indeed need to work at something" – I put up a hand as he began to protest – "communication. There are loads of examples. I can't understand why you think you are good at it. I have to

practically drag it out of you every single time. I think that is because
you enjoy the control element so much, you can't bear the thought that
it might be taken away from you. So you button your lip completely.
That must change. It is all very well you being efficient at what you do
but if you don't provide any information for anyone else to work on in
parallel, the end result is that things will be taken away because you can't
be trusted –."

"What!" he roared.

"I'm sorry," I said, acknowledging the mistake with a raised hand.
"'Trusted' is not the right word. You give the impression of not being
trustworthy so the perception grows that you can't be trusted. It's only a
perception but perceptions grow from something."

"I can be trusted," he said, simpering slightly.

"Okay. I will ask you to prove it."

"Eh? How?"

"There are democratically elected members or co-options to the
committee as per the articles of this organisation."

"What on earth are you going on about?" he interrupted.

"Given that there are people in those positions, why did you take it
upon yourself to proclaim yourself 'Secretary' in the programme for
America?"

"I didn't. I –." He stopped himself, looking down at the floor.

"Adrian, that is why I can't feel I can trust you. Any perception you
have that I am looking for ways to oust you from the committee or the
Chorus is entirely of your own making."

He sat in smouldering silence, glaring at me through frowning and
bushy eyebrows.

"You cannot continue like this. Take this as a warning. Sort yourself
out and we'll say no more about this."

The corners of his mouth turned down as he got up suddenly and
slammed his hand on the desk, as he had at the committee meeting at
my house. "You are an evil bastard. You have no idea about me. You sit
there spouting crap about the kind of person I ought to be in this
Chorus, lording it over the place, getting me to talk about myself. It's
not good enough!" He slapped the table again and pointed a finger. "You
just wait!" He glared at me for a few seconds, still pointing his finger,
stomped to the door and slammed it behind him.

I rubbed my forehead in exasperation. If I had not made that slip
about being trusted, things may have turned out differently and I might
not have been on the receiving end of Adrian's latest vitriolic excoriation.

I picked up the 'phone and called Gary, who picked up at the other end after four rings.

"Yeah?"

"Gary? Dave."

A silence other than the clicking on the line. "Yes. What do you want?"

"I've just had an interesting chat with Adrian Hilton."

Another silence, although I could hear laboured breathing. "So?"

"When I spoke to you earlier and we agreed to go carefully on this issue, I was not expecting you to bad-mouth me to him."

"I don't know what you mean," he replied innocently, although there was tension underlining it.

"Did you specifically tell him that I was looking to sack him? That he was useless?"

"Well, I had to say something to get him to give me the details on America," he whined.

"But not like that, Gary!" I said firmly. "I cannot believe that you undermined me in that way."

"Oh, lighten up, Dave. He's a prat, anyway."

"Who happens to be co-opted on to the committee and has been delegated an important role in this American trip. I want you to apologize to him and tell him the truth."

"Oh, bugger off, Dave," he continued whining. "Why waste energy on him?"

"Because that is my duty and responsibility."

"Duty and responsibility?" he scoffed. "Duty and responsibility? Where was this sudden duty and responsibility when you were getting an eyeful of that woman's breasts on the Paris stage? Where was this duty and responsibility when you were persecuting me during the recording?"

"For God's sake, Gary!" I thundered. "Grow up! You know damned well what I am referring to." I put my head back and slowly took in a breath. The old hatred and anger had resurfaced at the mention of my Parisian misdemeanour.

"You are nothing but an old woman, Loughton," he said tersely.

"Let's not get into another backbiting session, Gary. Are you going to sort this mess out with Adrian or not?"

"You are not going to tell me what to do. You can piss off back to whichever stone you crawled from under."

"Gary, that is not helpful."

"Gary, that is not helpful," he mimicked childishly.

"Gary?"

"Bugger off! I thought you were finally coming to see things my way but obviously I was completely wrong." He slammed the 'phone down.

I hung my head and closed my eyes. Placing the receiver back slowly, I reasoned that I did not want to keep going to Sir Norman to fight my battles and made up my mind to sort this issue out once and for all. The mood I had generated while working through the recording label details had all but evaporated for the moment and I decided to go home instead, taking the binder of papers with me. I needed to work through the major issue with Gary and Adrian – nothing and no approach appeared to be working.

PUPPET ON A STRING

CHAPTER 24

The next day, still concentrating on how to resolve the situation with Gary and Adrian, I had not come up with anything, which would help them see what asses they were making of themselves, while also protecting the commitments in which they were involved. I knew that I was making matters worse by trying to sort it out it on my own. However, I also wanted to avoid the potential loss of credibility by seeking out support from Sir Norman. Once was fine but they had both reverted back to character now. I had buried myself in personal rehearsal in the early morning and was now going back to the office to complete the paperwork for expressing my thoughts on the record label and to doodle a few designs for the label motif, too. Fortunately, there was no sign of either Adrian or Gary as I gingerly poked my head into the room and sat down at my desk.

Having worked through what I was looking for from a technical perspective, I drafted a business plan to present to the record companies to be approached with a view to setting up a distribution deal. I had done some investigation at the local library with the reference books and looking through the *Musician's Year Book*, for information on how to approach these companies. Essentially, what they would be looking for was saleability of the recordings to protect their distribution investment and increase their profits. I laid out the basics of the idea and approach we would adopt (assuming Bruce Carlton could confirm its feasibility), the genre of recordings we would undertake, information on target markets and a rough breakdown of areas, which required costs to be estimated.

Bruce arrived as arranged some two hours later just after lunch, knocking on the door as he opened it. He was a young man approaching middle age, with shoulder-length, brown, wavy hair, round, pink-glass spectacles and a tall, lanky body, which he folded into the visitor's chair, after shaking my hand.

"I hope you don't mind me asking you here," I started, handing him
a coffee poured from the percolator in the kitchen annexe.

"No problem, friend," he said, waving my concern aside with a
casual hand. "Do you mind?" he asked, picking up his cigarettes and
lighter. I shook my head, despairing that I had just been through this
pulmonary assault course the day before with Gary but I needed Bruce's
input.

"Not at all," I agreed, pushing the glass ashtray towards him.

He sucked his cheeks in on the cigarette once lit, crossed his legs and
breathed out, sweeping his hair away from his face. "Sounds like an
interesting project."

"I think it is. The idea is barely off the drawing-board but I need
some technical expertise and input before taking it on to the next stage."

Bruce nodded encouragement, taking another drag from the
cigarette and flicking the growing grey ash into the ashtray. "What do
you want to know?"

"Well, we – the *Coro di Londinium* – do recordings with the soloists
and orchestra at the same time."

"Uh-huh."

"Is there any way that the three separate entities can be recorded
separately and then fused together afterwards?"

He considered this, uncrossed his legs, stubbed the cigarette out and
leaned forward, clasping his hands over the desk. "Of course!" he
confirmed. "There are a number of ways of achieving that. You could
record each group separately, and then play the tapes simultaneously,
recording that output. Or there's a new process of being able to record
on to different tracks on the master tape. Up to a maximum of eight.
What are you thinking of?"

I leaned forward, mirroring him unconsciously. He was a very
intense sort of person, knowledgeable and intelligent, but positive too.
This was just the sort of input I wanted to make this work. "I'm not sure
how to explain it really." I pulled a piece of paper from the tray and drew
a large circle, with a small circle at the centre of it. Stabbing the pen on
the smaller circle, I said: "This is the listener to the recording" – Bruce
nodded and I added a small half-moon at the top of the circle, five
smaller circles in a semicircular arrangement between the half-moon and
the 'listener' and a corresponding reflection of the half-moon shape at
the bottom of the circle – "what I want to try to achieve with the use of
stereo is for the listener, with his eyes shut, to feel that the chorus is
directly in front of him in this half-moon, the soloists are between him

and the chorus but appear to be" – I stabbed the smaller circles in turn – "to his left, slightly further round, central, to the right and so on. And then the orchestra sounds as if it is directly behind him in this half-moon. Basically, the recording surrounds him and he is at the centre; I want him to feel that he has to look in the direction of the sound. Can that be done?"

Bruce pursed his lips and studied the drawing for a long while. He took my pen and made a few additions to the drawing, with lines pointing to incomprehensibly and technically jargonistic text. Then he sat back, frowned at the drawing, pursing his lips and nodded. "I think you have something here, friend. I tell you something: it'll sound refreshingly original and give a completely new take on the traditional sound. The good thing is that we can play around with it, I think, so reversing the orchestra and chorus, putting some of the orchestra in front and behind, same with the chorus; we can even put the soloists in such a position as if they were standing around the listener. Intriguing!"

"How do I move this forward?" I was excited at the prospect of seeing my idea to fruition and was now overtly pleased that I had not pushed Gary to take it on; in actual fact, I had had reservations that the whole thing would fall flat facewards if Gary had been involved but was willing to risk that for the sake of choral peace.

Now, Bruce was studying the drawing and shaking his head in a jaunty fashion as if to weigh up the pros and cons of doing it. "I think we need to run a few tests first," he suggested, "just to see how things pan out. And to see if there is anything here that is not possible or is too costly. Is it possible to book a studio somewhere for an afternoon?" He looked up, a flash of excitement across his eyes; a man champing at the bit.

"Of course it is," I replied, standing up, indicating the door. "We have one on the premises. See if it will meet your needs."

Bruce followed me down to the basement, through the efficiently tidy wardrobe area and towards the back, where the studio was situated. I pulled out the bunch of keys and tried one or two in the control room door before hitting success. The smell was not quite musty but smelled of newly sawn hardboard. This was not entirely surprising, since the walls were covered with makeshift boxes from that material to deaden the sound. The gleaming control desk winked as the reflection of the overhead lights hit it. "State of the art!" he exclaimed in quiet awe, running a finger along the edge of the console of sliders, buttons and gauges. There were three tape decks on the left side of the desk and right beside the glass screen which let out on to the studio itself. I opened a small cupboard by the door and flicked a few switches. Subdued light threw the studio into vision and Bruce stood, hands on hips, nodding slowly. He asked, indicating the studio: "Can we see?"

"Of course!" I replied and skirted the control desk to get to the interconnecting door. The other side was like an airlock, with a small space to stand and another door the other side, connecting with the studio proper.

Bruce whistled appreciatively as he regarded the serried rows of relatively unused headphones and banks of microphones and coiled leads. Stacked in the corner were a number of microphone and music stands. Running along the entire length of all the walls except the one connecting with the control room were several twin ports for microphone plugs and headphone sockets.

"What do you think?" I asked, bristling a little with pride.

Bruce was still looking around the room, which was big enough for a group of thirty of so to stand comfortably in front of a microphone. "Excellent!" he said softly. "We'll need to think about the logistics of recording the orchestra but it's fantastic!"

"Do you need anything from me?"

He was still nodding and looking around. "Right!" he said suddenly and made a move towards the microphone stands, pulling two out and positioning them four or five feet apart. He grinned: "Yes there is – you can make me another cup of coffee while I'm setting this up. Then I'll need you to do some singing, if that's okay, friend?"

"Perfectly," I replied, smiling, "you're the boss. One cup of coffee on its way."

When I had returned with a tray with two coffees and a plate of biscuits, Bruce was back in the control room and checking out the sliders and knobs on the console. "Thanks," he said, taking his coffee absent-mindedly and putting it on a small table to the side. "Right, friend! Are you ready?"

I saluted and smiled. "Reporting for duty. What would you have me do?"

"If you could stand in between those mikes about a foot back from them, I'll let you know."

I closed the connecting doors carefully, positioned myself as requested, pointed to the floor and raised a questioning thumb. Bruce responded with an enthusiastic thumb and pressed the intercom. "Can you hear me?"

"I can, Bruce. Loud and clear."

"Right you are, friend. What I want you to do is to sing a twenty-second snatch of something from where you are. Then we'll stop and you can move directly in front of the left mike and sing the same thing. Then we'll do the same with the right. Okay?"

"Fine. Let me know when you want me to start."

Bruce got up to check the tape reels and wrote something on a clipboard. He sat down again and leaned into the intercom microphone. "Dave Loughton's Aural Arena testing tape. Central position. Take one." He waved at me to start. I smiled at the label he had given it.

I breathed slowly, as I had been trained for the recording studio to avoid sharp and sudden sounds, and began singing the first thirty seconds or so of the tenor aria *Ingemisco* from Verdi's *Requiem*. The intercom clicked on, as Bruce thanked me and asked me to take up the second position.

"Dave Loughton's Aural Arena testing tape. Left position. Take one."

This continued with variations for the next couple of hours, as Bruce tried different things, with microphones set up in different positions, behind me, directly to the sides of me, above and so on. Eventually, we were seated at the console, supping a fourth cup of caffeine, adrenalin pumping. Bruce had placed the control room speakers at either side of the desk and began playing through the variants. It was odd hearing my voice coming through them with such crystal clarity. I knew I was on to something. Each take, Bruce asked me to shut my eyes and express how I was hearing it, making notes on the growing sheaf of papers.

Eventually, as darkness gathered outside, although our basement position precluded us from witnessing it, we called it a day. Bruce yawned and stretched, resting his clasped hands on his head. "Is there any way we can get more people in here to do further the tests?"

"Yes, of course," I agreed. "Just let me know when."

"How about tomorrow? Or is that too soon?"

"No, it isn't. Leave it with me and I'll give you a call."

"Thanks, friend."

We shook hands and Bruce left me sitting in the control room, a satisfied smile growing on my lips.

This was it! This is what it was all about! It was an exciting prospect that I had something I could pitch to some of the major companies for distributing our label once it had taken off.

I locked up, took the tray back to the kitchen annexe and called Pete before leaving to explain what I wanted to do.

* * *

As I drove into the car park the following day, Bruce was already pacing backwards and forwards, stooped forward, long hair covering his face and dragging on a cigarette. When he saw me arrive, he jerked his head to remove the hair from his face, dropped the dog-end and trod it into the ground.

"How're you doing, friend?" asked Bruce, holding out his hand, which I shook. "I could barely sleep last night, wondering how today would turn out. This is great!"

"I know what you mean," I agreed. "I was fretting a little about how we can get this off the ground, assuming this will work." I unlocked the door and stood aside for Bruce to go through. He took the stairs two at a time down to the basement. As soon as I had opened up the control room, he was magnetized to the console. He went back over the previous notes and marked positions on the sliders and knobs with a china pen. "Did you manage to find anyone, friend?" he asked as he worked.

"I did. He should be here any time soon." I checked my watch.

Almost on cue, I heard footsteps on the concrete stairs and Pete's voice. Following behind him were the lady-like, careful, pecking steps of stilettos. I squinted into the dark basement and recognized Beth Jackson. "Hope you don't mind me bringing Beth along," Pete said, shaking my hand.

"Of course not." I smiled at Beth and kissed her cheek. "Do you know Bruce? Bruce Carlton?"

Beth nodded and he shook both their hands as I introduced them. "Dave," she said, smiling sweetly. "I think we might have a surprise for you later on."

"What surprise?" I raised my eyebrows.

Pete tapped my chest with a pointed finger. "Well, it wouldn't be a surprise…"

"…if you told me," I finished for him, nodding. "Okay. I'll wait."

"So," said Beth, "what are we doing?"

I gave them a précis of what Bruce and I had done yesterday and showed them the now tatty diagram we had been playing with the day before. Pete and Beth nodded occasionally as I took them through what I was hoping to get out of these tests, asking the odd question now and again.

"This looks fantastic, Dave," said Pete, swivelling the diagram around in his hands, turning his head in the opposite direction, He looked up at my amused face. "No, really!"

"Thanks, Pete, I hope it will work. Right. Let's get into the studio and see what we can do."

Bruce had produced a set of diagrams detailing the arrangement of microphones and we started the same process as the previous afternoon but with a central person all the time (interchanging that central voice between the three of us) and moving the remaining two around. After the third or fourth option, I returned to the control room to see how things were going. Bruce described what he was trying to do and how he felt it was working. He was discussing the merits of putting microphones above everyone, when a pair of feminine hands came over my eyes. Initially, I thought it was Beth, playing around because I was aware that they might get bored during the down time. I reached up and took the wrists and I recognized the contours of the delicate skin. My heart leapt into my mouth. Turning around, mouth agape in a wide smile, I exclaimed: "Marie!"

Marie flung her arms around my neck and we kissed. We hugged hard and I parted slightly from her. "What are you doing here?"

"I'm your surprise! Beth called me last night to see if I were free to come to London for the day. She told me what you're doing here and I thought I might help out too!"

I looked through the interconnecting glass and saw Beth and Pete winking and pointing at me. Yes, they had got me! Turning back to her, I said: "But you said nothing when we spoke last night."

"It wouldn't have been a surprise if...."

"...if I had known you were coming," I finished the sentence for the second time, and kissed her, holding her head softly. I turned to Bruce. "Sorry, Bruce, very rude of me. Do you know Marie Duvois?"

"Don't mind me, friend. You two carry on. Course I know Marie. We've done – what? – five or six recordings together in the last two or three years?"

"Something like that," agreed Marie and shook his proffered hand. "Now, David, where do you want me?"

It occurred to me that we now had vocal representation from the four main parts – soprano, alto, tenor and bass. After discussion with Bruce, we abandoned the original plan and decided to do something a little more radical – if the listener were in the centre of the listening arena, to have each of the four voices in front, behind, to the left and to the right. We played around with different ways of doing that and all five of us listened to the results in the control room, shutting our eyes and imagining that the singers encircled us. It was working!

"It's great, David!" said Marie. "Don't you agree, Bruce?"

"He's the man!" Bruce opined.

"Now," I said, weighing up an imaginary substance in my hand. "I wonder if this will work. Bruce, is it at all possible to record the voices so that it sounds as if the singers are moving around the listener?"

"Let's try it. Do you mean all of you walking in a circle while singing?"

"If that's the only way. But I was wondering if any of these gizmos here would do that for us while we stand still?"

"As I say, let's try it. Sounds interesting, friend."

We all herded back into the studio and Bruce set up four mikes at the four points of the compass, initially facing out. Then we tried the same thing with them facing in. Each time we recorded the four of us improvised harmonies to a Beatles classic or some of the more popular and lighter operatic arias. Irrepressible giggling was also a feature from Marie and Beth; eventually, all four of us were lying on the floor, laughing until tears streamed down our faces.

During the playback, Bruce demonstrated an extraordinary thing. Not only was my idea working well, with the listener encircled by a song moving clockwise and then anti-clockwise, but he had also recorded us laughing when we had been lying on the floor, staring at the ceiling. He had taken it one step further and produced a kind of rolling sound, so that it felt as if the four voices were moving towards the listener but with one voice taking over from the previous one, followed by the next and so on. It was an amazing technical feat.

We continued trying different things out until early evening, when Bruce reluctantly had to leave. While Marie was in the ladies' room, I walked out with Pete and Beth. In the car park, in the distance, I heard several staccato clicks like a sluggard cicada but thought little of it.

Pete shook my hand. "Amazing, Dave. Great fun! I can't remember when I enjoyed myself so much."

"Nor me," agreed Beth, giving me a hug and kissing my cheek.

Pete frowned. "Put that young lady down now!"

Beth flashed a smile at Pete and went to him, giving him a kiss, just as Marie joined us, taking my hand. Pete looked at his watch. "We'd better get off," he said. "Thanks for a wonderful afternoon."

We bade them farewell, walked to the car and we set off for my house.

In the car, Marie put a caressing hand on my leg and said: "I'm very proud of you, David."

"Thank you, sweetheart. I had almost given this away to Gary to do but I'm glad I held on to it. It was great fun with the four of us."

"It was. Which should mean our holiday will be great, too. What made you think of this recording approach?"

"It was last week at EMI. I was looking at the structure of the layout and it is almost always the same for every recording I've done. I thought there must be a fresher way of doing it. I know that the rock and pop world is experimenting; the Beatles with their *Sergeant Pepper*, the Moody Blues with their *Days of Future Passed*, which has an orchestral accompaniment on it, but it is always so staid when it comes to the classical recordings, whatever the medium. So I drew out what I was looking for and contacted Bruce."

"You are very clever," she said, as we drew up towards the garage.

Pulling on the handbrake, I grinned and said: "I know!" We kissed for several moments and all my longing since she had returned home seeped away to nothing. "I'm so happy you came along today."

"So am I," she said sweetly and placed a hand on my chest. "Shall we...er...go inside?" she asked suggestively, cocking her head towards the house. "Feels like you're happy to see me the way your heart is racing!"

We got out of the car and that's when I noticed the smashed front-room window with a jagged shard jutting out accusingly in to the growing dusk. Swearing a little and thinking I had been burgled, I rushed to the door, struggled with the key, opened it and ran into the front room.

Marie ran in behind me and gently touched my arm, looking to where I had locked my gaze. "What is it, David?"

"Someone doesn't like me," I said grimly, looking at the half house-brick, lying in the middle of what was once a glass-topped table.

PUPPET ON A STRING

CHAPTER 25

The following morning, having boarded up the broken window and removed the remaining shards from the frame, I set about clearing up the front room. Isla had been banned from the room until it was confirmed that all the slivers had been picked up and she would not sustain any injury to her paws. Marie laid out newspaper to bundle up the glass and put it in the bin.

She was concerned that anyone would do that to me with no immediate threat but wanton vandalism. "It's just so strange," she said, washing the newsprint from her hands and drying them in the kitchen.

"I think I know who it might be but, as I said last night, there is no proof other than the chunk of brick so it's not even worth contacting the police."

She nodded, hanging up the towel. "I know. It's just so odd – that's all."

Marie's flight was due out of London Airport in the late afternoon and we had agreed to meet Pete and Beth for lunch. "If I ignore it, the perpetrator will get fed up because I haven't reacted. Now, let's go out for a walk and meet up with Pete and Beth." I put my arm around her, hand on her naked shoulder and kissed her head. "We can talk about the holiday."

Marie smiled and turned to kiss my lips. "You are a wonderful man," she said, turning towards the door.

A few minutes up the road from my house was the local park. It was a huge expanse of green, with trees dotted outside the perimeter, a wicket area cordoned off for the weekend's cricket in the middle and a small children's play area with swings, a roundabout and a slide. Today being Saturday meant that several parents were milling and watching their children shouting and screaming joyously in the sunshine as they played, demanding the roundabout to be faster and the swings to be pushed higher. A couple of men in white flannels and shirts were making their way over to the wicket area, carrying the stumps and bails. One of the best sounds of summer is the crack of leather on willow, in the hazy afternoon sun, followed by lazy clapping at the result. It all seemed so peaceful. Marie and I sauntered slowly through the park and wandered between the trees, sometimes in silence, other times talking about the fun we had had in the studio the afternoon before and the conversation inevitably turned to where we were going to live. I told her that I had received some interesting details from the south coast, which I was planning to go and visit the next day, Sunday.

We stopped in the shade of a tall oak and sat beneath it, Marie carefully pulling her skirt to avoid creases as we settled. I folded my legs at the ankles and rested on my elbows and Marie subconsciously did the same. Staring into the middle distance in comfortable silence, I turned towards her, appreciating her lithe form under her knee-length, pink, cotton skirt and white halter neck blouse. The athletic shape of her limbs I had observed on our first night together had lost none of their appeal. Her arms were taking on a deep tan now that the summer sun was with us and I noticed that her freckles were shown in starker relief as they tanned darker still.

"What's the dopey grin for?" she asked, squinting in the bright, dappled light coming through the trees.

"You are so beautiful," I replied, reaching out to stroke her arm. "And I love you."

She turned to me and placed a hand on my face and kissed my lips. "I love you too, David. Thank you."

I raised my eyebrows. "For what?"

"For being you and wanting and loving me." I cuddled her, kissing her neck and shoulder. She pulled apart from me slightly and placed a hand on my chest. "You are still responding to me nicely. Your heartbeat is doing a fine jig."

"It's the heat and the sun that do it. And being with such a beautiful woman," I grinned.

"Have we time before meeting our friends?"

I checked my watch. "We'll make time." We stood up, brushing off twigs and dried mud from our clothes and walked back to the house quickly, arms linked. Five minutes later, we were naked on the bed, clothes discarded on the way up the stairs. The heat of her skin from the sun made my passions rise further, as we kissed urgently. Marie manoeuvred herself on top of me. Sweat trickled down the sides of my face and beads of perspiration appeared on Marie's forehead and down the centre of her back. We kissed deeply, hugging each other tightly until our passion exploded together.

Drowsing in the coital afterglow, trickles of perspiration running down our bodies, I hugged her tightly and said: "Marie, my sweetheart, I can't find the words to express how much I love you."

She lifted her head and put a finger on my lips. "Actions speak louder than words, they say." She smiled impishly. "And that was some action!"

I laughed and uncurled myself from her embrace. In the background, I heard the telephone ringing but chose to ignore it. "We ought to get going or we'll be late." We bathed quickly and pulled on the discarded clothes and left the house at a swift walking pace, unaware that we were being followed.

We were only five minutes late as we bustled into the bistro, where Pete and Beth were already studying the menus. They looked up as we arrived at the table, apologizing profusely for our tardiness.

"Have you been running?" asked Pete, one eyebrow raised knowingly.

"No," I replied, trying to be calm. "We were just...running late."

The other eyebrow joined the first, as Pete kept quiet but nodded slightly. We sat down so that I was opposite Pete and Marie opposite Beth. I changed the subject, although our flustered entrance adequately covered the creeping redness of embarrassment at the question rising up our cheeks. "Any suggestions for a holiday destination, then?" I asked casually.

Pete threw his head back and laughed, as Marie stuck her tongue out slightly through smiling lips. Before anyone could respond, the waiter interrupted us to take our order. As we handed back the menus, Pete asked: "What sort of place are you thinking of? Sunshine? Romantic cities? Intellectual pursuits?"

Beth replied: "Oh, I think somewhere nice and hot. Lazing by a swimming pool, drinking ice-cold beer, slowly turning a darker shade and generally relaxing. What does everyone else think?"

Marie agreed readily and Pete and I nodded our acceptance. Pooling diary commitments, we calculated that the best time would be a couple of weeks or so after the American tour was complete. We talked through the various suggestions such as some of the Asian or Arabic countries, the west coast of America, the Caribbean or one of the Canaries. Pete and I offered to research the two main suggestions of the Bahamas or the Canaries with the travel agent on the Monday.

Two hours later, Marie and I were on our way to London Airport. At the departure gate, a few feet from the point I had gone on one knee just one week ago, I hugged her tightly and kissed her lips. "I'm really going to miss you," I said, sadness at the prospect deepening the furrows on my brow.

Marie put her hand over my heart and squeezed me hard. "I will miss you, too. Good luck with the house-hunting tomorrow. The sooner we can settle in there, the sooner we can avoid being apart from each other for so long."

I held her arms gently and looked into those beautiful brown eyes. A tear was appearing in one and it ran down her cheek. I wiped it carefully with a thumb and hugged her again. The Tannoy indicated that the flight was ready for boarding. She looked towards the gate and frowned. Then she turned back to me and said: "I'd better go. Call me tomorrow." She kissed me again, picked up her bags and made her way to the departure gate. Again, as I had the previous week, I watched her plane disappear to become a small dot in the azure sky from the terminal's window.

* * *

On the Sunday morning, I got up early and packed the car for my day-trip. The air was cool and goose-bumps pricked up on my arms as I loaded the small picnic I had prepared into the boot. The sun had only been up for thirty minutes and had yet to add its warmth to the day. Ensuring that the hardboard was firm in place of the smashed window, the door was locked and I had the fistful of property descriptions from the estate agents, I set off, pointing the car southwards towards Dorset.

The roads were beautifully clear and, as the sun rose in the sky, I had to open the windows to let a breeze through the car and put sunglasses on. Today felt good – I knew that a suitable property would be found.

At just after eleven o'clock, I was driving along the Swanage sea-front. It was exactly as I remembered from my childhood: the grey and white chalky cliff of Ballard Down on one side of the bay, the pointing finger of Peveril Point on the other and a placid sea, splashing waves on to the golden, sandy beaches with lazy effort. A few boats bobbed at anchor by the old pier and a motor-boat was carving up the water in the distance. I parked on the front and got out to stretch my legs, stiff from the continuous driving. I shaded my eyes against the sun's glare and looked to the horizon – the Isle of Wight was barely noticeable. According to local folklore, the weather would be fine if the Isle of

Wight could not be seen; bad if it could. Taking the agent's property particulars and the road atlas from the car, I sat on the edge of the sea-wall and looked out to sea at nothing in particular. The fresh smell of salty sea air met my nostrils pleasantly and I shut my eyes, facing the sun, feeling its heat on my forehead and cheeks and sighed.

Eventually, I looked at the property particulars, the slight wind occasionally lifting a corner of the paper. I organized the properties into a logical sequence according to their distances and juxtaposition to each other and stood up, brushing the sand from my hands, to get moving.

The first couple of properties in Swanage and Durlston, while typical of the local structures made from Purbeck stone, were too small for our needs. I struck them from the list. Another in Kimmeridge was a good size but had poor views, despite being close to the bay. It was only when I drove into Worth Matravers, with its central duck-pond and chocolate box arrangement of the houses and streets nestling into the foliage of trees and hedges that I knew I had found the place I wanted to live. There was only one property for sale in this village. I parked in the high street and got out to look around. To the left of the duck-pond was a street leading towards the sea and I noticed that this was where the house was for sale.

Taking just the relevant document with me, I sauntered down the small street, hands in pockets, drinking in the beautiful scenery and the stillness, interrupted by bird-calls from the song- and sea-birds. Halfway down the street was the house. A high, green privet hedge covered the entrance. Beside it was an alley-way, the sign-post for which confirmed that it was part of the coastal path. I walked down it and jumped up to look at the secluded garden, which was small enough for my lack of green fingers not to mangle but large enough to be able to amble around, with trees dotted along its length and at the bottom. I daydreamed of putting up a hammock between two of them, lying in it, a cool drink in my hand, a straw hat over my eyes shielded from the sun. It was perfect. I looked around the other side and saw that the garden and house were not overlooked by the neighbours' houses because of their position and judicious use of plants to secrete them from one another. Carefully opening the front gate, I went up the snaking garden path, also made from local stone and knocked on the door. There was no answer – I had not expected there to be anyone there on a Sunday necessarily, but it would have been good to look inside.

I cupped my face against two of the windows and looked through. One of the rooms was extended all the way to the back, so I could see the garden and, peeking just above the top of the trees, I could just about see the sea in the distance. It followed then that from the top rooms, there would be an excellent view of it. The room to the other side of the door was a large reception room with comfortable furniture in it. I stood back and looked up at the top of the house and nodded. This was the one.

I made my way back to the car and took the box of sandwiches from the boot. Throwing the house details on to the front seat, I locked the car up again and returned past the house and sauntered down the coastal path. Following it for fifteen minutes, I came across a secluded shale beach, which had large ruts carved into them. It had the romantic name of Dancing Ledge, according to the map. The ruts, I later found out, were from carts used to ferry loads to the sea edge and back again during the last century. At the back of the ledge was a high cliff face. At the bottom was a small cave and I wondered whether this was a place for smugglers, thinking back to the *Moonfleet* story, which was based in Dorset.

Lunch was had on one of the many large rocks, strewn around the ledge. I stared into the middle distance again, listening to the crashing waves on the slate, the gulls and terns calling to each other and the peaceful stillness in the air. This was definitely the place Marie and I would buy.

* * *

I arrived home at nine o'clock in the evening. As I reached my front door, I heard the telephone ringing. Pushing the door open and dumping everything in the stairwell temporarily, I grabbed the handset. It was Pete.

"Dave, there you are. I've been calling for the whole afternoon."

"Sorry, Pete, I stayed there longer than planned. I've found this beautiful cottage in Dorset. You should see it."

"That's great, Dave." There was an edge to his voice.

Snapped back to reality by it, I asked: "What's wrong, Pete?"

"Have you seen today's papers?" he replied eventually.

"No." I had not had the chance because of the jaunt to Worth Matravers.

Strained silence at the other end.

"Pete?"

"You're in it again." I heard Pete sigh.

I slumped on to a stair and, rubbing my forehead nervously, I said: "What does it say this time?"

Another sigh. "You're not going to like it."

"No, but go on anyway."

"There's a small picture of Marie with the headline: 'While the mouse is away dot dot dot, see page four.'"

I held my breath. What could they possibly have to say about me this week? "Go on."

A rustle of pages as Pete found the relevant page. "It repeats the bollocks that it printed last week and has a picture of you kissing Pippa Furzebrook at Bob's funeral and, what's worse, a picture of you kissing Beth outside our offices, with me looking extremely disgruntled in the background."

I recalled hearing that strange clicking on the night we had been playing in the recording studio. I said nothing.

"Then it goes on to suggest that, with Marie out of the country, you are playing the field a bit. Flirting with every piece of skirt you meet, is the basis. It also suggests that they tried to contact you yesterday – Saturday – to get your position on this but were obviously screening your calls in some way."

"Hmm." My mind was racing. When Marie and I were making love, the telephone had been ringing. I wondered whether that had been the reporter.

"What are you going to do, Dave?"

I thought for a while longer. "Pete, I'm going to do precisely nothing. There is no foundation to this scurrilous shit they are printing but I'm not going to blow it up either. If I contact them, they'll only dig deeper and I don't want to put Marie through that. I'm also secure in my relationship with her not to be unduly concerned. How is Beth on this?"

"Well, actually, she laughed, because she knows the truth, of course, so she's not worried."

"Good. Okay. We'll see if they come up with anything else next week. If they do, then I might act."

I changed the subject and described the Worth Matravers house and its position. Pete confirmed that it sounded ideal. We said goodbye and confirmed we'd meet up for private rehearsal in the morning prior to the first acting rehearsal later that day. As soon as the line was cut, I called Marie to tell her the opposing pieces of news. She agreed that the newspaper articles should continue to be ignored, while she was very positive and excited about my description of the Worth Matravers house and readily agreed that I should put things in motion the next day for its purchase.

PUPPET ON A STRING

CHAPTER 26

T he Monday was hot and sultry. Fortunately, we had our first acting rehearsal in a room shielded from the greenhouse glare of the sun and it was relatively cool. Pete and I had been talking about the holiday and the Dorsetshire house, for which I had put in an offer to the estate agents and was awaiting a response. Pete had picked up a number of brochures for holiday destinations and we were discussing a couple he had ringed, when a fraught Adrian interrupted us, cutting right across our conversation.

"Name?" snapped Adrian to Anthony Devlin, who was standing near us, lost in thought, arms folded.

Anthony perked up a little and droned: "Anthony Devlin."

Adrian noted something on the black clipboard he was carrying. "What are you singing?"

"First bass."

"Sing second bass," ordered Adrian, making another detailed note on the clipboard. "There are too many first basses and not enough seconds. Stand over there next to Richard Johnson."

Anthony nodded his agreement and did as instructed. Pete and I, conversation suspended by witnessing this extraordinary dictatorial attitude, looked at each other in states of mock alarm and nodded silent agreement to each other.

"Name?" Adrian barked at me, not looking up with pen poised over my name on his list.

"Pardon?" I asked gently.

"Name?" he repeated in exactly the same tone and still not looking up.

"What do you mean: 'Name'?"

"Come on, Loughton. What's your name?" For the first time he looked up at me. His eyes looked tired but spat venom energetically towards me nonetheless. I wondered momentarily whether he had been responsible for the brick through the window.

"So you do know my name, then?"

Adrian sighed and moved his leg as if he were about to stamp. It was a conditioned reflex, a childish movement but provided a window into his psychological make-up. "Look, Loughton. I haven't got time to mess about. I'm very busy."

I stopped myself from pointing out that his business was entirely of his own fabrication because I did not want to descend too far to his level. Nevertheless, winding him up may have helped him to understand how he was perceived. I ran a finger down the list of names, halting at mine. "That one'll do." I smiled sweetly.

Adrian sighed impatiently, shaking his head a little and ticked my name. "What are you singing?" His tone had taken on a suffering edge as if he were dealing with buffoons and incompetents.

"*Die Zauberflöte*," I replied, a slight smile on my lips. "Why? What do you think we should be singing?"

Another noisy sigh. I noticed that Gary had now joined Pete and was listening in on the conversation, smiling as if he were witnessing the bloodlust of the lions and the Christians or the spectacle of a car crash. It made me feel uncomfortable but I pressed on regardless. "No!" said, Adrian tersely, his brow rippling in consternation and inability to control the situation as he had with Devlin and others. "Part!?"

"You sound like Moses trying to cross the Red Sea," I said, causing Adrian's facial tic to make him wink involuntarily. "Okay, Adrian. I am singing second tenor. I have been singing second tenor for the last couple of weeks when we started rehearsals for these operas and I'm going to sing second tenor right up until the performance, when I shall, if the mood takes me, probably sing second tenor then too."

Adrian flinched when he heard Gary's mean laugh. It was not my intention to berate Adrian in public and certainly not in front of hyenas like Gary. However, I was pushing a point home and I was almost there. "Alright," said Adrian, resigned but with an edge of frustration, creeping into his voice. The control he thought he had was slipping away from him, by talking to me. He pointed with his pen to a space a couple of yards from where I was standing. "Stand there," he ordered and poised the pen over his clipboard.

"No."

Adrian slowly turned to me and frowned one eyebrow. "What?"

"No, I said."

"But –."

"Look, Adrian. You are completely out of order. You are not the director of this work. The New York Met. will have a different rehearsal hall from this one, so it doesn't really matter where we stand. This rehearsal is to get the basic idea for the actions clear in everyone's mind so that we don't start green when we get to America. Now stop being so damned officious."

Adrian puffed another disapproving sigh, the redness of frustration creeping up his cheeks and moved on to Gary. "Name?" he asked, in a quieter tone but still not maintaining eye contact with Gary, pen poised above the clipboard. Nothing I had said had made the slightest difference. I was frustrated that the point had not got across to him and knew that Adrian would treat it as another example of my antipathy towards him. Now that Gary was talking to him, it was likely to worsen the situation.

"You what?" Gary responded now. His mouth was turned down in a figure of disgust and he frequently glanced at Pete and me for moral support. Pete, for his part, was impassive, while I watched carefully, fearful that Gary would take things too far.

"Oh, not you as well, Gary. Name?"

"Benito Mussolini," smirked Gary, winking at Pete. "And he is Joseph Stalin and I think I saw Mao Tse Tung knocking about somewhere. You can call me Ben and him Joe, if that makes it any easier." Gary smiled cruelly, knowing that he had knocked Adrian hard, repeating the exercise that I had started.

Another sigh. "Will you stop messing me about?" he whined.

"Will you stop being so bloody bossy?" returned Gary, the cruelty winching up a broader smile.

"You appointed me to do this."

"Against my better judgment, it seems."

This time Adrian did stamp his foot. "That's completely unfair."

"I agree," I said, separating the two before they came to blows.

Adrian glared at me, breathing heavily, as Gary tried ineffectually to respond to me, unable to articulate anything. Adrian slowly took a deep breath and said, through clenched teeth: "Why don't you just bugger off and leave me alone to get on and do what I'm good at?" With that, he turned on his heel to order a group of sopranos to move a few feet sideways.

"What were –?" spluttered Gary.

"Gary!" I rounded on him. "That was completely unnecessary."

"Pots and kettles!" he needled defensively. "You were having a right go at him."

"Yes I was. But it didn't need you to continue the pantomime. I have had enough difficulty bringing him into line without you joining in and allowing him to think that we are ganging up on him."

"I thought we were."

"You poor deluded fool, Gary. The only reason I was treating him like that is because it appears to be the only level of social intercourse his repressed mind seems to understand. Now, thanks to you, it is going to be doubly hard to bring him into line next time."

"'Now, thanks to you, it's going to be doubly hard…'," Gary mimicked in a high-pitched, nasal and childish voice, screwing his face up as he did so. "God, Dave, you talk about Adrian being officious. Look at you."

"Dave's not being officious, Gary," Pete pitched in, watching the growing heat between the two of us.

"Could've fooled me," replied Gary after a moment and slunk off to smoke outside the building.

Pete raised his eyebrows and shrugged.

"I don't know what to do about them," I agreed to his unspoken thoughts.

"Just keep going, I guess," suggested Pete. "There must come a point when it is obvious to them that their behaviour is unacceptable."

I nodded resigned agreement and we returned to our earlier conversation.

At the end of the rehearsal – which had had us trying different ways of projecting the meaning of the words through actions, in different groups and in different positions, thus completely and amusingly nullifying the directions that Adrian had given everybody and he had been furiously trying to follow all this on his clipboard – while everyone was collecting their belongings, Adrian stepped forward and clapped his hands twice. With his head imperiously lifted, he bellowed pompously as if we were in the next room: "Ladies and gentlemen. All those doing the American trip"

("i.e. everyone," muttered Pete under his breath)

"there has been a change of rehearsal venue in America."

("I'm not listening to this drivel," said Gary, "I'm going to the pub.")

"We are now rehearsing in the St. Francis Hall on the Tuesday."

(Gary stood up noisily and made his way to the exit)

"Finally, I won't be here tomorrow, so could you sign my registers, which I will pin up on the notice-board?"

("What? The same procedure as you've dictated for all the other rehearsals," observed Pete quietly)

"It's a three-line whip, so please ensure that you sign up –."

The remainder of his self-important monologue was lost in the noise of everyone following Gary's example and preparing to leave for the day, giving up on listening to Adrian's inconsequential prattle. I told Pete that I would catch him up in the pub while I had another word with Adrian.

Adrian was putting the clipboard and other stationery neatly into his briefcase and he glanced up as I approached him. He sagged slightly and returned to playing in his case. "What do you want?" he asked morosely. "Going to tell me how to do my job again?"

"No, I'm not. But can I give you a couple of observations? I'm trying to help you."

Adrian scoffed and continued tidying his case, more out of distraction rather than necessity. "Yeah, right."

I ignored him and carried on. "Here's a fine example of what I was trying to get across to you the other day. For someone to be respected as a leader, that person has to bring people along."

"Eh?"

"Well, rather than dictating unnecessarily to them, they only need sufficient information pertinent to them to make intelligent decisions of their own."

"What *are* you on about?" He stood up and put his hands defiantly on his hips. "Are you having another go at me?"

"Adrian, that is the last thing I want to do. But you have to admit that you haven't got much control over the proceedings today."

"But I'm very good at managing things. You said so yourself."

"Things: yes. People: no."

"You don't know what you're talking about," he said dismissively and started pushing papers around his briefcase again.

"I do. Look, let me give you the example. Your announcements at the end of the rehearsal just now." I sat on the back of a chair so that there was no appearance of looming over him as he bent over his case. "That was too much information. It was either unnecessary or inappropriate timing. You saw people getting up and leaving before you finished."

"That was Gary. The others followed like sheep."

"Only because you haven't got their focus. They were itching to go and Gary was the catalyst."

"Okay, okay," he replied hotly and glared at me. "I'm crap at what I do."

"That's not what I'm saying, Adrian. What you need to do is create a rapport with the Chorus at large so that they are prepared to listen to you. Giving them useless bits of information, ordering them about and stamping your feet when you don't get your way is not the way to do it. Now if I were you –."

"And thank *God* you are not me. Now, if you'll excuse me, some of us have got work to do." With that, he pushed past me, deliberately banging into me to throw me off balance on the back of the chair. I unfolded my arms to grab the seat-back and called after him. It was met with terse silence and his retreating back. I stood with hands on hips and bowed head, frantically trying to think of another way to approach him, knowing that my options were now so severely limited that my normally inventive imagination was shrugging theatrically and saying: 'I dunno!'. Slowly, I went to the office to cogitate, slumped in the chair, fingers arched as I stared into the middle distance to think things through.

* * *

In the Goat and Dramatist, a furious Gary was remonstrating with Pete, drink slopping to the floor and ash cascading from a rolled-up cigarette as he punctuated his anger with overt gesticulation.

"Just who the hell does he think he is? The change of rehearsal venue is of no interest to us. The only person it affects is the Greyhound coach driver. We're going to have to do something about him, Pete." He dragged on his roll-up but it had gone out. Gary tutted, gave Pete his drink to hold and rummaged the contents of his pockets for a lighter.

"Gary, I know that he's a pain in the back-side but we ought to leave it to Dave to manage."

"And he's another one. Where does he get off telling me not to be so rude to poor little Adrian when he had been doing exactly the same thing."

"I think Dave was making a point to Adrian and he was concerned that it would go too far." Gary was about to respond when Pete put up a hand to stop him. "So what are you proposing for Adrian?"

"Well," said Gary, taken off-guard by the swift return to his original point. "Stop him becoming tenor section manager for a start," he blustered and sucked on the roll-up, which had gone out again. He muttered something under his breath and threw it carelessly towards the ashtray on the table beside them. Taking out a tin, he pulled out a paper and inexpertly lined up tobacco along its length, licked the paper and rolled it up. It sagged badly in the middle as he stuck one end in his mouth to light it.

"How do you suggest doing that? No-one else is standing as far as I know."

Gary cupped his hand around the lighter flame, closed it with a metallic click and it was in his pocket all in one accustomed flourish. He tipped his head back and breathed a plume of smoke aimed at the ceiling. "We ask – no, tell – someone to stand alongside him."

"It's got to be democratic, Gary. We can't force people to stand for the position."

Gary raised his eyebrows in innocence and spread his hands out to the side. "Of course, of course. I'm not suggesting otherwise. But some people might need a little convincing to stand."

Pete regarded him for a while, chewing slightly at his cheek. "Who should we ask?"

"What about Mike Shedson?"

"I don't think he's keen. He's standing in for Bob but I get the impression he's highly reluctant."

"Leave him to me. I'll discuss his concerns with him."

Pete pointed at him. "Seriously, Gary. Go carefully. I won't support anything that is underhand."

PUPPET ON A STRING

CHAPTER 27

The final orchestral rehearsal was scheduled for the day before our departure to the New World and was just for the choral parts of each of the operas without the soloists. Given that we were scheduled to perform four operas, this meant that we had a rehearsal in the morning, the afternoon and the evening. We were due to travel out of London Airport very early the following morning and I had already packed my suitcase, which was waiting by the front door. I had spoken to Marie the previous evening to let her know that I had posted the house details to her and that I had put in an offer for it.

Just before I left my house a couple of hours before the first rehearsal was due to start, I called the agents to let them know that I would be unavailable for the rest of the day and that I would be away for a week. I was stunned by the news that the offer had been accepted and made another call to instruct my solicitor to get things moving in my absence. With this good news, I walked to the office with a spring in my step.

Later on, tidying up last bits of correspondence and confirming meetings I had organized with major record companies to discuss distribution possibilities when the record label had taken off, I was interrupted by a sharp knock at the door, which opened tentatively. A head with shaggy, white, professorial hair poked around the side as it opened.

"Sir Charles," I said getting up to shake his hand.

"Ah!" he said opening the door fully. "Wondered if there was anyone about." He opened the door fully and limped in, leaning heavily on a mahogany cane, which was topped with a gold eagle-headed effigy. It was this that had rapped so sharply on the door. I remembered reading that he was a martyr to gout and it was obvious from his expression as he applied weight on the affected foot that it was hurting him badly.

I shook his hand and moved the chair for him to sit down, "I'm the Chairman of the *Coro di Londinium.*"

"I know who you are, dear boy," he said, a note of condescension bristling in his words, spoken with effort as he sat down in the chair. "That is the reason why I came to the rehearsal early. Marie gave me your address but I appear to have mislaid it."

I was suddenly a bit wary of him. I could not divine whether it was the foot or if there was something else but he was not treating me warmly. "Coffee?"

"Milk, two sugars," he said peremptorily, trying to position his heel on the floor to cause least pain, wincing every time he moved it and grunting slightly.

I disappeared into the kitchen annexe, wondering if he were testing me in some way, and returned with two mugs of coffee. "Milk, two sugars," I repeated, handing him one of them.

"No cups?" he said absently and sipped carefully, putting the mug on the edge of the desk.

"Marie tells me you conducted a good *Il Trovatore* in Paris last week," I said. An opening conversational gambit. Get him to talk about himself and defrost the ice that seemed to be between us.

"The critics seemed to like it," he agreed and then smiled wistfully. "It was Marie who made it, though." He turned to me and the smile vanished. "You are not going to hurt her."

"No, I'm not!" Alarm opened my eyes widely and I sat on the edge of the desk. "I don't understand."

"Mr. Loughton," he said, regarding me carefully, "I read the newspapers. Marie has not had an easy life and she cannot endure being treated badly."

I was completely taken aback. After a moment to collect my thoughts, I said: "Sir Charles. None of what was written about me in that rag is true."

He stared levelly at me. "If that is the case, why have you not responded to the paper in question?"

"Because I did not want them to bully me into a position where they were left thinking there wasn't smoke without fire. And not to get fired up by it so that they'd find some other poor sap to chase after."

"I would say that, by taking no action, it has already created a position where there is no smoke without fire." I was about to protest but he waved it aside with the flexing of the fingers holding the eagle-head and turning his head away. "The point is that I can see how upset Marie was in the photographs they published. And I do not want her upset any more."

"I don't know what to do about it, then."

"Respond to the paper, damn you, and prove that the allegations are without foundation."

An uneasy silence descended between us, broken by his occasional grunts as he moved his foot. Eventually, I said: "Sir Charles, I love Marie deeply and I would never ever do anything to hurt or harm her. In fact, I'm trying to protect her."

He rounded on me. "You have a funny way of showing it. Being discreet about dalliances with other women is one thing but to be seen cavorting with them in public is entirely different. It's just as well Marie is in France and cannot see what you have been up to."

I protested again. "This is completely out of proportion, Sir Charles. It is completely innocent."

"Not from where I'm sitting."

I thought for a moment. "Have you spoken to Marie at all about this?"

"What? And upset her. Besides, I don't have to."

"Do you know that we are getting married?"

He pursed his lips and stared at the eagle on his cane. "Marie has told me. But I have not given my permission."

My heart stopped momentarily. This was awful. My happiness with Marie was supposed to be a done deal but this appeared to be an unthinkable broadside to the establishment of our permanent union.

I thought quickly and said: "Sir Charles. Marie means the world to me and I know I mean the world to her" – Sir Charles regarded me bitterly and returned his focus to the eagle-head – "I would never knowingly do anything to hurt her. Those newspaper reports are completely untrue and without foundation. I have spoken to Marie about them, to ensure that she got it from me before anything more snide reached her. We agreed that I would take no action because it would be never-ending – by asking them to retract the comments or take legal action may cause further disruption to our lives while they dig around trying to find something that is just not there. Marie is the only woman for me and, while I know she loves you as a paternal or avuncular figure, if I can't have your blessing to our marriage, then so be it. But you'll be doing her a disservice and creating unnecessary disharmony between the two of you if you don't at least acknowledge that this is going to be."

I was breathing heavily as my exasperation increased the urgency behind the words. Sir Charles had watched me impassively throughout and said, finally: "I admire you for having the courage to speak to me in that manner, boy, but the fact remains that I am here to protect my dear Marie from making a foolish decision."

I folded my arms in defiance. "I'm sorry you feel that way, Sir Charles. As I've said, I feel that that is my job now. I can take over where you left off and you've done a great job. She is a wonderful girl, warm, sincere and genuine" – Sir Charles winced a little, maybe because of what I had just said or because the gout had pricked him again – "I will be marrying her. Marie has her own mind and is beyond the age where I have to ask for her hand. I was going to ask you as a matter of courtesy but I know what you'll say, now, I think."

"I will not stop her deciding her future but I'll make damned sure that you do not risk her happiness. I want her –." He stopped suddenly. The emphasis had been on the word 'want' rather than 'her'. With pin-dropping clarity, I suddenly understood. This old man was secretly lusting after Marie but recognized that it would be unbecoming of a man in his position to do anything about it. During the time Marie had had no paramour, there had been a very close link between her and Sir Charles; with me on the scene, he was expecting this to be put in jeopardy. I would be taking her away from him; the object of his misplaced affections. He stood up with effort and leaned heavily on the cane and cleared the hanging and oppressive embarrassment from his throat. "I've said my piece. You know where I stand on this newspaper business." He pointed an accusatory finger. "I'll be watching you, boy."

Not as closely as I'll be watching you, old man, I thought, as he limped towards the door and disappeared.

I was now in a quandary. I did not want to raise this ugly spectre with Marie because that would upset her deeply – the two men she cared about at loggerheads with each other – but I also did not want Sir Charles to pre-empt anything by feeding her dishonest titbits in an attempt to undermine our relationship.

The rehearsals were not enjoyable, since I had now seen him in a completely different light and I was thinking of Marie and how to get out of this situation. The best option, I figured, was to brazen it out with Sir Charles and talk with Marie about this newspaper issue once more.

* * *

During the break between the afternoon and evening rehearsals, avoiding Sir Charles as much as I could, I took Sir Norman aside to talk about the record label.

Sir Norman patted my shoulder and smiled. "Bruce told me what you got up to in the studio last week. Interesting way of looking at the recording medium. What are you going to do next?"

I told him about the meetings with EMI, Decca and others. "The idea of this swirling sound around the listener made me think of *The Creation*. I know Haydn wanted to get the effect of a maelstrom, for instance, at the beginning by handing off the tune to different parts of the orchestra but I think, using the technique we established last week with Bruce, we could inject more life into it."

Sir Norman nodded. "That's a good idea. I like it. And, when you think about it, given that it's a new venture, quite an apt opening title for the label."

I had not seen that and was struck by how easily it was all coming together, almost accidentally. "I was thinking of getting the recording kicked off after we return from America. I think I can secure Marie Duvois and Beth Jackson for the female solo slots. Just need to find a bass and tenor."

"Good idea. Let's organize that when we have a spare moment in America."

"Fine."

"Now, on the subject of America, Gary has just told me that there is a chance that President Johnson is going to join the Mayor of New York for one of the performances."

"Really?" I asked incredulously.

"Didn't you know?"

"I do now. That explains a lot. Gary and Adrian have been circling each other like wary fighting tigers for the last couple of weeks."

"That's what I was afraid of. The organizers say that they want minimal representation from each organisation involved to meet the President if he turns up."

"Who do you think?"

"I was going to suggest you and me but I'm aware that certain people might not enjoy that decision."

"Leave it with me, Sir Norman. I'll get it sorted out once Adrian is back and not so heavily involved in organizing this tour."

"Is he not here today?"

"No and I don't know why. Still, somewhat quieter without him."

Sir Norman grinned and nodded knowingly. "Well, keep me posted."

Sir Charles, I noticed, had been observing us throughout our discussion but smiled generously when Sir Norman came over to talk to him.

* * *

Later that evening, subdued from the efforts of rehearsal and the discussion I had had earlier with Sir Charles, I called Marie.

"Hi, sweetheart," I said, "I've got some good news. Well two pieces really."

"Okay, give me the good news first and then the good news."

I laughed. "First, the offer I put in on our house has been accepted."

Marie squealed and the line crackled. "Fantastic!"

"I've asked the solicitor to get things moving while I'm in America. I've organized the bank, so things should move swiftly as I don't have to sell this place before buying that one."

"And the other news?"

"Pete has sorted out a holiday for us in the first two weeks of August. We plumped for Italy."

"I thought we suggested the Caribbean? Or the Bahamas?"

"All booked up. It was a toss up between St. Tropez and Perugia. There's a nice villa in a remote village. It's at the top of a hill, splendid views and even has a swimming pool in its garden. You're not too disappointed, are you?"

"No," she replied genuinely. "Anywhere with you would be great and I've never been to Umbria or Tuscany. I'm looking forward to it."

"So am I. The only other thing," I said, recalling my chat with Sir Charles that morning, "is that I am still concerned about this rag of a Sunday paper trying to muck-spread our lives. Do you still think I should do nothing?"

"David, if you think you need to do something, then go ahead but I agree with your reservations. If we were to respond to it, they will just keep reporting on us. Ignore them and they should go away."

"I agree with you. Are you sure?"

"Yes."

"I had a talk with your uncle – Sir Charles – this morning."

"He's a nice man, isn't he?"

"He certainly dotes on you," I said, hoping that Marie had not noticed the slight pause before I answered.

"I know. He's a soppy old man when it comes to his feelings for me. He gets all paternal."

"I had noticed. I asked for your hand in marriage. You know, just to keep it on a formal footing."

"And what did he say?"

I thought quickly. "He said he's not going to stand in your way."

"Sweet," she said. I could hear her smiling as she said it. There was no way that I could express my fears and concerns to Marie nor give her a complete account of the words that had passed between us. It would destroy her and potentially damage our relationship completely.

We got off the subject of Sir Charles – deftly I turned the conversation back to Worth Matravers, when she would be able to see it (she would be in England shortly after I returned from America) and made plans for getting down to Dorset. We bade each other good night and I stumbled into bed. It was so good to hear her voice and the concerns I had over her mentor had lessened considerably.

Nevertheless, I had a fitful night's sleep.

PUPPET ON A STRING

CHAPTER 28

I was dreaming again. The same cyclical melodramas I had always suffered; irritating and nightmarish in their intensity. They were the same dreams that had disappeared since I had been with Marie but had now returned. Eventually, at around four o'clock in the morning, they subsided to be replaced by another, focusing on Marie.

We were walking along the fashionable side of the Seine, which obviously was not the Seine because of a curious Taj Mahal-like monument on one side and the predominance of hula girls in grass skirts playing bagpipes in small groups. Hand-in-hand, we came across a lovely house in a suburb of London (dreams are never sticklers for continuity), very spacious and an altogether des. res. In some respects, it resembled the house we had bought in Dorset. We were standing at the foot of the stairs, hugging and kissing, Marie placing her hand on my chest in the now familiar gesture.

"Marie," I said in the dream, "we should settle down and consider having some kids. What do you think?"

Before she could answer, a huge, hooded figure shadowed across the front door, momentarily darkening where we were standing. Something glinted in the sunshine outside through the glass panes, flashing brightly in our eyes, which looked like a gardening implement of some kind but not a scythe; it all seemed to be a grotesque parody of the Grim Reaper. The shadow passed again, flattening its haggard, white face to the frosted glass and pressed the doorbell. Incessantly the doorbell rang as Marie screamed…

…and I reached over to turn the alarm off, Marie's screams still echoing but receding in my head. It was one of those dreams that leaves a bad taste in your mouth; consigning an uncertain feeling to add to the general malaise that something is wrong but you cannot specify or identify what exactly. I shook my head and wandered to the bathroom, eyes almost closed with the effort of getting up at such an ungodly hour, especially after the fitful night, watering as they were every time I tried to open them fully. I felt jumpy and disconcerted by the remnants of the dream echoing in my ears and flashing before my eyes.

Downstairs, washed, dressed and feeling less than human, experiencing the odd sickness that comes with arising too early with insufficient sleep or the new phenomenon of jet-lag, I made a cup of strong tea to jar my nerves into some semblance of consciousness. I slumped into the armchair in the front room and went into a daydream about my weird nightmare, what I could now remember of it. I jumped violently when the doorbell rang, momentarily positive that the Grim Reaper itself was present in the room.

"Damn!" I whispered to myself, brushing spilled tea from my black trousers. Fortunately, the spillage would not notice appreciably and I decided not to bother to change. Gulping down half of its lukewarm liquid, the contents spurred my senses into some action, so thick and strong was the tea. I opened the front door as the bell intoned again and the taxi-driver gave me a smart salute.

"Taxi, Mr. Loughton?" he asked and smiled.

"That's right," I replied, wearily, looking around. "That suitcase only. The briefcase will come with me."

"Righto, mate," he said, cheerily opposite in mood from me.

While he deposited the case in the taxi's boot, I quickly washed up the breakfast things, made sure that the gas was turned off and threw the electricity mains switch for good measure.

The roads were very empty at that time of the morning. Dawn was breaking on the horizon as we approached London Airport and I joined the small group collected near the check-in point shortly before six o'clock. Our flight was scheduled to depart at half past eight but we had been advised to get there early to avoid disruption of plans and to ensure that everything made it on to the plane. Adrian had already organized for the wardrobe and props crates to be put in the cargo hold.

By a quarter past six, it appeared that everyone was there, mingling with each other in subdued conversation. Gary was counting heads quickly, while at the same time, on the opposite side, Adrian was doing likewise, only with laborious slowness, as if he had some trouble identifying the next number in the sequence as he counted. They continued counting and moved towards each other. When they met on the far side, Gary had almost completed his count and Adrian had achieved only a third of the Chorus. As he realized that Gary was counting too, he glared at him malevolently like a goaded bulldog.

"Gary," he whined childishly and stamped his foot, "*I'm* supposed to be doing the counting."

Gary put his hands up quickly in surrender and lowered them again. "But you're taking all day." His voice was rising in pitch. "We're supposed to leave at eight thirty *a.m.* not *p.m.*"

"Well, let me count, then," replied Adrian indignantly. "After all, unless you haven't noticed, I have done all the work for this."

"What a baby," Gary jibed, and closed his eyes in annoyance, putting his fists on his hips. Then he swept a hand towards Adrian, saying: "Go on then. Behave like a child. Go ahead and count."

Adrian smiled victoriously and began his headcount afresh, even slower than before. Gary walked over to Pete, wringing his hands as if strangling someone. "We're going to have to do something about that jumped up little prig."

"Like what?"

Gary snapped his fingers and his previously grave face let a light shine from somewhere in its depths. "I know. Let's hold the section manager referendum on the plane."

"Have you spoken to Mike Shedson, then?"

Gary gave Pete a sickly grin. "Of course I have. He's happy to stand."

"Okay, Gary," replied Pete uncertainly. "But it must be ethical and fair."

"Naturally," said Gary, hurt that someone would suggest otherwise.

"Have you spoken to Dave about this?"

"Yes, I've talked to him too," he replied, irritation barely concealed.

"…a hundred and thirty-two," counted Adrian, his head tipped back officiously. "Right, that's it. Everybody on the plane. Now!"

"Can we check-in first?" called one wag from the throng.

"That's what I meant," spat Adrian, thunderous brow weaving over the top of his eyes.

* * *

The aeroplane was a chartered jet from English Monarch Airlines, its patriotic colours of red, white and blue glinting proudly in the early morning sunshine. The beauty of chartering a jet was that it could be treated more like a coach outing rather than having to worry about other passengers with the inevitable boisterousness of the Chorus.

We would be lifting off at twenty-five past eight, according to the jocular pilot, into the clear blue sky, out west over Windsor Castle before turning north towards Manchester, across the Irish Sea and towards Greenland. With safety-belts securely buckled, the air hostess gave a demonstration of what to do if the cabin depressurised, the brace position in the event of a crash-landing and what to do if the plane came down in the water. With the vestiges of my dream still with me, I was far from reassured and tried to ignore any strange sounds – what did I know? I was no aircraft engineer – coming from the engines and regularly dug my fingers into the armrests as we bounced in pockets of turbulence.

Which was why, two-thirds of the way into the flight, I was happy to see Gary get up, walk to the front of the plane and, after a brief discussion, was handed the intercom 'phone by one of the stewardesses. I noticed Gary glancing down at her legs and following her hungrily with his eyes until she had disappeared, his neck eventually craning to watch her.

His voice came back to us, thin and reedy over the hubbub. "Ladies and gentlem… This isn't working." He called to the stewardess, who returned, pointed at a button, which Gary pressed and a light 'bong' over the speakers heralded its activation. Again Gary watched the stewardess until she was out of sight. "Ladies and gentlemen," his voice boomed over the speakers, causing me to wince a little. "Ah! That's better. Ladies and gentlemen, welcome to Gary Adner Tours, where we will be cruising at an altitude of approximately no inches from the floor of the cabin. Let's hope it stays that way."

This produced some ribaldry in response. Gary had taken to laughing at his own jokes just recently and it was becoming annoying and wearisome, but at least it was a distraction from listening to what I envisaged to be the plane falling apart.

"This is directed at the tenors," he continued, "As everyone is sitting there, my captive audience, waiting for the trolley dollies to break open the cocktails, now seems a good time to hold the tenor section manager referendum to replace our dear departed friend Bob." Insincerity was oozing from him and it annoyed me to hear him talking about Bob in that manner and frustrated me that he had not referred to me about his intentions. However, in the spirit of a good tour, it did not seem worth getting unduly upset about it and I let it ride.

"So, Pete will distribute the pieces of paper – well, pieces of my notebook – for the purpose of each tenor writing their choice for section manager on it. It's a closed ballot and the nominees are: in the red corner, Adrian Hilton and, in the blue corner, Mike Shedson. So, no hitting below the belt and, when I give the nod, come out fighting."

I was surprised that Mike had decided to stand after all. The last conversation I had had with him shortly after Bob's funeral was that he was not suited to the elevated position and did not enjoy the idea of stepping into 'dead men's shoes', as he put it (intended metaphorically but had a literal context too). Secretly, I hoped that he would win because I could not endure the thought of the aggravation that Adrian Hilton was likely to bring to me and to the Chorus.

"Here," Gary carried on in Vaudeville style as Pete handed out the paper to the tenors. "It feels like a cabaret up here. At last, I'm a star. Did you hear the one about the two fleas going out for the evening, when one turned to the other and said," – he changed up to falsetto – "'It's a lovely night, dear, shall we walk or take a cat?'"

Everybody laughed, even though this was the joke he told everybody, and which unfortunately spurred him on further.

"Remember," he said, his face straightening and his voice lowering gravely. "You can lead a horse to water but you can't saddle a duck."

More laughter.

"A white horse walks into a pub. As they do. My local is full of horses but that's just the female clientèle – nothing to do with equine matters. A white horse walks into a pub and the landlord says, ''ere, mate, why the long face?'"

Another loud ripple of laughter.

"No, no, he didn't," laughed Gary. "The barman said to the white horse, ''Ere. We've got a whisky named after you!' And the horse replies: 'What? Eric?'"

Now I did find that one funny, as did the whole 'plane. Gary was warming to his theme of music-hall comedian, while Pete was moving up and down the aisles collecting the slips.

"A grizzly bear walks into the pub. History doesn't relate whether it's the same pub as the white horse and, even if it is, whether the two animals are friends. But, nevertheless, he walks into the pub and the landlord says: 'Yes, mate. What can I git yer?' The bear ponders for a while, rubbing his stubbly chin and replies: 'I think I'll have a pint of'" – Gary broke off and stared fixedly at the ceiling. Eventually, people were beginning to feel uncomfortable, wondering what Gary was doing – "'...Guinness.' 'Certainly, sir,' confirms the barman, pulling the pint, 'but why the big pause?'"

Laughter again and applause. Pete was nearing the end of his weaving around the cabin. I looked at him quizzically, as he took the slip from me. He knew I was asking mutely about Mike Shedson and he pointed at me, equally questioningly. I shook my head to show that neither Gary nor anyone else had approached me about Mike or the referendum. Pete sighed, rolled his eyes and moved on.

"Which reminds me of the two city gents," Gary battled on, "standing next to each other at the urinal. Well, actually it doesn't do anything of the sort but I couldn't think of a more suitable link! So, these two city gents, standing there, performing their necessary ablutions, when one turns to the other and says: 'I see you've splashed out on a new suit.' And the other says: ' Have I? Oh, dear, I'm so sorry.'" Gary mimicked brushing something from his trousers.

Embarrassed, hand-covered giggling from Norm's Gorms was the predictable reaction to this joke.

"Well, Pete's finished collecting the voting slips, so I'll stop there. Besides I've run out of relatively clean jokes for the moment. Thank you and I love you all." He kissed his finger-tips and threw his arm out wide, handing back the intercom to the grinning hostess. Gary winked briefly at her as more spontaneous applause broke out.

Pete was counting the slips intently, separating them into two piles. He glanced over at me, when he had finished and said: "It's a complete rout."

"In whose favour?"

"Adrian Hilton – three votes to every one of Mike's."

I rubbed my eyes with outstretched finger-tips. "I wonder how much Mike wanted to stand. Can you hold off any announcement until I have had a chance to talk to him?"

"Of course," said Pete. "That bloody Gary! He's not going to like the result."

I nodded in rueful agreement.

PUPPET ON A STRING

CHAPTER 29

The rest of the plane journey was uneventful. Pete fell asleep in the seat beside me, while I worked through the business plan for the record label, in preparation for the number of meetings I had set up with record companies on my return. With the backing of both Sir Norman and Bruce Carlton behind the venture, it was shaping up very well as far as these companies were concerned and, judging from the interest generated, they were falling over themselves to be a part of this particular project. Having also secured the services of two singers – in Marie and Beth – of such great world-renown (and therefore pulling-power), it helped the cause no end. The meetings I had had with the record labels indicated that, even if it were unsuccessful as a venture, it would nevertheless be lucrative!

The 'plane touched down at John F. Kennedy Airport in the eastern part of New York State at half past four in the afternoon, British time, half past eleven, American Eastern seaport time and, if the in-flight literature were to be believed, half past midnight at Ayer's Rock in the Australian desert. Adrian remained at the customs hall, awaiting the wardrobe and props cargo, while the remainder of the Chorus made their way through Immigration and Customs to the Greyhound coaches thrumming their engines outside the Terminal to whisk us off to the hotel in central Manhattan. I noticed with interest that the process was swiftened by the complete absence of Adrian's self-important, ineffectual authority and posturing.

At the hotel, having freshened up and unpacked the suitcases to get travelling creases out of clothes, Gary was the first to the bar and was already supping a glass of cold fizzy lager beer, when Sir Norman joined him.

"You did well in your début as a stand-up comic," said Sir Norman, raising impressed eyebrows at Gary.

Puppet on a String 301

"Thanks, Norm," replied Gary, fingering the lapel of his jacket in an affectedly modest way, "it runs in the blood, you know."

"Does it?" asked Sir Norman, feigning lack of interest.

"Yes," laughed Gary, "like main-lining morphine."

Sir Norman ignored him. "What was the result of the Tenor Section Manager referendum, Gary?" He winced expecting bad news.

"Well, Adrian, unfortunately" – Sir Norman shut one eye slightly as Gary paused – "lost."

Sir Norman's face relaxed. "I can't say I'm not relieved. I know I set him up to it and all that but the more I've witnessed the way he works as a result of this tour, the more I thought that it was a bad decision. So, at least it turned out well and I don't have to live with the outcome of it."

Gary nodded and knocked back the remainder of his gassy beer and belched with blatant disregard to good manners. He turned to Sir Norman: "Drink?"

"I won't, thanks, Gary. I need a clear head for this afternoon. Don't let me stop you, though." Sir Norman stepped off his stool by the bar and muttered under his breath: "As if I could, anyway."

Pete and I acknowledged him as he passed us to leave the bar. I hopped up on one stool and Pete on another. Gary begrudgingly ordered drinks for us. When they arrived, he passed them to us and said: "Just think. This time next week, it'll all be over."

"Yes, it will," I agreed. "Seems to have been a bit of a long haul getting here but at least we're here now. Make the most of the next few days."

"I might have some time off when we get back to England," said Gary grandly.

"I'm going to sort out my rapidly overgrowing garden," said Pete.

Gary looked at me. "Me?" I asked, sucking the remnants of very sweet lemonade moustache from my top lip. "I'm not going back to England. I thought I might go to Paris to see Marie."

Gary's face creased. "Marie Duvois? Oh, you're not still sniffing around her, are you?" he said unreasonably. "She'll get sick of you following her to get a glimpse of her cleavage."

A direct reference back to my mistake on the Parisian tour but I was unfazed. I winked slightly at Pete and took another sip of bitter-sugar-in-a-glass. "You don't think I stand much of a chance with her, then?" I asked, putting the glass down on the bar, pursing my lips with distaste at its contents.

"Well, she's way out of your league," he replied, with a casual wave of his hand.

"You keep saying that. Do you think I'm wasting my time with her?" I asked with the appearance of genuine concern that I might have misread the signs emanating from her. "Do you think I've misread the cues she's given me?"

"Obviously," agreed Gary, tapping out a cigarette on the bar and putting it in his mouth. It waggled between his lips as he spoke, while he searched his jacket pocket for his lighter. "Take that Chinese meal we went to. She wanted to sit next to me. Not you. But it was only your deviousness that stopped her. I saw that she was upset by the way you handled her."

"Oh, my God!" I exclaimed in mock astonishment. "I hadn't realized. Do you really think she prefers you to me? Do you think that's why I have no chance?"

"Of course." The cigarette was now alight and performing semaphore in Gary's expressive gestures. "And what about that time when she came to the office? You could tell she completely changed when I came in. God knows what you had been saying to her. Boring the arse off her probably. But I could tell. There was something in her eyes."

"Probably dust." Gary was now becoming offensive to me so I thought I'd bring it to a close. "Well, if it's alright with you, I'm still going to go to Paris to see how the land lies."

"You're wasting you time, you know," replied Gary, arrogantly. "I might as well fly out there. I've got far more chance than you."

"Nah!" chipped in Pete to save me from Gary's inevitable tirade. "I'm putting my money on Dave."

Gary looked at Pete and appeared to get the message. "You have no faith in me," he said, more calmly and dragged on his cigarette, looking at himself in the mirror behind the shelves of alcoholic bottles.

I picked up the cue. "Well, I'd love to sit here and continue to swap the personal insults but I have a business meeting with Sir Norman. So, if you'll excuse me."

As I left, I heard Pete berating Gary for his unkind words. I grinned to myself when I heard Gary's expostulations to the knowledge that I was actually engaged to Marie Duvois, dismissing it as so much hogwash and 'pie in the sky'.

I took the elevator to the third floor and knocked softly on Sir Norman's door. There were two voices, which stopped. Sir Norman called for me to enter and I pushed the door open. Seated in the two armchairs, deep in conversation over a glass of room service red wine were Sir Norman and Sir Charles. Sir Charles grimaced when he saw who had interrupted their friendly conversation and the temperature appeared to drop a few degrees.

I made the effort and, with outstretched hand, greeted him. He looked at my proffered digits for a moment, briefly and limply shook hands using just his fingers and, getting up stiffly and leaning on his cane, he made his excuses to Sir Norman, who agreed to meet him later. Sir Charles then turned to me. "Please will you do me the honour of joining us for dinner after the performance on Thursday?" he asked.

I was taken aback. Despite the frosty atmosphere, he had, almost through gritted teeth, asked me to join them socially. "I would be honoured, Sir Charles."

He nodded efficiently and limped to the door, bidding us farewell.

"That surprised me," I said, as the latch clicked.

"Oh, he's a good sort," said Sir Norman. "I know he's protective of Marie but you'll win him around."

Sir Norman's astuteness surprised me. "I hope so."

"Now," said Sir Norman, briskly. "To business."

I resisted the urge to pick up the half-full wine glass and exult: "To business!" Instead, I highlighted the agenda for our meeting, including the record label, the first recording of *The Creation*, confirming that I had lined up both Marie and Beth for the female leads, adding that the traditional single female vocal part would be divided between them, and that they were willing to do it for a nominal fee. I asked him for suggestions for the tenor and bass.

He sat back and narrowed his eyes as he regarded me. Steepling his fingers to his pursed lips, he said: "I'm going to suggest something now and I don't want you to respond immediately until you've thought it through."

"Okay," I said carefully, putting a loose fist to my mouth and frowned in concentration.

"Before I do that, I want to clear up another point."

"Okay," I repeated, one eyebrow frowning a little more.

"I want you to take joint production credit with me," said Sir Norman eventually and appeared to kiss the fingertips near his mouth.

I protested immediately, sitting forward. "But I can't! I don't know anything about recording production."

Sir Norman continued in the same calm manner. "David, you know more than you think. What do you think a producer does?"

I sat back slowly again, thinking. "I don't know. I guess he makes sure that the recording is organized and completed on schedule. And I guess he also plays around with the mixing desk. But that's something I know nothing about."

Sir Norman nodded slowly, his eyes never leaving me. "You are correct in part. The producer does indeed co-ordinate the proceedings but he doesn't do anything with the recording console, without taking engineering credit too. That's what we have Bruce for. No, the producer expresses what he wants from the recording, while the engineer makes that happen."

I raised my eyebrows and nodded. "So, what you're saying is that, because this use of stereo was my idea, I should take some of the credit for this recording?"

Sir Norman nodded slowly again, fingers still pressed to pursed lips. "Yes. Except that I want you to develop it further."

I nodded in agreement. "Okay. That sounds like an opportunity I can't pass up."

"I will, of course, be on hand to help you with the traditional aspects of the record producer's role."

"Excellent!"

"And I also want you to take primary credit for it on the record sleeve."

"But what about you?"

Sir Norman waved the consideration aside with a hand and returned back to leaning on arched fingers. "Listen, David, this record label was your idea, you have done all the work in getting it off the ground and it is completely your idea to try this novel method of recording. I tell you what. How about something like: Producer colon David Loughton in association with Norman Pettinger?"

I spluttered a bit, embarrassed at his generosity of spirit in allowing me to take centre-stage on the recording, but there was more to come when I finally and – reluctantly with modesty – agreed.

"And now," said Sir Norman, regarding me even more carefully than before, "to the main question. Please don't reply immediately."

I nodded, wondering what he had up his sleeve.

"I want you," started Sir Norman, pausing to consider his choice of words. "No. I would *like* you to consider singing the tenor part on the *Creation* recording."

My stomach did a quick somersault and the world greyed out for a bit. I could have sworn Sir Norman had just suggested that I sing one of the lead solo parts on the recording. Astounded, I blinked and said: "Pardon?"

"I would *like* you to consider singing the tenor part," he repeated, still watching me intently.

"But...why?" I asked incredulously. "Surely, there are other soloists you would want to consider? Visconti? Estente? What about them?"

"If you really don't want to do it, I will of course talk to them and others but I wanted to give you the opportunity. I think you have an excellent voice – it has a lovely quality and a vibrato that makes what you sing interesting to listen to."

"But are you sure?" My incredulity was not allowing this to sink in.

Sir Norman finally sat forward and, almost confidentially, said: "David, I would not ask you if I did not think you were up to the mark and neither would I, if I did not think that your voice would add something to the recording."

"Well," I said eventually, "I'm honoured. When you put it like that, it would be churlish to turn down the offer."

"Excellent!" exclaimed Sir Norman, leaning forward and patting my knee once. "That's it, then. Now we just need to consider the bass. Any suggestions?"

I thought for a few moments and then asked: "I know this sounds a bit strange but would you consider another Chorus member?"

"I would if they were good enough. Who do you have in mind?"

I recalled the story of Hank Marvin of the Shadows being requested to play guitar as backing for Cliff Richard and he only accepted if his friend Bruce Welch could come along. But it was worth a try – 'you don't get anywhere in life if you don't ask, occasionally,' as my mother used to say to me. "I was thinking of Pete," I said, and put up a hand to ward off perceived objections. "I know he's my mate and all that but I think he has an excellent voice. It would be worth thinking about him."

Sir Norman started laughing. "Don't worry, David, I had already considered him and I'm glad you suggested it."

"Do you want me to talk to him about it?"

"Yes, if you wouldn't mind. I'm sure it's more likely he'll agree if you ask."

"And you don't think it's strange that we have two world-renowned female voices and two unknowns for this recording."

"Unknown for now," replied Sir Norman, obliquely. "No, I don't.

We need the big names to bring this to the forefront of the media so that this label idea of yours takes off. But I think your innovative approach will do that by itself. Now, what other business do we have to attend to?"

I looked down the agenda. I was so elated at this recording prospect that everything else paled almost into insignificance and I had to force myself back to the mundane. We discussed the protocols for meeting the New York Mayor and I agreed to find out from Adrian whether we had heard any more with regard to the potential attendance of President Johnson.

At the mention of Adrian's name, Sir Norman smiled with relief. "I'm so glad that Adrian didn't win the election. In retrospect, it was a poor decision to suggest he stood and I was worried that I was going to rue it. But it's worked out for the best."

"What?" I asked dangerously.

"Adrian. Not winning the election." Sir Norman was taken aback by my response. "You didn't think he was best positioned for it, did you, David?"

"No, I didn't," I replied and took a deep breath to keep the anger with Gary at bay. "Did Gary tell you this?"

"Yes, he did." Sir Norman was worried now. "What's the matter, David? You look ready to blow a gasket."

"That bloody Adner!"

Sir Norman shook his head. "I don't understand."

"I was with Pete when he counted the votes. It was almost three to one. In Adrian's favour." My voice had risen in pitch as I was expressing my disgust at Gary's underhand dealings.

"Oh, dear!" said Sir Norman quietly, burying his head in his hands and running his fingers through the silver locks. "Do you want me to say anything?"

"No, thanks, Sir Norman. I'll sort this out."

We concluded our meeting and I went in search of Gary, who had apparently disappeared shortly after I had left the bar. Pete told me that he was not in the least bit happy that I had, first, asked Marie for her hand, second, that she had accepted and, third, not involved him in any juicy gossip. Hot-headedly, he had stomped from the bar to find Adrian. My remonstration would have to wait and, glad for the reprieve to cogitate on the issues a little more, I planned how to approach Gary to clear this up.

* * *

The promoters had contacted both Gary and Adrian, confused as they were over who they should be talking to on the arrangements, and were no clearer by the initial dress rehearsal, planned for later that afternoon. They had eventually contacted Sir Norman via Sir Charles in exasperation and he had got a message somehow to Gary, who was now windmilling his arms in consternation and working himself up to a likely coronary as he loomed over Adrian in one of the dressing-rooms at the New York Metropolitan Opera House. There were a few chairs and a coat-rack, which had the polythene-covered costumes for some of the men dangling nonchalantly from it, and a long, brightly-lit mirror at the dressing-table for the make-up application.

"Look, Adrian!" spat Gary, pluming smoke from his mouth as he spoke. "I am the Secretary of this outfit. Not only that but *I* am a founding member."

"So!" replied Adrian petulantly, the corners of his mouth flickering a little. "You appointed me to this rôle."

"I know I did, Adrian, but that was when I was so busy with that damned *Carmen* recording. I can't be expected to do everything you know."

Adrian backed up against the dressing-table, his head bobbing away from Gary's sibilant consonants. "And neither can I," he retorted.

"Meaning?" Gary took a sharp drag from his cigarette and flicked ash from the end to the floor, by running his thumb-nail against the filter tip.

"Meaning that you have done sod-all for this American trip other than to get in my face. Between you and that bastard Loughton, it's a wonder I have my sanity left."

Gary stepped back and expressed innocence. "Don't have a go at me, Adrian. Loughton has given me just as much a hard time as you, if not more so. If you want to harangue anyone, it should be him. Not me!"

"He's going to get his come-uppance," muttered Adrian, morosely.

Gary launched back in on him. "But that still doesn't change what I'm saying. Loughton has instructed me to take this off you now so that I can concentrate on it."

"But you can't."

"I can, Adrian. As I'm the Secretary and to keep him off my back, you have got to hand it over to me. You can still do the boring stuff."

Adrian's eyes widened and he blustered: "But I've worked hard on this."

"Yes, you have, Adrian," said Gary through clenched teeth, the forgotten cigarette being waved manically between gesticulating fingers. "Maybe too hard. But as David Loughton has observed, you are strutting around like an egotistical dictator. No-one likes to be talked down to by a pygmy Hitler with a clipboard. You just can't handle people like that. They won't give you any respect."

Adrian scoffed and glared at the floor, the muscles in his cheeks working quickly as he clenched his teeth together. "You do it your way and I'll do it mine."

"That's not good enough, Adrian," said Gary, suddenly aware of the burnt-out cigarette, throwing it to the floor and stepping on it, crushing it into the thin carpet pile.

"No!" said Adrian, defiantly and folded his arms as an unconscious barrier. "You can't have it. I won't allow it."

"Look, Adrian," said Gary, levelling his voice to show that he was a smidgeon away from losing his temper. "Loughton wants to have that invitation. Now, if the President does turn up tomorrow, I want…Loughton wants to be there. Now, as Secretary of this outfit and overall manager of this tour –."

"Why?" said Adrian, aghast at what he had just said. "What have you done for this tour?"

Gary stood open-mouthed and stared at Adrian. "Why, you insulting little…" Gary was momentarily lost for words. As if his reasoning and logic were clear, he eventually said: "I'm the Secretary."

"So? That doesn't mean you have done anything, though, does it? And it doesn't give you or Loughton the right to ride rough-shod over the excellent job I have done."

"Let me tell you something, Hitler – Hilton, sorry," said Gary, with measured vehemence, turning vermilion, fists balling at his side. "I appointed you in my absence because, at the time, I had far too much else to do. I now have the ability to concentrate on this tour and am now assuming responsibility on Loughton's authority."

"But –."

Gary put up a hand to stop him and Adrian flinched. "Loughton showed me those Programme proofs." Each successive lie, if they had ever, bothered Gary less and less.

Adrian gulped and looked frantically around the room for a response but found nothing.

"By putting your bloody name in place of mine means that you owe me. I had to fight Loughton to allow you to stay in the Chorus for this misdemeanour. He insisted that you be cautioned at the very least but I forced him to drop it."

Adrian's mouth was working up and down but little was coming out. "But –."

Gary was unrelenting and he stabbed a pointed finger at Adrian. "And I'll tell you something else for nothing." He punctuated each word with the finger on Adrian's chest: "You – are – not – Tenor – Section – Manager. And that's democratic."

Adrian was suddenly crestfallen. His lower lip trembled as he looked up slowly at Gary. "But that means I've done all this for nothing," he whined, "the arrangements, the letters, the registers, the organisation – everything."

"Yes. And another thing I find myself agreeing with Loughton is on the subject of registers. You told two people who didn't turn up to one rehearsal – the first rehearsal – that they were dropped from the tour. You have missed two rehearsals – one of them, probably the most important of the lot and that you had the gall to say to everyone else was a three-line whip."

"But I had other things to do. He knows that. The bastard! He makes complimentary remarks about my organisational abilities and then he stabs me in the back by telling you tales. I had to sort out the wardrobe."

Adrian was getting desperate now and Gary knew he had him on the ropes. "Yes and the wardrobe. God alone knows how you wheedled and wangled your way into that one. But the fact remains that Loughton was right that you hadn't done enough rehearsal – private or otherwise – but you're still here. And that was because of me."

"What are you trying to say?" Some of Adrian's petulant composure had returned.

"That because of the favours I've done for you, keeping Dave Loughton off your back, giving you space to do your thing without his interpolation, you should allow me to take your place in meeting President Johnson." Gary smirked victoriously and added: "Alone."

"Oh, no! No, no! No!" said Adrian putting up a hand to Gary. "I won't accept that."

"What do you mean you won't accept it?" Gary's face was the epitome of disgust as he advanced again on Adrian, looming over him even more menacingly.

"Just what I say. Besides, the invitation has my name on it."

"That can be changed. Listen! I'm the one you are answerable to. I have fought hard to protect your position in this Chorus, stopping

Loughton having his undemocratic way. I might decide that the fight is just not worth it and let him have what he wants and sack you."

Adrian opened his mouth in shock at the sheer audacity. "That's...that's bribery." Gary raised an eyebrow and cocked his head briefly to the side. "I don't have to take that kind of shit from you or Loughton. You're both as bad as each other, you bastards." He stood up away from the dressing-table and reached into his inner jacket pocket, producing a thick, white envelope and waggled it teasingly in front of Gary. "And I *am* meeting the President, if he comes. *I* have an invitation from the organisers and you don't." His lower jaw was juddering up and down as if to combat a sudden drop in temperature.

Gary deftly swiped the envelope from his grasp and said: "Right. That does it. I've enough of protecting you any more. I am invoking David Loughton's commandment that, due to lack of rehearsal for this performance, you will not be allowed to take part. You will stay in the hotel until it is over."

"You can't do that, you bastard," cried Adrian desperately, displaying his limited vocabulary of expletives, grabbing and clutching at the envelope, which Gary kept tantalisingly just out of reach.

"I can and I'll have you for insulting behaviour too, which goes against the Chorus constitution."

Suddenly, as swiftly as a cat sneaking up on its prey, Adrian lunged out and grabbed a handful of Gary's facial flesh, digging his nails in painfully and viciously under the eye and scratching down his cheek, drawing welts filled with running red blood. Gary yelped and slapped blindly at Adrian's face but he would not release his grip. Tears of pain welled in his eyes, as he brought his arms back and landed Adrian a punch in the solar plexus. Adrian released his grip immediately and reeled backwards, doubling over and puffing like a long-distance runner in the final stages of a marathon race.

"That is it, Hilton!" shouted Gary, pawing at his facial wounds and looking at the copious blood on his fingers. "I have had enough of you."

"I'm sorry, Gary," he tried now, still bent over and getting his breath back.

"Dave Loughton was right about you. I should have listened to him but I thought I could make something of you."

Adrian tried to protest but Gary was hearing nothing of it. In frustration, Adrian lunged at him again but this time Gary was prepared. He caught his fingers and twisted them slightly, leaving Adrian yelping with pain, kneeling on the floor. Gary smiled evilly and slowly released Adrian's hand.

"On behalf of the Chairman, you are sacked from this Chorus, effective immediately. You will return to the hotel, pack your things and return to England. The Chorus will not pay for or refund your return ticket. Get out quickly and get out now!"

Adrian glared at Gary, mouth in a downward crescent, breathing heavily and noisily through his nose. He straightened up as far as he could, one hand on his stomach, decided not to say anything as a tear rolled down his cheek and ran from the room.

Pete and I were entering the adjoining dressing-room as Adrian slammed the door to the one he had just left Gary in. He stopped short in front of us and his face flushed and the tears tripping down his cheek. "Adrian?" I said, concerned that he was in such a state. I put a hand out towards him but he shrugged it off.

"Fuck off, you bastard! You'll pay for this!" he yelled, leaving a ringing in my ears, and pushed violently past me up the corridor.

I turned to Pete. "What, do you suppose, was all that about?"

Pete shrugged slightly and we went into the room to prepare for the dress-rehearsal.

* * *

It was a good hour later, Pete and I were slouched in the chairs, already changed into our costumes, talking about what we would do when we went to Perugia later in the Summer, when an harassed Sir Norman poked his head around the door, caught sight of us and came in fully.

"What's going on, David?" he asked, concern stitching his brows together.

I took my feet off the table and sat forward. "I don't know, Sir Norman. What's the problem?"

"Adrian."

"Ah! Well, I haven't had the chance to talk to Gary and, as far as I know, no announcement has yet been made."

Sir Norman waved that aside and sat down on a chair between us. He looked from Pete to me. "Adrian Hilton came back to the hotel, saying that you, David, had fired Gary up to sack him."

My mouth dropped open mirroring Pete's reaction. "First I've heard of it. Sack him, you say?"

"Yes, he's packing as we speak." Sir Norman wrung his hands

together. "I told him not to be hasty but he was adamant that he was not going to stay anywhere near you or Gary."

Pete and I looked at each other and comprehension dawned. "Sir, Norman," I said. "Leave it with me. I think Gary Adner has some explaining to do." My sunny disposition had clouded over and I was spoiling for a fight with him. Gary had gone just one banister length of steps too far this time.

Sir Norman stood up and said, as he was leaving: "Okay, David. If you need my support, you know where I am."

I leaned my elbows on my knees and sighed. "Pete, what the hell are we going to do with him? He's out of control. I wouldn't mind so much if he weren't blaming his inadequacies and ineptitude on me."

"Do you want me to come with you?"

"No," I said decisively and stood up. "This is one of my more unpleasant duties but I must do it on my own."

As I opened the door, Mike Shedson almost rapped his knuckles on my nose. I smiled sheepishly and greeted him. "Hi, Dave. Look, I'm sorry to do this across the committee but I don't think I want to take this Section Manager position."

"Marvellous. Why did you stand, incidentally, Mike?"

"I didn't. Well, I did but only after being forced to by Gary."

"Fantastic!"

"Sorry, Dave."

"No, I'm not angry at you really."

"Well, I was wondering if Adrian could pick it up as he came second."

"No he can't and no he didn't."

"Pardon?" Mike was looking confused.

"Nothing. Adrian has gone home, unfortunately. Look, Mike, for the time being, please can you stand in again as Section Manager and I'll organize a replacement as soon as I can."

Mike nodded and walked away, head bowed. I looked back at Pete who shook his head slowly. "Right!" I said and stormed off to the dressing-room that I thought Gary might be in. Sure enough, as I pushed the door open sharply, letting it bang into the wall for dramatic effect, there he was, not yet dressed for the rehearsal, feet up and crossed on the dressing table, a paper cup of Californian wine poured from a huge carafe on the side, the overfilled ashtray resting on his bloated belly. I stood in the doorway, hands on hips, wondering what to say and how to say it.

"Ah, hello, Dave," he said, breezily, oblivious to my mood.

"What have you done to your face?"

He subconsciously put up a hand to cover the claw-marks in his face. "This?" he tried nonchalantly. "I slipped in that fangled shower-thing and hit my face on the taps as I went down. Looks worse than it is."

"Talk to me about Adrian," I said, a serious edge glinting along the edge of my words.

"What about him? He's an obnoxious little git." Fear had crept into his eyes and he took a sip from his cup, surreptitiously eying me as he did so.

"I said: 'Talk to me about Adrian'."

He feigned understanding. "Oh, that!" He waved it aside and picked up the cigarette, which was resting on the ashtray on his belly and dragged on it. "I sacked him."

"Why?"

"What is this? The Spanish Inquisition?"

"Why?" I demanded more insistently.

"He hadn't done enough rehearsal."

"A bit late in the day to be doing anything about that. And, correct me if I'm wrong, it's not a sackable offence."

Gary sat up, placing the ashtray on the table. "What the hell are you getting at?"

"Why didn't you consult me before taking such a decision?"

"He attacked me," he said in a gratingly, whiny voice. "He tried to gouge my eye out."

"No. That was the shower-taps, remember? Why was I not consulted?"

"He insulted me."

"Still not a sackable offence. Why did you not consult me? Answer me!"

"Surely there's no point in getting involved." He picked up another paper cup and motioned to me. "Wine?"

I ignored the offer. "Talk to me about Mike Shedson."

"What about him?" He jolted the wine guiltily, temporarily thrown by the change in questioning. "He won the Tenor Section Manager job fairly and squarely."

"Where are the voting slips?"

"I...I threw them away. We don't need them any more."

"Not according to our constitution, which you have flouted gravely. Talk to me about Pete."

"Oh, what's he been saying now? You know, you two are so up yourselves, people will start gossiping about you. When are you two going to get married?" His tone had changed to be snide.

"Talk to me about rigged elections."

"Oh, come on, Dave! Lighten up. Adrian wouldn't have made a good committee member. It was just about alright with his co-option but to be elected? No way!"

"We don't know that. Who the hell do you think you are? You sit on cloud nine, talking out of your arse about how wonderful you are. You don't give a damn about other people or their feelings."

"But I –."

"SHUT – UP!!" I bellowed, shaking with the sheer force and vehemence. "You take it upon yourself to sack people, having rigged an election that's supposed to be democratic, rubbishing my name into the bargain, and then you have the temerity to sit there and say that Adrian Hilton is behaving like a despotic dictator. Has it ever occurred to you that you are behaving in exactly the same way? And that he might have learned that from you. Okay, so Adrian Hilton was wrong to attack you but I can't help feeling that you deserved it and that it is hardly surprising. The provocation you have given him over the last month or so would have driven anyone scatty and I can't help but feel you deserved it!"

Gary was now on his feet, oscillating between anger and defensiveness before settling on an amalgam of the two. He began shaking slightly and then looking at the paper cup he had just refilled with red wine, he suddenly threw it straight into my face, making my eyes sting and staining the front of my costume as the warm liquid cascaded down it. While I was blinking away the fermented acid, he advanced on me, fists clenched. At the last moment, I saw his arm going back but was too late to stop his fist connecting with the side of my face, sending me spinning to the floor.

Dazed but with my wits returned to me, I turned quickly to face him and got to my knees. I shied away from the first and second blow and batted the third away with my own fist and got to my feet, pushing him away, aggressively. "And that," I said levelly, pointing at him, fist at the ready as protection, "has just added insult to injury. By the rules of the constitution, I am invoking the regulation with respect to carrying yourself with decorum at all times and the associated regulation about not bringing the name of the Chorus into disrepute." Gary was momentarily surprised that I had troubled myself to read this document.

"I read it once I was elected," I spat at him, reading his thoughts. "You are officially sacked from this Chorus, effective immediately. You will return to the hotel, pack your things and return to England. The Chorus will not pay for or refund your return ticket." I was breathing heavily and still ready for him to assault me further. I relaxed my fist and looked down at the stains and the slight rip endured from being punched to the floor and added: "And you will be sent the cleaning and repair bill for this costume. Now get out!"

Gary's eyes took on a kind of malevolent supplication. "You can't do this to me. Look, I'm sorry."

I grimaced at his supplication. "It's too late, Gary. For far too long, I've been appealing to your better nature but today has brought it home with stark reality that that is completely impossible since you don't appear to possess one."

"Where am I going to get another job at my age?" That was a good point but I could not waver; I had to be resolute on this.

"You should have thought of that before you tried to treat this Chorus like your own personal *Mafioso*."

His eyes narrowed and then he was on me, slapping and hitting me. "You shitty, bloody... bastard!" he exclaimed, his ire narrowing down his list of insults to childish name-calling. He drew back his arm ready to punch me again but I side-stepped him, grabbed hold of his arm and took the follow-through momentum to twist it up between his shoulder-blades.

"You will not learn, will you?" I said, as Gary yelped with pain. I pushed him towards the opening door towards curious onlookers. "Get out. Now!"

Rubbing his shoulder, he turned and then pointed at me. "I'll get you for this! So God help me, I'll bloody kill you!"

He pushed his way through the gathered crowd, who parted and closed behind him, watching his flustered progress. I waved them all away telling them that the show was over and sank into the nearest chair, closed my eyes and rubbed my forehead, shaking like a timid kitten.

PUPPET ON A STRING

CHAPTER 30

My heart was not in the dress rehearsal, nor in the performance itself. This was partly because of jet-lag, partly because I was worried about the impact of Adrian's and Gary's outbursts and attitude on the Chorus but mainly because the adrenalin of dealing with the crisis brought about by the two of them was dissipating and had left me drained. I had also noticed that Adrian, in his infinite wisdom, had agreed to schedule the dress rehearsals in the evening on the same day as we had arrived. This meant that, although the Chorus was used to rehearsing into the evening, with the time difference on top of that we finished rehearsing at the equivalent of three o'clock in the morning, having been up since the early hours to meet at London Airport. But that seemed like in a different lifetime.

Nevertheless, the performances went well and we had the world's classical music press asking for interviews, taking pictures throughout the rehearsals and the performance. Adrian had kept the cards so close to his chest that I would not have been surprised to see the reverse imprint of the Ace of Spades on it. As a result, prior to the performance and at the last minute, I was requested to attend a press conference alongside Sir Norman and Sir Charles.

It became quickly apparent that the salacious news stories had traversed the Atlantic. It was not long before the questions of my private life impinged on what was supposed to be a prestigious occasion, concentrating on the New York Metropolitan Opera Houses, old and new, rather than trying to get hold of some untrue and inappropriate gossip. When the assembled throng began directing their questions at me, Sir Norman sat back arms folded glad of a reprieve from the promotional niceties. Sir Charles, however, was leaning forward on his forearms and regarding me irascibly. I knew that my responses had to be guarded; not only to protect Marie but also to satisfy her frustrated guardian and unrequited lover.

"There have been a number of reports in the British press," said one bespectacled journalist, standing up, initially holding his notepad and pen in one hand, while he pushed the black-rimmed, Buddy Holly glasses up his nose. "A number of press reports that all is not well between you and Marie Duvois. Would you care to comment?"

I glanced at the reddening Sir Charles and looked down at the table as I considered my answer. Flash-bulbs popped. I looked up and said, wittily, I thought: "You don't want to believe everything you read in the papers."

A few chuckles greeted this response and it heartened me a little.

"But this isn't about me," I continued, "this is about the inauguration of the new Opera House and the last rites of the old."

Frustrated, the journalist sat down. Hands went up and Sir Charles pointed to a blonde woman in a brown dress in the front row, who stood up. "But surely you have some response to the allegation that you are treating Mademoiselle Duvois badly?"

A chorus of supportive murmurs followed this question and I bowed my head again in resignation. "David?" said Sir Charles, tersely, wiping the corner of his mouth with a folded handkerchief.

I nodded a couple of times. "I am not treating Mademoiselle Duvois badly."

"But," protested this woman, "what about all these other women you've been seen with?"

"I have done nothing wrong." Sweat trickled down my temple and landed on my shoulder with what sounded like a loud 'bang!' to me, as the nervousness of the situation magnified the sensory input.

"What about the pictures of her in tears?"

I heard Sir Charles snort like a stampeding horse. "Our relationship is nothing for public consumption," I replied finally. "I wish to keep it that way as there is nothing wrong with Marie's and my relationship. Now please can we get back to the main purpose of this visit?"

The blonde sat down reluctantly and a grey-haired, wizened hack in a tweed jacket stood up, pointing his pen accusingly at me. "Last Sunday, the British papers – actually, my paper, to be precise – ran a story about you seeing other women. When we tried to contact you, you were nowhere to be found. Were you in hiding? Afraid of what had been found out about you?"

My temper slipped. "No!" I replied vehemently. "There is absolutely no truth in the lies that were printed. I happened to be house-hunting for my future wife" – a frisson of excitement ran around the room – "yes, that's right. I have asked Marie to be my wife and she has readily agreed. I was house-hunting so of course I was unavailable to talk to anyone about these stupid allegations. Now, please can we get back to the Opera House and the reason why we are here?"

"Just one more question, David" – my heart sank. They were becoming familiar with me, which meant that they were planning to skin me alive – "how does Marie feel about you seeing other women, especially if you are going to marry her?"

Another notch slipped in my temper gears. I covered my face with my hands. Flashbulbs fired again. I took a deep breath and looked at the assembled audience. "This has absolutely nothing to do with what we are here for today and you are trying to invent stories to sell your papers. Now I have done my best to be considerate and answer your questions and I am fed up with your insinuations. They are completely without truth and, in order to protect Marie, I am leaving this press conference now." I stood up and pushed away the microphone and stalked off to the door, cameras clicking and questions being called at me as I did so. Turning as I opened the door and looked at the journalistic throng, giving them a look of disgust, I slammed the door behind me. "Bastards!" I said to myself, although it worried me how Sir Charles and Sir Norman might have taken my response; worried that I might be perceived as petulant and childish but the concern was countered every time I thought of the impact that this nonsense might have on Marie and I knew that I had done the right thing.

* * *

After the performance, Sir Norman rushed on to the stage once the final curtain had fallen and pulled me aside. "President Johnson was present at the performance," he said breathlessly and coughed slightly. "We'll be in the line-up to greet him."

Ten minutes later, President Johnson, surrounded by burly, besuited agents appeared on the stage, moving along the line to congratulate everyone for a good performance and to thank Sir Norman and me for making it across the Atlantic Ocean to take part in it. Naturally, the press was present too and the cameras were clicking and flashbulbs electrifying the stage with blue lightning as the President made his way along the line. It might have been me but it felt like more photographs were taken when he reached me.

Two minutes discussion and it was all over but we had to remain in line, until his entourage exited with him stage right. I relaxed a little when the strained bonhomie was replaced with relieved chatter. "Well, that's that then," I said to Sir Norman.

"Bit of an anticlimax, really," he replied, brushing his nostrils with the side of a finger. "Can't see what Gary and Adrian were getting so fussed over. By the way, David, I think you handled yourself well in the press conference." He put a comforting hand on my shoulder.

"Thank you but I'm sure Sir Charles didn't see it that way. He didn't seem at all happy."

Sir Norman nodded ruefully and then looked up and smiled. "Sir Charles is very protective of Marie. I think he just wanted to make sure that there was no foundation in the rumours and press reports and that you would comport yourself in such a way as to protect Marie."

"Do you think I did as far as he is concerned?"

"Yes," Sir Norman confirmed, patting me on the back.

"Even though I lost my temper?"

"Yes," repeated Sir Norman. "To be honest, I'm surprised that you kept your anger at bay for as long as you did under such a barrage of insults. I wouldn't be at all surprised if Sir Charles doesn't now harbour just a little respect for you." He raised his eyebrows supportively and then patted my shoulder again. "Now, if you go and change, remember that we have a supper engagement."

I had completely forgotten about Sir Charles's invitation and I was now reluctant to attend. Tiredness and enforced melancholy had crept over me and, after the press conference, regardless of Sir Norman's perception of Sir Charles' reaction, I did not want more. "I might give it a miss."

Sir Norman looked up at me quickly. "You'd be foolish to do that."

"Why?"

"Trust me," he said and smiled. "Don't worry about Sir Charles. He'll come round."

I sighed and put my hands on my hips. "Are you sure?"

"You'll kick yourself. Trust me!" He raised an eyebrow smiling and held my gaze until I nodded agreement. "Good! Now go and get changed and we'll meet you out front."

I wandered off to the dressing-room to change and remove the make-up. More than ever, I just wanted to be alone with Marie by my side, cuddling up together on a comfortable settee, drinking slowly from large glasses of wine but I knew that was not going to happen any time soon. Before meeting the resident Knights of the Realm outside the stage door,

I sought out a public telephone and requested Marie's international number from the operator, who instructed me to pour several coins in the requisite slot.

I desperately wanted to hear her voice and tell her that I loved her. Expecting the transatlantic cabling to give me problems, I was holding out little hope. My heart jumped when the ringing tone could be heard. A smile spread across my lips, which disappeared by degrees the longer the ring-tone grated along the line. Eventually, the operator came back on to tell me that no-one was responding and did I want to place another call. Thanking her, I put the receiver back on its cradle and waited for the handful of coins to chug back out. Then, reluctantly, I made my way to the stage door, upset and puzzled that I had been unable to contact Marie. Even though it was two o'clock in the morning in Lyons, where she said she would be, I knew that she would have picked up the telephone if she had been there.

Somewhat depressed and a little bamboozled, I met Sir Norman outside. Even Sir Charles had cheered up and he slapped me familiarly on my back as he hobbled away from the stage door. It was five minutes to the chosen restaurant and, after dispensing with jackets and Sir Charles' pretentious black cloak to the waiter, we were shown to our table. Sir Norman kept the conversation flowing detailing his personal view of the excellence I had expressed in the Chorus record label. In many ways it was comforting that he was supporting me in this way to Sir Charles but it was also uncomfortable and my natural modesty kicked in.

"It's just an interesting medium," I said lamely in an attempt to turn the conversation to another subject. We were occasionally glancing at the menu and it had been twenty minutes since we had sat down. "Shall we order? I'm starving."

Sir Charles put a hand on my arm and smiled. "Not yet, dear boy. We are waiting for another guest and they said they might be a little late. Now, Sir Norman tells me that you will be taking joint production responsibilities for this Chorus label."

This seemed very strange. The conversation, though more polite than the throng at the press conference, was again trained on me. Nonetheless, since they were now talking about my baby, the record label, I was expounding on what I was trying to achieve in recording technique, when I noticed a knowing smile appear on both of their faces. I was about to turn around, when I was plunged into darkness by hands covering my eyes. She had done this before!

"Marie!" I exclaimed, jumping up and taking her hands from my eyes. Her eyes twinkled as she smiled. She was about to say something to me but I grabbed her and enveloped her in my arms and squeezed hard, which she reciprocated. "I love you," I said quietly to her and held her strongly. Releasing her slightly, I kissed her lips and she looked at my eyes worriedly. I felt a tear roll down my cheek and hugged her again, surreptitiously wiping away the wetness.

I held her hand and watched her intently, grinning like an over-excited baboon as she sat down. She was wearing exactly the same dress as she had to our first dinner date. I turned to Sir Norman and said: "Thanks."

"What for?"

"For convincing me to come out tonight. I now see why!"

"You deserve it. Especially after all that nastiness with Adrian and Gary."

Marie leaned forward, taking my hand, her brow furrowed questioningly.

I sighed and laughed with relief and squeezed Marie's hand. "It's nothing, really, Adrian and Gary are no longer part of this Chorus."

"What happened?" she asked, her brow relaxing slightly.

"Nothing much. It's quite complicated but it came to a head yesterday afternoon. The two of them have been spoiling for a fight for ages. Anyway, because this performance had the chance of meeting the President, they both wanted that opportunity. Gary, having rigged an election away from Adrian's favour, goaded him into a fight and then sacked him. I was perturbed that I had not been consulted about the sacking and the election-rigging so went in search of Gary. That was when things turned really nasty. He threw wine in my face and then attacked me." I laughed at the relief of telling this story. A black cloud crossed Sir Charles's face, which cleared as soon as Marie glanced at him, curious at what I was looking so querulously. "It was all rather silly, really. A bit like a pantomime. He punched my face" – I reached up to my cheek – "and I retaliated. To protect myself, you understand. Anyway, after a number of threats thrown at me, I had no option other than to sack him. He's had it coming for a long time and I've always tried to appease him. This time I got him good, as the Yanks say."

Another black cloud passed over Sir Charles' face but Marie diverted my attention by taking both my hands. "David, are you all right?"

Rubbing her hands with my thumbs, I smiled lovingly at her. "I'm fine. Just a bit of a trauma at the time." Then, turning back to Sir

Norman, added: "It suited Gary very well to have an ineffectual Chairman. When I came along and started taking control of the Chorus' destiny, when Sydney Althorpe left, it started showing Gary's inadequacies in sharp relief. But Sydney's method of running the Chairmanship also suited Gary and his over-inflated ego to tell everybody how wonderful he was, how much he was doing and to be in charge by proxy of the Chorus in martyrdom. Couple that with Adrian and his officious methods and the strain on everybody else including me becomes almost overwhelming."

Marie smiled but was still concerned and touched the cheek I had indicated that Gary had punched. "You poor man."

I took the hand she was stroking my cheek with and kissed the palm. "I'm fine. Honestly."

A waiter interrupted our conversation, pen poised over notepad and awaited our orders, forcing us to make our decisions quickly. Then the discussion returned back to the recording and the subject of Gary's and Adrian's appalling behaviour was gratefully dropped.

PUPPET ON A STRING

CHAPTER 31

Returning from Marie's apartment in Lyons after the weekend and just about over the jet-lag, I was confronted by two distasteful things. The first was easy to clear up. Some bored kid had obviously decided it would be fun to push dog excrement through my letter box. It had dried and a bit of hot water and elbow grease sorted out the smell, while the door-mat was despatched to the garden to dry off. Fortunately, Isla had been despatched temporarily to a cattery for the duration of my trip and subsequent holiday – thankfully, she did not have to endure this invasion of her house. The second was more difficult. Slightly stained from the first unpleasantness but still readable, Pete had pushed a copy of last Sunday's *The Investigator* through the door, with a large exclamation point in red ink beside the banner headline:

Breaking under the strain of our questions?

And there was the picture of me, face covered in my hands at the American press conference. The by-line and story written about me were more fanciful concoctions from a vivid imagination putting two and two together and getting three thousand and forty-two. The only difference this time was that the whole piece was couched in questions rather than a statement of fact – an insidious way of trying to avoid further accusations of making the stories up, which had, following the way that I had reacted, probably given them a whole hostess trolley of further food for thought. The first question they had written was about where I had been the weekend before the American trip and whether I was hiding from the press; the second, whether Marie was as forgiving as she seemed to be for my perceived indiscretions; the third, how I could justify two-timing her; and the last, and most important to me, whether I might be telling the truth. Still hurtful, but I decided to ignore it – if they had started to doubt the validity of their own accusations, it would soon peter out and they might drop it.

"Two loads of shit to come home to," I thought to myself.

After dealing with Gary and Adrian in America, the press conference and coming back to this rubbish, the stress had left me as tense as a coiled spring and I knew that I needed our holiday badly. I telephoned Pete and Marie to ensure and confirm that all the arrangements were in place, since we were due to travel in two days' time and I did not want to have further stressful surprises.

* * *

As soon as we had taken off from London Airport, the achy tenseness across my shoulders and neck began to ease and, by the time we were pulling out of Pisa Airport car park in a hired Fiat, my natural joviality had returned. As we headed out on the *autostrada*, with me behind the wheel, desperately trying to remember that driving on the right side of the road was not only acceptable but also essential to our safety, I glanced to the right and saw a familiar landmark.

Pointing it out, I said: "I wonder why the tower leans. Do you think it was designed like that?"

Marie, sitting beside me in the passenger seat, said: "Maybe it's tired."

It was something about the sweet way she said it but I doubled up with laughter and had difficulty keeping the car straight on the road. Marie asking me why it was funny did not help me get myself back under control.

When decorum was restored, Pete leaned forward, elbows on the back of Marie's seat and said: "I read somewhere that it was built on a bog. I think it's a folly built at the insistence of whoever owned the palace or whatever it is where the tower sits. And I think it was built in several stages, hundreds of years apart. If you look at pictures, you'll see that the top bits look crooked because the architects were making up for the lean that had already taken place and the extra weight of the building made it lean even more as its foundations dug into the marsh underneath."

Quiet greeted this interesting history lesson, until I said: "Mm. Mushy Pisa." Now it was their turn to giggle and guffaw helplessly. A good start to our holiday.

The villa we had rented was on the outskirts of a hilltop village, which was reached by zigzagging up steep roads and around sharp hairpin bends. In the secluded grounds of the house was a small swimming-pool, which glistened invitingly in the hot, early afternoon sun. Inside, there was a basic but clean and functional kitchen, three bedrooms, a living area, a bathroom, two toilets and a small shower room. Adjacent to the living area, through large French windows, there was a small veranda, with a wooden table, benches and a large parasol umbrella, jutting through the table's centre.

The main bedroom gave out superb views across the valley. Pete and I tossed coins to see who would take it, agreeing that, at the beginning of the second week, we would swap bedrooms. Pete and Beth won the right to the first week.

Settling in, we unpacked quickly. In the kitchen, I opened the bottle of wine, which the owners had kindly and generously left for us with four stubby glasses laid out on a tray. We took it out to the balcony and settled back to drink the wine and the scenery. Over the other side of the dividing hedge next to the swimming pool was a huge field of sunflowers, bowing towards us in the slight breeze. In the distance, we could see the square block of the thirteenth-century church with its single, exposed bell in the tower, which rang every quarter of an hour. All around us, the lazy sound of crickets communicating with each other, rasping their legs together. This was heaven.

"Prost!" exhorted Pete, raising his glass.

"Skol!" added Beth and sipped from hers.

"Derrières en haut!" I responded and Marie giggled.

"I wonder what the Italian equivalent of that would be," she pondered, flashing encouraging eyes in my direction.

I went inside to get the phrase-book and flipped through it, trying to work it out. "We'll have to try this on Guido Estente, Marie. I think it's" – I flicked between 'B' and 'U' in the dictionary section of the book – "Fondi su. I think," I said squinting into the sun. The phrase and its French equivalent stuck for the holiday and would continue beyond.

For the next two or three days, we decided that we would not travel anywhere and would stay at the villa being lazy. Each morning, we took it in turns – Pete and Beth, Marie and me – to walk the half-hour or so to the village to pick up fresh provisions such as bread, milk and meat. It was so still and quiet and I could feel the anxiety of the previous few days and weeks slowly drop away. When people say that they feel a weight is lifted from their shoulders, I had always thought it a prosaic way of describing being under pressure, but now I understood it. By the third day, I actually felt taller.

One morning, as we were walking back from the small market hand-in-hand, provisions clasped under my arm in paper bags, Marie stopped and turned me towards her. Leaning her head on my chest, she put her arms around me and cuddled me hard. "I love you, David," she said and looked up, one eye closed against the glare of the sun, her sunglasses perched above her forehead.

"Marie, I love you too. Without your love and support over the past few days, I think I would be in a nut-house right now." I laughed lightly.

She squeezed me again and reached up to kiss me. It turned into a passionate embrace and, when we parted, she put her hand on my chest and smiled. Looking up again, eye winking against the sun and dimple deepening with her impish smile, she said: "Mr. Loughton, will you marry me?"

I grinned. "I'm sorry, I can't. I'm afraid I've already asked someone else to marry me."

Marie slapped my chest playfully and then kissed me quickly. We continued our stroll back to the villa arm in arm. Pete and Beth had laid out the breakfast accoutrements on the table on the veranda by the time we returned and we had a long, lazy, leisurely meal. Having cleared away the crockery and sat back on the veranda as the mid-morning sun rose high in the sky, I stood up and sighed.

"Well, I can't sit around here and do nothing all day" – Pete raised his eyebrows. I pointed at the swimming-pool – "No. I'm going to sit down there and do nothing instead." Beth and Marie laughed and agreed that they would join me.

A high fence and an entrance gate to stop the local fauna getting in surrounded the swimming-pool. There was plenty of space around the sides for the sun-loungers, several upright chairs and a table with a parasol umbrella, for when the heat became unbearable. Marie and Beth had changed into bikinis and a cotton wraparound skirt, when they joined us, bringing the tan oil, books, hats and other paraphernalia for a day by the pool.

By the afternoon, I was almost groaning with the pleasure of doing absolutely nothing with the sun's deep heat on my skin. Both the girls had taken their bikini tops off, had rubbed oil into each other's backs and shoulders and were now lying on their fronts on towels at the pool-side, sun glistening off their skin, talking and giggling in low, conspiratorial voices.

"This is the life, eh?" I sighed lowering the sun-lounger another notch.

"I can't disagree with you there, mate," agreed Pete, putting his hands behind his head.

"I have not felt this relaxed…ever, I don't think."

"It has been a tough few weeks, hasn't it? What with Gary and Adrian and all their bollocks. And that press conference. By the way, I think you handled that with dignity."

"I hope that will be the end of it. Especially as I'm trying to launch this record label. I wouldn't want anyone or anything to taint that. Once it's got going, such brickbats will be easier to deflect."

"How is the label going?" said Pete, drowsy in the hot Italian sun.

Marie and Beth had turned over, bearing their breasts to the tanning elements. My heart skipped a beat at Marie's lissom beauty.

"It's going really well, actually. I forgot to tell you this because events took over. I was talking to Sir Norman in America and he asked me to take joint production credit on it. In fact, taking the prominent production credit."

"Blimey! How do you feel about that?"

"Well, honoured, of course. Honoured and scared. I've never done anything like that before."

Pete looked over at me. His eyes were inscrutable behind the dark, black lenses of the sunglasses. "You are too modest. You've got a natural bent for it. That was obvious that afternoon when we were in the studio, playing with different sounds."

Goose-pimples in reaction to the praise rushed up my back, down my arms and were gone, beaten by the heat of the sun. "Well, thanks, Pete." I thought for a moment. Naturally, I had spoken to Marie about this but I had not yet broached it with Pete. "Sir Norman also asked me to take up the tenor solo."

Pete sat bolt upright, shocked. "You're joking!" he exclaimed.

"I'm not. My gast was flabbered and my ox a little flummed, I can tell you."

"And are you going to do it?"

"I wasn't sure but agreed anyway and have now come around to the idea. I'll be singing with Marie and Beth and that's going to be fun."

"The 'Big Time'," said Pete, appreciatively, settling back on his lounger, hands back behind his head. "Any idea who is going to do the bass part?"

"Yes."

There was a pause before Pete looked over to me again. "Who?"

"Pete, how do you fancy doing the job?"

He was now bolt upright and facing me. "I couldn't. I've never done anything like that before."

I grinned and sat up to face him. "What were you just saying to me about record production?"

"That's different," he said, dismissing it with an absent-minded wave and then thought, pinching his lip between thumb and forefinger. "What will Sir Norman say, though? What if he wants someone else to do it? Torchev, maybe?"

"He doesn't want Torchev to do it."

"Oh, who has he suggested then?"

"You."

His hand dropped away from his mouth and he said: "No! You're joking!"

"I'm not. Because he had suggested that I do it, I mentioned that you would be in a good position to take the part and Sir Norman told me that he had been thinking of you anyway!"

"I don't know what to say."

"Say yes. It'll be fun. You, me, Marie and Beth. If I were being soppy about it, I would –."

"You? Soppy?" ribbed Pete.

"Thank you!" I laughed. "If I were to be emotional about it, though, I would say that it will be a testament to our friendship – the four of us." By the side of the pool, Marie and Beth had stood up and were stretching self-indulgently.

Pete was lost in thought again, rubbing his chin. "Actually, the more I think about it, the more I want to do it."

"Great!"

"Also, all four of us were there at the inception of your ideas becoming reality. Yes. I'll do it." Pete held out his hand and I shook it vigorously.

Marie came up and sat on the end of my lounger, Beth on the end of Pete's. "What's all this male bonding about, then?" Marie asked, resting her head momentarily on my shoulder.

"I've just been talking to Pete about his part on the *Creation* recording."

"And has he agreed to do it?" she asked.

Pete raised his eyebrows and pointed at Marie. "You knew about this?"

Beth cuddled his arm and said: "So are you going to do it?"

Pete turned towards her and, smiling slowly, said: "You knew about it too?"

Beth giggled. "She's my best friend. Of course we're going to talk about you. You should hear some of the things she says about David."

I opened my mouth in mock shock and turned to Marie, while Pete tickled Beth, her peels of laughter ringing out in the still, hot quietness of the villa grounds. "What have you been saying?"

I raised my hands and flexed the fingers towards her ribs. Marie giggled nervously and brought her arms into her body, hands out to protect herself from the threat; protection which, sadly, was inadequate. Marie's squeals and protests joined in with Beth's. Torture dealt out as was only proper and appropriate under the circumstances, Pete said: "I can't believe it. It's a conspiracy. I'll do it, of course, but it's a conspiracy nonetheless."

"Excellent!" I said, standing. "This calls for a celebration – as if we needed a reason." Five minutes later, I returned with a bottle of wine and four glasses. Passing them out, we laughed as we all said together: "Fondi su!" I added: "Here's to a successful venture with my very good friends!"

Later that day, Pete and Beth had gone up on to the veranda, leaving Marie and me down at the pool-side. We lay facing each other on the same sun-lounger, kissing and cuddling, feeling the heat of the sun on our skin.

"How did you get to be so lovely?" she asked and smiled slightly.

"I must have learned from the master. Or mistress."

She placed a finger on my lips and looked deep into my eyes. The familiar undertow feeling came over me as I disappeared into her eyes. I embraced her, her bare breasts pressed to my chest, the nipples stiffening against me as I kissed her.

"Oh, God! You are so beautiful," I said, eyes still locked, stroking her arm.

"When shall we get married, do you think?" she asked, putting a gentle hand over my heart.

I kissed her gently again. "How about on the first anniversary of us going out together? Twelfth of April, 1969. Does that sound like a good wedding date?"

"I love you, husband-to-be," she said, kissing me.

"I love you too, wife-in-waiting. Let's take some time out over this holiday to work out what we are going to do for it, who to invite and so on. I want it to be perfect."

"Thank you, David," she said. "Back to my original question: How did you get to be so lovely?" I grinned and kissed her fully again. She put her hand back on my chest and a twinkle came to her eye. "You had better get into the swimming pool and cool off."

I pretended to be disappointed and then said: "You're right. But you must come in too." I stood up suddenly, lifting her in the same movement, running to the swimming pool edge, Marie screaming and laughing, her fists beating lightly on my shoulders and back. And then we were in, the sharp contrast of hot skin and the cold water hitting us hard and quelling our ardour quickly. As we broke the surface, gasping, Pete and Beth were standing on the veranda, giving us a round of applause.

* * *

The holiday was just what we needed. To be close without the pressures of the day-job, to have fun when we wanted to, to relax and lie in, catching up on sleep, without the need to get up at specific times, and also to be with friends – something which I had been ignoring, so focused was I on Chorus business, the Chairmanship, the record label and Marie.

We visited several local sights – Assissi, Perugia (Pete wryly observed a good advertising slogan for the area: Umbria, it puts other Italian destinations in the shade), a day-trip to Rome, another to the newly-discovered, extended ruins at Pompeii and a memorable excursion to Florence. Wandering around the Ufizzi, we came upon Michaelangelo's famous statue of David.

"Look, David," said Marie, "that's you!" She looked up at the statue and looked from it to me and back again, introducing us to one another. "David? David. David? David." She giggled as I laughed.

"No, he's nothing like me," I said eventually, "I've got a nice deep tan going and he's a little pale. And, besides, mine is bigger." I winked at her.

Marie covered her mouth in shock. "You can't say that!"

"What? No, my head" – Marie laughed out loud drawing several frowns from our fellow gallery-visitors – "Why? What did you think I meant?" I asked innocently.

Marie pursed her lips to stop herself laughing further, grabbed my hand and dragged me off.

"What?" I was still protesting in mock innocence.

Outside, I was accosted by a loud, fat American, wearing too small shorts, his stomach spilling over the waistband, varicose-blue legs ending in grey woollen socks in brown sandals, a cigar squashed between his teeth, a camera slung over his shoulder and a brusque approach to asking for assistance.

"Hey, can you tell me where number eight is?" he asked, holding the cigar inches from his lips as he spoke, pushing his voluminous stomach towards me.

I thought momentarily that I ought to pretend that his language or accent was too difficult to understand, when I realized that indeed I had no clue what he was talking about and was intrigued. "I'm sorry?"

"Number eight," he repeated in the loud arrogance that many of his fellow countrymen adopt. If at first the question does not get through, try saying it louder, then slower, then louder *and* slower until they do understand. "Where is it?"

"I'm sorry, I don't understand what you mean?"

"Number eight!" he said louder and more slowly, as if I were a backward child unable to recite my four times table.

I looked blankly at him, shaking my head in bewilderment.

"Number eight!" He was almost deafening in his condescension and the enunciation of his words was at a snail's pace. "Where is it?"

It matters not how many times you say it in exactly the same way, it is no clearer what you want from me, I thought. I said: "I don't understand. What's number eight?"

The American sighed, stabbed the cigar back in his mouth and drew out the map from underneath his arm, unfolded it and pointed at it with a stubby finger. I looked at the map and finally understood the numerical reference. All the tourist spots were marked on the map and given a number. In this case, he was looking for the old bridge over the river with the tourist shops on it. Not only had he been arrogant enough to assume that I would know what he was talking about, he was too stupid to realize that there might be different tourist maps with different methods of pinpointing the locations of the sights. Further, if he had actually bothered to read the signs or the street names, he could have calculated it himself. So, helpfully, I pointed him in completely the wrong direction.

"Thanks," he spat around his cigar, as he refolded his map, "I've never been to Fy-renze before."

I shuddered. At least have the common decency to learn the pronunciation or call it its anglicized equivalent, I thought, but just smiled and pointed in the same direction I had already given. He stalked off, satisfied that *he* had taught *me* a lesson in manners, towards the centre of the town, oblivious of the stroke I had pulled. Marie giggled again as I said: "That'll teach the damned colonial!"

* * *

Sadly, the holiday passed all too quickly. What had started out as a huge number of days stretching out into the future had suddenly turned into just two or three days left. Although we had discussed our wedding plans – sometimes on our own, sometimes with Beth and Pete – we had not discussed it in fine detail. On the Friday, the other two decided that they wanted to go out for the day and asked if we would like to join them. On this occasion, we simultaneously turned down the invitation, citing the need to be on our own to discuss the wedding details so that we could get them moving once we returned home.

"Don't do anything I'd do!" said Pete, grinning.

"I think that would be a physical impossibility for us, Pete," I retorted and he laughed.

They left shortly after breakfast and Marie and I went down to the pool with some paper and writing implements to start our planning. As we were on our own and the garden and swimming pool were secluded, Marie took off not only her bikini top but the bottoms as well and I took great pleasure in rubbing the tanning oil in to her buttocks. Because of the sunbathing we had done, the only white marks were where this garment had been. The rest of her body was a delicious, deep, almost-chocolate brown.

"You are so brown," I commented, caressing the lotion in to her skin.

"So are you. In fact, if you ever get the opportunity to sing the lead in *Otello*, you won't need any make-up!" I laughed, as I massaged her back and shoulders.

Slapping my hand, I remonstrated loudly with myself to keep my hands off her and concentrate on the task in hand. Lying on our fronts on towels over the grass edge beside the pool paving, arms and shoulders touching, we worked our way through lists of things to be considered: invitation stationery, orders of service, hymn choices, wedding lists (both of us having houses or apartments, the list was predictably more luxury than necessity), catering, reception choices and finally the list of people to be invited. We started with the officers – best man, bridesmaid, ushers and so on. And then it hit me.

"Who is going to give you away?"

"Uncle Charles," replied Marie without a moment's hesitation.

I think my slight hesitation went unnoticed, as I wrote his name at the top of the list. By the time we had finished, we had taken the planning as far as we could without actually speaking to anyone. It had taken almost three hours and, happy with what we had come up with, I threw the pen down on the pad and closed it. Marie had turned on to her back and pulled her sunglasses back down over her eyes. The natural, lissom beauty of her body and limbs, enhanced by the deep tan was too much for me to resist any longer and I stroked a hand across her stomach.

She murmured slightly. "What do you think you are up to?"

My hand stopped moving. "I'm sorry, but you are so gorgeous and your body is just crying out to be touched and kissed."

She took my hand and moved it up her body. "I didn't say stop, though!" she said, devilishly, her dimple deepening as she did so.

With the hot, Italian sun beating down on our bodies, we made slow love with each other, sweat running down our backs, arms and legs, mingling together as I pulled her over on top of me, stroking her chest and legs until we exploded with a rapturous climax. She collapsed forward on to me, out of breath.

"You just get better and better, David," she said to me, breathlessly. The sweat was now running in rivulets from her body on to mine.

"I told you. It's the heat that does it. Entirely helped by a fantastic body belonging to a wonderful girl." I kissed her perspiring face. "Do you think we ought to cool down in the pool, before the other two get back?"

She agreed and we gasped as we eased ourselves in to the relatively freezing water. Marie was hunched up, elbows pressed in to herself as she tip-toed along the shallow end before taking the plunge and pushed herself forward in the water. She yelped with surprise until she got used to it. I followed suit and we swam to the deep end, where I held on to the side and Marie gave me a hug.

"I love you so much," she said, kissing my neck and squeezing herself in to my body.

I put my free arm around her and felt the heat of her skin below the coldness of the water. "I love you more than I can express, sweetheart," I said earnestly. "I cannot wait for the day when we are married and I become father to your children." I lifted her chin and saw that she was crying softly. "What's wrong?"

"Nothing," she responded, nestling back in to my chin. "I'm just so happy. I don't want this moment to go away and I don't know what I've done to deserve you."

We held each other for a few moments, when I heard the car on the gravel track leading up to the villa. A couple of hairpin bends and Pete and Beth would be back. I released Marie slightly, looked in to her still-shaded eyes and smiled.

"You're right," she answered to my unspoken question. "We ought to make ourselves decent for our friends." She reached up, placing a hand either side of my face and kissed me hard. "Thank you for a lovely day. It was perfection."

I lifted her on to the side, following her out in one physical exertion. By the time Pete and Beth had parked and come over to join us, we had covered our nether regions and were lying innocently on the loungers side by side. I looked up as they approached.

"Gah!" exclaimed Pete and looked at Beth. "I told you they would be lazing about doing nothing." He looked back at us. "Have you done anything I'd do?"

"And more!" I responded. Laughter rang around the garden.

We stayed outside until the sun went down. As the heat went out of the day, Marie put a white sleeveless tee-shirt on and it showed the deepness of the tan on her arms brilliantly. For the rest of the evening as we talked through some of the wedding plans, I could not take my eyes off my gorgeous Marie. You are troubled wondering what you've done to deserve me? I thought. Well, I certainly am at a complete loss as to what I have done to deserve you, my sweetheart.

PUPPET ON A STRING

CHAPTER 32

T*he Creation* is traditionally a choral piece for soprano, tenor and bass, with chorus and orchestra. I was adamant that, for the first recording, Beth should be involved, even though she is an alto (or mezzo-soprano), especially as she had been present at the initial vocal sessions, playing around with stereophonic sound. With Marie's complete agreement, Beth would play the part of Eve to Pete's Adam, while Marie, Pete and I played the parts of the angels Gabriel, Raphael and Uriel.

Having signed the English National Chamber Orchestra to accompany us, and leaving Sir Norman to rehearse both the choral and orchestral parts, the four of us spent a few afternoons rehearsing, occasionally having fun with it by doing different parts: Marie trying her best *basso profundo*, me doing a falsetto and Beth and Pete swapping their Adam and Eve roles. Although we were prone to playing around, we were also very disciplined to guarantee, as Marie said on one occasion, that we knew our parts backwards – when she used this quaint expression, it gave me an idea and I suggested that we ought to have a trail off at the end of the record with us doing something knock-about but in reverse. Throwing a few ideas around, we settled for a close-harmony version of Cliff Richard's *Congratulations*, since this had been a worldwide hit around the time that we had all got together with our respective partners, and it encapsulated the mood with Marie and me getting married, starting up the label and the general feeling that this was going to be big.

When we were not rehearsing, I was attending meetings with distributors and the mainstream record labels. I let little knowledge become public as to the plans of the recording – the rolling wall of sounds that we had tested with Bruce, for instance – but just let them know the main names involved: Sir Norman, Marie, Beth and Bruce. This was enough for the companies to bid ridiculous sums for the honour of distribution. I rejected their request to control the design and packaging as I had ideas on that too. Eventually, I signed a six-month contract with Sojourn Records, with a view to extending it for a three-year tenure dependent on the success of the venture. The larger companies had wanted just too much control in the whole fledgling process.

With that contract signed and a banker's draft to deposit in the bank, I was reminded that one of my election pledges was to look into having a Treasurer co-opted to the Committee, despite Gary's objection that we had always got by, without the need to change everything every five minutes. It was only going through the paperwork that it became abundantly clear why he had expressed his resistance with such vehemence. There was money missing!

"Oh, my God!" I whispered slowly to myself, as I double-checked my analysis to confirm that it was indeed missing and that my calculations had not been mistaken. Each month, our sponsor provided a statement of the monies he had provided. The corresponding receipts and cheque-stubs and bank account statements were seriously at odds with this information. As I dug deeper, to my horror, another name started creeping in – Adrian Hilton. Shortly after Gary's vainglorious acceptance of Adrian's co-option as Wardrobe Master, it appeared that Gary's wily ways had rubbed off on Adrian and he had begun siphoning money from the sponsor's monthly contribution. Small amounts to begin with – crediting the props cost by an increase of five or ten pounds. By the end of their tenure, the two of them were making off with several hundreds of pounds. I even found a letter from the sponsor confirming that, as Gary had requested, the monthly contribution would rise by 15% and still the coffers were empty. And another letter, addressed to Adrian, confirming enclosure of a cheque for more than was required to replace props items for the American trip. Again no sign of the deficit.

I mused, thinking back to a couple of instances when Gary had argued against appointing a Treasurer: the Committee meeting at my house, which had ended so abruptly. Gary and Adrian had been sighing heavily and generally making things unbearably uncomfortable. At the time, I had misconstrued this to be a childish attempt to undermine my authority and me at the meeting but it now seemed obvious that there was an altogether more sinister motive behind it. Perhaps they had been afraid that they might be found out. It would certainly explain the stressed outbursts, their surly demeanours and Gary's descent into further alcoholism. With the refreshing clarity of hindsight, I could count a number of other examples too.

I sank back in the chair in the office, thinking through the enormity of it all, and regarded the incriminating papers before me. I twiddled my thumbs, considering what few options I had left to me. The sponsor wanted to retain anonymity but there had been a serious crime – or crimes – committed here. I could probably avoid unnecessary publicity for our sponsor but knew also what had to be done and leaned forward to pick up the telephone.

Replacing the receiver after the brief conversation with the officer in charge, I tidied up the papers, placing them in a new binder ready for collection by the fraud squad when they arrived. The next person I called was Pete to tell him what I had uncovered and to ask him to help me through this interview with the police. Thirty minutes later, we were talking to two detectives, one more senior than the other, describing some of the conversations we had both had with Gary, which now made more and more sense given their propensity to resort to vilification. We provided them with the copies of the documentation for their analysis.

When they had left, confirming that there was a case to investigate if not to answer just yet, I turned to Pete. "What do you think?"

"It explains a lot, certainly," he replied, reaching for his now tepid coffee, left undrunk during our discussion with the policemen. He sipped and grimaced before putting it back down again. "I just can't believe that he's played us both for such fools."

I reflected on the enormity of change in our relationship with him in just two months. "God knows how he's going to react."

"That's not really our problem." He paused to reflect. "But I know what you mean."

I leaned forward and picked up another binder that had laid unopened since my initial discovery and opened it. "How did he think he'd get away with it?"

"God knows!" conceded Pete. "I hope they throw away the key for all the upset he's caused and for putting our future in jeopardy."

"Indeed! I might request an audience with our sponsor so that he's aware and can take any decisions he needs to."

"Do you think he'll withdraw funding?"

"If he does, I'm hoping that this record label will allow us to subsist. But I must be honest with him. Gary and Adrian patently haven't been. Thank God *The Investigator* has stopped its invidious assault on me. This would be all they needed to close us down!" Pete nodded in agreement and we sat in silence for a while. "As I say, I'm hoping the record label will give us more autonomy."

"Have you got all the contracts lined up, then? For this label?"

"I have," I confirmed, taking out a piece of paper. "What do you think?" On the paper was a rough sketch for the sleeve and label design. At the centre was a large, fiery, orange ball, which had just begun to explode, parts of the blackened crust being pushed outwards from the sphere. On one of the larger pieces in words of fire, was *The Creation*. Nothing else. I wanted it to be simple, effective and memorable. On the back would be all the sleeve-notes and the names of the participants and studio information. The circular label was similar, with the fiery ball exploding around the central hole, with the track information written in orange in the lower black area and the work title and participants above.

Pete turned it over and around and looked at it from different angles. "Excellent, Dave!" he said, finally. "I had no idea that you were a budding artist."

"Neither had I. Obviously something latent from my mother's genes."

* * *

Over the next few days, I worked more on the design and despatched it to a printer to get a proper mock-up created so that people could better see what the end product would look like. Work had also begun on the sleeve-notes, shying away from an academic description of the work but concentrating more on the history of the Chorus and its future endeavours in a generic way, so that it would appear current in years to come. My quirky sense of humour came out in the writing of the notes. The organisation of the personnel information was titled on one section 'The Without Whoms', covering those who had taken a key involvement in getting the label and the recording off the ground and 'The With Whoms' on the other to cover those with whom we would be working on the record, such as the orchestra and a few of the studio staff.

Then I turned to my Production duties and concentrated on how I would like the final recording to be heard in stereo. I wrote out each section of the work diligently in italics, with an idea of its sound:

Representation of Chaos – swirling and boiling around the listener
In the Beginning – starting light and distant and growing heavily with

an explosion of 'brightness' (like the sun coming out on a cloudy day) on *Let there be light*

And God Made the Firmament – furious, almost 'building site' intensity

And God Said, Let the Waters – I would like a sound effect included here growing through the piece but not oppressively obvious. Perhaps starting with a drip and then becoming a trickling stream or babbling brook

The Heavens are Telling – expression of joy and brightness, like the atmosphere at a children's birthday party

...and so on. Later on, at my pre-recording meeting with Sir Norman and Bruce, they would be taken through what I wanted, giving them a chance to air their viewpoints on what was appropriate and, more importantly, achievable. As it turned out, they loved the ideas, especially some of the techniques of presenting swirling fury but also the additional ideas of including subtle sound effects. They, too, wanted this recording to be different.

* * *

During this time of nurturing the infant record label through its first faltering steps, Marie had stayed with me at the house in Hertfordshire, taking on the responsibility of getting things moving on the Worth Matravers house. It transpired that it was a vacant possession. The previous owner had unfortunately died and her heirs had decided to sell it rather than use it themselves. I had taken Marie down to view it the first weekend after the holiday, this time with a key from the agent to view the inside. We agreed it was absolutely perfect, the views were wonderful and the neighbours did not overlook the garden in any way. Marie, excited by the prospect of moving into the house, made several trips to Dorset to ensure the estate agents were moving as fast as they could.

During one such trip, I took the opportunity for concentrated effort on the schedules for the sessions – we were not taping it in the standard way and, following a lot of aural design discussions with Bruce, we had established how it needed to be recorded; orchestra, chorus and soloists separately from each other group. While I was working through these plans, there was a tentative knock at the door, followed by a pause but the it had not opened. The knock came again.

I looked up, pen stopped on the paper. "Come in," I called.

A face poked around the opening door, sallow in complexion, now pitted with ancient acne, sunken eyes with dark rings surrounding them and painfully skinny, blanched limbs hanging from limp and dirty clothes. "Hello, Dave," said a barely recognizable voice.

It took a moment but it suddenly came to me and I stood up quickly. "Mandy!" I gained the other side of the desk as she came fully into the room. Shutting the door quietly, I took one bony shoulder lightly and gave her a friendly peck on the cheek. Her mouth was open, expecting more, which she shut and cocked her head to brush my hand with her cheek, but I removed it subtly and quickly. "How are you? Do you want a coffee?"

"No, thank you." The characteristic drone was present in her voice.

"So, how have you been keeping?" I had retreated to my side of the desk, feeling more comfortable with a large piece of furniture nestled between us.

"To be honest, not overly brilliant," she intoned and crossed her stick-thin legs. The kneecap was very prominent as was the definition of the joint between upper and lower leg. I resisted the temptation to confirm my perception that the lack of brilliance and health was obvious.

"Oh, dear." I tried to sound sympathetic but was unsure how successful it was. "What's been the matter?" What the hell had she done to herself in the last month or two since we had last seen each other, when she had thrown that tantrum in the office?

"I...," she started but stopped to clear her throat. She tried again: "I came here to say I was sorry for the way I reacted and for the horrible things I said." There was a tear perilously close to jumping off the lower lid. Her twigs of fingers were working nervously at a paper handkerchief, ripping small holes in its fabric.

"Think nothing of it," I said, "I behaved like a complete tosser myself. So let's call it evens?" I smiled but it was not reciprocated.

"I couldn't forgive myself. I couldn't eat. I was even taking mild antidepressants for a while and I couldn't summon up the courage until now to apologize."

That explained the mess she looked. Then there was also a pervading smell of stale alcohol assaulting my nostrils and it was all I could do not to screw my face up in disgust. "Look, Mandy, you don't have to apologize. As far as I'm concerned, it's long forgotten."

"Thanks, David," she said with palpable relief, looking down on to what could loosely be described as a lap. "Does that mean we can start again?"

"You can come back to the Chorus whenever you feel ready."

She blinked uncomprehendingly at me for a moment. Then it clicked. "No," she protested, "I meant us. Can *we* start again?"

I closed my eyes for a moment. How had I not seen this particular request marching over the horizon to a large brass band, twirling a majorette's baton, shouting at me? "No, Mandy," I said gently.

The tear gave up the ghost and committed suicide down her cheek. "Why not?" Her bottom lip was quivering and the paper hanky was being ripped to shreds in her hands.

"Mandy," I said, getting up and struggling to remove the hint of exasperation from my voice. I moved around to the other side of the desk and sat on the edge to look in her eyes as I said what I had to say. "Mandy, there will never be any 'we' or 'us'. We have been through all that already."

Tears were tripping freely down her face and a globule of fluid appeared in one nostril. She wiped it away with the back of her hand, rather than with the fragments of the tissue. "But there can be," she insisted. Her lip was quivering quickly and her once pretty brow was knitted together in anxiety. "We just have to try. We were good together."

I stood up to avoid showing my frustration and slipping temper. "There will never be any 'we', Mandy. *We* will not be getting back together again."

"Is it because of what I said? Or because I hit you?"

"No. Neither." I looked out of the window. There was the man, taking his dog for a walk. "Mandy, I'm going to be honest with you. There is no purpose to you wanting to get back with me. I've moved on and you need to as well." The dog had cocked its leg against the lamppost and was limping along in that position as his owner tugged at the lead. "Look, next spring, I'm getting married." I broke off suddenly with a clear sense of *déjà vu* – staring out of the window, stark but painful messages, a girl who thought she was in love me and felt that I owed her in some way. I turned in time to deflect a weak punch. She still knew how to move swiftly and soundlessly!

"You bastard!" she shouted, head down, flailing punches in my general direction with no control, hitting my hands as I protected myself. I managed to edge my way around the desk again so that it was between us and stood away from her pistoning arms, so that she fell forward on to the desk, hitting her chin on the surface. The shock or possibly the embarrassment of the situation seemed to bring her to her senses. I was standing away from the desk with hands raised in surprised surrender mixed with the need for protection. Her face was red and screwed up with pent-up fury. "It's you, you, you, all the time, isn't it?" she sneered, spittle flying from her mouth as she spat the words at me. "You cop off with me but I'm not good enough, so you go off with some other tart. When will you break up with her? When she's served her purpose as your sex-slave?"

I tried to calm her down but could not get a word in edgeways. Eventually, waving my hands slowly downwards, I managed to interpose with: "Mandy, please! There's no need for insults!"

She stood up defiantly and put her hands on her hips. The chin-crack on the desk had forced her teeth to break the skin of her lip and blood was now oozing from the wound. "Oh, isn't there?" she mocked, fury sparking from her eyes.

I was getting cross. "No. I'll have you know that Marie and I are very much in love –."

"Marie!" she scoffed and raised her eyes to the ceiling giving a hollow laugh. "So you finally hounded her into bed too?"

"Mandy!" I said curtly. "I will not have you talking about my fiancée like that!"

"Oh, Mr. High and Mighty now." She stood, purse-lipped, breathing heavily. "You abused me," she said quietly and poked her tongue warily around the wound.

I stopped breathing momentarily with the shock of the allegation. "I most certainly did not!" I protested, livid that this should be levelled at me.

"You latched on to me and conned me into bed and used my body for your own pleasure!"

I was going to protest again but knew it would be useless.

"And I thought you actually loved me, you bastard!" Fresh tears welled up in her eyes and dropped down her cheeks but she ignored them. With a cracking voice, she added more quietly, punctuating each word with a quick, sharp breath: "I – have – never – stopped – loving – you." She looked downcast, took her hands off her hips and slumped at the shoulders. "How could you do this to me?"

I moved around the desk, wanting to comfort her. "Mandy, since we broke up, I have never been anything less than honest with you, because that's only fair –."

It was a mistake, I realized, she slowly looked up at me, starting to growl and opening her mouth to give out a primeval roar. The letter-opener in her hand slashed out at me, catching the cuff of my shirt and ripping the sleeve. She raised her hand high to stab the knife into me but I reacted quickly, fear loosening my bowels slightly but making me quicker-witted into the bargain. Blocking her arm by catching her at the wrist, I twisted it hard over so that she dropped the knife, the tendons in her wrist creaking under my grasp. She yelped with the pain as her arm wrenched in a way nature had not designed, and I followed up with a punch to her jaw, which knocked her out and she slumped to the floor. Still holding her arm, I released the pressure but took her weight as she slid down in a heap.

The shock and dissipation of the sudden adrenalin shot left me badly shaken, taking in deep breaths as I hyperventilated and I scratched my head in anxious nervousness at what I had done. How had it come to this? The woman had tried to kill me! And, for that, I had left her in an unceremonious heap on the floor. "Oh, God," I said, before taking control of myself. Putting my arms under her armpits, I steadied myself to heft her on to the chair, but it was easier than anticipated such had been her dramatic weight loss.

Gradually, Amanda came round, moaning softly. Eyes still closed, she raised her hand to the side of her chin I had given the right hook. She blinked myopically at me as if to get me back into focus. "What happened?" she asked weakly, frowning.

I had picked up the telephone and had dialled one number already.

"You bastard!" she exclaimed coming round quickly, bewilderment crossing her eyes and being replaced by hatred. "How could you?"

I started dialling the second number.

She stood up and loomed over the desk, resting her fists on the desk and, spraying blood from the initial lip wound as she spoke, she said: "You bastard! I thought you loved me!"

I dialled the third number but did not release the dial. "Amanda! Listen very carefully. I only have to release this and I will be calling the police. I suggest you calm down and pull yourself together."

She glared at me, breathing heavily, her lower lip steadily covering in blood, fluid mucus darting in and out of her nostril. As quick as a cat after its prey, she leaned forward and swiped at the receiver, knocking it from my hand. In the surprise, I released the dial and heard the tinny voice coming from it: "Which service do you require: police, ambulance or fire?" Amanda reached out slowly and pressed the cradle down, shutting off the link to the operator.

I stood up to be in a less vulnerable position just as Amanda advanced around the desk towards me, forcing me to back off to avoid another unpredictable onslaught. "Amanda!" I said firmly. "Will you please understand that I do not want a relationship with you? I will never, ever love you and I am now with someone else. I'm sorry if that is upsetting to you but that is the position."

"Upsetting?" she snarled. "Upsetting? I'll give you bloody 'upsetting'!" Hatred sparked in her eyes. Another low growl metamorphosed into a scream. This time I was prepared, having learned from her previous attack. As far as I knew there were no harmful implements in her hands but I could not afford to take any chances. As she swung her right fist, I caught her wrist and twisted. This time she did not respond other than to flail with her left, which I caught and jerked in the opposite direction. With a deft move, I managed to turn her around, still holding her arms but above her head now and pushed her away with a foot to her lower back, jerking her head backwards. She managed to stop herself going face first into the wall with her released hands and she turned back to me, hair straggling lankly in the tear-streaks on her face. The wildness was ebbing from her eyes but I would still not trust her.

"I'm sorry, David," she tried.

"Amanda, for assault on a Chorus official, I terminate your contract, effective immediately. You will leave these premises forthwith and any return will be met with police resistance. Do you understand?"

"But, David, please! I love you. Don't *you* understand?"

"Actually, Amanda," I said, sweat popping on my brow with the exertion and fear, "I don't care. I gave you a chance to be reasonable but you tried to attack me." I reflected, anger rising hotly in my heart and brain, and moved towards her, causing her to flinch. "Actually, no! You tried to kill me!"

"I didn't," she protested weakly.

"You did!" I bellowed. I picked up the letter-opener. "With this!" With disgust, I threw it in the corner, deliberately away from Amanda.

"I'm sorry, David, I really am. I didn't mean to."

"I don't think you know anything any more. Now get out!"

"Please!"

"GET OUT!"

Suddenly, the flash of hatred and anger mixed and returned to her face. The flushes reappeared on her cheeks. "You bastard! Next time, I *will* kill you!"

I feigned a quick move towards her and she turned and fled to the door. "Get out!"

Standing in the open doorway, she turned to face me and, with finger pointing accusingly, snarled the warning: "Look over your shoulder, Loughton! No-one treats me like this. Keep looking behind you because one day....! If I can't have you, I'll make damned sure no-one else can! Just you wait!"

"Right!" I said, striding to the door and she escaped downstairs, without turning back. I heard the bang of the side door. Closing the office door, I sank to the floor, where I stayed for forty minutes or so, attempting to steady my nerves.

* * *

Naturally, this episode had seriously unsettled me. Marie had noticed immediately that something was wrong, asking me what had got me into such a state. I was worried, in a small way of course, that Amanda coming back might jeopardize what Marie and I had got together but decided that honesty was the best policy and proceeded to give her all the details of our sordid relationship, my misgivings, the feelings of betrayal towards Marie, culminating in the attack in the office. Throughout, seated forward on the settee at home, Marie had had a hand curled around my elbow but had not moved. She had stared at me intently throughout and when I had finished, a strong pang and the need to be sick hit me but I managed to control it. Marie was crying and I feared that what had been done and said had unravelled part of our relationship.

Swallowing hard and now with a dry throat, I said: "Marie, I'm sorry. I didn't mean to upset you."

She smiled and squeezed my arm towards her, resting her head on my shoulder. "David, I'm not upset." She sat up again, and wiped an errant tear away with the back of her hand. "I'm happy!"

I smiled with a little relief. "You have a funny way of showing it," I observed.

She positioned herself so that she could face me better and took my hands. "David, you are the most honest person I know. You are the most caring, wonderful, warm human being I know, too. I also understand that you must have been driven to the edge to have to take such action and would never knowingly harm anyone or anything unless you absolutely had to and, on this occasion, you very definitely did. And, while you might think that it needed a lot of courage to tell me all that – and I know that it probably did take a lot – the fact that you hid nothing and care so much for me to do so means so much to me. And if you were worried that I might think differently about you because of what you said or did, I don't. In fact, I love you more now than fifteen minutes ago."

Her eyes were earnest but truthful and a palpable and comforting emotion swept over me. "When you went out with her, you did it for understandable reasons." She put a finger to my lips as I began my protest. "And actually, your intentions were quite chivalrous. But you knew when to end it because of the hurt you knew you would inflict otherwise. I say 'understandable reasons' because I did something very similar when I returned to Lyons after our Paris *Tosca*. You were never far from my mind but, in my case, I was thinking that you would never want to go out with me because you might think of me as an aloof celebrity. So I tried to stop thinking about you by seeing another man. Like you and this woman, I knew pretty quickly that it just wasn't working but still took a long time to end it." She paused and smiled kindly. "At least my life wasn't threatened in my attempts to do so."

I reached up and stroked her beautiful face, tracing the indentation of her dimple with a thumb. "What did I ever do without you?"

Her smile trembled and tears fell down her face and she wrapped her arms around me, kissing with fervent desperation. "I love you," she repeated in between the kisses and before long, clothes were shed on the floor and we were lying in a bear-hugging cuddle, in the afterglow of our love-making.

"It's alright," she said, looking up at me. "I'm not going anywhere." She smiled an impish smile and returned to lie on my chest.

"And I'm not going to let you," I confirmed, cuddling her even more tightly into me.

Our relationship had more than survived its first big test and my heart swelled with relief, love and pride that she was going to be my wife, for better or for worse, and we had just proven it.

* * *

The recording took longer than standard, because we were not recording the musicians together. We laid down the orchestral pieces first, segregating the sections and even taping just individual instruments. This was particularly effective, with the techniques we had devised, on the maelstrom effect I wanted to achieve in the *Representation of Chaos* and I knew instinctively that this was going to be an interesting recording.

The Chorus, we divided into four sections, corralled into purpose-built booths to obtain the effects of ethereal movement around the listener. In some of the choral pieces, we used the electronic wizardry to make the voices sound mystical, by squeezing it to sound as if it were coming down a very long pipe.

When it came to the soloists' parts separately and with the Chorus, Bruce managed to make the angels sound as if they were floating around the orchestra and Chorus and even occasionally fluttering downwards. It was an excellent achievement.

But my favourite part had to be when the four friends were singing on our own. Because of the strangeness of it all, there were several retakes as one or the other of us would find something funny and it would set the others off. Marie (of course, without a hint of bias) was wonderful. Her method of making the production of her beautiful soprano notes, hitting each one with crystal clarity each time with a soft power, added a qualitative dimension to the recording. When singing on her own, she would adopt the same pose as she had when recording *Carmen* – hands placed in her back pockets, giving wonderful definition to her shoulders, arms and back. Sometimes we would be at different ends of the studio, facing each other, winking, making faces, other times facing away. On one occasion, we had the microphone dangling above our heads and Marie and I were back-to-back, shoulders and bottoms touching. She would try to put me off by moving against me and I would give her a playful tap and she would then grab my hand. Sometimes, we would stand in that back-to-back, hands placed in each other's back pockets and arms interlaced. The closeness we felt increased during the studio sessions and our love grew even greater each day – just when I thought it impossible for it to be augmented further.

The funniest and most enjoyable moment came on the recording of our improvised version of *Congratulations*. Pete was singing staccato bass accompaniment in the style of a barbershop quartet and we all joined in. I did some falsetto nonsense accompaniment and then extraordinarily, we sang one syllable in turn without any prior planning, collapsing in laughter before the end. That was the first and only take we did and decided to use it.

It was halfway through the hard editing sessions that news came
through that the deeds for the house were ready for our joint signatures
(I was determined that everything in our life would be shared equally).
Taking time out to visit the solicitor's office, Marie and I added our
scrawls in turn to the documentation.

When it was complete and fully witnessed, Marie turned to me, eyes
widening and a smile turning into open-mouthed joy, she reached out for
my hand, then jumped up and down, clapping her hands. "We've got it!"

I stood up and she kissed me passionately. "Yes, we have!" I grinned,
squeezing her.

Apologizing to the solicitor, who was looking through papers to hide
his embarrassment at the sudden lack of decorum, she looked into my
eyes. "I love you," she said quietly, kissing me again. "I've never been so
happy. Thank you!"

Bruce and I worked long hours to complete the edition of the
recording and, when complete and sequenced on the master, we invited
Sir Norman, Marie, Beth and Pete to listen to it.

Sir Norman was nodding appreciatively and making comments like
"That sounds good" and "Oh, yes, I like that effect". Pete and Beth were
giggling with enjoyment at the memory of the sessions but it was Marie
that affected me most. She was sitting forward, elbows on knees, chin in
hands, eyes staring widely into space, mouth open and she did not move
from that position.

As the final notes died away (Bruce and I decided not to let Sir
Norman in on the trail-off secret), Marie continued to be motionless. I
noticed a tear had run down her cheek and on to her fingers but she had
not wiped it away. Eventually, she got up and embraced my neck. "It's
brilliant!" she said and kissed me. "Absolutely brilliant! You are so clever!"
She kissed me again and turned to the others. "What did you think?"

Pete stepped forward and shook my hand and Beth kissed my cheek,
agreeing that the end result was certainly spectacular and that it was
worth all the effort I had put in. Sir Norman stood up, wincing as a
bone cracked. He put his hand out and cupped my hand with the other
as we shook. "My boy, you've brought a fresh approach to this type of
thing. I do believe we have a big seller on our hands. Well done!"

"Thank you," I said, abashed at the praise heaped on me. "I must say,
it's great to hear it without the clicks and pops you get from frequent
plays of vinyl. It's pristine."

"Klixxen Popps?" laughed Pete. "Isn't he that Finnish tenor?"

PUPPET ON A STRING

CHAPTER 33

The next few days were taken up with co-ordinating printing, the distribution process and the pressing of the records. Never having done this sort of thing before, I estimated conservatively that fifty thousand might be a suitable number, especially as it was unknown how it would be received. During this time, Marie had finalized the details on the house and was, even now, looking through colour charts and material patterns. It was on the last day of working on the recording – everything else on it was in the hands of the various companies and no more needed to be done by me – that we received the confirmation that we could move in, with the banks' financial exchanges and legal proprieties completed. I remember thinking that it was excellent timing with conclusion of the work effort. Although keeping an eye and ear on the progress of the recording, we could devote all our time to getting the house and garden straight.

During the last week of July and the first week of August, Marie and I whipped through the house, painting, hanging curtains and pictures, getting a little man (as Marie called him) into lay the carpets and another little man to burnish the parquet flooring in what was to be our dining-room. It was hard work, not least because of the heat, but we had fun getting it just how we wanted it. On one occasion, we were renovating our bedroom, the room with the magnificent view across the garden and down to the sea. I was in black shorts with aged plimsolls on my feet; Marie was in light yellow, cotton dungarees and pink canvas shoes and nothing else. Her tan had not faded since the holiday and the light colour of the dungarees showed the depth of it on her arms, shoulders and back in sharp relief – it was all I could do to keep myself from pulling the straps down and covering her in kisses. No, instead I had to concentrate on the painting (a sky blue colour) and ensuring smooth, straight lines along the tops of the walls and at the skirting board. It was then that I felt something liquid hit my shoulder-blade, but thought nothing of it, given that droplets of sweat had been dripping from my forehead and nose for most of the morning. Then I felt it again, this time on my forearm and there was a dollop of light blue paint. I looked up at the wall, wondering how the paint could possibly be falling off. About to say to Marie that something odd was happening, I noticed her standing on the other side of the room, paintbrush in hand as if holding a flag, a deep dimple in her impish cheek. She flicked the brush again and another spot of paint hit my chest.

I opened my mouth in surprise and then jumped across the room, catching her before she could get away, and held her with her back to me, threatening to daub her face with my brush. Marie held my hand away as strongly as she could, screaming and laughing. I released the pressure and she calmed down a little and then I pounced: a splash of light blue paint appeared at the top of her chest.

She yelled a little, getting away from me, looking down at the mark, her mouth, this time, open in surprise. "I can't believe you just did that!" she said and then giggled, flicking her brush at me again in an arc. A splatter of paint hit me from shoulder to stomach. "No!" she screamed as I moved quickly towards her, catching her around the shoulders.

"There's no point in struggling," I said, grinning, holding on to her with one arm cuddling her into me, as the other painted a blue line down her arm.

Marie screamed with laughter again, trying to break free, ducking down to the floor to reload her paintbrush, drawing a thick paint line down my thigh.

"Right! This is war!" I bent down, dipping the brush into the paint pot and spread paint across her naked back. This continued for some while until we stood apart, brushes poised, giggling like children at each other, covered in washes, drops and strokes of the paint. "Peace?" I offered eventually.

Marie grinned and nodded, as we both put our brushes down, watching each other carefully. "Look at the mess you made of me," she said, looking down at her arms and chest.

"Well, look at me!" I grinned. "You know something?"

"What?"

"You don't half look damned sexy dressed in splodges of paint."

"Blue suits you too," she said, moving towards me and wrapping her arms around my waist. "Give me a kiss."

I bent to kiss her lips, and stroking her painty arms, I pulled the straps of her dungarees off her shoulders and kissed the freckles left free of the blue colour.

"Why, Mr. Loughton! What sort of a girl do you think I am?" Marie was wide-eyed and grinning.

"I think I know what sort of a girl you are. You are beautiful, cuddly, soft, covered in paint and I want to make love with you now."

She half-smiled and said: "Well, Mr. Loughton, I thought you'd never ask."

Laying down on the dust-sheet, we kissed, cuddled and stroked each other and made love urgently. In the beautiful, close afterglow, perspiration trickling down our bodies, I cuddled her towards me and squeezed so that she gasped.

"Do you like me or something?" she asked, kissing my neck.

"Just a little bit," I agreed. My eyes wandered over her curves, which were slick with perspiration and squeezed her again. "Not only that but I love you."

She kissed my lips again. "I think I might just love you, too."

I picked up her arm and said: "You are a bit of a mess, young lady. However did you get into such a state?"

"I can't imagine. The same way that you did, probably." She grinned, stroking my chest. "Shall we have a bath to get rid of the paint?"

I agreed readily and we spent the next couple of hours languishing in the lukewarm bath, cooling ourselves down after the exertions of the morning.

* * *

The garden was extensive and was completely isolated with no neighbour overlooking us, which was perfect – the privacy was just what we needed. Down one side was a high brick wall and, on the other, a tall, wooden fence. At the bottom, luscious hedgerow plants protected us. In the stillness of the garden, you could hear in the distance the low crash and rumble of the waves advancing up the shale beach and retreating again. One of my first priorities had been to make my daydream true by hooking up a hammock between two trees, which provided shade from the hot mid-day sun.

When we had finished the decoration of the rooms and all the carpets and furniture were in place, Marie and I spent many a morning and afternoon lying in the sun, relaxing in the shade, drinking cool fruit juices through straws, talking and making plans. Marie took every opportunity to top up and deepen her tan and I took great pleasure in massaging the sun oil into her body, front and back – because we were not overlooked, she sunbathed completely naked and the white skin that had existed under her bikini bottoms on the holiday was now almost the same deep brown colour as the rest of her body.

During the long, hot summer – our last summer –four terrible and beautiful things happened to us that were to break our self-imposed idyll.

The first terrible incident that happened was when Pete called us in the early hours of the morning. We had deliberately chosen to be ex-directory so that a few select people could get in contact with us but we could not be easily traced by those not close to us. By the same token, the 'phone ringing at that time of night indicated that there was an emergency.

"Dave," said an extremely worried and harried voice as I blearily picked up the extension 'phone by the side of the bed. "I've got some bad news, I'm afraid."

His tone woke me up and suddenly I was upright, feet trying to find slippers kicked off the night before. Isla protested half-heartedly, yawned expansively and settled her head back down on her paws at the end of the bed. "Pete, what's wrong?"

"Um," he started and was obviously struggling to find a way to broach whatever he was trying to tell me. "It's bad news, as I say." Another pause and then a deep breath. "I'm afraid your house has been gutted by fire."

"What?" The hushed tones I had been using to keep from waking Marie up had now metamorphosed into shocked indignation. Marie was awake now and had put a comforting arm around me my waist as I sat on the edge of the bed.

"It's true," Pete continued reluctantly. "The police have been trying to trace you and found me by the emergency numbers at the office. They were worried that you might be inside." Another pause. "And thank God you weren't!"

Marie asked what the problem was and I cupped the receiver to tell her. Returning to Pete, I confirmed that I would leave immediately and drop by his house. Not that I could do anything other than survey the damage, of course, but I thought that some belongings might be salvageable if nothing else.

"That's not the worst of it," said Pete, obviously saving the last nugget to the last. Another maddening pause. "The police reckon it was started deliberately."

"Deliberately?" I repeated in shock.

"Yes," confirmed Pete. "Petrol poured through the letter-box followed by an open lighter according to the fire brigade. There are dead matches littering the front doorstep apparently so it was also a last resort."

"Pretty determined, then," I observed and checked my watch. "Look, I'll see you in three hours."

Ending the 'phone call, I repeated what Pete had told me to Marie, insisted she stay where she was and that I would return in a few hours, once the damage had been assessed.

"Be careful, sweetheart," she said, wide-eyed with shock and disappointment for me.

I dressed quickly in casual clothes, ran downstairs and, pausing only to check the door was secure, raced towards the north of London in my protesting Mini. Three and a half hours later, I was standing outside the charred and still smoking remnants of my old house, hands on hips, stunned into silence. The fire brigade and police were still there, tidying up hose-reels and packing the fire-fighting paraphernalia back into their truck. Pete was with me, equally dumbstruck. The roof had caved in, bringing down the lower floors as it did so. Being such an old house, the timber frames had served as kindling for the massive fire, which went on to gut the house. Only the walls remained standing, although now very unstable without the support of internal joists. Everywhere, blackened and wet timbers smouldered. Nothing was recognizable. Speaking with the chief fireman, he told me that the catalyst had indeed been petrol poured through the letter-box, but also that it must have been spread using a squeezy bottle, since the base of the start of the fire was not centred on the front door mat but was all the way up the hall and on to the stairs and up the walls. There was no way that the house or its contents could have been saved.

A policeman had cordoned off the front garden to prevent injury of anyone unwittingly approaching the house, while another took a statement from me as to where I was, dates and times and other helpful information, giving me a reference for insurance purposes. Pete offered his spare bedroom for the night, which I declined, preferring to get back on the road to Marie – I had severe misgivings about the start of the fire and who was responsible for it and did not want to be apart from her any longer than I had to be. I wanted to ensure her protection from whatever evil was now hounding me.

I arrived back to the Worth Matravers house by eight o'clock, drawn and exhausted from the driving and lack of sleep. Marie met me at the door and hugged me as I relayed the terrible details. If I had not moved a lot of the best furniture and some possessions down to Dorset, I would have lost pretty much everything I owned. It took the colour off the day and it was a good few days before I had resigned myself to the inevitable, letting the insurance company sort it out. Life was too short and I wanted to get back to having fun with Marie again in our perfect cottage by the sea.

The piece of balancing good news came just two weeks after the release of *The Creation*. A lot of the more serious-minded critics pooh-poohed the recording as sensationalist and dismissed it as an attempt to jump on the bandwagon created by the Moody Blues and Decca (with their seminal *Days of Future Passed* album). The critics view was that the recording was bringing the whole world of classical and choral music into disrepute and they wondered how Marie Duvois, Beth Jackson and Sir Norman Pettinger had allowed themselves to be roped into such desecration of the classics, especially with the two unknown singers (Pete and me). On the other side of the wall, though, there were several critics who applauded what we had done, raving about the fresh approach we had adopted, praising the techniques used to represent the drama in the piece, expressing wonder and amazement at the perfection of Marie's voice and making encouraging noises about Pete's and my first foray as soloists. There was no middle ground: they either hated it or loved it. This was better than I had hoped, because the provocation of such a reaction meant many column inches were devoted to the record, raising its prominence and thereby increasing the sales. True enough, by the end of the first fortnight with the critics writing attacking and praising pieces on it and then writing counter-attacks the following week, *The Creation* reached number one in the classical charts. Following that announcement, the *Gramophone* and other erstwhile publications went on the attack and counter-offensive to suggest that, since the record was not purely classical music (even though it was simply the recording technique, which was different), it did not rightly sit in the classical charts let alone at the coveted top spot. I had severely underestimated the demand for copies and had to order three hundred thousand more pressings to cope with it.

Two weeks later, Pete, Beth, Marie and I received gold record awards for the number sold as soloists and I received another for my production duties. The three plaques took pride of place side by side in the room that we had converted into a music room. From this success, I began drawing up ideas for the follow-up, which could benefit from the techniques we had already employed and looking to extend them.

The second uncomfortable situation happened to us – well, to me, more accurately; as a deliberate ploy on my part, I made sure Marie was unaffected by it – the second situation happened towards the end of August. Marie and I were enjoying a relaxing, long Bank Holiday weekend. We had taken walks down to Dancing Ledge, partaking in picnics, sitting quietly on the slate rocks, arms around each other, Marie with her head on my shoulder, looking at the placid sea, with the sun twinkling nonchalantly on the barely noticeable ripples on the mill-pond. At the sea's edge, half-hearted dribbles of waves broke but achieved little in their advance up the beach. It was as if the sea were bored or, like us, feeling listless in the hot sun. On one such jaunt, we continued along the coast path and, at a sort of hillock at the top of a cliff, we found a turnstile, which had a sign on it: 'Cuddle'. We did not require much coaxing to obey that instruction every time we went there and we returned there several times during our tenure as home-owners in this idyllic part of England.

On the Bank Holiday Monday, the dry heat was still present and even Marie could not bear to sunbathe for too long in the mid-day sun. I had retreated to the hammock, wearing only swimming trunks and wanting to remove another invisible layer. Marie, in her yellow bikini, had offered to get cold drinks and, moments later, with my hand lazily placed on forehead, I heard her footsteps on the dry grass as she approached. Squinting in the sun to thank her for the drink, I was too late to avoid the icy, cold water she poured on my stomach from a plastic beaker. Gasping with the shock of the extremes of heat, I fell out of the hammock. Marie was giggling at the trick she had played on me and I noticed there was still some water left in the beaker. In a sudden movement, I lunged for it and, so surprised was she by my obviously lithe and catlike movement, Marie let it go without a fight. Realizing that she was now going to get similar treatment, she turned on her heel and ran away from me, squealing at me not to splash her with the water. Gaining on her quickly, I launched the water at her, which landed squarely on her brown back between the shoulder-blades. Screaming with the cold, she slowed down. Throwing the beaker down, I grabbed her arms, pulling her towards me. Still screaming and giggling, she looked at me wide-eyed as I laid her gently on the grass, straddling her midriff and holding her wrists above her head. She played at fighting back, yelling at me to get off her. As I bent down to kiss her, a large shadow passed across us and a stick tapped my ribs. "Do as she says, son," came a voice.

Jolting so violently that it was almost an 'out of body' experience, I released Marie's arms and stood up – thank Heavens we were fully clothed on this occasion! Marie jumped up and hugged the interloper. "Uncle Charles!" she said, kissing his stubbly face.

Sir Charles reached his hand out and stroked up her arm to her shoulder and down her naked back, growling with satisfaction as he did so. I was shocked. This dirty old man was, to put it in the vernacular and parlance of the day, 'copping a feel'. My suspicions had been correct and warranted – Sir Charles wanted more from Marie than purely being her sponsor and his frustration with me came from unrequited lust for her.

Marie returned to the kitchen to get some drinks and I took my opportunity to say something to him. Moving him further away from the house and down the garden, I turned to him and said: "I would appreciate if you would keep your hands off my fiancée, Sir Charles."

Initially, he reddened and guilt spread across his face, which was then replaced with a deliberately controlled but apoplectic fury. "How dare you?" he almost whispered so that Marie would not know that anything was wrong.

"I saw you, Sir Charles, pawing her and almost salivating down the front of your shirt. Now, please keep your hands off her and, in future, tell us when you are going to visit us, so that we don't have to endure such distasteful surprises." Sir Charles began to protest but I put up a resistant hand. "Do as I say and I will ensure that Marie doesn't know about your sordid aspirations."

Sir Charles's mouth goldfished for a while as he searched for a suitable retort. "Are you blackmailing me?" Sweat had broken out on his forehead.

I laughed humourlessly. "In a sense, but only to protect Marie. She doesn't deserve to be heartbroken by your hideous secret."

"You are a cad, sir!" he spluttered as the back door shut.

"That I may be but for the right reasons," I countered, lowering my voice as Marie approached. "Do you agree to my terms?"

Sir Charles was forced to comply as Marie joined us, a cotton wrap now around her lower half, carrying a tray of glasses and a jug of ice cool lemonade. "Yes," he conceded.

"Which is great," I said, conversationally, as if I had been halfway through a different discussion. "Because it gives me the impetus to try something else in a similar style. I'm working on Britten's *War Requiem* next. What do you think?"

A little flustered but covering well, Sir Charles reluctantly acknowledged that it was a good idea.

"Especially at the moment, with so much unrest in the Far East. It seems appropriate to record something like that, expressing the futility of war. And none more so than in Vietnam."

Sir Charles harrumphed a little, a sickly grin on his face for Marie's benefit, and took one of the proffered glasses.

Marie placed the tray on the garden table and we sat down at it. She stroked my forearm and said: "David's very clever, isn't he, Uncle Charles?"

Sir Charles was caught on the hop. His obvious distaste and a sentiment verging on hatred for me were flickering across his features. It was only obvious to me because I knew it was there and what to look for. After a moment's hesitation, he beamed a smile at Marie, raising his glass. "I think what he has done is interesting and will turn the classical recording world on its head." We joined him in raising glasses and drank. To praise me in that way must have burned like acid; not only because it was about me but I knew for a fact that Sir Charles was a musical purist and would have been vehemently critical of what I had achieved, were he not on the receiving end of moral blackmail.

It was not as if I wanted to hold him to ransom necessarily but more that I really did not want him to go near Marie, compounded by the fact that she would have been very hurt if the two men in her life did not get on. After lunch in the shade of the large oak tree at the bottom of the garden, Sir Charles stood up stiffly and confirmed that he would be going and not to see him off the premises. He shook my hand briefly and then turned to Marie. He bent to kiss her and force of habit made his hand hover over the naked flesh of her shoulder. I cleared my throat subtly and he glanced in my direction, observing my admonishingly raised eyebrows. Clearing his throat in sympathy, he simply kissed her cheek and bade us farewell.

"He's a nice old man, isn't he?" said Marie, putting her head on my shoulder as we watched him hobble up to the side-gate without turning. She smiled wistfully.

"Yes," I agreed quietly. "Isn't he?"

This unwholesome episode was relegated into the lower divisions by the stratospheric joy brought about by the second absolutely wonderful happenstance. Marie had gone into the village for the morning, being very secretive about what she was up to. I took the opportunity to develop my ideas further for the *War Requiem*. Three hours later, feet up on one of the garden chairs, several pieces of paper weighted down with anything I could find to serve the purpose, it took me a moment or two to break the line of thought as I heard Marie rustling through the lawn towards me. She was wearing a white sleeveless tee-shirt and a pink cotton skirt, her chocolate brown limbs complemented completely by the clothes. She was smiling widely as she came and perched on the seat in front of me.

"Give me a kiss," she said.

I leaned to her and kissed her lips gently. "So what have you been up to? You look like the three-legged cat who got the cream."

She smiled and took my hands. "I've got something to tell you and I think you will like it." She sat straddling my lap, facing me.

It was not yet my birthday so I was wondering if she had organized another surprise for me. "I hope so," I said, a dopey grin on my lips, "I like surprises!"

Taking a greater hold of my hands so that we were clasped palm to palm, she looked into my eyes – oh, those beautiful brown eyes that could make me do anything for her – and said: "Right. Are you ready?"

"Do you want me to shut my eyes or anything?"

"Only if you want to. Ready?"

I took a deep breath and nodded once. "Yes. Hit me with it."

"I'm pregnant."

She was still smiling, looking deeply into my eyes. The world swirled away momentarily as the neurons in my brain tried to stop themselves short-circuiting and to comprehend the two words she had just spoken. "Pardon?" was all I could come out with.

She smiled more widely if that were possible and the edges of her eyes crinkled with happiness and amusement. "I'm pregnant," she repeated.

Slowly the world slotted back into place on the periphery but right now my sole focus was Marie. I looked down at her stomach and back to her face. "What…?" I started. "When…? How…?"

Marie gently placed a finger on my lips and said: "I've been wondering for the last couple of weeks plus feeling a little weird in the mornings. I made an appointment to see the doctor a few days ago and he confirmed it to me today."

A smile broadened across my lips and I jumped up from the chair, set Marie gently on her feet and punched the air, shouting: "Yes! Yes! Yes! I'm going to be a Daddy!" I grabbed her hands to join my dance. I stopped abruptly, concerned. "Sorry, sweetheart, I shouldn't shake you up in your condition."

"I'm only pregnant," she protested and giggled.

I pulled her to me and kissed her. "Pregnant with *our* baby."

She pecked my lips and smiled, raising her eyebrows. "Yes. Now, do you want your other surprise?"

Holding her away gently by her shoulders, I asked: "Another surprise?"

She nodded.

"Bigger or smaller than the first one?"

"Oh, bigger!" she acknowledged with mock gravity.

"Okay, I'll shut my eyes for this one." I squeezed my eyes shut and, for good measure, placed a hand over them, holding the other out palm upwards. "Right. Ready."

Marie lightly tapped my hand and said: "Sure?"

"Yes. Give it to me now. I like surprises, I told you."

A brief pause. "The doctor thinks it might be twins!"

The world swirled away again as I slowly removed my hand, mouth opening agape at the news. Pulling myself together, I grabbed Marie bending her slightly backwards and over to the side, kissing her face and forehead rapidly.

Giggling, she said: "I take it that means you're happy?"

I pulled her up straight, took her by the shoulders and foreheads touching, I looked into her eyes. "Marie, sweetheart, that is the best news since you agreed to marry me. Not only are you pregnant but you might be pregnant with two babies. And they are our babies." A surprised tear fell down my cheek, and Marie smiled as she wiped it away gently with the heel of her hand. I wrapped my arms around her and cuddled her strongly, which she reciprocated. "Oh, Marie. It's perfect. I love you."

We stayed in that position for a good few minutes. Now it was Marie's turn to have wet cheeks. "I'm not sad," she said, by way of explanation. "Quite the opposite. I'm so glad that the news has made you happy. Especially after the some of the nastiness in the last few months."

The last comment passed me by. "I feel like doing cart-wheels across the lawn," I said.

"Well," said Marie, wiping her cheeks with the back of her hand. "Why don't you?"

"Slight problem. I've always been useless at gymnastics."

Marie giggled and pulled me into another hug.

"Let's just say that I wanted to do a cartwheel but I don't actually have to do it."

Marie looked up at me and kissed me again. "You are such a lovely man. Strange, true, but lovely with it."

"And you are one girl in six thousand trillion." I paused. "Or possibly three girls in six thousand trillion."

Marie laughed brightly and slapped my shoulder. Kissing me again, she placed her hand on my chest and nodded contentedly. "Do you want to tell anyone?"

I considered it. "Let's just tell close people for now. We don't want to put the kybosh on it. You know, Sir Charles, Pete and Beth."

Marie agreed and went inside to change. Grinning like a Cheshire cat, I followed her and picked up the 'phone, dialling Sir Charles number. Asking him to be discreet with the information for Marie's sake, his irritation showed as he begrudgingly accepted that I was now inextricably linked with Marie. His ire was stoked by the news because it reduced the paucity of any chance that he might have had even more and it was all too prevalent in his chosen words. Marie came downstairs and, when I said that I would put her on, his tone brightened immediately and I left them chatting.

Marie called Beth next and she was ecstatic with the news. Then I called Pete. Melodramatically, after the news had sunk in, he said: "That's fantastic news, Dave! You? A father? I could scarcely believe it. Let joy be unconfined."

"Pete," I said in a serious tone, "what you do in your private life is up to you, but surely Beth would be put out?"

A shocked pause. "What? I don't understand."

"Locking up women for your own pleasure but poor Beth!"

"Locking up...?" Then he tumbled to it. "Ah, very good. Joy. Unconfined. Got you. Actually, she's a very nice young lady. By the way, that comment was supposed to be off the handcuff."

I groaned at the joke and we swapped further puns until I could take the pain no more. "Enough!" I said. "You've always been able to take it one step further. Or is that 'too far'?"

Pete pretended to be huffy. "And I always thought you liked my humour. Anyway, before you can respond to that one, let's get the conversation back to your news. Phew! That was subtly done! How's Marie?"

"Positively glowing," I confirmed.

"Well, look after her mate."

"I will."

Back out in the garden, Marie was in her bikini and cotton sarong, sitting at the table and looking through my plans for the *War Requiem*. She looked up as I came out. "Pete sends his love."

She smiled in response. "This looks good, David," she said, indicating a couple of drawings of the position of the listener. For the poetry spoken during the piece, I wanted to have it sound as if the listener were standing in 'No Man's Land' and I was proposing to use some battle sound effects.

"Thanks," I said, crouching by her side and bent forward to kiss her stomach three times and then looked back at her grinning. "One each!"

She giggled, taking my hand and kissing it. "The doctor says that I'm a month or two along the way. It's going to be touch and go as to whether I will have given birth before the wedding or not."

"Do you want to move the wedding?"

"No, David. I like your romantic notion of it being on the first anniversary of our meeting each other." I reached out and placed a tender hand on her stomach and stroked it softly, a distant, dopey grin on my face. Marie leaned forward and kissed me, a rascal glint in her eye. "I love you, Daddy."

I leaned into her stomach and said: "Hey! Did you hear that? Mummy loves me." Marie almost choked, she was laughing so hard.

* * *

Over the cooling days of September, as the trees and garden turned from lush green to a transient yellow and on to the browns, reds and golds of autumn, the babies began to grow and Marie began to show more prominently. The pregnancy was becoming difficult for her because with it came unusual but not unheard of sickness, which laid her low for a few days at a time. Nonetheless, even though she was not feeling brilliant, she still exuded the pretty glow of oncoming motherhood. My love for and appreciation of her continued to grow during those early stages. In a much earlier life, I had been bitter with reproach about my lack of success with the feminine gender – looking at my growing family now, that time seemed ancient and centuries ago, such was Marie's benevolent impact on me.

One evening, as the nights drew in earlier and earlier, cooling the heat of the late Indian Summer days, we were cuddled up on the couch, with me stroking her stomach, I swear I felt a movement and we grinned together, Marie confirming that she felt it too.

"We ought to think of suitable names," she said, hand on top of mine as it made its slow and circular movement over her stomach.

"How about something from nature? You know, like the hippies do? Leaf, River, Willow, Honey…Twig, Manicured Lawn… Turnip?"

She wrinkled her nose and shook her head. Thinking for a moment, she said: "We could choose the name of a flower, though. Erm… Rose? Or Daisy?"

"Petunia," I suggested. "Dandelion, Deadly Nightshade, Dogwort…"

She slapped my hand lightly and laughed. "You're not taking this seriously. Anyway, what if they are boys? We can't call them Daisy or Rose. Or Dogwort." She giggled.

"Of course we can. In later life, they'll have to be very tough to cope with names like that."

She giggled again. "So, really, what do you think."

I had given it some thought and suggested two girls' names and two boys'. Immediately, Marie agreed, saying they were lovely. "I can hardly wait to meet them," I said.

"Neither can I, sweetheart," Marie said gently and turned to kiss me.

PUPPET ON A STRING

CHAPTER 34

A drian and Gary had been quickly arrested within forty-eight hours of my original crime report to the police. They had been held for questioning, staying an enforced night in the cells to allow the completion of the interviews and necessary paperwork. Then they were formally and summarily charged with embezzlement – Gary also had the charges of perverting the course of justice and resisting arrest to add to his list of misdemeanours – and both were bailed to appear in courts, the dates for which they would be notified. To prevent them absconding and avoiding facing up to their fates, their passports were removed from them.

Gary's and Adrian's hearings were convened separately in late November and it was agreed by the judge, based on the Prosecution's evidence, that both had cases to answer but that it was his judgment that Gary's crime was the greater, especially with the additional charges brought to bear. Neither spoke during the proceedings, except to confirm their names, abodes and pleas of 'Not Guilty' – after which Gary let fly a vituperative tirade from the box, while Adrian fainted with gastric ulceration problems.

They were both arraigned to appear on separate trials on a date to be set at the court's leisure but by the end of April the following year. This was to enable their respective solicitors enough time to come up with a suitable defence and to establish any counter-evidence. I read the article on the arraignment with interest, secure in the knowledge that I had done the right thing by reporting them to the police.

As predicted, *The Investigator* left me alone after a while, preferring to take up a story of seedy happenings in a sordid part of the pop world. I had to bring myself up, when reading this change of focus because I was falling into the same salacious trap as others who would have read the libellous stories about me. From that point on, I decided that the paper was not even fit for use as toilet paper, such was the quality of the

ink and material, and that I would never read it again. And I kept my
vow, except for that final depressing headline.

As Marie's pregnancy advanced, she became very troubled by it and
was frequently sick and ill. The doctor confirmed that this was perfectly
ordinary and to be expected and that it may be connected to carrying
two babies – confirmed; he could hear two distinct heartbeats in the
latter stages – the two babies had increased the physical drain on such a
slender woman. Even though she did put on weight – her particular
peccadillo was baby pickled gherkins smothered in vanilla ice cream – it
was insignificant. It also started affecting her back as her stomach grew
with two very active babies inside.

At the first recordings for the *War Requiem*, she took several breaks,
sometimes looking pale and drawn, despite the remnants of her summer
tan, with a chair constantly at her disposal. Towards the end of the
sessions, the pain and sickness suddenly disappeared. She was so much
better and, at her own admission, could actually enjoy recording the way
I had planned it rather than treating it as a chore – something she
thought she would never feel about music. I had planned, at one
dramatic point, having the soloists (again using myself, Pete and Beth as
lucky charms), lying on the floor on our backs with a circle of
microphones pointing away from us, dangling from the ceiling of the
studio in a circle. That idea was temporarily abandoned because I did
not want to put Marie through the trauma. However, because her health
dramatically improved, she insisted on it and we went ahead as planned,
albeit carefully lowering her to the floor and picking her back up again.

Once again, at the end of the recording, Pete, Beth, Marie and I
recorded an impromptu *a cappella* version of *All You Need is Love*, again
running it backwards across the trail-off from the record, as a sort of
protest in keeping with the tenor of the main recorded work. Sir
Norman and Bruce Carlton joined the four of us and we sat through the
end-to-end recording (without the trail-off!) – Sir Norman was again
commenting on bits that he liked and what worked well. But this time,
Pete, Beth and Marie were sitting, eyes glazed over, in thrall at what was
coming out of the speakers.

"It's fantastic!" commented Pete, when the final chord had drained
away to nothing.

Beth hopped off her seat, showing me the goose pimples on her
forearms, and kissed my cheek. "That's what *you* did. It's brilliant!" she
exclaimed.

I turned to Marie, who was still in thrall, tears cascading down her cheeks. Standing in front of her, I took her fingers in my hands and asked: "What did you think?"

Still with a faraway look in her eyes, as if focusing on the madness of the Great War evoked by the music, she said. "They should play this version to anyone considering declaring war; it would make the world a much gentler place." She looked suddenly up at me and smiled. "It's beautiful and so thought-provoking. And I am incredibly proud to be a part of it."

Sir Norman got to his feet, looking increasingly grey around the gills, despite insisting that he had never felt better, and shook my hand. "Another sure-fire seller, young David. Well done!"

After all the ballyhoo created by *The Creation*, the next recording, regardless of its strength or banality, would always invoke a stream of its own publicity. Walking down Oxford Street, on the day of its release, in one of the big record shops, a full frontage of the shop was taken up with the simple sleeve design of a rutted and muddy field, with broken barbed wire, a discarded gun in the foreground, puddles reflecting the grey and overcast sky, and, in the middle of this, standing starkly in contrast to the destruction, a simple red poppy. There were several banners detailing those involved but there was one, which had the simple dedication written by me from the back of the sleeve: 'Dedicated to all the brave men and women who fought and suffered to rid this land of tyranny'. I bristled with pride when I saw all of this and knew that it would be a big seller, as Sir Norman had suggested, not the least because of the message held within it. In a now fairly rare moment of paranoia and unease, I had worried that the critics might tear the *War Requiem* apart as mawkish and overly sentimental.

This time, though, they were bowled over. While some begrudgingly accepted that the emotions created from listening to the recording should not be overlooked, they still criticised the stereophonic techniques and the trail-off and some of the subtle sound effects incorporated but had suggested that even purists might find this one worth listening to. As a result of such positive publicity, the record held the top slot in the classical music charts over Christmas and into the New Year, some of its impetus held up by the sentimentality of the season but mostly because everyone agreed that this was an extraordinary recording. More gold record awards were put up beside those we had already received from *The Creation*.

Over the Christmas period, we had agreed to take some time off to prepare for the birth of our twins in April. This time was well-spent getting the spare bedroom converted to a nursery and organizing the wedding. During this period too, Marie and I settled down as if we were already married. We invited Beth, Pete and Sir Charles to stay for Christmas. Our friends gladly accepted the invitation immediately but Sir Charles demurred and called me.

"I don't think that would be a good idea, do you?" he said stiffly.

"What do you mean?" I asked, guessing his motives.

"I don't want to be in your company any more than I have to. If it were Marie on her own, then of course I would dearly love to come down."

Ignoring a golden opportunity for a snide comment, I said: "But Marie will be upset if you're not here."

"Don't you worry about that, boy! I'll be talking to her."

And the line went dead. And indeed, he did talk to her. Apparently, his excuse was that he had a conducting engagement on Christmas Eve in Leipzig and was at an age when running around on various forms of travel was exhausting and that he hoped she would understand.

She was a little piqued that it sounded like an excuse rather than a genuine plan stopping him but our Christmas was not marred further by anything else. In fact, we had a lovely time with Pete and Beth, opening presents frantically like excited children, burping gratuitously after a fine dinner and a taking a refreshing walk along Dancing Ledge, until the twilight came in and we returned to the warmth and comfort of our house. On New Year's Eve, they were with us still, having agreed that we would see the New Year in quietly. I had a presentiment that this was going to be our year and I was looking forward to it with great eagerness. With the prospect of parenthood and the prosperity of the fledgling record label, my ambitions were being fulfilled quickly, which meant I could face what would have been an otherwise uncertain or sedentary future with energy and zeal, supported by the deep love of a gorgeous young woman.

It was at the stroke of midnight as we raised our glasses that Beth dropped her bombshell to Pete. She had fallen pregnant, too. "Only the one, I think," she had grinned at Marie. Both Marie and I had noticed that she had looked healthy and positively glowing so, sub-consciously, we had already guessed. Pete was grinning like a loon as he shook my hand, kissed Marie and hugged Beth.

"Both fathers in the same year, then," he observed, still a little shocked.

I put an arm around him and patted his shoulder. "It's all right, mate," I said in mock confidentiality, "I'll tell you all you need to know."

"Yeah!" he exclaimed. "You'll be an old hand by then with two of them."

I kissed Beth and congratulated her on her news. She and Marie went off into a girly huddle to talk babies and the effects of pregnancy, while Pete and I settled in the armchairs. Pete raised his glass again, saying: "To our year. It's going to be perfect."

I raised my glass. "I hope you haven't put the kiss of death on it," I joked and Pete laughed.

* * *

Over the next three months, in between visits to antenatal classes and the doctor for regular check-ups, I was planning the next recording as well as preparing for a number of *Coro di Londinium* performances in Covent Garden. Initially, I was undecided as to what the third recording should be, toying with the idea of a mass or requiem but there is not a lot of drama in them to benefit from the technique that Bruce and I had developed. Researching composers in the British Library, I came across an intriguing choral work by Edward Elgar called *King Olaf*. It was essentially an Old Norse saga set to music and seemed to fit in with the dramatic persona necessary for the recording. With due regard to the planning, I set to work in my spare moments, pulling the details together. Because it was an unfamiliar work, there was a risk to its popularity but figured that the success of the *War Requiem* would provide the sales impetus needed to keep it in the public focus.

In the early spring, the *Coro di Londinium* was invited to take part in a performance of *Tosca* in the Royal Opera House in Covent Garden before embarking on the now annual Paris tour. Marie was slated to take the lead role, while it was to be conducted by the estranged Sir Charles. The date was scheduled to be 11th April – the date before our wedding and, pre-eminently, the same opera we had performed when Marie and I had first dined out together. All the signs looked good for a romantic couple of days and I signed the agreement, sending it back to the organisers, making a note to inform Sir Norman of the need to dust off the wardrobe and props and prepare for the necessary rehearsals.

Almost like a premonition and spookily, the 'phone rang and a voice at the other end identified himself as Sir Norman's eldest son. I caught my breath momentarily and could not speak with the unease that had crept over me.

"Hello?" came the voice again.

"Sorry, yes, Stephen," I said finally. "What can I do for you?"

"I'm afraid to tell you that my father died this morning." Stephen's voice was distant and tight, in the effort to stop the emotion from the grief sweeping over him. I knew they were a very close family. Although Sir Norman was reputed to be a bit of an authoritarian and a disciplinarian where his family were concerned, there was a lot of respect and love, too. I had been concerned that Sir Norman had been looking ashen for weeks and recalled his unsteadiness at the *War* Requiem listen-through. But I had not done anything about it after his insistence that he was fine and that no-one should fuss over him.

"Oh, God! No!" I was shocked even though, to be truthful, I was half-expecting it.

"Brain haemorrhage; nothing they could do."

"Was he in pain?"

"They believe not because the end was quite sudden. He collapsed in his club in London."

"Please accept the condolences from me on behalf of the *Coro di Londinium* and Marie Duvois. If you need me to do anything, please, you only have to ask."

"Thanks," Stephen replied, his voice now thick with grief. "I'll let you know the arrangements for the funeral."

"Thank you." I put the 'phone down and buried my head in my hands. Not an auspicious start to the romantic interlude that was to lead up to the wedding. I called Pete and Marie to let them know and then set about organizing a stand-in choral conductor for this performance. As part of my original plan, *King Olaf* had been intended to be a tribute dedicated to his musical achievements and to his support for the record label. But now any new recording would automatically also be a tribute to his memory. I took the decision to revert back to creating a standard recording of a requiem mass as a testament to the vision and energy of the man who had guided the infant Chorus to musical maturity. His death was a setback – a painful setback, of course – but nothing that could not be overcome.

Towards the end of March, with Marie becoming quite large with the twins, we recorded Verdi's *Requiem* straight with no gimmickry and packaged it as a memorial to Sir Norman. There was a distinct passion in the record and this, coupled with the purpose for recording it, made it a good seller. Instead of using Pete's and my voice, we relented to allow Guido Estente and Mikhail Torchev do the honours. Having said that, it nowhere near met the targets of the previous two records on the label but I was neither surprised nor disheartened – we had recorded it as a personal obituary to Sir Norman and not necessarily to make money. Nonetheless, it did make a small profit, which was useful.

We also started work on the recording of *King Olaf*, which had been suspended for a while, to give the Chorus time to rehearse for the Covent Garden *Tosca*. On the first of April, I received an excited 'phone call from Marie, when I was in the offices organizing and finalizing some ideas for the recording.

"I've got good news!" she said, barely able to conceal her excitement.

"What news?" I asked, intrigued.

"Uncle Charles wants you to sing," she said. A bizarre image came into my mind of Sir Charles sitting on my knee as I crooned at him. Very odd.

"What do you mean?" I asked dumbly.

"He wants you to sing," repeated Marie insistent in her excitement. "In *Tosca*," she added.

My jaw dropped, while Marie called my name a couple of times. "I'm still here. For a moment I thought you said that Sir Charles wanted me to sing in *Tosca*."

"I did," she replied.

"Hey!" I suddenly realized the date. "You're not trying to make me a *poisson d'Avril*, are you?"

"What?" Marie was confused and then caught on. "No, I'm not trying to make a fool of you, silly. It's true!"

"Marie, will you do something for me?"

"Of course, David."

"Can you get a cab and come over and pinch me? I think I'm dreaming."

"If you want," she chuckled. "So what do you think?"

"My gob is smacked and my gast a little flabbered. Is it one of the minor transient rôles?"

"Well, sort of," she replied. I could tell that the minx in her was coming out now.

"Which one?" I asked guardedly.

"You know. That small part. Oh, what's his name? Cavaradossi!" She chuckled again.

I caught my breath and let it out slowly. "You're joking!"

"No."

"But Cavaradossi is a huge part. Why does Sir Charles want me to sing it?"

"John Shinkton has fallen ill and he could not find a willing replacement at such short notice."

I read between the lines and knew that a little kind engineering by Marie was also involved in the decision, but it did not bother me. In fact, I was incredibly flattered. "I don't know what to say."

"Say 'yes'!" she urged and then after a pause, added: "You do realize that we'll be singing together on the eve of our wedding?"

Nervous sweat had popped out on my brow and I wiped it away absent-mindedly. She had a good point. Having worried about the loss of romanticism in the performance following Sir Norman's death, this was a chance to get it back on track. "Of course I'll do it!"

Marie cheered and chuckled on hearing my acceptance and confirmed that Sir Charles would be talking to me in due course. 'In due course' was some twenty minutes later and I wondered momentarily whether Sir Charles was at our house and if he had judiciously chosen the timing of the visit. However, there was frenetic activity in the background, which proved that he was elsewhere. Another thought struck me that it was odd that, even in apparent desperation, he was using Marie as a kind of mediator. As he came on the line, his discomfort with being at my mercy for a second time was almost palpable with its hidden resentment that he had been forced into this position.

"My boy," he started, the words sticking in his craw and he cleared his throat. "Have you spoken with Marie recently?"

He was playing a game but I was not going to be a willing participant in it. "I have, as well you know, and I have agreed to sing the part, not because you asked me but because Marie did." I was surprised at the level of hostility in my voice but also felt somewhat undermined because he had not asked me directly, getting Marie to do his dirty work because of his stupid pride.

There was a pause and he cleared his throat. "And I thank you very much for stepping into the breech at such short notice."

"Believe me, it's a pleasure, but only for the reasons cited before."

"Yes, well, we don't have to like each other to get the job done. My voice coach will be in contact tomorrow to organize some rehearsals. How well do you know the part?"

"Word perfect!" It was true – since meeting Marie, *Tosca* had become my passion and I had troubled myself to learn the tenor rôle off pat.

"Good," he agreed reluctantly. "Until next week at the dress rehearsals then."

His end went dead, while I gradually held the receiver away from my ear, squeezing it in my fist. "Yes!" I shouted, looking heavenwards, and punched the air. The telephone crashed to the floor, since I was still holding it in my manic celebration. I laughed happily to myself.

* * *

The lead up to my first public performance was interesting and a few unsettling and odd things happened. While there was a lot of press surrounding my sudden elevation into the spotlight, there were many kind words about the new leading man affianced to the beautiful leading lady, positively blooming in the late stages of pregnancy. Even *The Investigator* was evidently surprised into publishing something positive about our relationship (though, of course, nothing of the more cerebral exploits of our performance together). This provided further publicity for the record label, of course, as *The Creation* and the *War Requiem* were the single points of reference for the journalists as to my musical abilities.

While I was enjoying the pressure of being a lead performer (without the ability to retake and re-record if there was a faulty performance), there was an extraordinary paranoid feeling that I was being watched. It was difficult to adequately explain it but, whenever I travelled into London, walking the streets towards Covent Garden to rehearsals, I had the unnerving feeling that a hidden person or people were observing me. It was not a paranoia built from casual people-watching in a busy city because there was menace underneath it. Several times I shuddered as I felt the icy presence but tried to shake it off. It was forgotten by the time I entered the rehearsal hall, only to be picked up on my return to the hotel where Marie and I were staying – its plushness redolent of the first hotel I had stayed in with Marie but without the modern expansiveness.

It was on my way to the final individual rehearsal that it dawned on me why I was experiencing these creepy feelings. Using the back streets from the hotel to the rehearsal hall for speed and expediency, my route took me past a darkened alley. At the brisk pace I was walking, it felt like something had wrapped itself around my ankles and I went down heavily on one knee, grazing the side of my left hand. Looking back to see what I had tripped on, I was flabbergasted to see Adrian Hilton standing over me with a length of four-by-two wood in his hand, slapping it in an intimidating way into his other hand.

"Adrian!" I exclaimed, suddenly worried about where that wood was going next. "How are you?" It was all I could think of to try and disarm him.

He gave a hollow laugh and looked up towards the sky. "How am I? 'How am I?' he asks. How do you think I am?" He looked back down at me and the wood-slapping intensified.

"I don't know. You look well," I tried, watching the slapping wood warily and wondering how I could get up to obtain a more commanding position than being straddled on my back on the pavement. The problem with the back streets was just the reason why I had chosen the route – it was clear of people.

"Ha!" he scoffed. "You've never liked me, have you, Loughton?" Slap! Slap! Slap!

"Adrian, what do you want?" My normal candour was returning and I was determined to take control of this potentially disastrous situation.

"You've ruined me." Slap! Slap!

I was sitting up now, dusting my hands off. "You ruined yourself, Adrian."

SLAP! He stopped. "What?" he asked. There was a dangerous edge to his voice.

"You can't blame me for your misdemeanours."

"What?" The same malevolence was in his voice.

"You committed a crime, Adrian. How can I possibly have been responsible for that?"

The slapping of the wood started up again, although more slowly than previously. "It was Gary who made me do it. But it was your threats to sack me that started it."

I had managed to position myself so that I stood up quickly, causing him to take a step backwards. The slapping stopped and he brandished it threateningly like a knight in a sword-fight. I made no further move other than to brush down my jacket. "Adrian, I have never tried or threatened to sack you. It was Gary's insecurity – and now I can see why – that was foisting the blame on me."

"Well, you would say that, wouldn't you?" The wood was waggling uncertainly above his head.

"No. But it seems to me that you have a good defence. Or at least a mitigating excuse for your actions."

"Gary may have been lying or setting me up but it was you who reported me to the police. Why did you do that?"

I looked at him and said bluntly: "Why did you commit the crime?"

That floored him momentarily. "But you didn't have to report it," he countered, a whine coming into his voice. "I had already been sacked by you." He stopped and reflected for a minute. "I might go to jail for this."

"If you can't take the punishment, don't do the crime, Adrian," I said.

"You bastard!" he said and swung the wooden baton towards me, but I was ready, deflecting his arm with mine and grabbing the wood and twisting it out of his hand.

I mimicked his stance of slapping the wood against his hand. "The boot is firmly on the other foot now," I said, eyes sparkling with victory. "I could report you for attempted assault, you know."

Something akin to fear crossed his eyes but was gone. He pointed a shaky finger at me. "This is not over, Loughton. I'm going to make your life hell. I'm going to kill you. You ruined my life." Petulance had made his eyes shiny and I raised the baton threateningly, upon which he turned on his heels and ran down the road.

I watched until he was gone and threw the wood to the side of the street, brushing my hands again and examining the graze on my hand and noticed with annoyance that the knee of my trousers now had a hole in it, while the sting directly underneath indicated that my leg had been grazed too. Another death threat, I mused resuming my journey to the rehearsal hall. Another couple and I will have the complete set.

* * *

Over the course of the next week leading up to the performance, Marie supported me in every way as my nerves took over, giving me the courage to confront them. This was all the more miraculous because she had begun to feel ill and tired with the pregnancy again and, despite my protestations that she should take it easier, she was resolutely determined to see this performance through. The joy of performing together and the romanticism of doing it on the eve of our wedding made it imperative for her.

A few minutes before the curtain was due to go up, I went to see her in her dressing-room. She was wearing a tent-bottomed ball-gown, loose at the midriff to disguise the pregnancy. I planted a kiss on her head and looked at her reflection in the mirror – she looked drawn and exhausted, dark outlines appearing around her eyes, which she was covering with make-up.

"You do look pale, sweetheart," I observed. "What did the doctor say?"

"I'm all right, sweetheart," she replied, turning to me stiffly as far as the burgeoning twins would allow and took hold of my hands. "Really I am. Just tired from these two." She patted her stomach. "And it's all down to an iron deficiency." She rattled a small pill bottle on her dressing table.

I crouched down, kissing her hands. "Please promise me that you won't overdo it. You'll shout if it all becomes too much. The understudy is on call."

She smiled wearily and stroked my cheek. "I know, sweetheart. Thanks for your concern but I'll see it through. The show must go on."

"Okay. I won't nag you any more."

"Nag all you want. It's nice to have someone caring for me so deeply." I smiled and kissed her hands again. "I love you."

"I love you too," she responded, her eyes glinting impishly. "Madly, deeply, stupidly, head-over-heelsingly." She pressed a hand lightly to my chest.

I laughed and kissed her again. "I'll see you on stage."

"Good luck!" she called as I opened the door. I turned to give a 'thumbs up' and smiled.

* * *

The performance was excellent. I cannot describe the freedom I felt on the stage, staring out into the blackness of the auditorium, knowing that there were several hundred unseen people watching me. What made it even more special was that my darling Marie was with me every step of the way. Everything went perfectly and better than I had expected. Pete reprised his silent role as one of Scarpia's henchmen and took great pleasure in dragging me off to be tortured. He and Beth had constructed a branding iron in the shape of a horseshoe with red foil attached to a rod. This he waggled at me menacingly once we were in the wings and it was all I could do not to laugh and to remember that I was supposed to be groaning because of the torture. Marie's understudy was employed only once – but it was planned – to take the dive off the battlements at the back of the stage.

As we stood stage forward taking the curtain calls, I looked at Marie and the professional glint in her eyes belied the level of exhaustion I knew she felt. She took my hand and squeezed it to indicate that she was fine and not to worry and that I should revel in the adulatory clapping and catcalls for encores. Dragging my hand forward, forcing me to take a step in front, she graciously moved back to allow me to take my own applause. Bowing self-consciously, I stood up and put out an outstretched arm to assembled cast and applauded them. Then I turned to Marie, wanting her to take my hand, which she did and I kissed her lips, which increased the level of applause. One of the stage managers ran on with a huge bouquet of flowers and I received a spontaneous laugh and more applause, when I pretended to be so surprised at receiving this gift. The stage manager faltered and went by me and I shrugged to the audience.

On the final curtain call, we exited stage right and Marie immediately sat on a chair that had been organized for her, holding my hand for support. I crouched beside her, concern rippling my forehead. Eventually, she raised her head and said: "I'll be okay in a minute. Just a rush of blood away from my head. These little darlings have taken to playing a football match." She smiled wearily.

I placed a gentle hand on her stomach and felt small knees, elbows, feet, hands all pushing at her. "I think they are dancing. Maybe they are happy that Mummy and Daddy have performed so well this evening. You were brilliant." I kissed her engagement ring.

"No, David, it is your night. You worked hard to get it perfect and it was. You are a natural performer."

"Thank you," I replied, modesty forcing me to blush crimson. "Do you want to go to the after-show party?"

"Yes, David. To support you but I'll have to see how I go." She stood up a little unsteadily. "I've got second wind."

We made our way back to the dressing-rooms and changed for the party. In her room, Marie relented. "Do you mind if I stay for the one drink and then return to the hotel. It's stupid me overdoing it and being unable to enjoy our wedding tomorrow. That's far more important."

"Of course I don't, sweetheart. You're absolutely right. Look, let's go for one and I'll walk you back."

"You don't have to."

"I do. You and the twins are far more important."

"Well, okay, but only if you promise that you'll return to the party."

"No, I –."

"That's final," she said and smiled sweetly. "Now you do as I say."

At the party, after the initial round of congratulations and a glass of champagne, I turned to talk to Marie and saw her sitting in a corner, a tear in one eye. Now was the time to get her back to the hotel. I excused myself, promising to be back and Marie and I made our way to the stage door. A few paparazzi were there, taking photographs, asking the usual standard of ignorant and impudent questions about what I had done to upset Marie (they had observed her unhappiness and the tears and had leapt to the completely wrong conclusion). Encircling us, their questions became even more urgent and I could see Marie becoming even more distressed. With no further ado, I pushed my way brusquely through the crowd, taking Marie's hand and guiding her quickly through the throng, demanding they got out of my way.

Back at the hotel, I poured Marie a glass of water and placed it on the bedside table. Marie was undressed, sitting up in bed, propped against several pillows. Moving to find comfort, she looked down and stroked her stomach. "They're still very active," she said and smiled.

I sat on the edge of the bed and linked fingers with her, gently stroking her belly, feeling the movement within. "The natives are getting restless," I said and she laughed. "Do you want me to stay with you?"

She took my hand and squeezed it. "No, we agreed. Or, rather, I agreed. Now get back to the party. You deserve the honours being foisted on you."

I was reluctant to go but she was insistent. "I'll see you in a while. Now, you two, look after Mummy while I'm gone."

Marie held her belly in both hands and looked down. "Mugwort? Nipplewort? Did you hear what Daddy says? You've got to look after me."

I laughed out loud and joyously. Marie's sense of humour was returning and that gave me comfort that I could leave her for an hour or so without having to worry. With a guard up, it is always difficult to let your sense of humour through.

I returned to the opera house and was accosted by the same paparazzi, who had upset Marie when we had left for the hotel. They grouped around me, asking more deeply personal questions, including why Marie had been upset, why I had been gruff with *her*, why I had not returned with her and whether the marriage was on the rocks before it had started.

"Piss off!" I observed, after attempts to counter some of the stupid accusations being levelled at me had crashed on take-off and brushed past them, deliberately banging shoulders as I went by, listening to the tuts of being put out as I did so. Rejoining the party, I enjoyed another couple of glasses of free champagne and modestly accepted the plaudits being heaped and pressed on me but my mind was back at the hotel, worrying about Marie. It was soon crystal clear that I was not enjoying revelling in the corpulence of such a superficial affair and eventually decided to leave after forty or so minutes.

Slipping out of a side door to avoid the press again, I set off for the hotel. As I turned the corner, a hand pushed hard at my shoulder and the surprise, shock and force threw me to the ground, sprawling ungainly.

"I knew you would come out at some point," said a voice I recognized.

"Gary?" I guessed, squinting at the silhouetted figure against the streetlights.

"You are a complete bastard. You have fucked up my life."

Scrabbling with my heels slipping on the pavement to get away from him to get a better look, I shielded my eyes to see if he had any weaponry on him. After Adrian's attack, I was very wary. However, he appeared to have nothing and I relaxed a little, aware that this was almost déjà vu lying on a London pavement being threatened. "No, Gary, you did that all on your own."

A strong hand reached down, grabbed my lapels and hoisted me to my feet. His drink-scarred features, bloodshot eyes and whisky-sodden breath were inches from my face as he contorted into rage. "It's my fault, is it?" he spat and I flinched as the spittle landed on my lips and chin. "It's my fault that you put me in an untenable position, where I had to sack Adrian bloody Hilton. It's my fault you then engineered it to sack me? It's my fault that you are so up yourself that you wanted to take the glory?" His voice was strident and his eyes bulging with apoplexy. "How dare you?"

I brought my arms up swiftly and out to the sides, forcing him to release my lapels. "Yes, Gary, it was your fault. Not mine. I gave you so many chances. But it's your fault that you are in the mess you are in now."

"You didn't have to grass on me."

"I did, Gary. It was too obvious what was going on."

"Call yourself a friend? Now look at you. We have gone up in the world, haven't we?"

"I was in the right place at the right time."

"Who did you have to bribe? How many people did you sleep with?"

"Gary! That's not fair. Tonight was on my own merit with a little luck."

He stiffened and swayed slightly as he did so. "Nice little lady, you have there."

I was nonplussed by the comment and tried to ignore it.

"Shame I didn't have her when I had the chance, before you got her up the duff. Shotgun wedding is it?"

"No!" All the old hatred and impotent rage was returning and I was reminded of the *contretemps* we had under the Paris stage when I was trying to see Marie on the second night.

He grabbed my lapels again and pulled me towards him so that our noses were touching. "Shame if she met with an accident. Shame if she lost those bastards she's carrying."

Red mist descended and when it cleared, Gary was lying on the pavement himself, a trickle of blood oozing from a nostril. I pointed at him. "Don't you dare to ever threaten my wife and children again!"

Gary made a good deal of standing up and dabbed at his nose, looking at the red droplets on the end of his fingers. "I could have you for that," he warned, malevolence on the edge of his voice.

"Do you think it will do you any good?"

"You are a smug git, aren't you? You think you have it all. You think you know it all. Well, you know nothing. You have fucked up my life and I'll have you over for that. Mark my words. You think you're protected? Well, look over your shoulder and I might be there. I'll run you down. I'll fucking kill you and that tart you've been paying to sleep with you!" He had backed off, shakily pointing at me, his voice shaking and breaking with the effort and then he fled from the scene.

Hmm, I mused again, full house. I have the complete set now. First Amanda, then Adrian and now Gary. I figured that there was a lot of substance behind what appeared to be an idle threat and decided that the embezzlement case needed to be followed closely. For now, getting back to Marie was my priority and I began running back to the hotel. Out of breath by the time I got back to the room, I awoke Marie from her doze by banging the door open against the wall, as the door-handle slipped in my sweaty fingers.

"Sorry," I said hoarsely, "I didn't mean to startle you."

"That's okay," she said, yawning and stretching and then looked at me properly and frowned. "David, what happened to you?"

"I was mugged and threatened."

Marie sucked in breath and her eyes widened in alarm. "Who was it?"

"Remember Gary?" I asked, pacing up and down on the carpet, trying to get the frustration out of my mind and the abject hatred he had conjured up in me again after all this time. Marie nodded. "Well…" I spent the next fifteen minutes giving her chapter and verse of what I had to put up with, including his unkind power exertion under the Paris stage, his cheap and underhand methods of working, his sulking at the prospect of my being Chairman, the lead up to the fight in America, the discovery of embezzlement and finishing with his most recent attack, blaming me for his ill-fortune, and the unkind words about our relationship, Marie specifically and our unborn children. During this tirade, I had called him all names under the sun and more, frustration raising my voice to the point that our immediate neighbours felt obliged to bang on the wall to protest at the volume. I had subsequently reduced my voice to a whisper but, before long, the volume had increased again, leading to a more pissed off banging from next door. Marie had made soothing noises and occasionally gasping and exclaiming at Gary's audacity and then I started on Adrian, revealing that I had been similarly attacked the previous week. Another five minutes of venting my spleen brought a third volley of hammering on the wall. Pacing up and down, waving my hands to express my anger and frustration, I now took that opportunity to calm down and came to the bedside.

"I'm sorry, Marie, I didn't mean to lay all that at your door. It was just seeing him again that set me off."

Marie pulled me towards her, put her arms around my shoulders and kissed my head. "That's okay, sweetheart. You need to let it out or it'll eat away at you."

"I'm so tired now. Especially after all that pacing," I grinned and kissed her lips. "We have a big day tomorrow so let's get some sleep." I stood up and shed my clothes, climbing in beside my beautiful fiancée, still reclined upright as this was the only comfortable sleeping position. Snuggling up to her, an arm across her and stroking her arm and belly. "How have Bramble and Leaf-Mulch behaved themselves?" I asked and Marie laughed.

"They're fine. I think all the excitement of being on stage got to them and they're now sleeping," she giggled and added: "Like babies."

After the pressure of the evening and the fracas with Gary, I was looking subconsciously for anything that required a release. Since making love was out of the question (however aroused I was by Marie's beauty in the later stages of being with children), humour was a good substitute and I was yelping with laughter at her comment. Another battery on the wall from next door sobered me.

"Thank you," I said, circling my hand over her protruding belly. "I am so glad that tomorrow we are getting married. I can't understand how empty my life was before you entered it."

She blushed prettily and smiled. "Your life will be pretty full soon," she said, patting my hand as it circled.

I bent and kissed her belly twice. "Goodnight, Cowslip. Goodnight, Toadstool. See you soon." Marie laughed and I kissed her lips. "Goodnight, sweetheart. I love you."

*   *   *

We were in a park. Marie was on a boat in the middle of a lake and I was at the water's edge, trying to reach out to her unsuccessfully. I could see that the boat was filling rapidly with water; Marie had her arms outstretched in supplication for me to reach her, shouting my name and for help. I was trying to find a suitable purchase point on the edge of the lake and was about to dive in when, suddenly, an iron railing fence shot up before my face, missing it by inches, apparently rising to infinity and stretching out on either side to the horizon.

The skies were darkening as I ran along the perimeter of the fence looking for a way in, around, over or under it. In the background, I could hear an old crone cackling and she appeared from nowhere, standing at the water's edge on the other side of the fence, pointing a gnarled finger at Marie and cackling mirthlessly. Then she stooped and picked up a couple of pebbles, throwing them at the boat. A few of them hit, leaving sizeable holes in the bulwark.

The ground began to rock and I struggled to keep my balance. The boat was listing dangerously and Marie was crouched trying to avoid being dumped in the water. Mist rolled in from nowhere, threatening to envelop the boat and her screams had risen to fever pitch. "David, she's going to kill me. I'm going to –." The remainder of her plea was lost in the rising howl and pitch of the wind. It was now almost too dark to see, as I banged helplessly on the wrought iron uprights of the fence, shouting: "Marie! I'm sorry!"

Suddenly, a gate appeared in the fence. I looked up and noticed that the top of the boat was on the verge of being submerged. As I fumbled with the catch, Marie's screams seemed to be getting nearer and nearer.

The ground rocked me violently and the old woman still cackled fit to burst. Then the gate opened, there was a bright flash accompanied by a clap of thunder and the rain started coming down, splashing on my suddenly naked flesh, the boat disappeared and Marie was swallowed up. I shouted something incomprehensible and –

- and I sat bolt upright in bed, the vestiges of the nightmare still present around me, dissipating slowly into the shadows of the room. I saw a chink of light, which meant that the door was open, and a figure at the end of the bed. At first, I thought that it was still part of the dream and I squeezed my eyes shut, shaking my head to clear the image. Opening them again, the figure remained in front of me, dressed head to toe in black, cursing under its breath, clinking with something in its hands. I felt a strong sense of danger and bounced out of bed in one swift movement, grabbing the person's shoulder. It wheeled around and I felt a stinging blow across my chin, which left a burst of stars flowing around my head. Looking back at the figure, now silhouetted against the chink of light in the door, I saw that the implement was a handgun, which it was having difficulty with. Wanting to protect Marie, I lunged forward again. It gave up with a frustrated sigh, throwing the gun at me, which I caught to prevent it from connecting with my head again and the figure ran from the room. Following it, I saw the emergency exit door flapping. Because I was naked and as the hallway was filling with shocked people, I decided not to pursue whoever the mysterious figure was. I realized that the physical exertion had made me break out in a sweat because trickles of liquid were running down my left side. Scratching myself, I looked absent-mindedly at my fingers and was shocked into reality by dark red blood on the tips. Frantically, I searched myself for a wound and then the enormity hit. "No!" I screamed and ran back into the room, throwing the light switch as I did so, the door banging shut loudly with the force of my re-entry.

I was frozen to the spot, paralyzed momentarily by the scene. Marie was lying slightly to one side, towards where I would have been if I had been in bed. Her eyes were closed and blood was flowing steadily from a large wound just below her right breast. Her right arm and the bed on that side was completely covered with sticky blood. I was still holding the gun and, with a shudder, threw it into the corner not caring where it ended up and dashed over to Marie, shaking violently. "Marie?" I croaked, thinking that she was dead.

She stirred slightly and moaned softly. "David?" she asked weakly. Her eyes stared into nothingness before coming to focus on mine.

"Marie, I'm sorry."

"Why would this be your fault?" she asked and attempted to smile.

I reached for the 'phone but she stopped me. "But I should call an ambulance."

A weak but protesting hand pressed on mine. "David, it's too late. Please hold me."

I sat on the bed, taking her in my arms, rocking her slightly. Tears were flowing freely now. "I love you," I whimpered. "Please don't leave me."

"It'll be all right, David. Kiss me."

I bent to kiss her lips of ice, brushing her hair away from her face. "No, no, no," I implored.

"I'm cold. Please hold me tighter," she said, her voice now very quiet. I did as she asked, rocking her still.

I felt her go limp and I stopped. "Marie?" I was shaking uncontrollably now.

She came to slightly and looked up at me, raising a finger to my lips. "David, I love you. I'll always be here for you." I bent to kiss her lips and her hand dropped to my chest and she smiled, nodding a little – the small gesture that I had loved so much – then the smile faded and she went limp again.

This time she had gone.

PUPPET ON A STRING

CHAPTER 35

It was ten minutes later when all hell broke loose around me. I had been cuddling Marie's lifeless body to me, tears of grief and despair dropping from my eyes on to her naked shoulder. Moaning softly, I had kissed her head and apologized frequently, because I had not been able to stop this violence against the woman I would never talk to again, except through her inert body here and now and, in the future, in my dreams. I was still kissing her and apologizing when the door was viciously kicked in by a policeman, wielding a truncheon, a whistle in his mouth, which he blew three short, sharp times. He let it drop, dangling at his thighs and he crouched, inching towards me.

"Now, don't do anything silly," he warned. Given that I was utterly oblivious to him, it was extremely unlikely. I just wanted to hold my Marie and make all the nastiness go away; to return to just twenty minutes ago; or to the poolside at our Italian villa; or to our beautiful little house in the Dorset coast; anywhere but here with Marie dead in my arms. Tears were flowing still and I had begun rocking her lifeless form, apologizing and stroking her hair away from her face. I bent and kissed her nose when the constable grabbed me violently by the arm and yanked me on to the floor. Landing face down, I was suddenly winded but, with the pain of breathing already, scarcely noticed. Marie's body slipped down with the force of me being dragged from her and her head hit the bedside table. I screamed to stop them hurting her.

"Stop!" I yelled as my wrists were pulled together behind my back, pushing the air further from my lungs. Others joined the policeman, shouting at me to keep still and not make any sudden movements. It was only later that it was revealed that they had guns. The first policeman was now kneeling in the small of my back and sharp lights of pain burst in my head.

One of the other policemen was yelling at me to get up and not to make any sudden moves. A third policeman commented under his breath: "Well, 'e certainly done a bloody good job 'ere. Where's the gun?" A brief search revealed it to be in the corner, where I had flung it earlier.

"Crime of passion, do you think?" asked the first policeman, as he stood up.

"Most likely," agreed another, who pulled me painfully to my feet by my handcuffed wrists. "'Ere," he said, getting a good look at my face for the first time. "It's that bloke in the papers. Marrying that operatic tart."

"Yeah," concluded the first, "that's 'er there in the bed." He looked over at Marie's lissom, pale and dead body. "Why the 'ell would anyone want to play away when you 'ave something like that to come home to?" He shook his head at the ignominy of it all.

"I didn't kill her," I whimpered, when I realized where this conversation was leading. "It wasn't me. I love her. Never harm her."

"That's what they all say, sir."

Anger rose in me as I saw one of them manhandle Marie's naked body from the bedside table back on to the bed. Generating a low growl, reaching a scream, I ran at him, head down and knocked him into the wall headfirst, causing him to sink to his knees. "How dare you?" I yelled and drew back a foot to kick the fallen comrade but the darkness descended as two truncheons connected with the back of my skull simultaneously.

As I came around, head thumping, face raw from carpet burns as I went down, I heard one of the policemen say, with underlined relief: "Thank Gawd! I thought we'd killed him! Look, it was resisting arrest and assaulting a police officer. Understood!"

"Oh, yes!" agreed the other two, and they turned as the door opened to let the forensic officers and ambulance people into take Marie's body away.

Again, they pulled me up by my chained wrists and I heard my shoulders protesting with the abuse they were getting. But the sharp pain was nothing to the dull thudding in my head. What I wanted more than anything was just to go to sleep, never wake up and let this nightmare play itself out. Two of the policemen, the ones with the now-holstered guns put a bath robe around my shoulders and tied the belt in front, the arms of the garment flopping loosely by my sides, while the first policeman stood menacingly behind me, warning that they did not want any trouble. All the time that they were playing at stereotypical cops, their words reached me as if through a thick gauze. I could only gaze forlornly at my lost love for the last time. As I was pushed and shoved out into the hallway, with roped-off onlookers rubber-necking to see what was going on and gasping as I appeared, something wrenched from my heart as I realized I would never see Marie's earthly form again and I struggled to get back into the room. The policemen jostled with me, threatened me some more and that was it – it was indeed the last time I saw my beautiful Marie.

In the foyer, a barrage of television lights and camera flashes met me. Held back but lined up, I saw Pete's and Beth's ashen faces. When they saw me, they tried to reach me but were held back by a burly policeman.

"It'll be all right," called Pete over a policeman's shoulder. "We'll get you out of this, Dave."

Towards the front door of the hotel, I saw Sir Charles Minton, tired and shaken in a maroon silk dressing gown, leaning on his ever-present cane. I looked imploringly at him as he raised his head, his mouth turned sharply down.

"Oh, you stupid bastard!" he said, shaking his head. "What have you done? She was my little girl!" A tear brimmed and fell down his orange-peel cheeks.

I was not allowed to respond as the policemen bustled me out into a waiting van.

* * *

The full enormity of what had happened hit me hard, when we reached Charing Cross police station, where another bevy of press was awaiting my arrival. The shock, the grief, the unbearable loss of such a big and important part of my life, the knowledge that I would never kiss her freckled nose again, never feel the cute way she used to put a hand on my chest to feel my heart beating, all struck me completely dumb and immobile.

Having been processed in the system, with fingerprints taken, they finally removed the handcuffs completely. Two red wheals of painful flesh appeared around my wrists, but I was ignorant to the pain and sat motionless in my cell, still in the hotel bathrobe, and still splattered by Marie's blood. Meals and cups of sugary tea came, turned cold and grey and disappeared again. Still motionless at night, sitting up but resting uncomfortably back on elbows, all bodily functions apparently suspended for the duration, I stared into space, remembering the twelve short months Marie had had with me and the depth of passion we felt for each other. A tear would occasionally slip from one eye or the other but I left it to dry, not even being aware of the tickling sensation as they ran down my cheeks:

The autograph – how I had been taken by how down-to-earth she was and completely unstarry as we conversed in her dressing-room;

The dinner – how over-awed I had become by events and Marie's beauty and that first touch of her silky skin;

The aberration – how Gary had used my mistake on the second night to stop me from seeing her again and the point that I realized he was just manipulating me as a puppeteer does his charges;

The 'affair' – how I had gone with Amanda Begley in a twisted attempt to shun Marie completely from my mind and daily thoughts;

The election – how I had started the chairmanship campaign to stop Gary in his tracks, before conceiving that I could become my own puppeteer and wondering secretly what Marie would think of my ambitions;

The re-meeting – how I had felt when I heard that I was going to meet her again so shortly after I had given the quest up for lost in Paris;

The tea-room – how I had enjoyed the frisson of attraction that still appeared to be present when I took the soloists and Christoph Schmidt to tea across the road;

The faltering dinner – how Marie and I had received mixed messages from each other and had made a hash of our initial attempts at a relationship;

The agitation – how Marie had tried to convince me that we should get together and how it had all gone spectacularly wrong, followed by a sleepless night;

The apology – how Marie had made the first move to try again with the relationship and succeeding in identifying how crassly stupid we had been;

The play – how Marie had cuddled into me during the thriller play we had seen;

The first kiss – and the electrification of the first kiss walking her home from it (even now I can feel the warmth and smoothness of her lips on mine and my mouth waters to this day);

The ebullient dinner – how Marie had taken me back to her hotel to treat me to a meal there;

The stealth – how we had engineered a plan to get me up to her hotel bedroom and the achingly funny giggling bouts subsequently endured;

The champagne – how the bottle had exploded open and how we had left it after the one sip;

The first time – the exquisite, painful ecstasy of our first union;

The bath – how we broke down any further physical barriers by bathing each other;

The death – how supportive Marie had been during the terrible death of my friend, Bob;

The press – how they had interpolated their way into our lives by printing scurrilous and wholly untrue rumours regarding our relationship and the kind words of strength she had given me whilst dealing with it;

The American surprise – how she had surprised me as she became wont to do while dining out with the Sirs Charles and Norman;

The holiday – how energized we became just by relaxing with Pete and Beth in the sunny villa in Italy;

The house – how we found the ideal house and location for us;

The decorating – how we had found fun while executing a potentially boring and laborious set of tasks around the house in preparation for moving in;

The garden – how we loved the garden and the specific memory of our water-fight and its interruption by Sir Charles;

The record-label – how excited and full of awe Marie had been for my achievements and triumphs in this area and how we had played surreptitiously with each other during the recording;

The pregnancy – how dumbstruck I had been by Marie's news that she was carrying our babies – not just one but two of them – and the fun we had had with suggesting names;

The final performance – the romanticism of performing together on the eve of our wedding and the joint adulation we had received;

The gesture – all of this was painful and joyful to remember in equal measures, but it was the simple gesture of Marie placing her hand over my heart to check the pulse-rate that ripped at my innards and made me feel like I was turning myself inside out with the grief.

* * *

On the second day, I was found different clothes and forced into the shower, being hosed and washed down by policemen wearing rubber gloves on their hands and a permanent look of distaste on their faces. Several times I was asked if I wanted to call a solicitor but still being too dumbstruck to react to the question let alone think of my rights, it went unanswered. Eventually, Pete organized *[the lawyer M.S. – name removed for personal reasons]* to stand for me, the brilliant young lawyer, who had acted for us when we were setting up the terms and conditions of the record label. He came to visit me several times and, as if to prove that I was not meting out my silent and motionless reaction to selected people only, I was helpless but to ignore him too, since my thoughts were very firmly with Marie, remembering the freckles across the tops of her shoulders, the deep all-over tan from the summer, her sense of humour with calling our children Dogwort and Nipplewort – the memories flooded back and circled and they were embraced rapturously.

As a result of my inability to raise communication above the occasional monosyllabic and Neanderthal grunts, I was charged with murder and it was agreed and scheduled for me to stand trial at the Old Bailey. And it was the news of the arraignment, which allowed the shit-rag of a newspaper, *The Investigator*, to revel in its delight that they had apparently been right all along about my alleged nasty and vicious streak and that I cared little for Marie's feelings. It was the first policeman from the night of Marie's death, who came into my cell and threw the paper on the floor in front of me, muttering that everyone had me banged to rights.

*   *   *

Still unable to speak or react and, with little or no sleep leading up to the trial, I sat in the dock with head bowed, not giving any affirmative or negative answers to the court questions, which my solicitor had to answer on my behalf, entering a plea of 'Not Guilty'.

What followed, looking back on it, was a travesty of justice and an insult for our mutual deep love. There was a lot of circumstantial, although very compelling, evidence brought before the court by a very astute prosecution lawyer. *[M.S. the barrister]* struggled dutifully, given that I had not provided any counter-evidence nor explained my position entirely to either the police or him. Still in a semi-catatonic state, at that point, I cared not what happened to me. As far as I was concerned, my life was over at the point when I lost Marie and our unborn children.

*   *   *

[What follows is an edited transcript of the evidence provided over the course of the trial. It is the circumstantial evidence to which David Loughton refers in the preceding paragraph. It is presented here to help the reader understand

*the enormity of the miscarriage of justice against him and to provide the
suitable narrative to complete the story. M.S.]*

*The following is a list of formal admissions agreed by both the Prosecution
and Defence Counsels:*

The gun found at the scene of the crime was the gun used to shoot
Marie Duvois

The single bullet fired caused Marie Duvois's death

David Loughton's prints of his right hand were found on the gun

David Loughton had had a sexual relationship with Amanda Watson
(née Begley)

David Loughton had been involved in physical and verbal fights with
Gary Adner, Adrian Hilton and Amanda Watson

David Loughton had been involved in an altercation with the
arresting Police Constables on the night of the crime resulting in the
charge of resisting arrest

The photographic evidence was a true and accurate reflection of
what was found at the murder scene

All evidence had been presented properly and in accordance with the
regulations

* * *

On the subject of David Loughton's alleged propensity for violence:

The Prosecution's case was built upon the precept that, not only was
David capable of violence, but that he had exhibited it several times. The
next logical step was then to place the gun in his hand and imagine him
firing it at a woman. In particular, at a woman, whom he bragged about
loving although it could be proven that he had had a few dalliances with
other women during the period of their relationship. But the driving
purpose was to convince the jury that, at heart, David was a highly
volatile and violent man, especially towards women.

Amanda Watson took to the stand to confirm four pieces of critical
evidence. All the time she was giving her evidence, she had torn
nervously at a paper handkerchief, occasionally bowing her head, always
in tears. She confirmed under oath, following reminders of the penalties
of perjuring herself, that she and David had had a relationship after he
had met Marie Duvois, in the knowledge that he was being unfaithful
to her. She further attested that he was rough with her sexually (just
drawing short of accusing him of rape) and that he would not accept

that their relationship was over, despite her protestations that it must be ended. More importantly, she provided the detail of two attacks in the offices of the *Coro di Londinium*, including the descriptions of the injuries to her head and face sustained at the time, which had since cleared up. It was her assertion that she only just managed to get away with her life. Finally, she confirmed that David Loughton had sacked her from the Chorus. When pressed as to why this was, she made testimony that, at the time, she had threatened to go to the police and that he had sacked her to prove his power over her. She had then become depressed and decided not to do anything about it as a result. It was only during the past few months that she had pulled her life together again. Now, seeing 'that monster' in the dock, she hoped that he would rot in prison for what he had done to her, to Marie and to women everywhere, although the last remark was requested and agreed to be stricken from the record.

Sir Charles Minton, looking very aged and saggy-faced as if he had had a minor stroke, took to the witness stand and sat on a chair to compose himself for a moment, before taking the bible and swearing the oath. What he had to say compounded the evidence provided by Amanda Watson. He confirmed that he had witnessed David Loughton chasing the deceased around the garden at their home in Dorset, threatening to 'get her', before throwing her to the ground roughly and forcing himself on her, despite Marie Duvois's protestations to stop. It was only fortuitous that Sir Charles (in his version) had been there to stop the abuse going further. He went on to describe how he had witnessed David pinning Marie's wrists above her head as he tried to force her to kiss him. Later, when Marie had gone in to the house, he testified that David Loughton had made threats to stop Sir Charles from reporting him to the police. He also noted, with some candour and undisguised glee, that the pictures in the papers of late had either shown Marie pale and drawn or in tears in great contrast to the effervescent personality she had had prior to meeting 'that damned Loughton'. When pressed to give his opinion on the relationship between David and Marie, he confirmed that he considered it to be one-sided and that some threat or other always thwarted his attempts at intervention. It was one such threat of blackmail, he further attested, which forced him to give a starring role to David Loughton the night before Marie Duvois's death. When asked what the blackmail was, Sir Charles faltered momentarily but confirmed that it was to do with allegations of his (Sir Charles') relationship with Marie, suggesting that it was sexual and that the papers would hear about it. When questioned why it had not been reported to the police, Sir Charles simply answered that he was an old man and did not possess the energy to combat the claims. Any such publication of 'Loughton's lies' could ruin him regardless of their veracity. Sir Charles also gave detail of the discussion he, Sir Norman Pettinger and David Loughton had had in a restaurant in New York earlier the previous year, when he had glamorized a story of a fist-fight with Gary Adner and had subsequently sacked him – 'he seemed to relish telling the story,' he had added.

The prosecution served up pictures and reports from various newspapers showing David grim-faced and Marie upset, with a narrative expounding on his rude treatment of the press and that, on the night in question, he had physically pushed a photographer to the ground.

Gary Adner and Adrian Hilton were asked to provide evidence based on the allegations provided by Sir Charles with respect to the fight in the New York Metropolitan Opera House. Gary Adner confirmed the detail and alluded to the reason for his dismissal was to cover up David Loughton's own involvement in the embezzlement, the trial for which was still ongoing. Further, he provided information that David Loughton had sought him out the night before Marie Duvois's death and picked a fight with him because no-one else was around, leaving him scared for his life, when all he (Gary) had wanted to do was to appeal to his (David's) better nature and get him to confess to his involvement, so that Gary would receive a lesser charge. Once again, this comment was stricken from the record, although further information was sought and noted on the attack. Adrian Hilton provided testimony by proxy, since he was in hospital, to confirm that David Loughton had attacked him too outside the Royal Opera House in a similar manner to the attack on Gary Adner.

The final piece of evidence to verify David Loughton's propensity for violence came from one of the arresting police officers on the night of the murder, who had confirmed that David Loughton had turned very violent, resisting arrest and causing injury to himself and another police officer, who was now on sick leave because of the stress. The witness rejected the Defence Counsel's protestations that this might also have been attributable to the grief and emotions circulating around David Loughton on the night in question. He preferred to opine that it was something David Loughton would say to protect himself.

* * *

On the subject of David Loughton's alleged murder of Marie Duvois:

The most damning, but equally the most controversial, evidence came from all of the police officers, who had attended the scene on the night, backed up by the circumstantial forensic evidence. The gun found in the room was confirmed to be that used to kill Marie Duvois as the bullets fired in test matched the single bullet retrieved from the mattress, which had penetrated Mademoiselle Duvois's body. The evidence given that only one set of fingerprints, which belonged to David Loughton, had been found on the gun in blood clinched the guilty verdict in many people's minds, despite cross-examination showing that his fingerprints on the gun did not prove that he had fired it. There was no forensic evidence, for example, of gunshot residue on either David Loughton's firing hand or on the other. There was also some stricken evidence – due to inadmissibility – regarding blood found under David's fingernails; the assertion being that he had attacked her with his hands before shooting her dead. Cross-examination of this point proved that no bruises or other supporting evidence could be found, which Defence suggested that this was a further fabrication by the Prosecution to ensure a 'Guilty' verdict. Simply, the cause of death was the loss of blood from a single shot.

Several of the hotel's residents had confirmed their testimony that, when they peeked into the corridor after the loud bang, all they could see was a naked Mr. Loughton, covered in blood, looking wild and angry and holding the gun, before running back into his room when he had realized what he had done. This last subjective comment was stricken from the record on a challenge and the objection was noted. The immediate neighbour of Mr. Loughton and Mademoiselle Duvois confirmed that he had heard David's voice – later corrected to 'a male voice' – arguing and ranting loudly, although no specific words could be determined. In this witness's opinion, the male voice was very upset. Again, the supporting evidence of this, in the minds of the jury, was the corresponding confirmation that he had also heard Marie Duvois's plaintive appeals for calm and quiet. The voice was accepted as belonging to her because of the French accent. Despite being cross-examined that, if the words were not clear, the accent would be unclear too, Marie's 'protestations' were admitted as evidence. Further evidence was provided to support these testimonies, such as photographs of black arcs on a wall. The neighbour banging the heel of his shoe against it to appeal for silence had created these. There were also diagrams of the layout of the adjoining room to highlight where these marks were in relation to the bed. The Defence's assertion that it was equally likely that the murder might have been perpetrated by a third person was scorned by the Prosecution, principally because there was no forensic or testimonial evidence to place a third person in the room on that night (remembering that David Loughton had not been able to be forthcoming on these points).

Several other witnesses were brought forward to testify that they had observed Marie Duvois's state of mind on the evening prior to her death. There were several accounts, including those of Sir Charles Minton and various members of the Chorus Committee and orchestra, to raise sufficient doubt as to her happiness during that evening. Sir Charles had even suggested that David Loughton's stratospheric rise had temporarily sated his massive ego and that it was his own self-importance, which had led to the argument and subsequent shooting. Again, this was stricken from the court records but, no doubt, not from some of the minds of the jury. The general impression given, nonetheless, was one of uneasiness between the dead opera star and upstart singer hanging on the dress train of the star.

The final piece of extraordinary evidence to establish his guilt in wanting to cause Marie harm (but not necessarily her death) was that, given many opportunities to provide his side of the story, he had waived the right by being uncommunicative. The Defence Counsel painted a different picture of grief at the loss of a loved one in very violent circumstances. It might be hardly surprising that he had no wish to say anything because the depth of anguish, distress and bereavement made him incapable to do so. This was derided by the Prosecution Counsel as an attempt to protect the client.

*   *   *

On the subject of personal testimonies for and against David Loughton's previously unblemished character:

The alleged treatment of Amanda Watson has already been chronicled but her testimony was used and expanded by the Prosecution Counsel to paint a picture of an exceptionally violent man and sexual predator. Because of her tearful act in the witness box, breaking down every so often as she came to a particularly 'painful' part of her story, the melodrama was used to great effect. Cross-examination of this witness – now segregated as 'hostile', because of her vituperative asides – showed that there were some holes in her story. These were not stricken from the court record because the Defence Counsel was warned that it was not Mrs. Watson who was under trial, despite attempts to convince the judge that the veracity of her testimony would help to provide the jury with the facts in the case.

Gary Adner's witness statement, removing the assertions and allegations of David Loughton's involvement in the embezzlement against the Chorus and its sponsor, was used to great effect by the Prosecution Counsel to underline the periods of violence attributed to David, but was also examined further to help the jury understand that David Loughton was a megalomaniac, who would stop at nothing to gain control. Gary Adner also provided his own insight into David's relationships with women, aggrandizing the initial meeting between David and Marie away from what you read at the beginning of this book to one of a man stalking his prey and wearing her down until she agreed to partner him. His assertion of lack of surprise if David had coerced her into agreeing to marry her was stricken from the record after an objection lodged by the Defence Counsel.

The Prosecution Counsel used Sir Charles Minton's testimony to give it the appearance of wisdom that is conferred on the aged to help guide the jury's understanding of David Loughton's alleged motives for murder. His jealousy and covetousness of Sir Charles's strong relationship with Marie was a powerful argument, despite contentions that it could be considered to be the protection of an unrequited consort. Sir Charles asserted too that many people felt that the lack of response to the newspaper reports was seen as 'no smoke without fire'. Defence objected to this as hearsay but the question was turned around for Sir Charles to form an opinion, which he did with relish. Despite questioning as to the exact relationship he endured with Marie Duvois, Sir Charles gave nothing away to presume that there might be anything more than an avuncular, caring attitude. The latter parts of this book have, of course, shed new light on this.

The final witnesses for David's defence were Beth Jackson and Pete Phillips. Beth reiterated that she had never seen the couple ever have a cross word between them nor an argument and that, from what she had witnessed, there was too deep a love between them for either to want to cause the other harm. The Prosecution Counsel objected that this could be treated as hearsay, forcing the Defence Counsel to reword the question for her to form an opinion. Pete Phillips had a more difficult time with his testimony. Starting off, he let slip that David Loughton had taken on the Chairmanship on a whim. This was pounced by the

Prosecution Counsel, forcing Pete to backtrack and add that David had taken every opportunity to sort out the various conflicts within the Chorus and in his personal life. He further said that David Loughton was, by nature, a very gentle person and confirmed Beth's view that the two were very much in love and that he had never witnessed an argument between them. Prosecution made him stumble a number of times as he tried to protest the questions being asked. They grabbed at the suggestion that he was a man of a 'gentle nature' with alacrity, indicating that it had already been proven beyond doubt that David was prone to indiscriminate fits of violence against both men and women. Flustered, Pete retorted that those fights were only self-protection and that he had not started them. This was countered with a further assertion that, regardless of who had started it, he had been involved, to which Pete could only agree. The next point of ridicule was that, just because he had never witnessed an argument between Marie Duvois and David Loughton, it did not mean that one had never happened. Again flustered at this, but before he could answer, Prosecution suggested that, in the face of so much damning evidence, maybe he and Beth had colluded on their story to protect their friend. This was stricken from the record after a protest from the Defence Counsel but asked in a different (more acceptable) way so that it stood and cast doubt on the rest of his testimony. *[It should not be underestimated too the level of grief that both Beth Jackson and Peter Phillips were experiencing at the time for the loss of their friend. M.S.]*

* * *

The summation of the prosecution case made by the Prosecution Counsel [edited]:

Ladies and gentlemen of the jury, we have seen that the defendant is a highly volatile character, prone to fits of violent outburst and, on occasion, causing actual bodily harm. We have heard testimony from three people, who were so attacked. Unprovoked and unnecessary in the extreme as they were and with a wealth of evidence to support it, we also heard the Defence Counsel attempting to deny the allegation, preferring the argument that he was not the one who started it. But, surely, how can three people – one an eminent Knight of the Realm; another a member of Britain's police force – how can they be so wrong to the point of perjury and so wrong to the very same degree?

We have also heard testimony of the defendant's callous attitude

towards women. One witness described the abuse she had endured over
a period of months. And another has testified to witnessing the defendant
attacking the deceased in a very provocative and sexual manner.

With that in mind, we further heard testimony from the police
officers attending the awful scene that night in the hotel room and from
the forensic scientists that place the defendant at the right place at the
right time. We heard that it has been suggested that the defendant
argued profusely with the deceased on the night in question and we have
also heard that the defendant's fingerprints have been found on the gun,
also proven to be the one that shot the deceased.

It is obvious to me and every one in the court that the defendant is
not the same character as the Defence Counsel would have us believe. A
thug, a bully, a sexual predator are just some of the epithets that might
be used to describe him.

Therefore, with this overwhelming evidence laid before you, I urge
you to return a verdict of 'Guilty as charged'.

* * *

The summation of the defence case made by the Defence Counsel [edited]:
Ladies and gentlemen of the jury, we have heard the Prosecution
Counsel refer to the defendant as a thug, as a bully and as a sexual
predator. This 'overwhelming evidence' he mentions is paper-thin at
best and purely circumstantial at worst.

It has been suggested that he is a thug because of the violent attacks
he has been party to. Let us be in no doubt that each of these attacks
took place with no witnesses, so we are forced to rely on the testimonies
of two people, who are in court themselves on different charges and who
have an obvious grievance against the defendant. Two colleagues
corroborate the evidence of attacking a police officer and you have to
consider whether the attack was provoked or not.

The suggestion that he is a bully stems too from the testimony of a
hostile witness, who has most to lose, should he not deflect some of the
blame of embezzlement on to the defendant. Two character witnesses
have supported the view of the gentle man he really is.

To the third allegation that he is a sexual predator, again it relies on
the testimony of one witness, which is not corroborated by others, so
may be questionable, especially if that witness is seen as wanting to take
grievance against the defendant. Maybe the sexual predator was not the
defendant in this case.

We have also heard flimsy evidence placing the defendant at the crime scene at the right time. You must think whether this is so strange, given that the defendant and deceased had an ongoing relationship and, indeed, were planning to be married the following day. Maybe there was a third person there that night, who slipped away before anyone saw them. And we heard that the gun used in the crime had the defendant's – and only the defendant's – fingerprints on it. If this theoretical third person were present, may they not have worn gloves? The forensic analysis shows that the firing mechanism is faulty and I believe that the perpetrator was intending to kill both the deceased and the defendant but was thwarted by the poor operation of the gun. This fits the facts much better than the Prosecution's fabricated suggestion based around such circumstantial evidence.

We heard character witness statements supporting the converse emotion the defendant felt for the deceased and you have to ask how such violence could be perpetrated in such a relationship.

The evidence is not at all clear and I urge you to return a verdict of 'Not guilty'.

* * *

The summation of the judge prior to giving the jury leave to consider their verdict [edited]:

You have heard a number of witness statements regarding the varying levels of malevolent violence attributed to the defendant. You have also heard from others that the defendant is a gentle man. You have listened to testimonies of the various fights in which the defendant was involved. You, the jury, must decide whether he is a naturally violent man, as the Prosecution has portrayed, or if his involvement in those fights was an act of self-defence in each case, as purported by the Defence.

It is also the jury's decision whether the reported raised voice heard on the night of the crime was one of anger or, as the Defence has stated, an expression of frustration at recent events.

You have heard – and it has been accepted by both Prosecution and Defence – that the gun found at the scene was the weapon used to kill Marie Duvois. You have also heard evidence that there is only one set of fingerprints on the gun and that those belong to the defendant; again, acknowledged by both Prosecution and Defence. Defence has also suggested that there was a third person present in the room, which has been countered by the Prosecution Counsel as a fabrication since there is no witness statement to back that assertion. It is you, the jury, who has to decide, beyond reasonable doubt, whether such a figure could or could not been at the scene of the crime and, if you do so decide, whether this third person carried out the shooting.

With all that in mind, you must decide whether the defendant is capable of carrying out the murder, based on all the evidence submitted – if that is agreed, you must return a verdict of 'Guilty'. If you feel you cannot agree that the defendant is capable of such a crime, beyond reasonable doubt – and I must make it clear *beyond reasonable doubt* – you must return a verdict of 'Not Guilty'.

I will accept a majority verdict to be where ten or more of you are in agreement.

* * *

The summation of the judge on receiving a majority 'Guilty as charged' verdict:

A jury of your peers by majority vote has found you guilty of murdering Marie Duvois on the night of the eleventh of April, 1969 in the Castleton Hotel, in the Strand, London.

The evidence that has been presented shows that you are a dangerous individual, prone to violence with a short fuse for anger to subsume you. I have listened to the counter-evidence with interest and it seems to me that you have done yourself a disservice by not presenting evidence in your defence. But so be it – you must live by your decision.

The murder of Mademoiselle Duvois was a particularly brutal one for someone who was apparently in love with her and planning to get married to her. I find it astounding and disgusting that you should prey on women in the way that has been heard in the court and that you decided to murder this woman in such a callous and unnecessary way. What has been kept from the court until now is that not only did you murder Mademoiselle Duvois but you paid scant regard to the two unborn children she was carrying for you.

Because of this dreadful crime and your unpredictable nature, I am sending you for psychiatric reports. When those reports are received, this court will reconvene for sentencing. It is unfortunate that the death sentence as an option has been repealed, as I would have no qualms about using it in this case.

PUPPET ON A STRING

CHAPTER 36

Well, that is pretty much it for my story. I was sent, as the court directed, to a couple of psychiatrists, who unanimously decided that I was mentally fit and could stand for sentencing. That my depression and subdued manner was entirely down to grief – whether from losing a loved one or from carrying out the dreaded deed – they were unable to divine because I had given them no new information.

I was transported back to the courts, put in the dock, this time flanked by two guards and given the sentence of life, with a recommendation that I should not be considered for parole for at least twenty years. From there, I was driven to a dank, grey prison in the far north of England and mixed with murderers, sexual abusers of women and other human scum. But I was still unable to fight because of the introspection caused by my dreadful loss. I was allowed to attend neither the burial nor the memorial service in Marie's honour, because of concerns over the inevitable security risks created by the media attention. The hardest times to contend with have been the anniversaries of key moments in our short time together and I have always made time to remember her – not with God but for myself. I cannot believe that a benevolent God would allow such a violent and premature end to the life of a woman such as Marie – no, the thanks are always to the spirit of Marie herself.

I was not granted parole on the few occasions it was reviewed because a few other inmates have taken a dislike to me, seeing my sullenness as weakness. As a result of the fights, it was agreed by the parole board that my inherent violent temper had not been quelled any by incarceration.

The location of the prison also made it difficult for Pete and Beth to visit but they managed it nonetheless. The visits became more infrequent once they were married and children came along – with shock, I have just realized that their four offspring are adults themselves and the eldest is the age that my twins would have been had they lived. Pete took up a solo career, guided and assisted by Beth and is now in great demand for recording performances and I wish him continued success and happiness. I hope that both he and Beth will forgive me for what I am about to do.

The scandal surrounding Marie's murder and the embezzlement case was too much for our sponsor and the life of the *Coro di Londinium* was immediately blighted and therefore limited. The record label was wound up, although extra copies of our first three records flew off the shelves in the period just after Marie's untimely demise. It is a true observation that the best career move in music is to die.

What really drove me to writing down my story? Well, it was partly the significant anniversary of twenty-five years since meeting, but mainly because I was spurred on by two events. The first was a succession of stark and vivid dreams. I had always had the dreams, remembering the night that Marie died in my arms, the nightmares of the blood and the subsequent personal loss but just as I started writing this, they changed gradually to something gentler and it became essential for me to get it down on paper.

The dream was quintessentially this: Marie would be standing in the garden of the house in Worth Matravers, exactly as I had remembered it, bathed in a brilliant white light. At the start of my scribblings, the dreams consisted of Marie standing in the bright light and then disappearing. This has evolved over the time of writing this biography of our relationship into just about being able to make out a worried frown and then eventually to a smile until, last night, she was close enough to touch and I could see the beautiful freckles across her nose, her shoulders and I could reach out and stroke the silky smoothness of her bare arms. It was in this same dream that she reached forward and placed a hot hand on my chest, smiled and nodded. For the first time in the dreams, she spoke: "The children are fine. Chloë and Michael would like to meet their father. But only when you are ready." The message was very clear to me.

Over this same period of time, the second event occurred. On the same day as the later stages of the recurrent dream, I was working in the laundry – the latest in a succession of jobs given to me, failing in all of the others because of the ruckus that always ensued when another prisoner decided to pick on me, especially if they were disparaging towards Marie in any way – when a familiar voice piped up behind me: "Well, well! Look who we have here!"

Turning, I saw Gary's wizened face but chose to ignore him, returning to the chore of emptying out the big drum of washing from the industrial machines. Gary punched me on the shoulder and stepped back: "I'm talking to you, Loughton."

I stood up and stretched my aching back. "I wish I could say it's great to see you but I would be lying."

Gary put on a mock expression of sadness. "Oh, dear. Feeling a little precious, are we? Missing our little tart still?"

Red mist again. "How dare you!" I bellowed and moved towards him, fist poised.

Gary stepped back and smiled as two big men stepped in front of him, choreographed perfectly, from behind the washing-machines. "I dare because I can. Now, you and I, Loughton, have some unfinished business. Something to do with being reported to the police as I recall. But first, I'll let my two friends soften you up a little."

Attempted rape and another beating saw my latest prospects of parole, such as they were, gurgle down the plug-hole, but I knew that life was going to be very difficult with Gary on the scene. Coupled with the wonderful dreams of Marie, I resolved to end it here once I had completed this story. I have enjoyed remembering most of it and it has renewed my affection for my friends and especially for Marie.

This open letter to her encompasses how I feel now that I have opened some rancorous sores and the softly perfumed petals of brilliant memories:

To my darling Marie,

Nothing prepared me for the rude way that you were torn from me. A fatalist would presume that things were going too well and that it was only a matter of time before they began falling apart. I do not see it that way – the twelve months from our meeting until your horrific death were the most precious and fulfilling of my entire life and, if I had to choose between not experiencing them and being free from prison, I would gladly choose to be incarcerated without a second thought.

The time is almost nigh, my darling, and we will be together forever.

With all my love. xxxxx

The other day, while clearing out the drains in the laundry, I found a long shard of broken glass. This has been secreted away in my room, which I share with no-one because of my oft reported temperamental nature. Once I have finished this epistle, I will move nearer to Marie and my children.

*   *   *

I guess that all that remains, for those who are interested, is who killed my Marie and our babies, if it were not I. Marie always wore a very delicate perfume, which used to thrill me and allowed me to picture her every time I smelled it, regardless of whether Marie was in nose-shot or not.

    I have always known who did this despicable deed but was always too grief-stricken, depressed and confused to express my knowledge and thoughts. On the night of her death, I smelled a cloyingly sweet perfume, which disappeared along the corridor when I took chase. As with Marie's perfume, the memories of situations were evoked with the slightest tease of it. This sickly pong threw me back to a flat with satin sheets on the bed and an attack with a paper-knife in the Chorus offices.

I am not afraid. God, if he exists, be –

No! Marie be with me!

PUPPET ON A STRING

EPILOGUE

David Richard Loughton took his own life by cutting his wrists with a shard of glass. From the attached document, it will no doubt have felt like a blessèd relief from the hurt, the grief and the self-torture he had put himself through.

With the information provided within this document, the case was reopened and retried. David Loughton was given a posthumous Royal Pardon for the imprisonment, for which he had served almost twenty-five years of his life unnecessarily.

The police constables on duty that fateful night have all retired except one, who has been subsequently suspended on full pay while the allegations laid down in David's hand are investigated. It is unlikely, thirty-five years on that it will result in any prosecutions.

Sir Charles Minton died from a stroke shortly after the original hearing and his recordings are still held in high regard, despite the advances in recording technology.

Adrian Hilton had been a frequent visitor to hospital following his trial and imprisonment, suffering from gastric complaints. On the final visit, two years into his sentence, where he was being treated for stomach ulceration, he died after one of the ulcers burst.

Gary Adner has had his prison privileges removed, following the investigation into his manipulation and abuse of authority with respect to the beatings of David Loughton and other inmates. Following his embezzlement case in the late Sixties, he was tried and convicted on all counts and has never left prison for any great length of time, slipping further in to a life of crime. Rumours persist that he continues to operate scams from prison; allegations which will continue to be analysed.

Pete and Beth Phillips have had an enduring marriage and burgeoning joint and solo careers. Beth now hosts her own Saturday night television show, providing a show-case of the lighter side of opera, on which Pete regularly appears. A special show will be broadcast on the

BBC in memory of the shortened lives of David Loughton and Marie Duvois. Pete has also tried to revive the recordings just recently from the early days on the *Coro di Londinium*'s own record label, which is soon to be released as a boxed set retrospective in all formats for purists and technophiles alike, along with the only complete but unreleased recording from the *King Olaf* sessions – *As Torrents in Summer*.

Amanda Watson had married into the higher echelons of the Scotland Yard police force but this relationship had fallen apart within a year, although she had kept the name. An habitual user of alcohol and drugs and a frequent visitor to various rehab clinics in Britain and America, she was arrested, tried and convicted for the murder of Marie Duvois and her unborn children. Breaking down in the witness box at her trial, she revealed that she had perjured herself during David Loughton's trial and confessed that it was she who had been chasing David Loughton rather than the other way around and that she had instigated the attacks at the offices of the Chorus. She has also confirmed the detail provided in David's writings with respect to attempting to kill him with the paper-knife and that she would have killed him on the same night as Marie were it not for a jamming trigger mechanism. She had bought the unmarked gun on the streets of London that night, having watched the performance of *Tosca*, which had featured both Marie and David.

And Isla? Isla lived her remaining years as the family pet with Pete and Beth Phillips.

God rest the souls of David Loughton and Marie Duvois and of their children Chloë and Michael and protect them now that this ordeal is over.

M.S.

Printed in the United Kingdom
by Lightning Source UK Ltd.
100375UKS00002B/37-51